EREC REX

THE DRAGON'S EYE

Praise for Kaza Kingsley's *The Dragon's Eye*

"*Dragon's Eye* is a fantastic tale of a boy who gets caught up in a world he never knew existed and finds out he's part of something much bigger than he knew. It is a magical story filled with suspense, intensity, heart, and courage. I loved this book . . . and I'll be waiting for a sequel."

—Devon Werkheiser, "Ned," star of Nickelodeon's popular daily sitcom *Ned's Declassified School Survival Guide*

"This title is a solid addition to the juvenile fantasy collection. The main character, Erec Rex, travels to a secret world hidden within our own (a la Neverwhere) to save his mother from an evil king. . . . The story becomes more complex and compelling as trust is questioned, friendships forged, and magical abilities are discovered. The story touches on issues of social justice, politics, and sportsmanship, and would be useful in a social studies class. Young readers will enjoy this story and eagerly anticipate the next book in the series."

—Meagan Albright, *Children's Literature*

"Erec finds himself competing for one of three nefarious schemes, a crew of sneering bullies, sumptuous feasts, allies for Erec, a surprise villain and magic worked by everything from explosive 'nitrowisherine' to push-button remotes. Kingsley speeds her tale along to a climax involving an impulsive dragon. . . . Closing with the news that the young hero still has twelve tasks to fulfill, this light but not insubstantial outing definitely belongs aboard the Potter wagon, but merits a seat toward the front."

—*Kirkus Reviews*

"This is an action-packed fantasy filled with rich characters kids will really relate to. Erec Rex is poised to take over Harry Potter's long reign."

—Maria Schneider, senior editor, *Writers Digest*

"A very good book. Vivid descriptions . . . a riveting storyline. . . . [and] a great sense of humor. I highly recommend it!"

—*Wands and Worlds*

"Erec Rex contains elements of magic, conflict, and other-worldliness. . . . Kingsley delivers her tale in a light-hearted yet compelling style like that of J. K. Rowling or Diana Wynne Jones. . . . Erec finds friendship and bullies, magic and trickery, and clues to his own identity that make for as compelling a read as any Hogwarts adventure.

"The quirky setting is as much a star of this fantasy as any of the characters. A castle tipped onto its side, mazes and magical creatures, and cleverly devised competitions create an atmosphere any fantasy fan will long to visit. The story is peppered with delightful gadgets. . . . The book concludes with the news that Erec has more tasks to fulfill . . . good news for fantasy readers of all ages."

—Carolyn Bailey, *ForeWord Magazine*

"*Dragon's Eye* tells of the magical trek of a young boy trying to find his mother. Along the journey, he also discovers shocking knowledge about himself. This is a great story with such incredible detail that you will find yourself enjoying the journey."

—Autumn Lynn, *River Reader Books*, Lexington, MO

"A great read! Author Kaza Kingsley is one to watch!"

—Jeff Bowen, USA Book News.com

"Welcome to the world, Erec Rex. Your readers have long awaited you. *Erec Rex: The Dragon's Eye* is a fun, fascinating book that makes you want to chill out for a while and just read. Plus, this book's brave new world is chock full of nifty magical gadgets; cute, dorky, and even scary magical critters (fluffy pink kitten, anyone?); and spellbinding people who are mean, magical, or possibly dimwits. These lively creations found a platform all their own. Grade: A."

—Sherryl King-Wilds, fantasynovelreview.com

"The Bottom Line: A good read for fans who . . . can't get enough of magical adventure tales. I bought three copies for Christmas gifts. . . . I found myself engrossed in the mystery of Erec and Bethany's secret magical past. . . . accessible for teens and adults to enjoy as well."

—Epinions.com

Check out the other books
in the Erec Rex series

The Monsters of Otherness

Coming in summer 2009:

The Search for Truth

THE DRAGON'S EYE

KAZA KINGSLEY

Illustrations by Melvyn Grant

Simon & Schuster Books for Young Readers
New York   London   Toronto   Sydney

SIMON & SCHUSTER BOOKS FOR YOUNG READERS
An imprint of Simon & Schuster Children's Publishing Division
1230 Avenue of the Americas, New York, New York 10020

First Simon & Schuster Books for Young Readers paperback edition April 2009
Originally published in 2007 by Firelight Press, Inc.
SIMON & SCHUSTER BOOKS FOR YOUNG READERS is a trademark of
Simon & Schuster, Inc.
Book design by Jeremy Wortsman
The text for this book is set in Adobe Caslon Pro.
The illustrations for this book are rendered digitally.
Manufactured in the United States of America
2 4 6 8 10 9 7 5 3 1
Library of Congress Cataloging-in-Publication Data
Kingsley, Kaza.
[Erec Rex, the dragon's eye]
The dragon's eye / Kaza Kingsley ; illustrations by Melvyn Grant.
p. cm.—(Erec Rex)
Originally published: Erec Rex, the dragon's eye: Cincinnati : Firelight Press, 2007.
Summary: Twelve-year-old Erec Rex stumbles upon a world where magic has not
been forgotten, and must survive the ultimate test in order to save the magical
kingdom he was born to rule.
ISBN: 978-1-4169-7933-3
[1. Fantasy.] I. Grant, Mel, ill. II. Title.
PZ7.K6153Drc 2009
[Fic]—dc22
2008031841
erecrex.com

5408

For Sarah, Kelsey, and Ethan, who are fountains of laughter and the source of all smiles. And for Neil, who made everything possible.

CONTENTS

CHAPTER 1
Mrs. Smith

I T WAS EARLY, far too early to wake up in the summer, when Erec Ulysses Rex's alarm clock went off. The thing paced on its tiny metal legs until it could not stand to wait anymore. Then it kicked a marble that hit Erec right in the cheek, just below his glass eye.

Erec rubbed his face and moaned. He opened his good eye. His alarm clock was doing a kind of end-zone dance. It pirouetted toward a pen and booted it expertly into Erec's ear. Erec groaned. The obnoxious thing would pounce on him if he didn't get up fast. He could always throw it across the room, but it would only find its way back. And then tomorrow it would wake him even earlier.

"Leave me alone. I *told* you I can sleep late. It's summer." As Erec pried his head from his pillow, something grabbed his mouth. It was his toothbrush, another annoying gift from his mother. It shook its brush head over Erec's teeth, gripping his lips with its thin arms and legs. Erec almost choked.

He yanked the toothbrush from his mouth, threw it on the floor, and watched it run from the room. Last night Erec had jammed the alarm clock in the back of a bathroom cabinet. He wondered if the toothbrush had helped it escape.

Long ago, when they could afford such things, his mother had ordered these strange, lifelike objects from some store named Vulcan. As he grew up, he became used to these creatures and thought of them almost as pets. But his mother insisted on hiding them from visitors, who if they saw them might think they had completely gone crazy.

It was the start of another bad day, in a bad week, in what Erec thought was a very bad year. His large family kept moving to smaller and smaller places, and growing poorer and poorer. In fact, they had moved nine times this year alone. That left hardly enough time to make friends, let alone say good-bye when he moved again.

A few days ago, twelve-year-old Erec, his siblings, pets, and their adoptive mother, June O'Hara, moved into what the landlord called a "very modest apartment" in New York City. "Of course," he added, "legally, this is too small for you all to live here." Erec thought the landlord was being generous in his description. Rather than crowding on the couch with his brothers, Erec slept in a small closet with the washing machine. He hoped his mother didn't find more strays—for that's what they all were.

All of the children in Erec's family were . . . well, unique. Erec had a glass eye (which was really a sort of plastic). Eleven-year-old

Nell needed a walker. Trevor, nine, rarely spoke. The thirteen-year-old twins, Danny and Sammy, were found alone and abandoned. And four-year-old Zoey could be more than a little wild.

Erec was tall and thin with dark hair that was straight in front and wildly curly in the back. His glass eye did not quite match his blue one. But Erec had another problem, far worse than his odd hair and eye. It was something he called "cloudy thoughts."

Erec's cloudy thoughts left him dizzy and hazy, like polluted clouds were spinning through his brain. They made his stomach leap into his throat and threaten to hold a Boston Tea Party, dumping its contents out while singing a war chant. But worst of all, once a cloudy thought popped into his head, it was like an order. It would grab him like a sumo wrestler, terrifying him until he followed its command. He felt like a puppet, out of control. No matter how hard he fought, he had to obey.

So far the odd things he was ordered to do were good, like putting pillows at the bottom of the stairs moments before Zoey crashed down, or grabbing her before she ran in front of a car. He was glad to help, of course, but mostly felt like an unpaid, nauseated babysitter. And a freak. It was like coming down with an extremely annoying combination of ESP and the stomach flu. But, worse, he was haunted by a fear: What if someday he was commanded to do something terrible?

Erec had not slept well. A loud click had woken him in the middle of the night. He'd figured it was probably a new apartment sound. His stomach had churned for a bit, but, luckily, he'd fallen back to sleep.

He combed the front, straight part of his dark hair, not bothering with the tangled curls in back, and stepped over his sleeping dogs, Tutt and King. The coat rack, another of his mother's purchases from Vulcan, nearly bumped into him as he stumbled by in the hallway. It tried to get attention, tap dancing on the carpet, flapping its wooden arms. Erec waved it away.

Sunlight streamed into the small kitchen, glinting off the twins' sandy brown hair: Danny's standing on end, and Sammy's pulled into a ponytail. Long and lean, Danny wolfed Flying Count cereal from a box. He rolled his bright blue eyes at Erec. "She woke me up."

Sammy hunched in her chair with a frown. "You'd have woken *me* if that big . . . clown was in your room staring at *you*."

"Yeah, right." Danny munched more cereal.

"What are you talking about?" Erec asked.

"That." Sammy pointed at an immense woman overflowing a plastic folding chair by the front door. She did look like a clown. Unnatural white powder coated her face. Her orblike cheeks were decorated with bright red circles of makeup like great balls of fire. Her nose bulged, and thick blue war paint surrounded her slitlike eyes. Slick black hair clung to her wide face, coming to a point at her first chin. A small wedge of bangs in the middle of her forehead made her already heart-shaped face look like an ill-conceived valentine.

"Who is she?"

"The babysitter. Must be magic she doesn't break that chair," Sammy whispered. "I woke up, and she was standing over my bed staring at me. I thought I was in a nightmare."

"Did she wake Nell and Zoey?"

Sammy shook her head. "She was only staring at me."

"Another admirer. Clowning around." Danny batted his eyes and fanned himself with his hand.

"Shut up." A grin took over Sammy's face.

Danny lowered his voice. "Clown convention gathers in honor of Sammy Rex. Awed by her beauty, they crown her Clown Queen." He raised his eyebrows. "Oh, no! Your nose is starting to puff!"

Sammy giggled, the morning's bad start forgotten.

"Mom doesn't go out this early," Erec said, looking around for her. "And she doesn't get sitters anymore. Where did she go?"

Danny shrugged. "To find work, I guess." He shoved his cereal at Erec. "Want some?"

Erec took a handful of miniature flying counts. His mother had to work several jobs to support them all, he knew that. But it felt like he never saw her anymore.

The toaster, another Vulcan special, shot two pieces of burnt toast at Erec's chest. He caught them, looked them over, and put them on the counter. "I'm sick of toast." The toaster puffed smoke and plopped on the counter.

"Mom forgot to hide the Vulcan things," Erec pointed out. "The coat rack is wandering the hall. What if the sitter sees?"

"She'll think she's crazy," Danny said, liking this idea. "It could be fun."

Suddenly the room started spinning. Erec grabbed the counter and took a deep breath to steady himself. His stomach twisted and did somersaults like an acrobat. In the distance, it sounded like Sammy was asking if he was all right.

Fear filled his chest. It was happening again. He would be ordered to do something, yet he would fight it with every ounce of his being because it made him feel so terrified and out of control.

Then the cloudy thought commanded him: *Go find your mother.* Where?

Outside the east entrance of Grand Central Station. The hot-dog stand. She would not be there, he somehow knew, but he had to go there to find her. She was not hurt but lost.

Erec dropped into a chair and crossed his arms. The dizzy feeling was gone, leaving him gagging. This was ridiculous. His mom was fine. Now he had to run across town because she got lost on the way to a job interview? No way. He was staying right here. His mom could buy a map. It was bad enough having to help little Zoey. This was not fair.

Erec grabbed his seat, fighting his body's urge to run to Grand Central Station. His feet danced around him, and his legs shot under the table, trying to push him up.

Danny cocked an eyebrow. "Are you getting one of those cloudy things again?"

Erec nodded. He gripped the chair, fighting the urge to stand, until his hands ached. He had to give in. He would not rest until he followed the command. "I gotta get out of here," he said. "I have to find Mom." He got up.

"How will you find her?" Sammy said. "She didn't leave a note."

Danny shrugged. "He'll find her, all right. He'll crash into her by accident. Remember when he was studying, and he had to run outside in his pajamas and pick up a garbage can, and he didn't know why? And it turned out that scrawny cat was pinned under it."

Erec wished he could forget. It was bad enough to be forced to do things for other people, let alone every animal around. Was he servant to the universe?

He ran without thinking through his sisters' room, into the closet where his mother slept, and picked up a picture of his mother holding Zoey.

Nell stayed asleep, but Zoey stood on her cot, blond curls falling messily over her purple nightgown and around her wide hazel eyes. She looked at the picture and danced around the room. "It's me! It's me!"

So this cloudy thought involved taking a picture of his mother to a hot-dog stand where she was *not* going to be in order to *find* her. Erec shook his head and shoved the picture in his pocket.

The fortresslike babysitter perched by the front door. Her eyes widened when she saw Erec and then settled back into serene, feline watchfulness. She reminded him of a strange dream where one of his cats grew huge and tried to eat him. "I'm going out . . ."

The sitter raised a finger, watching the tiny television. A news story blared: "Thanatos Baskania, the self-dubbed Crown Prince of Peace, continues his push for peace on earth. He says our world leaders need a larger power guiding them to bring us the peaceful existence we deserve. Baskania and his many multinational corporations are putting enormous amounts of money and people power into this 'larger power,' the new world peace organization, Eye of the World. Today, amid much controversy, Eye of the World has been accepted as the ruling body of the United Nations."

The babysitter nodded with a thin-lipped smile. "Good man," she croaked. Red-haired Trevor snoozed, oblivious, on the couch.

Erec's toes were tapping, ready to run. "I'll be back soon." As he reached for the door, though, the clown-woman flicked an umbrella from under her chair and whacked the knob. Erec jerked his hand away just in time.

"Nobody leaves the apartment." The sitter's voice sounded like a rake scraping gravel. "Don't you introduce yourself, young man?"

"I'm sorry." He reached for the doorknob again, and as he did the umbrella rose in the air. His hand dropped.

"You're Sorry. Okay, Sorry. Call me Mrs. Smith. What are the twins' names?"

"Danny and Sammy."

"Hmm. Danny and Sammy."

Just then the coat rack sauntered into the room juggling three hats. Erec held his breath, waiting for the sitter to scream. He should have thrown the coat rack in the closet.

The sitter's beady eyes, swimming in blue makeup, coolly stared at the coat rack without a trace of surprise. The coat rack seemed offended and threw a fourth hat into the air, as if to get more attention.

"I have to go. We're out of food." Erec touched the knob just before the umbrella smacked it, this time grazing his fingers.

"No OUT!" rang like a jackhammer from her lips, and then a bland smile took over her face.

"But there's no food." The cloudy thought gripped him and his knees knocked.

The babysitter shrugged. "I don't think you'll starve to death." Her eyes narrowed to slits. She sucked her puffy cheeks in as if she was trying not to laugh.

Erec tried to grab the doorknob with an arm up to deflect the umbrella. This time, however, its unusually large handle caught him around the waist and yanked him in front of Mrs. Smith. "Do that one more time," she rasped, "and I'll have to tie you up." Her tight frown turned into a small grin. "But don't worry. We're all going soon enough. So run along, Sorry."

Erec flew into the kitchen, where the twins sat gawking.

"She's batty," Sammy said. "Don't worry. We'll get you out of here."

Erec was ready to jump the six floors to the sidewalk. "Where's Zoey?" Danny asked. "We could sic her on Mrs. Smith, and you can escape while she runs away in terror."

"Look." Sammy pointed. Mrs. Smith angrily swatted her face while Zoey, by her feet, chewed and stuffed paper into a pen shell. A spitball sailed into Mrs. Smith's puffy nose. She tried to kick Zoey without getting up from her chair, but Zoey rolled away, laughing. Danny and Sammy giggled.

Zoey steadied herself and blew a spitball into Mrs. Smith's open mouth. Mrs. Smith spat into her hand. She tried again to kick Zoey, but missed.

"It's like she's glued to that chair," whispered Sammy. She picked Zoey up. "You're going to get hurt, honey. Let the sitter rest. Did you go potty yet?"

"She's such a mom," said Danny.

"And you're such a pest," said Erec. The drive to leave was so overwhelming, Erec could hardly breathe.

"Shh." Sammy winked at Erec. She took Zoey into the bathroom and called, "Mrs. Smith, Zoey needs help."

The sitter filed her nails.

"Mrs. Smith! We need you." Sammy sounded desperate.

Mrs. Smith held out her hand to admire her filing job. "Bathroom help is not in my job description."

"Please. She's getting sick."

"Is she really," the sitter said in a gravelly voice. It sounded more like a statement than a question. She hummed quietly and filed the nails on her other hand.

Zoey left the bathroom, obviously needing no help, trailing a long stream of toilet paper. When Erec looked into the bathroom, his breath left him. It was as if he had been plunged into ice water.

His mother's glasses sat on the bathroom counter. The thick black frames were held by a thin, silky chain. His mother never went anywhere without those glasses hanging around her neck, although she rarely used them. In fact, Erec had never seen them off her. She even slept with them, and he often wondered how she kept from crushing them.

Erec grabbed the glasses. His feet moonwalked toward the front door under the control of his cloudy thought, until he stamped them a few times. "Look what I found."

"Wow," said Sammy. "I've never seen those off her before."

"She never even uses them," Danny said. "Maybe she's finally sick of them."

It was true. The only times Erec saw his mother actually put the glasses on her face was when she was alone and thinking. She would stare into space. Afterward, her eyes would be red. When Erec asked why, she would say they made her eyes water.

He looped them around his own neck, sure she would want them when he found her. Danny tried to pull them off for fun, but the chain caught.

"I have to get out of here." Erec looked around, breathing fast.

Danny winked and picked Zoey up. "I'll be under my bed," he whispered. "If this works, run for it."

In a few minutes Zoey skipped back, a delighted grin on her face. "Danny's climbing out the window. He's probably already gone!"

Mrs. Smith shot from her chair like a coyote after a roadrunner into Danny's room. Her thick, stubby legs and long feet flew over the beige carpet.

"What are you waiting for?" Sammy asked. "Go!"

Erec felt for his mother's picture and made sure the glasses were around his neck. "Come with me?"

"Nah. I'd rather see what the sitter does when she finds Danny under the bed. Now go!"

Trevor snored on the couch, gripping his action figures of Franklin Stein, the Super A springball team guardian, and a Cyclops. Erec was sure they were duking it out in Trevor's dreams. He darted down the stairs and ran three blocks before he dared look over his shoulder. There was no sign of the babysitter chasing him.

Little did he know that he had taken only the first few steps of a very long journey.

CHAPTER TWO

Where the Sidewalk Opened

AT THE END of the block, a crowd formed behind a barricade. Super A Team sports celebrity Mighty Joe Liath strolled out in shorts, a muscle shirt, and the Super A eye patch, flexing his huge biceps.

Erec wished Trevor could be there. Trevor owned all the Super A Team cards and figurines, knew the players' statistics, and had seen all of their movies. He even liked the greasy food at the Super A King fastaurants. A man followed Joe Liath with a movie camera and another threw him a barbell, which Joe tossed high like a baton. He caught it behind his back and spun to flash a toothy grin at the camera.

Erec wanted to stay and watch, but his shoes tapped the sidewalk, ready to go. He pushed through the thickening crowd until the way was clear. He let his feet direct him down an alley.

A boy his age walked by with his parents, laughing. Erec wondered what it would be like to have a real father. His had deserted him when he was three. What would it be like to have happily married parents, who bought him ice cream and went for walks with him? He knew his father was alive somewhere, but he had no interest in finding him.

A long line led to the hot-dog stand outside of Grand Central Station. People were walking fast everywhere. His mother was nowhere in sight. He stopped in front of Herman Howl's Finest UnderWear in the World and looked around.

This was great—being rushed by a cloudy thought to do nothing. Then his hand, on its own, shot into his pocket.

Of course—the picture. He had to ask if anyone had seen his mother. The short, chubby man at the hot-dog stand had been there last night when they had bought hot dogs together. Maybe he'd remember her.

"Want another dog, kid?" The vendor ran sausagelike fingers through what was left of his oiled black hair.

Erec pulled out the picture. "Actually, I'm looking for—"

"Whadda ya want?" The man looked past Erec at the forming line. Erec held up the picture. The vendor's mouth dropped and then returned to its original scowl. "Never seen her." He fidgeted with his tongs.

"How did you know I was looking for her?"

He glanced at the next customer. "What else would you be asking? Next!"

THE DRAGON'S EYE

"But we were just here yesterday—"

"*Next!*"

The man behind him stepped up to the cart and ordered a soft drink. Pushed to the side, Erec kicked a chunk of concrete into a gutter. The hot-dog vendor didn't remember his mother. Asking any stranger about her would be pointless.

Still thinking, he crossed the street and almost walked into a man working at a newsstand. The man was thin, with wild-looking dark blue eyes and sparse brown hair. Something about him made Erec cringe. He was strangely familiar, like a person from one of his nightmares.

A girl Erec's age with long, wavy, dark hair and butterscotch skin bounced over from the newsstand after helping a customer. "Let me guess," she said. "I'm a great guesser. Candy, right? No, it's more serious. Something for your mom, I think. Headache medicine?"

The newsstand man said roughly, "You buying something?" Erec shook his head and the man crossed his arms. "What? You're wasting my time, kid."

Erec reached into his pocket for the picture and held it up. "Have you seen her?"

The man grabbed it. "Where did you get this?"

The brown-haired girl peeked at the picture. Her eyes widened.

The man stepped closer. "This isn't a lost-and-found service. You're pretty young to be out here all alone." He moved closer, too close. "Are you lost? What's your name?"

The man's cologne smelled familiar and awful. It gave Erec a chill, and his stomach rose into his throat. He grabbed the picture and quickly walked away.

"Wait!" The girl chased him. Her dark brown eyes sparkled as she waved a candy bar over her head. "You forgot this."

Her dress was too small, Erec noticed, and all different colors.

He had never seen clothing patched so many times. "I didn't buy any candy," he said.

She stuffed it in his hand and whispered, "I've seen her. The picture. Meet me in front of Water Lilies around the corner." She hurried away.

Erec eyed the candy bar and looked up at the girl. He couldn't believe she recognized his mother. As he rounded the corner he saw the man yelling at her.

Time seemed to stop as he waited in front of Water Lilies plant shop. Right when he was sure she wasn't coming, the girl dashed around the corner, eyes flashing. "I'm Bethany Evirly. My Uncle Earl can't see us talk. Believe me, you don't want to know him. And I didn't like the way he was looking at you."

"That makes two of us." Erec glanced up the street, almost expecting her Uncle Earl to charge around the corner.

"It's okay. I'm supposed to be getting his favorite coffee." Bethany pointed at a small, dark coffeehouse called Drips. She stared for a moment at Erec's glass eye and quickly looked away.

"Let me see the picture again." Erec handed it to her. "Yup, definitely her. I've worked here most of my life. I don't miss much. Especially the weird stuff."

"What was weird? Where did you see my mom?"

Bethany paled. "It was your *mom*? I should have guessed." She looked down. "Well . . . I saw her this morning. She went into the underground place. I always notice when people do that."

"What, the subway?" Erec asked.

"No. It's like a secret passage underground. I told you weird things go on here. Two big men were with her. It looked like . . ." Her voice trailed off.

"What?"

"Like she was being taken somewhere," Bethany said. "Like

THE DRAGON'S EYE

she couldn't get away from them. This morning Uncle Earl brought me here an hour early, at four. It was awful, dark and cold. I had to set up the newsstand by myself, and Uncle Earl just sat around until these two huge men with eye patches showed up with her. She looked really angry. My uncle ran over to meet them. I think he was expecting them."

Air slipped from Erec's lungs. He felt like he was collapsing. His mother was not okay after all. "Are you sure it was her?"

"Positive. They were under a streetlamp."

"Show me where that underground place is. I'm going to find her."

Bethany crossed her arms. "It's not that easy."

"What are you talking about? Let's go."

"You can't just walk in."

"Why not?" Erec grabbed Bethany's wrist and pulled her toward Grand Central Station. She yanked back.

"Listen. I'm trying to tell you. It's not part of the normal subway system. It's a . . . special subway or something. I've seen people using it for years. It's hidden. My uncle watches it all the time. He must know all about it, but he won't admit anything."

Her face softened. "Anyway, I figured out how it works. I've spied on Gerard, the hot-dog man. He makes it open. People tell him a password and he pulls a lever in his cart. The sidewalk opens at the bottom of some steps, and more steps go down. After people go in, the sidewalk slams shut over their heads. It's strange, people walk by like they can't even see it, but it's clear as day to me."

Erec put his hand over his face. So, this was why he was here. His mother was in danger. The cloudy thought told him she wasn't hurt. He hoped it stayed that way.

"Do you believe me?" Bethany looked at him sideways.

Erec nodded. "How do I get in?" He wasn't sure why, but he had a feeling she wouldn't lie to him.

"We tell Gerard the password and run down the steps. But my uncle can't see us, or it's all over."

"Us? We? I don't think so. I better go alone."

Bethany shuffled her feet, but looked him in the eye. "I'm going with you. That's the deal. Or no password."

"But you could be stuck under the sidewalk."

"So could you."

"I have to find my mom. You don't have to go. And the last thing I need is your uncle chasing us. I'm sure he'll look for you."

"He doesn't know I can get in there." She grabbed his arm. "I've thought about escaping forever. Earl doesn't care about me. He's just stuck with me because my parents died when I was little. He makes me work night and day, and he won't even buy me another dress." She looked down at her dirty, patched frock.

"But what if we get stuck? What if it's a criminal hideout?"

"I'll risk it. If I'm running away, I'm going somewhere totally different, and I think this is my best bet. I've always wanted to see what was down there. Plus, what better way to begin than by helping you find your mother?"

Erec did not like the idea of Bethany's Uncle Earl chasing them, but going underground alone wasn't so great either. "How can we get in without him seeing?"

They peeked around the corner. Earl was searching up and down the street. "He's looking for me. Let's go around the block. We'll hide behind people and duck when we get to the hot-dog stand. Pretend you're tying your shoes."

Luckily, Grand Central Station was growing more crowded. They walked behind three men in blue suits to Herman Howl's underwear store and ducked beside the hot-dog stand. Bethany pointed at empty concrete steps near a wall. They appeared to be a dead end.

Gerard, the vendor, peered over his cart at them, thick eyebrows raised. "You again? You buying this time? If you want to play games, kids, go find a park."

Bethany looked up. "There is more to the earth, wind, and sea. Old magic remember me."

Gerard's eyebrows shot up and back like two fuzzy boomerangs. His face softened. "You gotta be kidding. You're a couple a kids."

Bethany looked as worried as Erec felt. She looked at Gerard and said, louder, "There is more to the earth, wind, and sea. Old magic remember me."

Gerard raised his hands. "Aright, aright. You got your sixty bucks?"

"What?" Erec stuffed his hands in his empty pockets.

"Thirty each. You don't think it's free anymore, do ya?" He looked at them suspiciously.

Erec frowned. "We don't even have that much at home."

Bethany smiled broadly. "I have ninety-eight dollars and sixty-three cents in my money belt."

Erec was impressed. "How do you know the exact amount?"

She shrugged. "I'm good with numbers."

Erec shook his head, not liking the idea. "We might have to pay to get back. Maybe another sixty. One of us could be stuck in there."

"I won't come back." She grabbed Erec's wrist. "I promise, if there's only enough for one ticket back, I'll give it to you." She counted out sixty dollars.

Gerard pursed his lips and drummed his sausage fingers on the cart. "Are you two, perhaps, hiding from someone?" He looked over his shoulder at the newsstand.

"Is that any of your business? Here." Bethany shoved the money at him.

"Hmm." Gerard's face smoothed out. "I guess it isn't my business." He took the money and then helped two customers who looked down at Erec and Bethany with amusement. When they left Gerard smiled. "Password again?"

Bethany took Erec's hand. "Ready to run?" She nodded at Gerard. "There is more to the earth, wind, and sea. Old magic remember me!"

Gerard pushed away a red vinyl cloth in his cart and pulled a shiny metal lever. "Aren't you kids taking anything with you?"

"No," they both said.

Bethany and Erec darted behind passersby. The sidewalk opened at the bottom of the steps, before their eyes. More steps descended into the darkness. Erec and Bethany flew down moments before the concrete slammed shut.

Erec was sure he had heard Gerard shout something about great new underwear at Herman Howl's if they needed it.

CHAPTER THREE

In FES Station

THE CONCRETE SLAMMED shut over their heads so fast Erec wondered what would have happened if they had gone down the steps slower. Bright lights flashed on in the low, sloping ceiling. Bethany and Erec ran down to a landing where more steps led down. These led to another landing, then another. Growing tired, they slowed down to a walk.

"You don't suppose these go on forever, do you?" Bethany asked.

Erec glanced back the way they had come. "It'll feel like forever when we're climbing back up."

Bethany, though, was looking the other way. "I've been wondering what's down here for years."

The air felt thicker as they went downward. It was heavy somehow, almost lifeless. The farther they went, the more unpleasant it became, until each breath felt contaminated. Erec craved the fresh air he'd left behind. He had an urge to run back up, but he remembered his mother needed him. Bethany's lips were pinched together, her eyes squinting.

After countless flights of stairs, the passage ended at a knobless gray metal door. Both of them pushed, but it did not budge. A sign at the side read WELCOME TO FES (FEE EVERY STOP) STATION, OUR NEW AND IMPROVED HUB OF TRANSPORTATION, WITH NEW AND IMPROVED FEES, MONITORED BY PRINCE, INC. Below the sign was a red button.

Erec gestured. "After you."

Bethany solemnly pushed the button. The door slid open long enough to let them in, then slammed behind them. They walked into an oval station that seemed as big as Grand Central was above. People of all shapes, colors, and sizes rushed to and fro: men in business suits, teachers with classes of children, couples, and families. Kids roamed in small packs. Some wore odd clothing, shiny silver jackets and pants, or long black or blue hooded cloaks and robes.

"It must be an underground part of Grand Central," Erec said, thinking out loud. The air around him still felt strange, wrong. It was almost as if it weighed more, not in his chest exactly, but on his mind. "This place is stressing me out. I don't know why, though."

"I feel the same way. Everything seems creepy. It's like all of a sudden, the whole world feels sad . . . or angry somehow."

The ceiling was around sixty feet high. Shops and restaurants lined the walls. Some were familiar: Super A King fastaurants and Burger Rama. But most were new, with interesting names like Sky High Chilly, A Fine Kettle of Fish, Animals or Minerals Vegetarian Cuisine, and Molten Lava Sundaes. There seemed to be a lot of underwear shops.

"This is so much cleaner than the rest of Grand Central," Bethany said. "And look at that shop, No Fear Flying Gear. How could that stay open in a train station?"

"Yeah, and all those underwear stores. I don't get it."

"Maybe it's because people are traveling. They might forget to pack underwear." Bethany shrugged.

Erec peered through a shop window. "I don't even see underwear in those stores. Just weird, shiny clothes."

"Maybe they hide it in the back so nobody will laugh at the people who forgot it."

Erec laughed. "You've got to be kidding." The strangeness of the station almost made him forget the pressing sadness in the air. "Hey, check out that store, Cavern in a Canyon. And . . . what was that?" His finger froze.

"What?" Bethany nudged him nervously. "I don't see anything."

"A door disappeared." He turned to her. "I thought I was seeing things, but then I saw another. Look." All around the walls, people walked into thin doors that vanished when they shut. New doors appeared, and people casually strolled from them, sometimes buying coffee at Under Grounds and going back into the same door, which disappeared.

The doors all looked the same: plain brown wood with gold doorknobs and small gold plaques. Sometimes they appeared in front of a food stand, and then they would shrink to half size to fit in the short wall under the counter. People would crawl through, spilling their coffee and grumbling.

"Let's check them out," said Bethany.

"We'd better look for my mom." Erec turned to see if the door he and Bethany came through had disappeared. It was still there, thankfully. Made of painted metal, it looked quite different than the wooden ones. A big green neon sign over it flashed UPPER EARTH. Erec pushed to make sure it opened back to the concrete steps. It would not budge.

A computerized voice sounded from the door. "Password?"

Erec repeated the password they had told Gerard, but the door remained closed.

Nearby, Bethany slid her hands over a wooden door, shaking the knob. "I can't open it."

A tall man with a pinched nose and hair greased over a large bald spot squinted at her through a monocle. "Excuse me? Are you trying to break into my house? Need I call the police?" He pointed to gold numbers on a plaque reading 2211.

"No. I'm so sorry." Bethany's face was red. "I've never seen one of these. I just wanted to see how it worked."

The man's eyebrows shot up. "Never seen a Port-O-Door?" He whipped out a camera and took their picture. "Just in case." He patted the camera and murmured a code after they walked away. The door slammed behind him and vanished.

"Bethany, the door from the stairs is locked. We're stuck here."

Bethany looked shocked. She pounded on the door, saying the password and as many variations of it she could think of. Finally she gave up.

"Well, I don't care. I don't ever want to go back, anyway." She bit her lip. Erec took a breath of the heavy air. This better be the right way to find his mother or he was really in trouble. They wandered farther into the huge station. After a few steps, Bethany stopped and pointed up. They had walked past a lower ceiling rim and could now see all the way to the top. It was moving, full of changing, swarming colors.

"What's that?" Erec asked in awe.

Bethany looked pale. "People."

Erec looked harder. She was right. There were people . . . yes, he was sure they were people, *flying* by the ceiling. Most were alone or in pairs; no children were up there. While they were doing something he had always dreamed of, they looked as busy and bored as commuters in rush hour. They glanced at their watches as they sailed by, occasionally bumping into one another and shaking fists. Tunnel holes near the ceiling led them in and out. A few landed on a tall slide that led them to the station floor.

Erec wondered if they were lifelike computer images put up for fun. They seemed amazingly real.

Bethany's eyes were glued to the sight too. "Do you think they're held up by cords?"

A flying man landed on the slide, sailed down to the floor, and ran by Erec, bumping him with his briefcase.

"Bethany," Erec said slowly, "I don't think we're in Grand Central Station anymore."

"I've seen strange things my whole life, living with Uncle Earl," Bethany said, "but never anything like this."

They walked in a daze, bumping into people because they could not stop staring at the ceiling. Crowds thronged toward large neon signs. One glowed ALYPIUM in huge white letters.

"I wonder what Alypium means. Do you think it's a place?" Bethany asked. A gigantic red neon sign further away read AORTH, and a third in blue read ASHONA.

"Ashona sounds like a sea-animal zoo," said Erec.

"Ooh, let's go there!"

Erec shook his head, not moving. He could not imagine how

he would find his mother here. His cloudy thought had vanished, like so many clouds and thoughts do. "Look at all the kids going to Alypium. It seems like a lot more is going on there." Masses of kids headed toward the Alypium sign. He could hear some of them talking about contests, but not well enough to understand. Under the Alypium sign, fast-moving lines led under huge arched doorways marked SKYWAY and ARTERY.

The Artery line was long, but not the Skyway line. A man with a blue business suit and a briefcase looked at his watch, strolled into the Skyway entry, and jumped. Instead of landing on his feet, he continued to sail upward, one hand holding his briefcase at his side and the other above his head, like a rudder, steering himself in the wind. He flew over an arched curve and out of sight.

"Wow," Erec said, "did you see that?"

A tiny old woman tapped Erec's shoulder. "Move it, honey. Go on or get out of the way." Erec looked at her frail figure in surprise. He was about to offer his arm when she shoved him aside with her cane. In the Skyway entry, cane tucked her under her arm with her shiny black purse, she flew up into the wind tunnel.

"I wonder if we could do that." Bethany tossed her long dark curls over her shoulder. They watched others sail off. Erec, overcome with curiosity, ran to the takeoff spot, raised his arms over his head, and jumped. His feet hit the ground. He jumped again and again, first with one arm up and then the other, until he noticed the people in the growing line watching him with snickers and shocked expressions.

Erec's face grew hot. He grabbed a giggling Bethany and walked past someone saying, ". . . think he's five years old or something . . ."

"The Artery then?" Bethany laughed.

"Fine."

Erec gladly left the Skyway, and they found the end of the Artery line. It was set with metal rails like a line for a roller coaster. "I still don't get this place. Do you think the Artery is a ride?"

"Mmm." She shrugged. She was listening to some boys standing in front of them.

A short, slim boy with shaggy red hair was talking fast. "My dad said *everyone* will be there. Even some of the Super A Team's kids. But they don't have any better chance than we do. I wonder if they'll bunk with us in the castle." The boy wore one of the silvery-gray jackets. It moved like shimmering lava.

A tall boy with blond hair, also around Erec's age, answered. "They'll be in the castle, all right, but in real rooms, not with the likes of us."

The red-haired boy looked disappointed. "We'll still see 'em though."

The line started moving again and the boys rounded a corner. After a few turns, Erec heard the blond boy talk the red-haired one into riding the Lift instead of the Artery. "I know it takes longer, but it's supposed to be beautiful, and I've never done it. Look, you've still got underwear on."

"Oops!" The red-haired boy laughed and pulled off the jacket. The fabric melted around his fingers, yet somehow stayed together. He stuffed it into his back pocket, even though most of it slid out again. As he turned the final corner of the queue, his jacket caught on a post and was yanked out of his pocket. The boy didn't notice. Instead, he ran with his friend through a small archway marked LIFT.

"Hey," Erec shouted. "Your jacket!" The boy disappeared through the archway.

Erec grabbed it as he passed the metal post. It felt surprisingly cool, soft and sleek like liquid metal.

"Might as well go this way." Erec and Bethany went through the small archway too.

It looked like an amusement park ride, which seemed even odder with the sad feeling that radiated through the place. A man with a striped vest that said "MagicLine" asked "How many?" without really looking at them.

"Two." The man pushed them toward a white line painted on the floor. In a moment, something that looked like a ski lift scooped them up. The seats were padded and comfortable. A wide pole connected to a cable that disappeared through a gap in the ceiling. The man strapped them in and pulled a padded bar under their arms. He stuffed paper bags into their hands and threw thick blankets with fuzzy hoods over them.

Their lift chair soared through a long, dark tunnel. Bright lights rhythmically whizzed by in the darkness, and wind pelted their faces.

"Wow," said Erec after a while. "This is some tunnel."

"I bet it's all underground," shouted Bethany.

Then there was a blinding burst of light. A huge green face appeared before them. Erec gasped. Could it be? Yes. It was the Statue of Liberty. They must have come out of her torch, but they were going too fast to be sure. Erec and Bethany looked back, open jawed, as the statue and the whole city of New York fell from sight.

CHAPTER FOUR
Losers in Alypium

ET DUST PUMMELED Erec's and Bethany's faces, and all was white until they burst from a cloud over the ocean. No land was in sight. They sailed so fast Erec was thankful he was covered with blankets. There were sandwiches in the paper bags, and Erec ate his right away. Huge white waves rolled far below. Birds darted over the waters and fish jumped from the waves. The blond kid was right, the ride was beautiful.

The awful, heavy air Erec had felt at FES Station was gone. Still, he had an uneasy feeling that they should have turned around long ago. "When do you think we'll head back?"

"I don't. See way out there? I think that dot is the lift ahead of us. Have you looked up?"

Erec turned his head to see everything with his one eye. With the excitement of sailing in an open chair over the ocean he had not noticed the pole attached to their chair. It hung unsupported in the air, with no cable in sight. Seeing that, he grabbed the bar, knuckles white.

"Don't worry, we would have fallen ages ago. We've been riding about a half hour, and it's been like this the whole time." Bethany smiled. "I think we found someplace . . . different. I mean, flying people, this ski lift, that jacket that melts in your hands. Even the password to get here, 'old magic remember me.' And the people operating the lift had 'MagicLine' on their vests."

She stared out over the waters. "You might think I'm crazy. It's just . . . I've always thought there might be someplace like this. Something *more*. Magical, exciting, different."

Erec shook his head. "I used to feel that way. My mother saw magic everywhere. It was like a game. But it became ridiculous because I got too old and she wouldn't stop playing." His mother still treated him like a baby, even singing an awful lullaby, an endless source of embarrassment.

"It was the opposite for me. My uncle wouldn't admit anything was unusual, even when it was right in front of my eyes."

They stared into the expanse of blue beneath them, teeming with life and mystery. Low clouds clung to their faces like dew. For several more hours they sailed over lush land with rolling hills, dotted with farms and villages, cities and forests.

"Where could we be going?" Bethany asked. "Around the world?"

"For thirty dollars?"

They crossed more water and gorgeous countryside. The sun warmed the air around them, and Erec took his hood off. A tremendous mountain range towered ahead, rock faces and jagged cliffs shooting into the clouds. They glided, slower, through the peaks. Waterfalls cascaded nearby. Hawks swooped around the lift. Deeper in the mountains, a glowing golden dome covered a huge plateau that was hidden by sharp cliffs. Although enormous, it was hard to see, blinking in and out of sight as the sun glinted off it.

The hazy dome felt like mist on Erec's face as the lift slid through. They stopped on a platform in a station house. A tall young man unbuckled them with a smile. "Good luck in the contests."

Erec pulled his mother's picture from his pocket. "Have you seen her?"

He shook his head. "I see too many people, though, to swear it. Most use the Artery, anyway."

Erec's insides tightened when he walked into Alypium station and his lips curled down. That sad, heavy feeling in the air at FES station was here, too. This station looked like a smaller version of FES, complete with flying people and disappearing doors.

Bethany walked to a ticket counter. A bald man behind the desk narrowed his eyes at her. "Going sssomewhere? It seemssss nobody elsssse isss. They're only coming in."

"How much are tickets back to New York?"

"New York?" The man raised a puff of skin where his eyebrow should be. "But thatsss in Upper Earth." His eyes narrowed. "Ooooh. Ssstrangers. How interesssssting."

"How much is it?"

"You can't *go* to Upper Earth. Thatsss not allowed. You know the rulessssss." The man started to sway.

"Well, how much to that station under Grand Central?"

"You mean FESsss? Sssssuch a good name. Ssssso much better than its old name, the 'Heart.' An Artery going back would be three ssssilver sssshires." His torso waved as if he were about to strike.

"How much is that in dollars?" Bethany asked.

"American dollarsss? But of courssssse." A smile snaked across his face. "Thirty dollarsss apiecesss." Erec noticed he had no arms. "But what are your namesssss?"

The armless man was hissing and waving so wildly, Erec and Bethany backed away.

Erec whispered, "What are we going to do?"

"I told you." She handed thirty dollars to Erec. "I don't want to go back."

Erec would not take it. "You've helped me enough."

"No." Bethany stuffed the money, folded up, in his pocket. "Don't worry. I'm great. I've never had a day like this in my life. Just compare it to slaving for my uncle."

Erec slipped the three ten-dollar bills into a machine and got back three silver coins with a crown on one side and a queen on the other. Bethany put her remaining eight dollars in and got back eight paper bills, printed with the word "Bil." She turned one over and gasped. On the back was a picture of her as a small child, hard at work in her uncle's newsstand. Erec took a Bil, and the picture changed to him with some friends at his old school.

Bethany pointed. "Look."

The tall blond boy and shorter red-haired one from FES Station were walking by. Erec pulled the silky jacket from his pocket and ran to catch them. "You lost this in the lift station."

The red-haired boy grabbed it. "Did you steal this?"

"I doubt that, you dope," said the blond boy, "seeing as he's returning it to you." Then he stepped back in shock. "Oscar, look at these guys." He held his thumb and finger in an *L* over his forehead.

A smirk spread over Oscar's face. "Losers! I didn't know they let Losers in here! What, are Losers coming to the contests now?"

The blond boy stared.

Insulted, Bethany grabbed the jacket back. "Didn't he just return this to you?"

"Give me that!" Oscar shouted. "It's not our fault you're Losers." He tried to take his jacket, but Bethany backed away. "See, Jack. My dad said there was a reason they were Losers."

"My parents said they should be treated fairly." Jack looked at them, frowning. "I guess they don't like to be called Losers."

"No kidding," said Erec. "Maybe you two don't like to be called stupid morons."

Oscar started to rush at Erec, but Jack held him back, laughing. "Please, don't be offended. We're sorry, really. We just don't know what else to call you."

Oscar giggled. "Yeah, with those big *L*'s on your forehead."

"Say what you want about me," Erec warned them. "But if I hear another word about Bethany, you'll be sorry you were born." He knew he should walk away, but fighting was a reflex after years of defending his sister Nell, with her walker, and his brother Trevor for being slow.

Bethany saw how mad he was. "Let's go, Erec. These guys aren't worth it." She pulled him away, leaving Oscar laughing.

Jack ran up, his face white. "Please. Don't go. I am sorry, really."

Erec looked at him skeptically. Bethany's nose was in the air, her face red.

"Look," said Jack. "Is it safe to say you're not from around here?"

"Yeah, I guess."

"I really want to help make up for the . . . mix-up. I'm Jack Hare, and this is Oscar Felix. We can tell you're from . . . up there." Jack jerked his thumb upward. "Where people forgot magic. You stand out here."

Erec was confused. Sure, some people were dressed a little oddly, but Jack himself wore shorts and a T-shirt.

Bethany's chin puckered as she looked at her patched dress. "It's okay, Erec. He's talking about me. I'll never fit in anywhere with these old rags."

"No," said Jack. "It's not your clothes. You have *L* marks on your foreheads. It's a spell put on your kind, since President Inkle passed the Loser Identification Law. A lot of people think it was a great idea, but my parents say it's not right. People should have privacy, even people from up there." He jerked his thumb upward again.

"You jerk," Oscar said. "It's not up there. We're not in Aorth anymore. We're in Alypium. From here we all live down there." He jerked his thumb downward with disgust. "I want to know how they got in here."

Both Jack and Oscar had extremely pale skin. Jack looked at Erec with interest. "Your eyes are different colors. Is that normal where you're from?"

Erec shook his head. "I have a glass eye." He paused. "My name's Erec Rex."

Oscar laughed. "That's a funny name."

"Leave him alone," Jack said. "You're named after your dad, which is funny knowing you and him."

Erec looked closely at Bethany's forehead. "How come I can't see the *L*'s?"

"I think only the Keepers can see them," Jack said.

"Keepers?" Erec asked.

Bethany said slowly, "They're the Keepers, and we're the Losers."

Jack nodded. "The Keepers of magic and the Losers of magic."

Bethany and Erec stared at each other. At last she laughed. "Well, if this place is really magical, then we *are* losers to be missing out on it."

Erec asked, "What do you mean we forgot magic? I never knew any."

"We learned in History that the Losers forgot magic five hundred years ago."

"Were *made* to forget it," said Oscar. "Because you were killing each other with it."

"Shut up, Oscar," Jack said. "I'll call my dad on my cell and see if he knows how to get rid of those *L*'s."

"*My* dad would say turn them in," Oscar said.

"Except your dad's never home," said Jack. "So, can it." He held a finger up, shook it, and put it in his ear. Then he spoke quietly into it and put it back in his ear.

When he finished, Bethany asked to see his phone. "You can't see it without a microscope," said Jack. "Don't you use cell phones in Upper Earth?"

"Um, yes," said Erec. "But they're a bit bigger."

Jack looked at him strangely. "My dad said to get hats on you quick. The *L*'s should fade when you adjust. Let's get you out of here, in case someone else noticed."

Oscar looked appalled. "You're hiding them? They shouldn't even *be* in the contests. What if they win?"

"Then it was meant to be," said Jack. "Let's get our bags."

"What are the contests for?" Bethany asked. "Are there prizes?"

"You don't know about the contests?" Jack looked amazed. "I thought that's why you were here."

Erec shook his head. "I'm looking for my mom." He showed her picture to Jack and Oscar. Looking at it made his heart sink. What if he never saw his family again? What if his mother was lost forever?

He should never have come here without knowing where he was going.

The luggage counter was piled high with suitcases and trunks. Jack called, "C'mon, boy." A huge duffel bag hunched and twisted on a shelf until it flopped onto the floor and scooted like a humongous inchworm toward Jack. A uniformed man ushered it around the corner, patting its back.

Oscar whistled, and two blue suitcases tipped onto their wheels and sped to him. The duffel rolled at Jack's feet as he lazily scratched its belly—if a duffel can have a belly—before unzipping it and finding an Alypium Team springball cap.

He gave the hat to Erec. "Wear it low to cover the *L*." Oscar looked annoyed, but he found a Super A Team springball cap and tossed it to Bethany.

The hat fell to the ground. Bethany's mouth was open as she stared at Oscar's suitcases jumping on him like frisky puppies. "That settles it," she said. "This has all been a great dream. I suppose now I'll wake up."

Erec grinned and handed Bethany the hat. So this was where his mother had found his toothbrush and the other odd things in his house. He wondered why they had to keep it a secret. It seemed like everyone would want to know about this place. "It's real. I've seen things like this before, but not suitcases that roll on their own wheels."

Oscar raised his eyebrows. "I thought everybody had suitcases with wheels now. They're much less awkward."

"Where did you get these things?" Erec asked.

"Vulcan," Jack shrugged. "Vulcan stores are everywhere, only they're hard to track down when you need one. They sometimes wander into the lands beyond and show up years later. Best to get them online."

"My mom bought our coat rack at Vulcan online," Erec said.

Oscar looked confused. "You have computers in Upper Earth but don't have suitcases with wheels?"

Erec said to Bethany, "We found it. Something more . . . like you said. You knew it was out there, right? Well, here it is."

All around the station, people walked with suitcases and bags. Only now Erec noticed no hands pulled them as they rolled along.

"Why do you call that 'underwear'?" Bethany pointed to Oscar's jacket.

"Aorth is real hot 'cause it's underground," Jack said. "UnderWear keeps out the heat."

"You mean all those underwear stores in FES Station sold clothes for Aorth?" Erec laughed. "But what are the contests for?"

"You know. To pick out the next three kings or queens."

"Kings or queens of what?" Bethany asked.

Jack squinted at them. "Don't you know anything about the Kingdoms of the Keepers?"

"The what?" Erec shook his head.

Jack sighed. "King Piter of Alypium, King Pluto of Aorth, and Queen Posey of Ashona are triplets. They've ruled for five hundred years . . . the whole time the kingdoms have been here. Bea Cleary, a great seer back then, said that they were the rightful rulers days before they were born.

"King Piter was supposed to have triplets that would be the next rulers. He did—but they died when they were young. His wife, Queen Hesti, died later that morning: sizzled somehow. There was nothing left except her crown and a smoking spot on the floor. It was really sad.

"And now there's nobody to take over. The kings and queen are tired of ruling, and King Piter is really sick. Someone decided to hold contests to find new rulers to take their places. The beauty is, anybody could be the next king. Someone poor, homely, genuine."

"Stupid, mean, or rich," Oscar added.

"Tomorrow is the big assembly, and then the contests start the next day. Are you coming to the castle?"

Erec had no idea where to find his mother, and the castle seemed as good a place as any. Anyway, it would be somewhere to eat and come up with a plan. Hats on, Erec and Bethany followed Jack, Oscar, and their luggage to a bus stop.

"Do you have buses in Upper Earth?" Oscar asked.

It was nearly dark. Erec remembered his brothers and sisters. They must be worried. Plus, maybe his mother was home by now. He asked to use Jack's cell phone.

Jack laughed. "Use mine? That's good. Don't you have one? Did they mess up when you were born?" He spoke into his finger, listened to it, and then shoved his hands in his pockets. "There's a ban on calls to Upper Earth." Seeing how disappointed Erec was, he added, "Maybe you'll find a way at the castle."

The seven, including the duffel and suitcases, climbed up a steep mountain road whose top was lost in clouds. The evening air was chilly. The same feeling of despair seemed to hang in the air that Erec had felt inside FES and Alypium stations.

Jagged cliffs towered over the huge fir trees. The golden dome they had flown into seemed invisible from inside. Scattered houses and stores with boarded windows and chipping paint marred the scenery.

Jack looked around. "This is nothing like Aorth."

"I heard there are ghosts in the castle basement," Oscar said. "And rooms that trap you, and secret passages."

"Do you feel it too, that terrible, sad feeling in the air?" Erec asked. "It feels like the world is about to end."

"And like it knows it, and it's scared and upset," Bethany said.

Jack stared at him. "You must be sensing the change. When people used to be able to go from Upper Earth into the Kingdoms of the Keepers, they could feel the problems in the Substance. I heard they got depressed, unless they took a breather bag of Upper Earth air with them and broke in real slow. After a few hours you shouldn't notice it much anymore."

"The Substance?" Bethany squinted at Jack. "What the heck is that?"

He rolled his eyes, sighing. "Don't you guys know anything? It's the energy that fills the world, the thing that holds all the magic." He shook his head at Oscar in amazement. "The Substance flows around the Earth, through the Aitherplanes."

"But we don't have Substance and Aither . . . things in Upper Earth," Erec said.

"You have them, but you can't use them for magic."

Erec wondered how Jack knew about Upper Earth if he had never been there. "So they don't do us any good?"

"You need them to live."

"But there isn't this awful feeling where I'm from, like there is here."

"The Substance is more messed up here. We know it's a problem, but nobody knows why, or how to fix it."

"So," Bethany said with a frown, "when we get used to it, this will feel normal to us?"

"Usually. It still hits you every now and then. You feel that the Substance is wrong and trying to fix itself but can't. We still know it's happening, but we try to forget about it."

A bright blue bus waited at the stop. Jack and Oscar's bags scooted into a trailer and the group scrambled aboard. The bus driver's skin and clothing glowed hazy silver. The harder Erec looked, the harder the guy was to see, as if he was only light, but when Erec turned away he snapped into focus. The driver batted his eyes into the rearview mirror and played with his silver hair.

Bethany nudged Erec, putting two Bils in the slot for them. When she saw the driver she screeched and leapt backward into Jack. The driver glared at her as she hurried by. The four plopped onto one of the two roomy benches in front.

"What *is* that guy?" asked Bethany.

"A silver ghost," said Jack, shrugging.

"A real ghost?"

Oscar frowned. "You don't have ghosts in Upper Earth?"

"No. Are they safe?"

"Usually," said Jack. "You can't trust 'em, though. They're pretty much out for themselves. Don't like humans too much."

"Silver ghosts? Are there other colors too?" Erec asked.

"Sure," Jack said. "Golden ghosts are great if you can find one. But you don't want to run into a bronze one. Then there are human ghosts, who stay on Upper Earth after they die. They look just like regular people."

Two identical boys about Erec's age with black, windswept hair, pale skin, and steely blue eyes were complaining to the bus driver. They wore long blue cloaks, and one sported a droopy gray hat.

"I don't care." The boy had a petulant voice. "Maybe this will help." He handed the ghost something that glittered through his silver hand.

The driver stood, pointing at Erec, his friends, and the people on the bench across from them. "Get in the back. Now."

They froze at the order.

"Now!" The ghost roared so loud Erec's ears rang. Oscar stood, followed by Jack and the kids on the other bench. Obviously the spoiled boys had paid off the driver so they could sit on the long benches in the front. It rubbed Erec the wrong way.

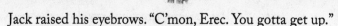

Jack raised his eyebrows. "C'mon, Erec. You gotta get up."

The ghost growled, "Last chance."

Bethany stepped away. The identical boys laughed.

Erec crossed his arms. He knew he should get up. This ghost thing could be dangerous. But these laughing rich kids sending everyone else to the back of the bus lit a fire in him. "You can't order us around."

"Oh, yes I can." The ghost's arm turned into a giant silver scoop. He swung it fast at Erec.

Erec winced, waiting to be flung at the door. Nothing happened. The ghost looked shocked. He swung again, his arm stopping inches away from Erec's body.

It was as if a shell was protecting him. The ghost tried prodding Erec, but it could not touch him.

The passengers stared. Erec looked down at himself, not sure what had happened.

CHAPTER FIVE

The Seeing Eyeglasses

T HE GHOST SNEERED. "Something is shielding him. Maybe it's those glasses." He marched back to the driver's seat. The identical boys sat on each side of Erec, staring hungrily at the glasses as the bus pulled out.

"I'm Balor Stain," said one of the boys, "and this is Damon. You can tell us apart because I have this"—Balor pointed to a bronze whistle around his neck—"and Damon always wears that goofy hat.

How much you want for those?" He touched the glasses.

"Hands off. I'm calling my friends back up here."

"No, you're not," said Damon. He spoke much slower than Balor and poked Erec hard on the shoulder.

"You can't." Balor smiled. "They aren't allowed up when the bus is moving. Anyway, we're sorry, right, Damon? That was obnoxious of us to want a whole bench each to stretch out on. Really, we're just tired. Up late last night packing, then traveling all day. We thought it would be fun to come by lift and bus like everyone else."

Erec glared, arms crossed.

"You're still mad. We'll make it up, I promise. Big pizza party at the castle, on us."

Damon's face twisted into a crooked smile. "Pizzaaa." He sang, "Damon had a little pizza, little pizza, little pizza . . ." to the tune of "Mary Had a Little Lamb."

"You're twins?"

"Triplets. Our brother Dollick doesn't get out much."

The bus slowed. A huge wall of clouds blocked the street, shooting up fifty feet. The swirling vapors reached far in both directions like a fortress. A bus ahead of them disappeared through an opening.

Balor grinned. "Aah, the Citadel of Clouds surrounding Alypium."

"Weren't we in Alypium?"

"Nah. That was the Outskirts."

Bright green light flashed under a rim of cloud and a small gap appeared. The bus drove through a long, dark tunnel and then burst into a sunset streaked with yellow and rose hues. Twisty streets wound around lakes, trees, and perfectly kept homes and parks. Narrow lanes with crooked overhanging signs looked like they came from a fairy story.

In the center of the village, a stately mansion with lovely gardens towered over the homes and shops. "What's that?" Erec pointed.

"The Green House. That's where President Washington Inkle lives."

Shops and theaters were crammed onto a smaller plateau up a hill. They were in the shadow of an enormous, oddly shaped building that stretched over many blocks in all directions. It was even taller than it was wide. One of its sides shot straight up like a smooth skyscraper. Long, irregular brick tubes and golden cones jutted from the other side, making stripes that glowed in soft pastel hues. Short, wide windows gave the building an ultramodern look. It gleamed in the sunlight like a gorgeous giant comb.

Doors ran up the straight edge of the tall building, not only leading into thin air, but sideways. In fact, as Erec looked harder, the building started to look like an enormous castle on its side.

"Is that King Piter's castle?"

Balor looked bored. "Of course. The famous."

"Is it supposed to look like it's on its side?"

"Not really, no. But it is on its side, nonetheless. King Piter is sick. He is old and confused, and he isn't able to keep the castle up anymore."

"What?"

"He muttered a spell by accident one day, almost ten years ago, and the castle went sideways. Nobody else has the power to upright it, and King Piter's not up to the job. He's really let the place go."

Erec frowned. "Do you need ladders to get from room to room?"

"No. King Pluto rearranged its gravity. It's a little tricky getting in and out, but once you're inside it feels all right."

"Usually." Damon giggled.

Balor laughed. "Every now and then a book shoots sideways off a table or someone falls. There are a few rooms that didn't take to the gravity spell. If you go into them, you fall onto the wall." He glanced behind him. "Don't tell the new kids. Damon and I want to push a few in and watch them figure out what happened." Damon and Balor burst into laughter. "Even better, what if someone walked out the wrong door, say, way up in the air." Balor giggled.

Erec cringed at the idea. "Real funny." These two were something else. "What are those?" Erec pointed to dark creatures flying around spires sticking out the side of the castle. "Bats?"

"Nah," Balor said. "Bats come out later. Those are gargoyles."

The bus pulled in front of six huge stone monsters that sat to the side of the palace. Balor and Damon climbed out. Erec waited for Bethany, Jack, and Oscar.

"How did you do that, with the ghost? Keeping him off you?" Oscar asked. Erec shrugged. Oscar looked Erec's glasses over before calling his suitcases from the trailer.

An eager young man with sandy blond hair, green eyes, and a big grin waved and blew a whistle. He wore a royal blue cape with a big white star. "Right this way, folks, future kings and queens. Grab your bags and come on in. I'm Spartacus Kilroy, one of King Piter's AdviSeers. Pick an open room in the temporary dormitories and sign your room number into my book." He paced back and forth, rubbing his hands together. "This is so exciting."

The dormitory wing was upright, with doors on the ground. It was attached to the flat underside of the castle.

"I'm starving." Erec sighed. If he paid for a meal, he could not afford to go home.

"Free food and shelter for contestants," said Jack. "Say, want to bunk with us?"

Oscar made a face.

"All right," said Erec. "But just for tonight." Tomorrow he planned to scour Alypium for his mother and head back if he didn't find her.

Each room had two sets of bunk beds. Jack, Oscar, and Erec signed their names into Spartacus Kilroy's book and took room 323. When Jack and Oscar left to find the cafeteria, Erec plopped onto his bed, exhausted. Kids bustled through the hallways, laughing and making noise. The sadness in the air seemed less pressing now, but Erec could still feel it.

He took the glasses off his neck. Why did the bus driver think they could have protected him? Curious, Erec slipped them on.

In a flash, the room was smaller and more crowded. Even more confusing, it looked like he was sitting in a chair now, not on a bed. It was the glasses. They were making him see strange things. He whisked them off just as he noticed a woman in the room with him.

He was back in the dorm room. Erec froze at the image that stayed in his mind. The woman looked oddly like his mother.

He put the glasses back on. Again, he seemed to be in the small, cluttered room. With his mother, who was knitting. She did not notice him.

"Mom?"

Startled, June O'Hara dropped her knitting. She looked wildly around, right through Erec. "Who's there?"

"It's me. I'm right here." Erec looked down and saw only the chair under him. He jumped when he realized he could not see himself at all.

June looked around, worried. "Where are you?"

"I'm here in the room. In the chair by the couch. I can't see myself."

She glanced around nervously. "How did you get here?" she said, suspicious. Erec wondered why she wasn't happier to see him (or not see him).

"I don't know. I just put your glasses on and I was here."

Color rushed into June's face, along with a huge grin. "Yes!" She

THE DRAGON'S EYE

threw a fist into the air and fell back, laughing, onto the bed. "Thank goodness. It *is* you. Erec, this is fantastic. What a smart boy to find my Seeing Eyeglasses. I was praying that one of you would find them. What a relief. Are you okay? Where are you?"

"I'm fine. I'm here, with you."

June smiled. "No, honey. When you put the glasses on, you can see me, but you're not really here. Anyone watching you would think you were talking to yourself. Are you home?"

"No. I went looking for you this morning. I had a cloudy thought. Now I'm in a place called Alypium. I got here from under Grand Central Station. Mom, people were *flying*. I thought I'd never find you."

June seemed stunned. "You're in Alypium," she murmured. "I can't believe it."

Erec looked around the small, comfortable room. "Where are you?"

June turned toward where he should be. "Erec, I don't want you to get upset, but you have to know. I've been . . . caught. Captured by people I've avoided for a long time. I am *fine*. They can't hurt me. But they can trap me here, I'm afraid. I'm in a dungeon—Pluto's dungeons."

She swept her arm across the tidy room. "I hoped if I kept moving we would stay hidden, but when they got our money it was so hard. The funny thing, now that they have me, it seems they don't even know who I am. They just know I lived in Alypium ten years ago and I have twins. Don't worry," she added, "I'll figure a way out of here."

Erec was shocked. "What? You *lived* in Alypium?"

June sighed. "Yes. I lived there, and you were born there. Now the fates have brought you back. Thank goodness you're okay."

Erec's head was spinning. Maybe this was a dream. "You're telling me I'm *from* this place? Why did we leave?"

"It got dangerous." She leaned forward eagerly. "Are the twins with you?"

"No."

"Oh?" June looked disappointed. "They're not at home. My friend here has been checking. She found Trevor, Nell, and Zoey a babysitter since I'm stuck here. They're fine."

"Mrs. Smith? She's terrible."

"Who's Mrs. Smith? The sitter is Lynette Wool."

"Mrs. Smith was the woman in the house when I woke up. She wouldn't let me go. I had to sneak out."

"I don't know who that was," June said, worried. "Lynette's there now. She's the one that my friend here got in touch with. I'm lucky there's someone here I can trust." She sighed. "If only I knew where the twins are. Maybe they went looking for us."

"Maybe they're home now." Erec looked around. "This doesn't look like a dungeon."

"It is." June looked sad. "I can make it look how I want."

"That's pretty nice of whoever captured you."

"Not really." June examined her fingernails. "They just can't stop me."

"I don't understand."

June hesitated. "I know magic, Erec. That's why I can't be harmed, and I can make my cell look like this." She tapped her finger on the table, muttering under her breath. A box of milk chocolates appeared, and June popped one into her mouth.

Erec gasped. This could not be real. "Do that again."

June shrugged and another box of chocolates sprang into the room. Erec was struck dumb. Nothing was right. He was in Alypium; he was seeing his mother in a dungeon through magic glasses. This had to be a dream.

"Erec? Are you okay?" June asked. "I thought that with your

THE DRAGON'S EYE

magic alarm clock and toothbrush, this wouldn't surprise you this much."

"Yeah, right. I grew up with those things. I'm used to them. But you . . . Why didn't you *tell* me? And where did you get these glasses?"

June smiled. "An old friend had them made for me. They let you see the one you miss most. Don't tell anybody about their power, Erec. Keep them safe, and don't let anyone see you using them. I'm sorry I didn't tell you all this sooner. The time just wasn't right."

Erec heard muffled footsteps and a key scrape into the lock. "Someone is coming." He didn't want to take the glasses off.

"Erec, if you're okay, maybe you should stay in Alypium for now. Maybe you could help me get out of here. But don't tell *anyone* who you are. Now take the glasses off before anyone sees you, but keep the chain around your neck. Only put them on when you're alone. And if you see a guard in here questioning me, don't say a word."

"Can't I stay with you?"

"You're not really here. Go before someone there sees you."

Erec took the Seeing Eyeglasses off. Oscar stood before him, gawping with an open mouth. "Are you okay?"

"Uh, yeah." Thoughts were racing through Erec's muddled brain. His mother knew magic? She was a hostage? He was born in Alypium?

Oscar stood before him, eyes narrowed. "Who were you talking to?"

"I was just . . . daydreaming."

Oscar stabbed his finger at the glasses. "Those *are* magic. Like the bus driver said. I could tell they were important. Can I see them?" Oscar tried to lift the glasses over Erec's head, but they stuck at the level of his chin. No matter how hard he pulled, they would not budge.

"They're nothing special. Really," Erec said.

Oscar scowled. "Whatever." He grabbed a jacket and left the room.

Erec found Bethany, Jack, and Oscar in the cafeteria. "I might stay in Alypium a while longer," Erec said. Bethany grinned.

"Great," Jack said. "You can enter the contests."

Oscar narrowed his eyes. "Aren't you looking for your mom?"

Erec shrugged. "She's probably fine. I'll call her tomorrow."

A huge salad bar was piled high with fruits and grains Erec had never heard of. Cold pureed red pepper and carrot soups colored the ends. Multicolored bowls of some pasty fluff covered a table. "What's that?" he asked a boy who scooped some onto his plate.

"Cloud loaf. There's spinach, corn, strawberry, pumpkin, and plain." The boy wrinkled his nose. "Where's the beef?" Erec felt sick to his stomach staring at the colored goo. For a moment he worried he was getting another cloudy thought.

Bethany called from across the cafeteria. "Hey, Erec. Real food's in the corner." She pointed to a table heaped with hamburgers, pizza, and muffins.

A tall, thin woman with a sharp nose, sharp eyes, and black hair spiked with gray in a bun appeared with a tray of sushi. "Anyone from Ashona? Help yourself." She cackled. "Aorth? Meat and pizzas for ya. I figured our fine competitors might be craving their local fare. You'll get used to our food soon. Much better for you, you know. That's why we live so long."

She regarded Erec critically. He was eyeing the food with pure greed. "Well, take some, then. I'm Hecate Jekyll, head cook. Been here forever. Say 'Heck-a-tee.' Won't have my name butchered." She put her hands on her hips.

THE DRAGON'S EYE

Oscar appeared, reloading his plate. "Can we get hamburgers here all the time?"

Hecate Jekyll cackled. "I'll try to sneak more up, but you should eat the other stuff. It'll make you stronger for the games. There ain't nothin' better for ya than grains, greens, and cloud grinds." She shook her head. "Let me know if you want anything particular. Of course, I'm way too busy, what with cooking special for King Piter every odd hour of the day. That man's on a strict schedule. Just look for me in the castle kitchens if you need anything."

One of Hecate Jekyll's eyes was light brown and the other was a bright, shiny blue. Erec looked harder and saw the blue eye was glass. "Hey, you have a glass eye like me."

Hecate Jekyll chuckled. "I'm old as the hills, boy. It's amazing I have any of my original parts."

Jack came munching on cloud loaf. "I love this place. You don't know how hard it is to find decent vegetarian food in Americorth North. I practically live on french fries."

"How long have you been vegetarian?" Bethany asked.

"Since I was little. Most people here have some sort of gift. Mine is talking to animals. I got so involved in their lives I lost my appetite for them."

"What's your gift?" Bethany asked Oscar.

"I can spot valuable things." He eyed Erec's glasses.

"So is that the magic you have, that we forgot?"

"There are three kinds of magic." Jack leaned forward, obviously excited to teach a Loser about magic. "One kind is inherited. We call that a gift—or sometimes a curse. You get it from your mom's side or your dad's. If you're lucky, sometimes both. It comes naturally."

"A second kind is bought magic, like heli powder that lets you fly, potions, hats that make your memory better, shoes that help you run faster, or my duffel bag that moves on its own."

Erec frowned. "Are you saying my walking coat rack at home is magic?"

Jack laughed at how little he knew. "What did you think it was? The third kind of magic is learned. That's the hard kind. Some people can do it, and some can't. If you want to try, you have to apprentice a sorcerer. It takes years."

Erec pushed his hat up to scratch his forehead, trying to sort out all this information.

"Hey," Jack whispered, "your *L* is lighter. It's fading already."

Erec grinned.

After eating, the heaviness in the air, or the Substance, or whatever it was, seemed to be gone. Or maybe it was just farther away, like a child crying in a distant corner that was easy to ignore.

Exhaustion filled Erec when he went back to his small dormitory room. He left the glasses chain around his neck, lay down, and fell fast asleep.

Erec's eyes flashed open in the darkness. He shivered in a cold sweat. It was his usual nightmare. He was stranded, maybe three years old, walking in the streets at night. He had no place to go. He walked until he was too cold and tired and then curled up under a bush.

His father, who he could only vaguely picture, and his father's boss found him somehow in the dark. The boss called his father stupid. His father mumbled that Erec was useless, but his boss yelled that he would be quite useful, and Erec's father fell to his knees apologizing. The dream always ended with the boss saying that Erec would be made to forget this.

That was the strange part. He obviously had not forgotten. Because not only was this a recurring nightmare, but it was also Erec's only memory of his father.

Erec felt the darkness all around him. He was amazed that he was really in a dorm in Alypium, not his little laundry closet. He wished he had a watch, though. He tried to fall back asleep, but his mind was spinning. Had he really traveled across the ocean? To a strange place where magic was normal . . . where (impossible!) he had been *born*? So, his mother had adopted him here then. Yes, his *magical* mother. His magical, *kidnapped* mother. Everything was all wrong.

Erec's mind buzzed with questions as the minutes slowly ticked by. Were the twins okay? Where should he keep the glasses at night? Who had kidnapped his mother and why? Did the glasses protect him from the silver ghost? Why did his mother take him from Alypium when he was little? Did he get his glass eye in Alypium?

June had always said his father was alive, implying that his birth mother had died. Maybe he was here in Alypium. His heart raced at the thought. Would he want to meet his father if he could? His one memory of him was terrible, and it seemed obvious his father wanted nothing to do with him, so probably not.

CHAPTER SIX

A Castle on Its Side

JACK SMILED. "HEY, that *L* on your forehead is even lighter. I'd keep the hat on today, though. Let's eat breakfast."

Erec stretched. He had finally fallen back asleep sometime last night. "You two go. I'll meet you there."

When the door closed, Erec quickly locked it and put the Seeing Eyeglasses on. His mother was reading in bed. "Mom?"

June dropped her book. "Erec? You scared me. Are you okay?"

"I'm fine. How are you?"

"All right. The dungeon guards were just here. Same questions as last morning."

"I have some questions. First of all, the glasses. My roommate tried to take them off of me, but he couldn't do it. Why is that? And did they protect me from the silver ghost?" Erec told her about the bus ride.

"If the chain is around your neck," June said, "nobody can take them from you. I don't think they could protect you from the ghost, but they will protect your neck, at least, as long as they're on you. Just don't take them off."

"What if I smash them when I sleep?"

"They're protected by a charm. An elephant could sit on them and they wouldn't break."

"Why couldn't the ghost hurt me, then?"

June thought a moment. "Let's just say *you're* charmed, like the glasses."

"So, an elephant could sit on me and I wouldn't be crushed?"

"Yes! Well . . . no. But ghosts can't hurt you. Something about the past not harming the future."

June looked uncomfortable. Erec pressed her. "Who gave me the charm? My birth parents?"

"You could say that. It's from your family lineage. Erec, there are reasons I have not told you more, and I'm not sure this is the time to start."

Erec fought the urge to argue with her. There were other things he wanted to know. "Did you work here in Alypium? What did you do?"

June waved a hand to stop him. "Erec, do you understand? I can't get into all this yet. This is enough for now."

"No, it's not enough." He caught his breath. "Just tell me, is my father in Alypium?"

June nodded sadly. "Erec, I don't know how to say this. Try to forget about him."

"Why wouldn't I?" He thought a moment. "And my birth mother is dead?"

"Erec!" June's face flushed. "*Enough* for now."

He had expected a simple yes. "Is she dead? You always said—"

"I never said *anything*," June snapped. "Now, remember the glasses stay on your neck. Don't put them on in front of anybody." Erec nodded even though she couldn't see him. Then she went on. "I've been thinking. Can you get into King Piter's castle?"

"I'm staying there. They attached dormitories to the castle for the contests."

"Perfect." June smoothed the sheets around her. "I'm going to ask you to do something. Find King Piter. You need to be extremely careful. I hope he remembers me." She shook her head. "If only you had my picture."

"I do. I took one with me."

June's face lit up. "Wonderful. Show him my picture. Tell him I'm locked in King Pluto's dungeons. He'll get me out of here. I've been having a bit of trouble doing it myself."

"This still doesn't look like a dungeon to me." Erec looked at the gingham curtains and fluffy pillows.

"Thank you." June smiled. "Nonetheless, I'm stuck."

"Why are you in King Pluto's dungeons?"

"His people captured me. Be very careful of him, Erec."

"How do I find King Piter?" Even saying it sounded strange. He was supposed to ask a king for a favor?

June thought about the question for a moment. "He'll be in the west wing. Bring him a pomegranate. He loves them. It might put him in a better mood."

"A pomegranate? Where will I find one?"

"In the kitchens. Now, go. Eat well; you'll need your energy. And find a toothbrush in town. Just because you're in a dormitory you still have to brush—"

"Mom! I'm fine. As long as I'm here, I probably should enter the contests. It would look strange if I was here and not in them. You think it's okay?"

June considered the idea. "Hopefully you won't be there long, but I don't see the harm. Maybe the fates put you there for a reason. Just don't attract a lot of attention." She paused. "And don't tell anyone you're from Upper Earth. Or that your name is Erec Rex."

"It's too late. What's the deal? Is somebody out to get me here?"

June coughed and looked at the ceiling. "No, not unless certain people find out you are there. Let's see Erec . . . call yourself Rec . . . Rick. Rick Ross, how's that? And say you're from . . . Americorth South. It's part of Aorth, big enough that nobody will wonder why they don't know you."

Erec didn't like the sound of this. "Mom, I can't believe you know magic and never told me. And that I'm from Alypium." He felt his throat getting tight. He was an idiot, really. Why didn't he suspect there was something strange about her all along? She brought home toasters and alarm clocks that came to life. He guessed that growing up with them made it seem natural, like a normal mother could buy such things. "And you're not answering all my questions. Can't you imagine how I feel?"

June gazed sadly at the chair he sat on. For a moment it seemed to Erec that she was staring at his stomach, but when he looked down he remembered he was invisible. He took the Seeing Eyeglasses off, and his small, drab dorm room sprang before his eyes.

* * *

Bethany was in the cafeteria nibbling on fluffy white pudding with swirls of honey, sprinkled with nuts and raspberries. "They call this ambrosia. It's not bad. All they have for breakfast is this and nectar." She held up what looked like a sparkling glass of honey. "Whatever it is, it's good. I'm feeling much better, too. That awful feeling from the Substance is gone, unless I really think about it. How was your night?"

Erec told Bethany about the glasses and his mother. "Don't forget, I'm Rick Ross from Americorth South."

"All right, Rick Ross. But what will you tell Jack and Oscar?"

Erec shrugged. "I'll tell them I'm changing my name to hide where I'm from. They might think it's crazy, but I think they'll go along."

"Did you sign 'Erec Rex' in Spartacus Kilroy's book?"

Erec's eyes widened. "Oh, no. I need to cross that out—quick."

"The book's not out anymore. There is an assembly in a few hours about the contests. Maybe Kilroy will have it there."

That reminded Erec of something else. "Maybe King Piter will be there too. It seems like a good place to start."

The entryway into the castle looked like a big porthole in the wall. Erec tried to step through, but the gravity pulled him sideways. He found himself lying in thin air and fell right back through what now was a trapdoor in the floor. Bethany doubled over laughing until Erec shot her a squinty-eyed look. He cautiously stuck his head through the trapdoor, rested his chest on the castle floor, and pulled himself through.

Entering the castle from the drab stone dormitory was like going from black-and-white into color. Huge, gorgeous tapestries covered the walls with scenes of old battles, heroes holding snake-haired gorgon heads, dragons flying, and unicorns running through forests. Erec stared at a rather gory tapestry showing a dragon roasting an armored knight with fiery breath. The cloth waved in a breeze, and Erec watched, amazed, as the picture changed to show a happy dragon resting on a treasure chest, picking its teeth with the knight's sword.

Three enormous chandeliers hung in the tremendous room, many of their candles unlit. Dirt spattered the floor, and cracks ran through the walls and ceiling. There was an overall appearance of incredible beauty gone to seed. Huge wooden doors led outside. One was open. Erec went to look out but staggered back when he saw an expanse of air before him, with sky to his right, green grass far to his left, and trees crossing horizontally in the distance.

An annoyed maid scurried over and waved a duster. The door flew shut. Maids and janitors, all looking frustrated, ran around with brooms, dustpans, mops, and rags. They muttered spells and even scrubbed with all their strength, but dirt just hopped from one place to another.

Bethany asked a maid why she kept trying to wipe smudges off a vase when they only moved to another spot.

"Because that's what I'm paid to do; what do you think?" The maid looked angry. "I'm not incompetent. *Nobody* can clean this place since King Piter let it fall into disrepair."

"How did he do that?" Erec asked.

"Oh, the castle just hasn't been right since he let it go sideways. It knows something is wrong and has been completely uncooperative. King Piter used to *insist* the place was spotless." She smiled and sighed. "Those were the days. Now he's just too old and sick." She whispered, "We're all hoping after these contests . . . one of you may make this place stand upright again."

The vase suddenly shot sideways, and the maid caught it and set it back again. "You'd best be careful," she said to their wide-eyed stares. "This fake gravity doesn't always work. Don't stand by any open doors, lest you fly out."

Erec and Bethany walked down a hallway into a huge, ornate atrium where the four wings of the castle met. The west wing was blocked by ropes and a large guard with long stringy hair and an armored breastplate. He held a spear and something that looked like a remote control.

King Piter was somewhere in there. If only Erec could get through . . . When he leaned over the ropes, though, the guard scowled. "These are the king's private quarters. He is not to be disturbed. Now, off with ye."

"Could I please just use a bathroom in there?" Bethany said.

"No," the guard growled. "You'll find one in the south wing."

Two boys walked by, laughing. One pushed the other, and he fell and slid underneath the ropes. Springing into action, the guard aimed his remote control at the boy on the ground. The boy froze mid-laugh with his knee in the air. The guard slid him back under the rope and pressed another button. The boy looked around, stunned, and got up.

Bethany cleared her throat. "Is King Piter there? We wanted to meet him."

A tall man with black hair appeared around the corner behind the ropes. A crease rode vertically up the center of his bulging forehead. Thick eyebrows slanted from his sharp, thin nose, almost meeting to form a bushy *V*. He wore a scarab amulet on his black cape and carried a beautiful walking stick carved with figures in dark wood. A smell drifted from him that reminded Erec of rotting garbage.

"And whoo are yoou?" he sneered, his whisper fierce and bone chilling.

"Uh . . . Rick Ross. And Bethany. We're from Americorth South." Erec took a breath. "Is the king in? We wanted to meet him."

"Wanted to meet him," the man's voice rose in a mocking tone.

THE DRAGON'S EYE

"The king is not himself lately, and the last thing he needs is to be bothered by *fans*." His eyes narrowed. "And don't you think of sneaking in for a visit. The king is not leaving my sight. If I catch you two in the west wing, you're straight in an Artery back to Americorth South. Now get back with those other brats to your stupid competition—that is, while it lasts," he said, snickering.

Erec and Bethany walked away. "Who was that?" asked Bethany. "He was horrible."

"Whoever he is, the king never leaves his sight," said Erec. "Now what am I going to do?"

"Don't worry," said Bethany. "We'll figure something out. Let's go to the assembly."

Plush red velvet seats and humongous chandeliers filled the beautiful theater in the east wing. Several people sat on stage, including Stoney Rayson, a Super A Team bouncer. Murmurs of excitement echoed through the room.

"Look," said Erec. "It's Stoney Rayson! Now I've seen two Super A Team members in person."

Bethany squinted. "I recognize him from articles at the newsstand."

"What? You haven't seen him on television a million times?"

Bethany blushed. "I don't see much television. Uncle Earl says I have to be useful. That means cook and clean all the time."

Bethany pointed as the man with the creased forehead who yelled at them in the west wing slid across the stage with his walking stick. With him was Spartacus Kilroy, who had greeted them at the bus, still wearing the royal blue cape with the white star. Erec did not see Kilroy's book.

They were helping an elderly man on stage. Long gray hair lay limp around his craggy face. He was large but stooped, as if he was somehow folded in on himself. Kilroy and the man with the creased forehead both tried to help him sit, but they pulled him in two directions at the same time. The old man's arms yanked outward, and his eyes bugged as he looked wildly about. The dark-haired man snarled and seated the old man next to himself.

Spartacus Kilroy approached the microphone, and the room burst into cheers. He laughed and held his hands in the air. "Thank you! For those who do not know me, I am Spartacus Kilroy. Call me Sport, Mr. Kilroy—whatever you like. I've been one of King Piter's AdviSeers for the past ten years, and what a great decade to be here! This!" He waved an arm across the audience. "This is amazing. A first in history! A time for all of our youth to come together as one: rich and poor, smart and dumb, young and . . . younger, from *all* the lands of this beautiful earth!"

"Except Upper Earth," Bethany whispered.

Kilroy continued. "These contests are not only the highlight of my career. As you all know, they will forever change the lives of three youngsters in this very room. Three boys and girls, right here today, will be our future rulers. What would you do if you were king or queen, with your own scepter, and all that power at your fingertips?"

The black-haired man scowled more fiercely than ever. He looked like he wanted to jump out of his chair and beat off the contestants with his walking stick.

Kilroy said, "Six hundred and twenty-one of you signed my book. After tomorrow, only two hundred will remain in the games. The next two contests will bring the numbers down to one hundred, then fifty. Those fifty will move on to games of greater difficulty, one devised by Queen Posey of Ashona, one by King Pluto of Aorth, and one by our King Piter and his staff. These will narrow down the group to twenty-five, then ten, and finally three.

"You are all invited to stay and enjoy the games. Three days after the contests we will dissolve the castle dormitories, so please make sure you are not in them at that time. In the meantime, there will be parties and even a Super A Team Alypium springball match for your enjoyment."

After the riotous cheering quieted, Kilroy continued. "Before you is the panel of seven judges, including myself.

"Mr. Richard Rayson, known as Stoney Rayson from the famous Super A Team." There was wild applause as Stoney flashed a smile, revealing stunning white teeth.

"Olive Umpee, the games referee." A gray-haired woman nodded to scattered applause.

"Our lovely Queen Posey." Kilroy nodded back at a dark-haired woman with dark circles under her eyes and a silver crown, who waved regally.

"King Pluto." The room howled with applause as a thin man in thick coats and a bronze crown smugly waved.

"King Piter." The applause hitched up a notch. The old man with limp gray hair blinked as if he had no idea what was going on.

"And King Piter's other AdviSeer, Balthazar Ugry." The dark-haired man's face slid into a slick smile as the applause died down.

"We will see you all tomorrow at the first game, which is called the Monster. Ten o'clock behind the castle maze." More cheers broke out as Kilroy waved and took his seat.

Stoney Rayson walked to the podium in a gray tailored suit, wearing the black Super A Team eye patch. The room went wild. Rayson obviously enjoyed the attention. He smoothed his slick gray hair and soaked up the crowd with his steely gray uncovered eye. Then he posed, knees bent and arms out, fists flipped back, so that he looked remarkably like one of his action figures. In the movies, he turned people to stone by tilting back his fists and opening gorgon eyes in his wrists.

Rayson's deep voice boomed. "If it weren't for these wristbands, kids, you'd all be *rocks* out there!" Kids went wild as Rayson posed again, moving his wrists to point at the entire room. "Okay, kids. I'll be meeting you in person. I'm one of your judges; that's right. Remember—no touch." He dusted his sleeves as if to wipe off dirty kid fingerprints. "He who touches the Stone Man is disqualified. My son, Rock, will be with you all tomorrow. Now, good luck, fight fair, and play to win!" Stoney flashed his wrists one last time in a quick pose that again set the room on fire and then went to his seat.

Olive Umpee, squat and muscular with thick silver hair cut in a short bowl style, walked to the podium. Her lips pressed tight so they were almost invisible. She surveyed the crowd with distaste and blew her silver whistle loudly into the microphone. The room fell silent. Erec's ears rang.

"Well," Umpee yelled into the microphone, "I hope there are three of you out there somewhere who can control yourselves. This is not a contest for lily livers or screaming meemies. In fact, those who know they are unfit to rule, please excuse yourselves right now!"

Everybody looked around, but nobody stood. Umpee continued, quieter. "You will address me as Miss Umpee, or Referee. I am King Pluto's assistant. There are rules. No remote controls or bought magic unless otherwise specified. No second chances. I'll have my eye on you." She leered over the audience before abruptly turning and sitting down.

Queen Posey—a beautiful woman with long, wavy, dark hair and a rippling silver crown—rose, picking up a long golden scepter that sparkled with jewels. She wore a shimmering aqua dress and a white shawl that fluttered and swirled around her as if it were made of tiny floating feathers.

"She needs more sleep," whispered Bethany. "Look at the lines under her eyes."

She cleared her throat into the microphone and the room fell silent. "Quiet, please. I am Queen Posey of Ashona. My brother Piter wants these contests, so I am behind him. Please enjoy." She blew a kiss to the audience. Her soft accent sounded mysterious. "I have nice prizes for winners of my contest." She waved and sat down.

Next to her, King Pluto picked up his scepter and walked to the microphone. He was pale and bundled in a thick black coat, scarves, and a black knit hat. A thin, coppery crown perched on the hat. He blew his nose and held up a hand until the clapping died down.

"I'm King Pluto of Aorth, as you must know. Hey folks . . . man it's cold up here." Erec did not think it was cold at all. King Pluto spoke fast, sounding very unlike his sister Posey. "Reminds me of the Cyclops who ran into a store and stole a thermos. Had no idea what it was. A friend told him it keeps hot things hot and cold things cold. He showed it to his wife, and she asked, 'What did you put in it?' He said, 'Three snow cones and a cup of hot chocolate.'

"Listen, have a great time. I can't wait to meet the new rulers so my brother and sister and I can finally retire. King Piter used to talk about this great little seaside condo on Miami Beach, right by the ocean for Queen Posey. I'm ready." He chuckled and sat down.

Erec was puzzled. Was this the King Pluto who put his mother in a dungeon? That Erec was supposed to stay away from? He seemed so nice.

Kilroy whispered in King Piter's ear and walked to the microphone. "As you know, King Piter is not well. You have his blessings. He wants you to know he is very excited about the contests." King Piter stared, fascinated, at his hands.

Balthazar Ugry, King Piter's other AdviSeer, with the bulging, creased forehead, went to the podium. The room fell silent and a few people gasped. Erec felt his stomach rise into his throat.

Ugry hissed, "I cannot tell you how . . . delighted I am that you are in our palace. My name is Balthazar Ulrich Theodore Ugry. I must, of course, attend to the king as my main duty, but believe me, I will be watching all of you. Nothing shall escape me." He spun around and his black cloak fanned behind him. Everybody in the audience stared, forgetting to clap.

"Okay! Tomorrow morning, ten o'clock, behind the maze. First game," Spartacus called into the microphone. He ran back to King Piter, but Balthazar Ugry was already walking the king off the stage.

CHAPTER SEVEN

The Maze

WANT TO COME find a pomegranate?" Erec asked.

"All right." Bethany shrugged. "But I can't imagine King Piter helping your mother. Did you see how ancient he looks?"

"I have to try." Erec was doubtful too. "Maybe he's changed since my mom knew him. Kilroy said he was sick."

"I thought King Piter, King Pluto, and Queen Posey were

supposed to be triplets," Bethany said. "King Piter looks like he could be their grandfather."

Walking to the kitchens in the east wing, Erec felt a pang of sadness. It took a moment before he realized the feeling was not his, but part of the atmosphere around him—the Substance. But the minute the kitchen doors opened, the feeling disappeared.

Wild noises flew from the kitchen: banging pots and pans, knives hitting chopping blocks, and clunking equipment. A giant black oven strolled through on short metal legs. It swung jointed arms through piles of food, scooping handfuls of eggs and flour into its door. Seconds later, it spit eggshells onto the floor. Servants ran through, sweeping up the mess. The oven dumped piles of sugar and butter into its belly with abandon and collapsed with a hum that sounded like a bad rendition of "A Spoonful of Sugar." In a moment it was quiet. The two lights on its hood blinked off, making it look asleep.

Balor and Damon Stain, whom Erec had met on the bus, and a tall blond boy with dark blue eyes sat on a counter. "It's the poor little rich kid," said Balor. "Never heard of Port-O-Doors, but he owns this nice little piece of work." He pointed to Erec's glasses and squinted. "I bet that funny eye does something clever too. Can I see the glasses?"

Erec shook his head. "Who's your friend?"

Balor shrugged. "Ward Gamin. Ward, this is . . . what did you say your name was?"

"Rick Ross. And this is Bethany Evirly."

"Evirly. That's familiar." Balor smiled. "You'll both be on my team."

"Your team?" Erec asked. "We have teams tomorrow?"

Balor and Ward's eyes met. "Not tomorrow. In the second contest." He looked Bethany over skeptically. "Got anything good up your sleeve?"

Bethany's eyes narrowed. "You think I want to be on a team with someone who threw me out of my seat on a bus?"

"Ooh, she's got spunk," Balor said. "We'll take her all right."

"Yeah," Ward grinned. "Just to make her mad, if nothing else." He high-fived Balor.

Damon strutted around the floor, flexing his muscles and singing, "Just to make her ma-a-ad, ma-a-ad, ma-a-ad. Brother is a little lamb." He stopped and stared into the distance. "I want the donuts." His mouth hung open and a strand of drool slithered out.

"Who says it's up to you, anyway?" Bethany asked, crossing her arms.

Balor, Damon, and Ward burst out laughing. "I do," Balor said. "I have connections. Who were those other two with you on the bus?"

"Jack Hare and Oscar Felix," Erec said. "How do you know we'll all make it through the first contest?"

Balor grinned. "Just follow me—if you can. I know the way."

Ward shoved Balor's shoulder. "Shut up, already. Here's our stuff." Hecate Jekyll walked over carrying trays loaded with cookies, cakes, popcorn, and candy. Balor and Ward grabbed the trays and Damon followed them out, stuffing food in his mouth all the way.

"Haven't I seen you kids before? What can I do for yeh?"

"Do you have any pomegranates?"

Hecate Jekyll's hands fell from her hips. "Pomegranates, eh? You're a pomegranate fan? What's your name?"

"Um, Rick." Erec's mind blanked. He could not remember his new last name.

"Rick what?" Hecate Jekyll stared intently.

Erec glanced at Bethany, mind racing. Rick Rose? Rick Rent?

"Rick Ross," Bethany put in. "He's a little distracted, new place and all. We also wanted some hamburgers, please. And if it's possible, those dessert trays Balor Stain had looked awfully good."

Hecate Jekyll smiled. "Well, sure. Balor and Damon have their own menu plan, but they're still down here changing it every day. I guess I don't see any harm in sending you two up with a plate of treats. All right, two burgers, two pomegranates?"

Erec and Bethany nodded. Hecate disappeared and returned with hamburgers and pomegranates. She whispered something to the big black oven. It swung open its door and stuck a rack out like a big tongue. She picked off treats and put them on a tray.

Hecate shook her head when she handed Erec the pomegranates. "Now, you kids eat some healthy Alypium food tonight. It'll give you more energy for the race tomorrow."

Erec cradled the pomegranates in his arm and Bethany carried the plate loaded with doughnuts, brownies, cookies, and muffins. As they ate their hamburgers, Bethany whispered, "Did you hear her say 'energy for the race'? I guess it's a race tomorrow." She bit her lip. "I'm not a runner."

"Remember, Balor said he knows the way. It's not a regular race."

She frowned. "He's the last person I'd follow."

"Unless you wanted to win. Balor obviously gets special treatment."

"No way," said Bethany. "You heard Kilroy. Everyone has an equal chance. 'Rich and poor, smart and dumb,'" she said, giggling.

"Did Hecate Jekyll look at me funny when I asked for the pomegranates?" Erec grabbed a cupcake with sprinkles.

"Nah." Bethany munched on a brownie. "She just wondered why you didn't know your last name."

Erec looked at his frosting-smudged T-shirt. "I wonder if Jack would lend me clothes."

Bethany brushed brownie crumbs off her dress. "My roommate, Melody, told me there's a free laundry in the castle. You wouldn't need many."

Erec told Bethany about his "cloudy thoughts" as they passed the roped-off west wing. The guard was muttering to himself about missing lunch. When he saw Bethany walk past with a plate full of treats he threw his hands in the air. "Blast it. Where's Ugand?"

Bethany held a finger to her lips as they walked around a corner. Three boys walking by ogled the treats. "Want some?" she asked.

"Sure."

"You can have the whole tray if you play a joke on that guard," Bethany whispered.

One boy lifted an eyebrow. "Are you sure that's a good idea?"

She nodded. "It'll be funny."

Erec and Bethany watched as the boys walked close to the guard, tossing donuts to each other. When they were right next to him, they shouted, "Aaargh!" and threw food at his face.

While the guard swatted at the food and cursed the boys, Bethany and Erec darted past the rope. Keeping an eye on the guard, they slipped in and out from the suits of armor that lined the hallway, holding swords, axes, and nunchucks. One held a teddy bear. As they walked by, it squeezed its teddy tighter and turned away.

Hallways led from hallways, and huge doors lined the long walls. A torrent of noise spilled from behind one closed door. It sounded like bowling balls were dropping, pots and pans clashing, and jackhammers hammering, with wild singing mixed in.

"The king could be anywhere."

They peeked in rooms and dodged maids. Erec saw a thin wooden Port-O-Door with a gold handle like they had seen in FES Station. Then Bethany pointed into a room.

King Piter was sitting on a red velvet couch near a fire. He seemed unnaturally gaunt and stooped for such a large man. Spartacus Kilroy was coaxing him into drinking coffee. "C'mon, King, open up. Here you go." He pushed the cup to the king's mouth. King Piter turned away.

"You know it's coffee time. It helps you so much. There you go." He poured the coffee into King Piter's mouth and dusted his hands. The king slumped into the couch. "You rest. I have everything taken care of." He pulled a blanket over the king and walked out.

Bethany and Erec flattened themselves on a wall behind a suit of armor. Kilroy walked out without seeing them. Erec held his breath when they went into the room. He stopped before King Piter, unsure how to wake him. He put his hand on the king's shoulder.

The king's eyes flew open. He looked at Erec in shock. Erec removed his hand, and King Piter's eyes started to close.

"I need your help. My mother, June O'Hara, is a prisoner in King Pluto's dungeons."

King Piter looked confused.

"Do you remember my mother?"

King Piter tilted his head as if deep in thought. Erec held his mother's picture out. The king looked at it and sniffed.

"Would you like a pomegranate?" Erec held one out.

The king wrinkled his nose as if it disgusted him, but Erec pushed it into the king's hand. As their hands touched, the king said, "Erec?"

Erec jumped back in surprise.

"What is the meaning of this?" Balthazar Ugry stormed into the room. "So, it's you two cretins again. Had to upset the king, didn't you? Pack your bags. You're going straight home. You kids think you can come here and take over, be the next king or queen. Well, that's not about to happen."

"Oh, Balthazar, I see you've found my friends," said a voice from the doorway. Spartacus Kilroy winked at Erec. "Is there a problem?"

Ugry hissed, "You know these wretches?"

"Sure. They volunteered to help. King Piter wanted to meet a few contestants, and these two agreed."

"That's funny," Ugry retorted. "I haven't heard the king *say* a thing in years."

"It's all in your approach," said Kilroy, smiling.

Ugry glared at Erec and swept from the room.

"Thank you," said Bethany, very relieved. "I would have died if I had to go home."

Kilroy shook his head at the thought. "Balthazar tends to overreact. If it was up to him, all you kids would go home. I'm not sure who he thinks the next kings and queens will be. But he's a little set in his ways. I think the world stopped for him when King Piter got sick.

"Meanwhile," Kilroy added, more serious, "don't bother the king again. One time, no harm. But he needs his rest." Kilroy pointed Erec and Bethany out the door and out of the west wing.

The gardens around the castle were immaculate, unlike the castle itself. Beautiful plants that Erec had never before seen were arranged without a weed in sight. The roses lining the path were taller than he was, with blooms as big as his head. A terrace full of huge, brightly colored daisies whirred with activity. The daisy heads took off into the air, spinning like little yellow, purple, and orange helicopters, and landing on different stems.

Small green reptiles with big back legs hopped by. When one jumped on Bethany's head, she shrieked and pulled it off. "What was that thing?"

A girl nearby said, "Leaping lizards. They're harmless." The girl ducked as another leaping lizard sailed past her own face.

Near the back corner of the palace, hundreds of flags waved from every country in Upper Earth and the Kingdoms of the Keepers. A few kids ran between the flagpoles, touching one, then another. Seeing this, Erec touched one too. A silence fell and a beautiful tune played. Erec guessed it was the national anthem of that country.

Behind the castle was a great maze made of shrubs too high to see over. "Oh, how fun," Bethany said. "Let's try it."

A sign in front of the maze entrance said it was closed for the day. "How can a maze be closed?" Erec asked.

"You're right. Let's go." Bethany tugged his arm.

Nobody was looking so they went in. Once inside they discovered that all the passageways looked alike. They quickly got lost. With so many twists and turns, the maze seemed like an endless trap. Erec started to wonder if they would ever get out.

Finally they heard a loud howl and cursing. Alarmed, they followed the noise. A gap in the shrubs revealed a courtyard in the center of the maze. A man was chaining a strange, sleeping beast to a pole. Another man sat on the ground, swearing. Blood covered his left arm, which hung limp at his side.

"It's okay, mate," the first one said. "They'll fix you right up at the palace, they will."

The man covered with blood groaned. "Why do they want a minotaur here, anyway? All these kids around. Someone's going to get killed, you just wait. Look what it did to me in its *sleep*."

The first man shrugged. "This is what the king's AdviSeer wanted, and he knows better than us. Said something about a surprise."

"Well, do we leave food for it?"

"The AdviSeer wanted it hungry."

The sitting man didn't like that idea. "This thing would eat a kid for breakfast."

Erec and Bethany tried to get a better look at the minotaur. It had the head and body of a huge bull, but its lower legs looked like a giant, hairy human's in racing shorts.

"Let's get out of here," Bethany said. "If you follow the right hand wall of a maze you'll eventually get out."

The sun was sinking and the maze seemed endless. Knowing that around any corner they might run into the kid-eating minotaur again made it even worse. When they finally got out, Erec was shaking. They ran into the dormitories and collapsed in a sitting room.

Later at dinner, all Erec could think about was asking his mother more questions. Why did she lie to him his whole life? He didn't know what to believe. He wanted to put his glasses on right then in the cafeteria, but kids were everywhere. His dorm room was no better with Jack and Oscar popping in and out. He closed his eyes. "I was stupid. Why didn't I put my glasses on in the maze?"

"Put them on now," Bethany said. "Nobody can hear us. I'll pretend we're talking."

"Someone could sit with us and I wouldn't even know."

"Don't worry. I'll kick you if someone comes too close."

Erec slid the glasses on his face. His mother was knitting and reading a book with a television blaring. "Mom?"

Taken by surprise, June dropped her knitting and spilled her lemonade. She put her hand on her heart. "Erec?"

"Yeah, it's me, Mom." A wave of embarrassment passed over him as he realized he was looking at Bethany and saying, "Mom."

"Are you all right?"

"I'm fine. I may have to leave at any second, though." He did not add that he was sitting in a busy cafeteria. He could imagine what she would say. "I have a lot to ask you. First, why didn't you tell me all of this before? I don't even know which way is up now. I find out my own mother knows magic. I was born in Alypium. People were after me here for some reason. I want the whole story."

"Erec, stop. I know," she said, picking up her knitting. "I'm sorry I didn't tell you I knew magic. I had my reasons. Then you would have wanted to know everything . . . like you do now. And you *can't* know much more." She twisted a pen she was holding so hard that it broke. "Don't be impatient. You'll find out when it's time."

"Why did King Pluto capture you?"

June sighed. "He's had a hard life. He was a sweet man, but he could only take so much. He wasn't as powerful as Posey, and not nearly as powerful as Piter. Not that that should matter, but he was always compared, and I know he felt bad.

"He's suffered, too. His scepter is weaker. That's what keeps them alive so long. It goes into everything they touch. That's why King Piter's wife lived a long time, before she and the triplets were killed. Queen Posey's husband and kids are several hundred years old. But Pluto's families . . . he's had a few, but they grow old and die while he keeps on living. His scepter isn't strong enough to keep them alive. That's been terribly painful."

His mother sighed. "Plus, he uses his scepter far too much, probably to make up for his lack of power. Those scepters can warp the strongest soul unless treated very carefully. And Thanatos Baskania is always at his side, making him feel worse, promising him power he never had. I'm afraid he's finally gone to the wrong side for good."

It seemed like his mother had skirted around his question, but he was curious. "Thanatos Baskania? You don't mean the Crown Prince of Peace, do you?"

"The very one." June frowned. "You may as well hear this now, for your own safety. Baskania, the Crown Prince, is not from Upper Earth. He is to be strictly avoided. In fact, of all people, he must not find out that you are there. He's a dangerous man."

"Where is he from, Alypium?"

"He created Alypium, and Ashona and Aorth, too. He's from the old times, when magic was everywhere."

"But what is he doing in Upper Earth, then?"

"Good question. I have a bad feeling about it. He's power mad

THE DRAGON'S EYE

from hundreds of years of trying to perfect magic and do things that nobody can do. Taking over Upper Earth wouldn't be too hard for him, and that's what I'm afraid he is trying. When he bought those huge corporations that spread across the world, I wondered if it was about the money, and all the things and people it bought. But now, with this politicking for 'peace' and getting involved with the United Nations . . . I don't know.

"But he'll be stopped before he gets too far. The rulers in the Kingdoms of the Keepers will never let him take over."

"What rulers?"

"Well, King Piter, of course. And Queen Posey, I suppose."

Erec faintly heard Bethany laughing as if he had told a joke. He felt grateful for her efforts.

"Mom, King Piter is no help. He didn't remember you. And he didn't want the pomegranates."

June was shocked. "But he does know me. Maybe he didn't hear you. Was he busy?"

"He was propped on a couch staring at the wall."

"Was he asleep?" June bit her lip.

"No," said Erec. "But he's sick, and he's really old and confused. I don't think he knows where he is."

June picked up her knitting, studying the stitches. "This can't be. I knew he was . . . not feeling right and that something was terribly wrong, but I had no idea . . ."

Erec wondered how she knew, but she didn't look like she wanted to talk about it. He could hear Bethany chatting nearby.

"Unless . . ." June said loudly.

"Huh?" asked Erec.

"You say he's confused, doesn't know where he is?"

"Yeah. He's let the castle go. It's lying on its side."

"Something isn't right, Erec. I think someone put him under a spell. He doesn't sound sick to me. I have an idea . . ."

Bethany kicked Erec hard on the leg. "Ow . . . bye!" he said and whisked the glasses off.

Ward Gamin, Balor Stain's friend, was marching to Erec's table with a sneer. Muscles rippled under his shirt.

Bethany whispered, "Your nectar glass shot over to that wall. It must have been a gravity lapse. It got all over Ward."

Ward wiped his shirt with Erec's napkin. "Think you're funny, huh?"

Erec bit his lip, trying not to laugh. He offered another napkin. "Sorry, Ward. I guess the messed-up gravity did it."

Bethany nodded. "I tried to grab it, but I missed."

"Yeah, sure." Ward looked back and forth between Erec and Bethany. He seemed confused how to turn their apologies into a fight. "Well, I don't like you anyway. I don't care what Balor thinks. He only wants those." He pointed to Erec's glasses. "But you're a bunch of nobodies, I can tell." He walked away, chuckling. "You bozos won't make it through the first game."

Bethany stuck her tongue out at Ward's back.

Erec slumped in his chair. "I feel like I should be wearing a target on my back. The only person I can trust is stuck in a dungeon . . . except for you." Then again, he wasn't sure he did trust his mother now. "I'm turning in," he said. "See you in the morning?"

"Ten o'clock behind the maze," said Bethany. "Ward Gamin is wrong. We *are* going to win."

CHAPTER EIGHT

The MONSTER

AFTER SHOWERING AND putting on clean clothes that Jack lent him, Erec felt like a new person. Jack said the *L* on his forehead was so light now he could barely see it. Erec decided to wear the cap just in case. They found Bethany in the cafeteria, no hat on, eating ambrosia and nectar. She looked completely different in her roommate Melody's orange shirt and blue shorts instead of her raggedy dress.

"You look great," Jack said.

Bethany's cheeks turned pink. "I don't feel like me. I feel so much . . . better. Why do some of the kids wear blue cloaks?"

Jack said, "They're apprenticing to be sorcerers. Sorcerers wear black cloaks—at least they all used to. It's getting old-fashioned. A lot of sorcerers wear street clothes now, except the ones who want attention. Funny, the ones who are the least powerful often are the ones who wear the cloaks."

As they walked together to the maze, Erec asked a question he'd thought of yesterday. "Do you know what the magic box was that the guard had? It looked like a remote control."

Jack laughed. "That's just what it was. They concentrate your energy, let you do magic you couldn't do unless you were really good. All the apprentices use them. A lot of people never could do magic without them. It all depends on how much power you have inside, really."

Erec thought that was great. "Do they let you do anything you want?"

"Nah. Only mid-level magic, like moving things or people, making things invisible, destroying things, making people feel different, starting fire, stuff like that."

Erec and Bethany looked at each other. "That sounds like a lot. What can't they do?"

"Plenty. They can't heal things, change things, make things grow, make force fields, enchant objects, read minds. To do those you have to learn a lot, and get past needing a remote."

A crowd gathered behind the maze where Erec and Bethany had been lost. He shuddered to think of the minotaur inside. "You don't think we have to go in there and . . ."

Bethany grew pale. "We won't do it. You heard what the man said. That thing would eat us for breakfast!"

Erec's stomach dropped. "Someone's going to get hurt, I know it. I'll go in and do what I can to help."

"You're not afraid?"

"I didn't say that." Erec would not think about being afraid. There was no room for that now.

Spartacus Kilroy, in his bright blue, starred cape, stood by a large metal archway with a dome on top. At his side, Queen Posey tapped her scepter on the ground. A thin stream of water sprang near Erec's feet, curving around the large group of contestants.

Kilroy blew his whistle. He seemed uncomfortable. "Now that we are all together, I have an announcement. There have been reports that, um, some of you are not who you say you are. We've had a few calls and . . . just to be safe, you understand, everyone will have to walk though this Identdetector. You will notice the water wall surrounding you, provided by Queen Posey, in case anyone was to try to"—he cleared his throat—"escape. Now, form a line, and let's get this over with."

A buzz immediately arose. Bethany grabbed Jack by the arm. "What's an Identdetector?"

"It shows your true identity and appearance, and exposes people who changed shape."

"How can people change shape?" Erec asked.

"There are spells," Jack said. "Not a lot of people do it, though, because you can never look like your old self again."

"Why not?" Bethany asked.

"You'd have to use the spell again to make yourself look like your old self, but it never works as well the second time. You'd only look similar. And if you change more than once or twice, you start to look strange. Pointy ears, pink eyes. People don't do it too much."

Kilroy was trying, unsuccessfully, to form a line. Occasional spurts of water shot above the crowd to appreciative laughter.

"Erec." Bethany pulled him aside and whispered, "You better hide. He's going to see your real name. And what if it shows where we are from? It could be all over."

"Maybe we should get out of here." Erec wasn't sure how the tiny stream could keep them penned in, so he put part of his foot over the water. It shot into the air with such force that he was thrown onto his back. A roar of laughter went up around him, but Bethany looked panicked.

A line formed near the Identdetector, which was the only way out of the circle of water. Erec and Bethany drifted near the machine, but avoided the line. Kilroy ushered kids one by one under the Identdetector's tall blue dome.

A boy walked under the dome. "Name?" asked Spartacus Kilroy.

"Bo Garth," the boy said.

Spartacus repeated "Bo Garth," and the pages of his ledger book flew open to Bo's name. Erec could see the screen on the side of the Identdetector comparing two identical pictures of Bo's face and his name. No address or other information was listed. Spartacus put a check by Bo's name.

Erec jabbed his thumb toward the book in Kilroy's hands. "I guess it's a good thing I didn't change my name in his book. I signed in as Erec Rex, so I should be okay."

"But what if Kilroy recognizes your name?"

Erec idly kicked a pebble into the water wall, and a small jet shot it back. "It's not like I have much choice."

The crowd in the water wall was thinning when a rumble of chatter erupted near the Identdetector. "Well, I think we have our culprit," Spartacus Kilroy said. Erec squeezed into a tight crowd peering at the pictures on the side of the machine. One showed an angry boy, about fourteen, now cursing inside the machine. The other picture was of a balding middle-aged man. "Queen Posey, your

THE DRAGON'S EYE

highness, we've found him. A grown man trying to sneak into the contests." Kilroy shook his head.

Queen Posey appeared with a splash, dark brown hair hanging in ringlets and shimmering blue robes draped around her. Now that she was close, Erec saw that the dark circles under her eyes were made from three thin black lines. She frowned and wagged a finger at the boy-man whose name was Tyrone Rant. In a moment Rant was sitting near her, penned in by a small water wall.

Kilroy looked shaken. "Good thing we checked. Your highness, should we let the rest of these kids go?"

Queen Posey thought a minute. "No. I think they should all go through."

Erec's heart sank.

Not many kids were left inside when shouts erupted. Two others joined Rant in his water wall: another man, posing as a boy, and a woman who looked like a ten-year-old girl. Queen Posey did not look pleased.

"I'm getting this over with," Bethany announced. She walked to the Identdetector with Erec behind her. After a short wait, she walked in. "Bethany Evirly," she said.

"Bethany Evirly," Kilroy repeated, sounding tired. He looked up. "Oh, hi," he smiled. His book flew open to a different page and he marked a check by her name. "You changed your name once, I see." he said. "Hmm. Are you related to Earl Evirly?"

Turning pale, Bethany shook her head.

"Too bad," said Kilroy. "He's in big around here lately. Always at important meetings." He shrugged. "Next."

Erec walked in. "Erec Rex."

"Balthazar's friend," Kilroy chuckled. He looked at the machine, puzzled. "Your majesty, I'm not sure what to make of this. Can you look? He *is* a kid, but his pictures don't match."

The queen stared at the pictures for a long time, then at Erec with a look of disbelief. Erec wondered what was wrong with his picture. He could not see it from inside the machine. Could his name be confusing everybody?

"Your majesty? Should we let him stay in the games? He's not an adult trying to sneak in. Who knows what happened to him?"

Queen Posey cleared her throat. "You are right, of course. He may stay."

Erec felt a surge of relief, though his legs were weak from the waiting. "AdviSeer Kilroy?"

"Call me Sport." Kilroy winked. "Saved you twice now."

"Uh, I like to be called Rick Ross, not Erec Rex. Could you change my name in your book?" Erec held his breath.

Kilroy was clearly surprised. "Well, I don't know. That's rather odd."

"You heard the boy," said Queen Posey. "Call him Rick Ross."

"Well, okay then." Kilroy smiled politely and drew a thin line through "Erec Rex." "Rick Ross it is."

"Thank you." Erec nodded to the queen and darted away to where Bethany stood waiting.

"What happened?" Bethany asked. "I couldn't see the pictures from this side. Did they recognize your name?"

"I have no idea." Erec shook his head in amazement. "They said my pictures didn't match. How could that be? I didn't have a shape-changing spell. Queen Posey was staring at me. I wonder if she recognized my name. Kilroy didn't seem to." A heavy weight settled on Erec's shoulders. He had been safe, but now he wasn't sure what was going on.

Bethany bit her lip. "It sounds like my Uncle Earl has been here."

"All right," Kilroy shouted. "There will be no more entries. The games have officially begun!" He blew his whistle and the crowd erupted in cheers.

"The first contest," said Kilroy, "is the MONSTER: the Multi Option Non Stop To End Race. The track is divided into half-mile segments, each splitting into branches. At the ends of the segments will be a sign with a question. Each answer choice will point you down a different path. Only one is correct. If you pick the right answer and go down the right track, it will split again in another half mile with another question. If you pick a wrong answer, you either come to a dead end and go back or, worse, you may go on to another track split, where there are two wrong answers leading to two dead ends. If you come to a question where you know both answers are wrong, turn back and take another track choice.

"You will not be able to see the dead ends until you are on top of them. They look like forks in the track. When you return from a dead end, you must wear vanishing caps, which will be in big boxes next to each sign." Kilroy plopped a black cap on his head and disappeared. Then he pulled it off and reappeared. "This keeps your competitors from knowing they are on the wrong path.

"If you make each choice correctly, you can win in five segments. That's two and a half miles. If you make every choice wrong, the race can be up to seven and a half miles forward plus five miles backward. Don't wear yourself out too fast. Decision making is more important than speed. And don't worry. This is hard, but two hundred of you out there will win the Multi Option Non Stop To End Race. Good luck!"

Erec thought of his sister Nell and her walker. The contest did not seem fair. Still, he was relieved it did not involve the minotaur in the maze.

Erec watched as Bethany was counting on her fingers. She saw him staring and looked sheepishly at him. "Just figuring out the odds

of winning by randomly guessing answers, with this many kids and the number of segments." She shrugged. "I like math."

The judges, minus King Piter, huddled nearby. Balthazar Ugry stood to the side with a scowl. King Pluto waved his scepter, and numbers appeared on the backs of everybody's shirts. Erec was 441 and Bethany was 398. Erec wondered if the numbers would stay on their shirts permanently.

The huge crowd followed Spartacus Kilroy around the maze and crowded around a wide starting line. Kilroy blew his whistle, and everybody ran, bumping into each other for a half mile to the first sign. A boy and a girl who looked like they were around sixteen flew above the crowd. A girl pointed up, saying, "There go the Calais twins."

A boy zipped by so fast Erec almost fell over. His feet skimmed over the track like ice on glass. A few kids bounced as if they were walking on the moon. Erec was the most surprised, however, to see a cheetah speed by like lightning. When it reached the signpost, it turned into a girl with long golden hair and freckles.

Erec saw Balor Stain look at writing on his palm and dash down the left fork without stopping, Damon, Ward, and Rock at his side. They all bounded with long strides, as if their shoes had rockets or springs.

A gigantic beast with long snakelike necks and big fangs jutting from its heads hissed from the first signpost. Erec jumped back when a head shot toward him, jaws opened. A slick, futuristic woman's voice spoke in calm monotone above the commotion. "You have come to a Hydra, which arose from a lake. It is charging at you, fangs bared. Go down the left path if you throw a sack over its middle head. Go down the right path if you chop its heads off with your sword."

Kids ran to the right and left, sometimes changing their minds and turning the other way. A snake head shot at a girl facing away from the sign. Erec rushed to push her out of the way, but the monster melted into the air when it touched her.

A tall, thin boy jumped twenty feet in the air and looked over the sign. Whatever he saw must not have helped him, though, because he looked disappointed when he landed. A dark-haired girl was somehow able to make the Hydra jump up and down. Although it was interesting to watch, it didn't help her at all.

"Well," said Bethany, who had kept up easily with Erec, "it's cruel and disgusting to chop off its heads, but I suppose that's the right answer."

"I don't think so," said Erec. "Balor ran to the left without even reading the sign."

Bethany put her hands on her hips. "Then we should go the other way."

"And lose for sure?" Erec wasn't sure why, but he wanted to win. Maybe it was his competitive side taking over. Then again, his mother did say that fate might have put him here for a reason. Anyway, it seemed best to try his hardest.

Bethany made a face and ran up the left track. Balor and his friends were out of sight. The track was less crowded, and they ran the next half mile at a decent pace. At the next sign, a huge crablike beast snapped long pincers at them. It had one eye and a large mouth with sharp teeth.

The same calm female monotone said, "Congratulations. You threw a bag over the Hydra's middle head, which holds its little brain, confusing it so you could run away. If you chop off a Hydra head, two grow back in its place right away.

"Now a hungry ginglehoffer sees you in a forest. It is dinnertime. He runs to catch you. If you use a marshmallow, take the path to the left. If you use a sword, take the path straight ahead. If you use a leash, take the path to the right."

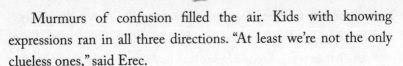

Murmurs of confusion filled the air. Kids with knowing expressions ran in all three directions. "At least we're not the only clueless ones," said Erec.

"Well," said Bethany, "it seems like swords don't work well with these things. And a marshmallow sounds ridiculous. Want to try the leash?"

Erec thought a leash sounded as ridiculous as a marshmallow, but it was as good as anything else. They ran to the right, slower now, to the large sign a half mile away. On the signpost a dragon roared and clawed at the air, wings spread. A path forked behind it.

The woman's voice said, "What would you do with a leash if a ginglehoffer was chasing you? Become a delicious dinner. Put on an invisibility cap behind this sign and leave it at the ginglehoffer signpost."

Erec and Bethany looked at each other in disgust. "I'm getting sick of running," Bethany said. From behind the signpost, the raging dragon looked like motionless cardboard. Bethany put a cap on and disappeared.

"How can we run together if I can't see you?"

"We can't." Bethany's voice was near Erec. "Don't wait for me. I'm getting tired. I don't want to lose this for you."

"Forget it," said Erec, putting his cap on. "Run your best. You may beat me, anyway. We'll wait at the signpost for each other. I won't mind a break then."

Running while invisible felt strange. Bethany appeared a minute after Erec took his cap off by the ginglehoffer sign.

"We've only run two miles," Bethany said. "We better slow down. Remember the tortoise and the hare?"

Oscar and Jack tore up to the sign, red and winded, and leaned on their knees, panting.

Oscar scowled. "We cut off the Hydra's heads, then we came to a giant mosquito and tried to throw a net around it. Wrong. Jack talked me into coming back here before we tried riding the mosquito. Who knows what's right?" He glared at Jack. "If we were supposed to ride the mosquito . . ."

Jack held up a finger. "Shh . . . We got it right, doofus. Listen to the sign." Erec didn't hear anything. He realized the woman's words must sound in the runners' heads when they came to the sign.

Oscar spat. "We've run three miles. You two look pretty good."

"We just ran two. We're going slower," said Erec. He went to drop the vanishing cap in the box, but turned around when Bethany loudly cleared her throat. She stuffed hers in her pocket and pointed at it. Erec put his cap in his pocket too.

Oscar and Jack saw him. "Good thinking," said Oscar. "That could come in handy."

Jack frowned. "I don't think that's smart. It's stealing. Is it worth getting sent home?"

Oscar's nose wrinkled. "Just say it was a mistake. They can't prove anything."

After a moment of doubt, Erec decided he should keep the cap. It could end up helping him save his mother. He stared at the ginglehoffer, claws snapping, while the woman's voice again sounded in his head.

"I still don't like the sword," said Bethany. "The leash path was a dead end."

"It's a marshmallow," said Jack.

"Are you crazy?" said Oscar.

"No. My dad said something about it once, I'm sure."

"No way. Give me the mighty sword." Oscar took off down the path straight ahead. Bethany, Erec, and Jack took the marshmallow path to the left. Running wasn't bad after the short break. They jogged at a steady pace, then jumped back when a giant minotaur in racing shorts appeared, towering over them. His bull-like upper body reared up to smash them.

"Eeek!" Bethany turned away.

"Look," Jack said. "It's just fake. It can't hurt you."

The infuriatingly calm woman's voice echoed in their heads. "Congratulations. Ginglehoffers can't resist marshmallows but are terribly allergic to them. Yours eats the marshmallow, gags, and throws up while you run away."

"I guess the theme is escaping and not killing the monsters," said Erec.

"Of course," sniffed Bethany. "One should always be kind to creatures." Jack nodded.

"Hmm, why don't I want to be kind to a minotaur?" Erec said, laughing.

The woman's voice continued. "A giant minotaur is tearing at you across a field. If you plead with the minotaur for your life, go left. If you shoot an arrow into the minotaur's eye, go straight. If you throw water on the minotaur, go right."

"I don't think pleading with a minotaur would work."

Bethany scrunched her face at the awful creature. "I don't like shooting it in the eye, though. Water, everyone?"

Erec looked at Jack. "Has your father said anything about minotaurs?"

"No." Jack shrugged. "Water's good as anything to me."

They took the right fork. After about an eighth of a mile, Jack struck something hard in the air. He fell onto his back, feet up.

"Darn it," a voice echoed behind them. The three looked at each other.

"Is that what I think it was?" Erec asked.

Jack stood and dusted himself off. "It was someone running back with an invisibility cap. We're on the wrong path."

"That saved us a mile." Bethany wiped her forehead.

"Or more," Jack said. "It could have split again."

Erec and Bethany took their vanishing caps from their pockets.

"Ugh," Jack said. "I didn't take one. Now what do I do?" He looked longingly at the cardboard back of the minotaur sign.

Bethany said, "You don't need it. Just run back without it. You've only gone down here a little way."

"No," said Jack, "it's not worth the risk." He looked sadly at the path ahead as kids ran by.

"Here." Bethany threw her cap to Jack and ran back without one. Erec and Jack looked at each other, put caps on, and followed her back.

"Thanks." Jack smiled and tossed Bethany the cap.

She shrugged. "I guess it's the arrow, then. Pleading with a minotaur is ridiculous." They walked slowly but picked up their pace as they came to an enormous, muscular man at the end of the track. Holding a club, he had one huge eye in the middle of his sloped head.

The woman's voice sounded in their heads. "Congratulations. You shot a bull's eye. Your arrow stunned the minotaur, letting you shoot another at its other eye, blinding it, or its heart, to kill it."

"So much for kindness to animals," said Jack.

The voice said, "Finally, at the end of your journey, an angry Cyclops swings his club at you as he climbs down a mountain. If you grab his ankles and trip him before he has time to react, go to the right. If you offer him your watch and all your valuables, go to the left."

Erec frowned. "Something tells me bribing the guy might work better than fighting him." Bethany and Jack agreed and they started slowly down the left fork. A few kids ran by, so the three put on steam and ran hard to the finish line. "We went seven segments. That's three and a half miles," said Erec. "Not bad."

Olive Umpee wrote down their shirt numbers as they crossed the finish line. Erec asked Umpee what his place was, and she pointed at a large board behind her, where runners' names appeared next to their numbers. Erec, Bethany, and Jack were listed as ninety-five, -six and -seven. They cheered and fell onto the grass.

"Look at the first four winners." Bethany pointed. "Balor Stain, Damon Stain, Rock Rayson, and Ward Gamin. Surprise, surprise."

Hecate Jekyll handed out cloudsicles, pollen sundaes, honeycomb, snow cones, and spring water at a refreshment stand. Erec tried a berry peach nectar swirl cloudsicle. Frozen purple mist moved around the stick. It was cold and delicious, and twirled in his mouth before it melted. Bethany ate a maple cloudsicle. "Look," she said, "it melts up!" As the cloudsicle thawed, it spun faster and bits puffed off the top. Jack had a honey cocoa swirl and a pollen apple swirl before flopping onto the soft grass.

"Spread the word," said Hecate Jekyll, "Sport Kilroy has planned a winners' party tonight in the agora. Winners meet at six at the dormitory entrance, and we'll walk down together." She winked. "We'll have pizza and ice cream, candy, sody pops—some Aorth treats for ya. And a pomegranate for you." She pointed at Erec then tapped her head. "See, I'm old, but I've still got it all up here."

Balor, Damon, Ward, and Rock Rayson walked by, laughing. Somehow they had bags of Super A King fastaurant burgers and sodas. "So, you made it," Balor said. "Good. You'll be on our team, then." He laughed. "Probably. You going to the winners' party tonight?"

"I guess," said Erec. "Are you?"

"Oh, we have plans," said Balor.

Damon grinned. "We have some *spying* to do."

Balor looked crossly at Damon. "Shut up, bonehead." He turned to Erec and laughed. "Have a good time tonight." They walked away.

"Did you hear that?" said Bethany. "They've admitted to spying. That's how they know so much about the contests."

"It seems to me," said Erec, "that whoever gave them those fastaurant burgers could just as easily have given them contest secrets."

Oscar walked over, red and panting. "You look like you spent all day relaxing on the grass."

Jack, Erec, and Bethany's eyes met. Nobody wanted to ask if he came in as a winner. Oscar plopped down. "Well, aren't you going to even ask how I did?"

"Uh, how'd ya do?" asked Jack.

Oscar scowled. "One ninety-five."

"You're in!" Jack shouted.

"Barely," said Oscar. "My dad will kill me."

Both Oscar and Jack's skin glowed bright red. "You guys are sunburned." Bethany tapped Oscar's nose. "Don't you get any sun in Aorth?"

Oscar glared at her as if the answer should be obvious.

Stoney Rayson appeared, looking cool in a gray suit, black wristbands, and eye patch. Kids ran up, searching for paper and pens for autographs. Rayson ignored them, announcing into a microphone, "The contest is over. The judges are leaving and the track is gone." Suddenly, a wide field of grass and wildflowers blew in the wind where the track had been a second ago.

"Winners, get your prizes here." Rayson pointed to a large pen where balls of different colors and size were scattered over the ground. "Everyone gets an aniball." Rayson checked off winners' names as they entered. "Only one each—just one. You can keep it or let it go."

All around balls popped, turning into rabbits, hamsters, lizards, dogs, squirrels, pigs, and even a platypus. Erec recognized Bo Garth from the Identdetector. He touched a small red ball and it popped, leaving a small mosquito in its place. He shooed it away, dejected.

Bethany was glowing with excitement. She eyed a small group of balls carefully. "I've always wanted a pet. Uncle Earl would never let me have one."

Jack touched a multicolored ball that turned into a big, beautiful butterfly and flew away. He shrugged. "I have too many pets at home, anyway."

Balor, Damon, Rock, and Ward checked in, and Rayson pulled out a burlap sack, rolling four black aniballs before them. The boys touched them and they became four identical shining black stallions. The boys high-fived and laughed. Rayson pointed a thumb to a pile of bridles and saddles.

"Hey," Bo shouted. "Why do they get special ones?"

"Top four winners," grinned Rayson, dusting his hands.

Bethany carefully chose a pink ball, which turned into a very fluffy small pink kitten. She oohed and aahed, picked the kitten up, and looked happier than Erec had ever seen her.

Oscar ran by with his hand cupping a tiny fish, which was gasping for breath. "See any water?"

Erec did some searching himself. There were a fair number of aniballs left, and kids roaming through the pen seemed afraid to pick. He finally touched a gray ball that turned into a fully grown dog, wagging his tail. He was shaped like a large Labrador, except triangular pointy ears stood straight up from his head. His back and face were a dark, flecked gray, and his underside, legs, neck, and snout glowed white. A white stripe slid down his face.

The dog jumped, paws hitting Erec's chest, almost knocking him over, and licked his face. His eyes were a shocking blue, with vivid intelligence. Erec wrapped an arm around his neck and rubbed his head, laughing.

Suddenly there was a scream. Kids and animals ran, shouting

and squawking, as a huge rhinoceros charged through the pen. Upset aniballs popped into birds and newts around them. Erec grabbed his dog and Bethany's arm and ran to the gate.

Bethany and Erec's dog both stared at him in shock. "How did you pick that dog up? Wasn't it heavy?"

Erec realized he was still holding the dog and set him down. He shrugged. "I'm stronger than I look."

Stoney Rayson watched the pandemonium, not moving. Three kids lay on their backs in the pen, and others were trampled. Erec wondered if Rayson was frozen in shock.

Finally, after the pen was mostly cleared, and the rhino had charged back and forth a few times, Rayson shouted, "Everybody stand back." He pulled a wristband off his right wrist, flipped his fist up, and suddenly the rhinoceros turned to stone, head lowered and poised to charge.

A girl and several animals near the rhino were also turned to stone, along with Bo Garth's left leg, which had been in the air. Bo screamed.

"It's okay," Rayson covered his wrist again. "We'll get you kids to the royal hospital in the south wing." He scooped Bo in his arms and started carrying him to the castle.

Balthazar Ugry appeared, glowering. "I knew someone would get hurt," he said. "These contests must end *now*."

"Nobody asked you, Balthazar," said Rayson. "And nobody got hurt in the contest. Stay out of it."

Ugry waved his walking stick toward the pen. The girl who had turned to stone, a few children lying limp, and some stone animals rose above the field and drifted alongside him to the castle.

"Did you see Stoney Rayson turn that rhinoceros to stone?" Erec asked. "He must really have gorgon eyes in his wrists."

Bethany also was dumbfounded. "Could all the Super A Team

members really have the powers that they do in the movies and comics?"

Jack frowned at them. "Of course they do. What did you think? Some of those guys are pretty scary. I'm surprised you've heard of them at all in Upper Earth."

Erec thought of the comics showing Mighty Joe Liath crushing his enemies, Franklin Stein bringing deadly things to life, and Mel Timan with his melting heat rays, and shuddered.

The pizza and ice cream at the winners' party tasted so much better than the cloud cuisine Erec had for dinner. Hecate Jekyll laid out trays of desserts and had brought a soda machine in.

Spartacus Kilroy quieted the room with an announcement. "First of all, congratulations. You demonstrated intelligence, strength, and, I'm pleased to say, good sportsmanship. You are all invited to the next contest on Wednesday. That's in two days. It's called the Pro and Contest. We'll meet behind the maze again at ten in the morning. Now give yourselves a hand."

The kids cheered. Kilroy quieted them again. "Unfortunately, as you know, there was a terrible accident in the prize pen today. Somehow, one of the aniballs turned out to be an angry rhinoceros. Three winners were mauled, Bo Garth's leg was turned to stone, and Sue Penne was turned entirely to stone by Stoney Rayson, who was trying to help.

"Ezzy Mumbai, our castle doctor, is excellent. She assured me everyone will be fine. I'm sure you can imagine how disappointed these kids are not to be able to go on to the next contests, so please visit them. And anyone who did not get an aniball because of the accident, see me."

Music filled the room. Kids talked about the contest, each sounding as if they knew the answers all along. It was a room full of conquerors.

Erec went to the dessert table for another brownie. He had not spoken to his mother since the contest because Jack and Oscar had been in the room. He was worried that Queen Posey had recognized his name. Would she find him and lock him in a dungeon? Since he did not know magic, dungeon life might not be as comfortable for him as it was for his mother.

Spartacus Kilroy bumped into Erec on his way out the door, mumbling something about being needed in the castle. Bethany's pink kitten perched contentedly on her shoulder. It was so fluffy it looked stuffed. "I named her Cutie Pie. I found a shoebox for her bed, but I'll probably let her sleep on my pillow. What's your dog's name?"

Erec hadn't thought about it. "I don't know yet."

Suddenly there was wild screaming at the other end of the room. Something was terribly wrong. Erec's fists clenched, and he ran toward the noise. In the dim glow he saw kids running aimlessly, crashing into each other.

A girl had blood on her face. Were the screams because she was hurt, or was she hurt from the commotion? Had there been a fight? Erec took a deep breath. More shrieks rose, and kids ran around him, frantic.

Then Erec heard a groan so deep it sounded like thick rust-covered hinges scraping open. Chills ran through him as the noise turned into an unearthly howl. Then, between running kids, Erec saw it. The minotaur. The same creature that had been sleeping in the maze was now in the party room, awake.

The minotaur looked wild-eyed, as disoriented as the kids. It knocked over tables, clawing chairs and children. It thrust its horns toward a boy and charged. At the last second, someone yanked the boy to safety. The minotaur paused for a breath and looked around into the chaos. Kids shook the doorknobs and kicked the doors, but they were all locked.

Erec pounded a window, trying to break through, but his arms jerked to a stop. A pair of chilling eyes appeared on the other side: Balthazar Ugry. Ugry had a horrifying look on his face, eyes flashing. For a moment Erec was more afraid of Ugry than he was of the minotaur.

In the confusion, kids filled a bucket with water and threw it on the minotaur, making it angrier. Of course . . . the MONSTER race today told us how to stop a minotaur, Erec thought. What was the correct answer? Not water. The minotaur grabbed a girl and almost bit her, but someone threw a table at its head. It dropped her and roared, spinning around.

Bethany shouted, "Stab its eye!" but there was no sword.

Suddenly, Erec felt faint and dizzy, like he was drifting over the crowd. His eyes jolted open. It was a cloudy thought. He dreaded the feeling, the loss of control. A mixture of sickness and quiet command took over him. He tried not to fight it.

The next thing he knew, he picked up a ceramic plate and threw it into the glass shelves behind the bar, smashing them. The minotaur was crushing a boy in its giant hands. It turned to look for the cause of the noise and then faced the boy again, licking its lips.

Erec leaped over the bar, grabbed a long glass shard, and charged. The beast looked at him right before he plunged the glass deep into its eye. The beast howled, dropping the boy, whimpering and pawing at the glass.

Just then a door burst off its hinges, and Spartacus Kilroy ran in with Balthazar Ugry glowering behind him. Kilroy ran toward the minotaur, remote control outstretched, shouting strange words.

Nothing happened.

Ugry pointed with his staff and boomed, "Aphantos."

Ugry pointed at the minotaur with his staff and it disappeared. "Out!" Ugry shouted at the contestants. "Out!"

They ran to the doors, some limping and others crying.

Kilroy scooped up the boy who had been squeezed by the minotaur. "Anybody hurt? Oh, my goodness," he said, stunned by the disaster. "I'll take you to the royal hospital. Come with me."

Ugry stood in the doorway, a foul look on his face.

"What an awful night," whispered Bethany. "Remember what those men in the maze said? The king's AdviSeer ordered a *hungry* minotaur for a surprise. Some surprise."

"Well, Ugry wants to end to the contests. Maybe this was his plan."

Jack looked shocked. "But Balthazar Ugry is one of King Piter's AdviSeers. He's been dedicated to the king since before we were born. He wouldn't hurt us."

Erec wasn't so sure. "Have you ever seen him close up? He creeps me out. There's something not right about him. It almost feels like he is looking right through me."

"Did you see his face at the prize pen after the rhino appeared?" Bethany asked. "I wonder if he planned that, too. Maybe he's trying to scare everyone off."

Erec said, "I saw him in the window when the minotaur appeared just now. He looked evil."

Bethany said, "Maybe he called Kilroy out so he couldn't help us, then magically locked us in."

Jack shook his head. "You have no proof. Anybody could have done that."

"Like who?" asked Erec.

"Maybe a sore loser," said Jack, but he did not look too sure himself.

CHAPTER NINE

The Sneakers

AMBROSIA AND NECTAR are growing on me," Bethany said, walking with Erec after breakfast the next morning. She was wearing another of her roommate's outfits. "And I feel so great after eating it."

Erec gave her a sideways glance. "Maybe they'll start to sell it at the fastaurants." Bethany laughed. "I'll have a Super Star ambrosia meal, please. Hold the bacon." He had taken a bag of ambrosia for his new dog, but doubted he would like it.

Melody walked by and waved, black curls cascading over her dark shoulders. Bethany said, "Now's a good time, if you want to use my room to talk to your mom. I'll guard the door for you."

Erec walked into Bethany's room and shut the door. A loud screech made him jump, and then something flew at him. He put a hand up and knocked Cutie Pie out of the air, but not before she scratched his face. She leaped onto Bethany's bed and glared at Erec, hissing and saying, "rawwwl, rawwl," as if she were trying to imitate a dog.

Erec glared at Cutie Pie until she settled on the bed. He slid the glasses on, and jumped back to his mother's room. June sat on her bed, reading.

"Mom?" Erec said quietly.

June jumped and dropped her book. "Erec?"

"I'm on the blue chair." Even though she couldn't see him, it was nice for her to look in his general direction.

"Are you okay?"

"I'm fine. I won the first contest, Mom! It was a race, and you had to know about monsters. It was fun. Maybe I might win some more. And I got a dog as a prize.

"But a minotaur attacked kids at the winner's party. Luckily I had a cloudy thought, or one of the kids would have been eaten."

June looked appalled. "I can't believe this. Piter . . . King Piter would never allow this to happen. He *had* to know about this."

"Mom, the king doesn't know anything. He's dazed."

She didn't understand at all. "Something fishy is going on. If Piter was really sick, Ippocra Asclep, the castle doctor, would fix him immediately. There is nothing that woman can't cure."

"She's not here. Now the castle doctor is Ezzy Mumbai."

June shook her head. "Somebody is messing with the king. Who do you think could be behind this?"

"Balthazar Ugry, one of his AdviSeers, always seems to be around when bad things happen. He gives me the chills when he looks at me."

"Balthazar was always faithful to the crown," said June. "Still, things seem so topsy-turvy now."

"Queen Posey found out my name. And she looked like she recognized it. Her eyes nearly bugged out of her head. Was she . . . out to get me when I lived here?"

June shook her head. "No. I'd like to think you could trust her, but I really don't know now. Just keep your distance."

"Why are people after me? What's going on?"

June sighed. "Please, it's been a bad day. We'll talk about it later. Just be careful. Danny and Sammy still aren't back. Lynette Wool, who's watching the other kids, said they called a few times and they're fine, staying with friends. They talked to everyone, so I'm pretty sure it was really them calling, but it doesn't make sense. They don't have friends in New York yet." June made a glass of ice water appear and took a drink.

"Erec, I need to get out of here. Obviously King Piter can't help me. But maybe you can." Erec jerked back in surprise, but she didn't see him. "I hate to ask. It could be dangerous. I just have no other choice." She held up a finger, thinking. "You can make a formula that will blast through the force field around my cell. It takes a while to brew, so you better get started. Most of the things we need are around the castle." She smiled as her plan came together. "There is something you need to help you collect the ingredients. They're special shoes called Sneakers."

"I'm already wearing gym shoes."

"No. These are *real* Sneakers, Erec. They let you walk fast, in perfect silence, no floorboard creaks or anything. And if someone is nearby you can stamp your feet and they will throw sound into another room or make a clatter down the hall to lead them off your track."

Erec liked this idea a lot.

"They're under a floorboard in the linen closet outside the royal chambers. There is a bag of money with them for emergencies. Take that, too. Go into the west wing ... let's see. Take the third hallway to the left, go to the end, turn right, go to the end of that hall, then turn left. The closet will be on your right, right by a big double door."

Erec said, "Third hall left to end, right to end, then left."

"Exactly. Get those, and then we'll talk about the ingredients for the force field–blasting formula."

"Mom, if you can do magic, why don't you make the formula?"

"I tried. The force field keeps me from bringing magical things in, like some of the ingredients."

"How will I get it there?"

"You'll have to bring it. There are several ways. I'll think about it. Also, keep an eye on King Piter. If you figure out who is spellbinding him, let me know."

When Erec came out of the room, Bethany got Cutie Pie and fed her something strange.

"I'll wait over here," Erec said, "away from your attack cat."

"You're kidding," Bethany said, laughing. She talked to her cat in a baby voice. "You are such a soft fluff bundle, you wouldn't hurt anyone."

"Oh, yeah?" Erec pointed at his scratched face.

"Maybe you did that to yourself." Bethany shrugged.

"Uh-huh. What are you feeding her?"

"Ambrosia and sushi. She loves it."

Erec told her about finding the Sneakers, and when he was done, she said, "We can use the vanishing caps to sneak into the west wing." Bethany pulled her cap from a drawer and popped it on and off a few times, watching herself disappear. Noticing the new clothes she was wearing, she added, "I need to find the laundry. Thank goodness it's free. I don't ever want to wear that awful dress again."

That gave Erec an idea. "Clothes will be a good cover. If we get caught in the west wing, we could say we were looking for the laundry. And we could hide the shoes and money in the clothing."

Erec stuffed his cap into his pocket and went to put his dirty clothes in a bag. When he put the cap on, the bag disappeared with him. As he stumbled through the sideways gravity into the castle, two socks and a pair of shorts fell out of his bag. They became visible in midair as they fell. A boy nearby stepped back in shock. The falling shorts and socks vanished when Erec scooped them up. The boy said to his friend, "I am very tired. I'm going to lie down." Erec and Bethany tiptoed away.

It was difficult darting around people who did not see them. Spartacus Kilroy walked by in his bright blue cape and looked right through them. When they were near the west wing, Balthazar Ugry swept close. He stared right at them. His scarab amulet glinted in the light. Erec grabbed in the air for Bethany's arm, and pulled her to the wall until Ugry went by. He held his breath. Ugry came closer, eyes blazing.

Erec's stomach turned over. A musty smell wafted over Erec, and he tried not to sneeze. Ugry stared at him. Erec glanced down. He was still invisible.

Ugry's brow furrowed into a knot. "Did you *steal* those vanishing caps? Take them off now."

Erec and Bethany took the caps off and saw each other's red faces.

Bethany said, "I'm sorry, sir. We just found them . . . in the dormitories." She held hers out to Ugry.

Ugry's eyes narrowed to slits. "Return them to Spartacus. If I catch you using those again, you'll find yourselves home immediately, or somewhere worse."

Erec and Bethany walked down the hallway, breathing fast. "How did he see us?"

Bethany shrugged. "Nobody else seemed to. We better not wear them again." She stuffed hers into her pocket.

"Shouldn't we give them to Kilroy?" Erec asked.

"Ugry didn't say we'd be kicked out if we *kept* them," said Bethany. "Only if we wore them again."

Balthazar Ugry and Spartacus Kilroy were glaring at each other nearby. Erec heard Kilroy say, "You don't know what's right for Alypium. I'm warning you not to meddle, Ugry."

"What are you going to do?" Ugry hissed. "Kill me?"

Bethany snuck past them, unnoticed, and signaled Erec to follow her to the west wing. "I'll distract the guard and you run in."

"I guess since Ugry is still out here I can use the vanishing cap," Erec said.

"I wouldn't. If you're caught in the west wing, you can say you got lost, but if you have that cap on, it's all over. Ugry would love to send us home. Go, quick. I'll distract the guard."

"How?" Erec was amazed Bethany saw this as an opportunity, with a guard, Ugry, and Kilroy nearby.

"I'll ask him about the laundry. Go while they're still arguing." She went to the other end of the rope and called the guard over. Erec glanced down the hallway at Ugry and Kilroy and darted under the rope, laundry bag in his hand.

He ran on his toes past the room where loud noises boomed from behind a door and turned left at the third hallway. When the hallway ended, he looked to the right. Two maids were leaning against the wall, talking.

Erec hid around the corner, waiting for them to go. Instead they started walking toward him. He touched the vanishing cap in his pocket. Could they see him with it on, like Ugry? Better not risk it. He opened a door and stepped into a dark room.

The minute he was inside, a tremendous force slammed him sideways into the wall. He was pinned, like the wall was a magnet and he was made of iron. He pushed his body away as hard as he could, but then his hands were stuck to it. He could pull one hand off, but the minute he lifted his other hand, his body flung back into the wall.

Footsteps clattered and voices rose outside the room. He realized how loud he had been, crashing into the wall. The door burst open and light streamed in. Without a thought, Erec grabbed the vanishing cap from his pocket and put it on.

A maid flipped the light switch and peered into the room. She seemed to know not to step inside. "Well, I'll be. It sounded to me like someone was in here."

"Yes," another giggled. "Someone who didn't know what they were doing."

"Well, I'll go get Ugry," the first one sighed. "He'll want to know about this." They closed the door, leaving the light on.

Erec whipped the cap off. Ugry was on his way and he was trapped. He looked around the room. The only furniture was a small sofa and chair. They seemed stuck to the wall he was trapped on.

As he tried moving, he realized that his feet easily lifted off the floor. Amazingly, he could scoot on his side all the way up the wall, straight to the ceiling. It was as if there was no gravity, or . . .

Erec remembered how Balor Stain told him that the gravity change didn't take in some rooms of the castle, and how they led kids into these rooms and watched them struggle on the wall. What an idiot he was. The gravity was sideways, that was all. He stood up on the wall. Now the question was how to get up the floor to the door.

He dragged the sofa along the wall, leaned it onto the floor, and climbed up the cushions. Standing on its side, he reached around the door frame and pulled himself out, falling with a clunk on the floor.

Voices echoed down the corridor. Erec was sure he heard Ugry. He ran down the now empty hallway to the right and then turned left. The closet was supposed to be on his right, by the big locked double doors. He ran by the gold-knobbed Port-O-Door. Several doors looked like they could be closets. Which was the right one?

Ugry's voice was getting closer. Erec dove inside a big door next to the double doors. Thankfully, he did not fly against the wall. Sheets and towels were piled in long rows on shelves. Maybe this was the right one. He slid his hands on the floorboards but felt nothing unusual. He tried prying some up with his fingers. It seemed impossible.

A maid twittered, ". . . around here somewhere. 'Seer Ugry said he probably has a vanishing cap on."

As Erec's eyes adjusted to the dark, he saw that a floorboard by the wall was slightly uneven. He pried it up with a pop. Underneath lay blue suede sneakers and a canvas bag full of coins and bills wrapped with rubber bands.

"He can't be far. Probably hiding somewhere." Ugry's voice sounded very close.

Erec pulled the shoes on. Luckily they fit. He hoped his mother was right about how they worked. Right as the doorknob started to turn, he stomped his feet.

A huge clatter arose down the hall. The doorknob stopped.

Ugry said, "Hmm." Erec heard the maids' loud footsteps and Ugry's cursing drift down the hallway.

Erec stuffed his gym shoes into his bag. Just to make sure, he jumped a few more times before peeking out. Nobody was in sight. He tore down the hallways, running in complete silence, thanks to his Sneakers. As he rounded the final corner, though, he ran smack into Spartacus Kilroy, who was carrying a tray of milk and cookies. The cookies fell to the floor, smashing into pieces, and some of the milk splashed onto the tray. Kilroy stared at the tray, stunned.

"Uh, sorry." Erec dusted off the cookies and put them back on the tray.

"I didn't hear you coming. My fault. No harm, only a bit of milk spilled. The king's ten o'clock cookies and milk." Kilroy suddenly grew concerned. "Say, what are you doing back here?"

Erec held up his laundry bag. "Trying to find the laundry. Someone pointed me back here. I think it was a joke."

Kilroy smiled. "I'll show you the right way. Now, no coming in here anymore, okay?"

"Yes, sir."

Kilroy led Erec past the guard. "The laundry room used to be in the basement, but since the castle is on its side that's impossible to get to. Now it's near the kitchens."

He headed off with the tray, and Erec spotted Bethany talking with a group of kids across the hall. When she saw Erec, she ran over. He pointed to his feet.

"You did it!"

"They work great. You know, I was thinking. If I was born here, I might have some sort of magic, too. Maybe *I* can do something, like send Balor and Damon home, or disappear without a vanishing cap." He scratched his head. "I wish I remembered more about being here."

"Better work on it fast. The Pro and Contest, whatever that is, is in the morning."

The laundry room, when he found it, was dimly lit. At first Erec had to squint to see the dark rows of machines lining the walls. Although the room seemed empty at first, Erec heard sniffs and panting. He wondered if someone was hiding.

With a loud creak, several washing machines swung around and walked toward them. As they got closer they came faster, and the ones at the other end of the room followed. Their lids opened and shut, giving them a menacing look, like they were about to gobble Erec and Bethany up. The sniffing noises grew louder. Erec realized they were coming from the machines.

Bethany backed away, but the machines closed in. A small washing machine, up to Erec's waist, nipped at his bag of dirty clothing. Erec opened its lid, and it straightened up. He pulled the money bag out and dumped his clothing inside fast, as much to make it leave him alone as anything else. The small machine plopped on the cement floor and hummed contentedly.

The rest of the machines walked faster toward Bethany. They reminded Erec of a group of huge ducks fighting over bread from a child they towered over. Bethany screeched, dropping her clothes as she ran for the door. One of the machines flipped her bag into the air with its foot, and they slammed against each other waiting for it to fall into one of their mouths.

The lucky machine made satisfied gurgles while the others slowly dragged back to the walls. A machine walked by Erec, sniffing him as it went back.

"That's it," called Bethany from the door. "I'm never seeing these clothes again. If anyone thinks I'm going to stick my hand in and try to get them back . . ."

The gurgling, humming machines with their clothing soon fell silent. The smaller one trotted to Erec, circling him playfully. It nipped and pulled at his shirt with its lid.

"Is it still hungry?" Bethany asked from the doorway.

"Maybe it wants to play," said Erec. "Or maybe the clothes are done?" He peeked under its lid while the small machine held still. His clothing was perfectly clean and folded inside. He lifted it out, and the machine trotted back to the wall.

The large machine with Bethany's clothing was still. A small noise came from it that sounded a lot like a snore. Erec peeked in and Bethany's clothing was also clean and folded. He took it out, leaving the machine to its nap.

Oscar and Jack were gone when Erec got back to his room. He opened the bag: There was more gold, silver, and bronze than he had ever seen, as well as rolls of the funny Bils he had seen in Alypium station. The gold coins had holes in the center. He took a deep breath and sat down with the bag in his lap.

His dog nuzzled his hand and gazed at him with its blue eyes. "Good boy. We can get good food for you now, and a collar." Erec opened a napkin and gave his dog fish, an apple, and some bread. With the dog happy, he locked the door and put his glasses on. "Mom?"

June jumped, but not so much this time. She was knitting, and her fingers were covered with huge diamond, ruby, and emerald rings. "Oh, Erec, thank goodness. I've been so worried—sending you off alone in the castle with things all topsy-turvy and Posey knowing you're there. Are you okay?"

"I'm fine, Mom. I got the money and the Sneakers. They're great."

"Already?" June said. "Wonderful. Did you have any problems?"

"Not at all. Don't worry about me." There was no need to worry her about how he was almost caught by Ugry. "Mom, where's the jewelry from?" If they'd had those rings before, they could have bought a house.

She tapped her finger and they vanished. "I just miss the finer things. It's a small consolation, though, for being stuck."

"If you could just conjure those up, why didn't you do it when we needed money so badly?"

"I couldn't. Magic is not allowed in Upper Earth. And if I had tried it, we would have been even easier to track down. There are homing devices." She popped a small emerald ring back on one finger. "So, are you okay with finding ingredients for a formula to blast me out of here?"

"You bet. What are they?"

She had a list ready. "We'll need a used horseshoe, wolfsbane, gunpowder, nitrowisherine, an eagle feather, three lion hairs, warthog essence, and grain alcohol. You better write that down."

Erec's heart sank. "And I'll have how many years to find all that?"

"Oh, it's not that bad. You can find a lot of it in the castle."

"Okay."

Erec took off his glasses, found some paper, and leaned back against the door before putting them back on.

"Get about four handfuls of wolfsbane, ten drops of nitro-wisherine, three cups of grain alcohol, and five drops of warthog essence—be careful with that. You can get these in the ingredient storerooms; at least you could in the past. The old head cook, Hecate Jekyll, kept everything well stocked. Is she still there?"

"Yup," said Erec.

"Good. She'll be a real help. Ask her for those four things. I don't think she knows enough about formulas to figure out what we are making. If she gives you a problem, let me know, and I'll tell you how to break into her storerooms. Then you'll need two cups of gunpowder, that's about two heaping handfuls. There are bags of it in the conventional armory. I'll tell you how to sneak in there later."

That struck Erec as odd. "Why is there an armory? Does Alypium have wars?"

"It never has. It's mostly a precaution. Now, the eagle feather and the three lion hairs are more unusual. I'm pretty sure Hecate Jekyll won't stock those. You'll have to order them on the Net." She looked anxious. "Can you do that?"

"Mom, I'm not stupid. Remember you said we could use the Internet at other people's houses? It's easy. I doubt I'll find lion hairs and eagle feathers, though."

June waved away that idea. "I'm not talking about the Internet. I mean the MagicNet. Same idea but a little different."

"Is it easy to use?"

"Easier. Someone should have access there." She snapped her fingers. "Ask around. It's new since I lived there. I don't know how we did without it." Her face filled with a smile. "You can even buy things over it. And you have money now. But be careful, there are some scam artists out there. If you need more money I'll tell you how to break into the castle vaults."

Erec wrote, "Eagle feather and three lion hairs—MagicNet." He couldn't believe what he was hearing. His mother knew how to plunder the castle vaults? He guessed that should be no surprise after learning she could loot Hecate Jekyll's storerooms and burgle the armory. She knew an awful lot about stealing things. He started to wonder what she was locked up for.

"That leaves the used horseshoe. Hmm. I suppose you can get almost anything on the MagicNet; you might as well try there."

"Don't worry. I know where I can find one." Erec wrote, "Used horseshoe—Balor's aniball horse."

Swiping the horseshoe would be a pleasure.

CHAPTER TEN

The Pro and Contest

I T HAD BEEN hard to convince Bethany to take money for clothing, pet food, and a collar for Cutie Pie, but once Erec did she was ecstatic about having new things. They dangled their feet in a large circular fountain. Kids were swimming around in the water spurting from a large stone whale, sea monster, and mermaid in its center.

Cutie Pie pawed the water by Bethany's side. After watching her, Bethany looked to see if anybody was listening and said, "Cutie Pie can talk. Really. She jumped onto my shoulder and whispered that the boy with the glass eye—that's you—talked to his mother in my room. I am so proud of her. I couldn't get her to say anything else, though."

"Great. First she attacks me. Then she spies on me." Erec glared at the fluffy pink kitten that was innocently licking her paw.

"You're just jealous because your dog can't talk. Does he have a name yet?"

"No." Erec was itching to go in the water himself, and he said, "We should have bought bathing suits."

"To swim?" Bethany stared at the water, blushing. "Did you know I have never gone swimming? Never had a bathing suit? I feel like an idiot. I don't know about anything."

Erec threw a rock, and it skimmed the water until it hit the sea monster. He was not sure what to say.

Bethany hugged her knees. "Uncle Earl thinks swimming is a waste of time, parties are frivolous, and if I'm relaxing I'm not earning my keep." She kicked the water, making a loud splash. "I hope I never see him again." Suddenly, she jumped into the waist-deep water in her clothing, tripped, and fell in over her head. She came up coughing and sputtering, eyes wide. "This is *great*!" She splashed back under again.

Smiling, Erec jumped in in his shorts. "Don't feel bad. My mom's great, but even she drives me nuts sometimes."

Bethany stood, dripping. "You're kidding. I'd give anything for a mom like yours. I guess I had one once. I have something to help me remember my parents. Earl never knew I had it, or he'd have taken it for sure." Bethany fumbled at something on her shirt and then held out two oval pictures connected by a gold clasp.

The picture on the left showed a smiling man with tan, pancake-colored skin and chocolate chip–brown eyes and hair. On the right

THE DRAGON'S EYE

was a red-haired woman holding a giggling, dark-haired baby. "That's my mom and me, and that's my dad. I've had this invisible locket ever since they died. You're the only one I've ever shown." She closed it and it disappeared.

"Kilroy said Earl Evirly comes here for important meetings. Do you think that could be your uncle?"

Bethany sighed. "He does go on business trips sometimes. I had to work twice as hard when he was gone. I always wondered what kind of business trips a newspaper vendor went on. Of course he'd never tell me. But it is hard to imagine a street vendor in meetings at a castle."

"With an invisible locket like that, he's more likely going to Alypium than Hoboken."

Bethany tilted her nose to the air. "*He* didn't give me the locket. My parents did."

"I know." Erec shrugged. "But he is your uncle. Your parents could be from here and then he would be too. Maybe you were born here, like me."

Bethany stopped splashing around and sat back on the wall. They both stared into the water. "It's funny," she said as he joined her. "When you've had something your whole life, even when it's strange, like an invisible locket, I guess you don't question it much."

Erec nodded. "I've been thinking that my mother may have been some sort of . . . outlaw."

Bethany's eyebrows rose. "No way."

"Way." Erec pointed out the reasons. "Bethany, she knows how to break into the castle vaults, and into Hecate Jekyll's storerooms. Don't you wonder where the money in the bag came from? We're not rich at home. What if she's locked up for a reason? What if she stole money and was on the run? We were always moving. She knew they were closing in. It would explain why we used to have money and she didn't work when I was younger. Plus, she won't tell me what she used to do in Alypium."

"You're still going to break her out, right?"

"Of course. She's my mom. She adopted me. I guess that makes me an outlaw too. That's probably why I'm not supposed to spread my name around. Maybe I'll get arrested unless I can pay back all the money she stole." That idea made Erec frown, and he fell silent.

"I wonder if I *am* from Alypium." Bethany's fingers twirled an invisible locket. "Maybe my parents were important. Maybe that's why Uncle Earl gets to visit with important people."

"Maybe your parents were the king and queen."

Bethany chuckled. "If King Piter was my dad, I'd be a hundred. Plus, my parents died. Plus, King Piter's triplets were killed."

"Yeah, yeah." Erec stood up, dripping water. "Come on, let's go back."

Erec sloshed to the dormitories to change. Talking about his mother reminded him of the night before he had come to Alypium, and he felt guilty. He almost never had time alone with her, with all of his siblings and all of her jobs. That night, they had finally gone on a walk together. A man had been following them. Erec told her, but when she turned around, the man had vanished.

June laughed. "What an imagination. I wish I was little again."

"I'm not little anymore, Mom."

"Of course."

Erec had gotten a hot dog, and an old man had sat next to them on a bench. June pointed at a bed of flowers crowded into a small plot of soil. "I bet if you look real hard you could see a flower fairy in there. There aren't a lot of places for them to go here."

The older man raised his eyebrows and chuckled. Then, to Erec's complete embarrassment, she started to sing the lullaby she had written for him ages ago. This, unfortunately, happened all too often. He supposed it was to try to make him feel better about being given up by his father and for having a glass eye. The man on the bench looked at Erec with pity.

Hush and quiet my sleepy child
And follow your dreams to places wild.
Safe within your snuggly bed
Let thoughts of magic fill your head.
You can be an explorer, a knight so brave
And find a dragon in a mossy cave.
He's guarding a gift that is just for you.
It came from your daddy, with love so true.
And this special gift, I tell no lie,
Is your very own dragon eye.
It was made for you, it fits right in
So your new life can now begin.

The man on the bench left.

"Mom, I'm too old for lullabies."

"Uh-huh," June said dreamily.

Not only did she treat him like a two-year-old and not believe him about the man following them, she also wasn't listening.

Erec snapped, "I hate that lullaby."

June threw him a sharp look. "Oh, really? I seem to remember you begging me to sing it."

"That was years ago. I can't stand it now." Part of Erec felt bad saying this, but another part needed to.

June straightened on the bench. "And why is that?"

"It reminds me I don't have a dad. And I'm missing an eye. And it doesn't make me feel better about it."

"You do have a father."

"Not really. He's never even bothered to send a birthday card. I've never even seen a picture of him or spoken to him. He's glad he got rid of me."

June put her hand over Erec's. "Your father loves you very much."

This put him over the edge. "Do you think I'm stupid?" Erec could not stop himself. "Why don't you ever tell me about him? And about my birth mother? She died, right? You never say *she's* alive and loves me. That's why my father gave me up for adoption. He didn't want to deal with a kid. Why don't you tell me the truth? You won't talk about the real stuff; you only talk about 'flower fairies.' You treat me like a baby." Although it felt good coming out, Erec immediately felt horrible.

June's eyes welled up and Erec's heart sank. She worked so hard and wanted everything to be good for him, and he had to go and make her cry.

They had walked home in silence. She had bought him a chocolate chip ice-cream cone even though Erec knew they shouldn't have been spending the money. It had tasted great, but it was tinged with the flavor of sadness.

"I wonder if Hecate Jekyll will have that crazy stuff. What is nitrowisherine?" Bethany and Erec both fell on their sides as they climbed into the castle. On their way to the kitchens, Queen Posey appeared before them wearing a silky blue-green gown of scales and holding a scepter carved with eels and sea dragons. They stumbled to avoid crashing into her.

Queen Posey pointed a long finger at Erec. "There you are." Her voice was slow and deep. "We need to talk."

Erec glanced at Bethany in desperation and turned, without

thinking, to run. Queen Posey grabbed his wrist. "Not so fast." Instantly, the hall around Queen Posey and Erec morphed to a large, round room with a high ceiling. Dolphins jumped and played in a pool in the center. A huge circular skylight the size of the pool was overhead, circled by a fresco of eels, stingrays, octopuses, sea serpents, and starfish.

The Queen of Ashona sat on a chair that looked like a huge oyster shell on a pedestal. She motioned for him to sit in a similar chair. It was surprisingly comfortable, although it made him feel like a pearl.

"Why is your name Erec Rex?" Queen Posey asked.

Erec's breath caught. Was it all over? Would he be sent to the dungeons because he could not pay back his mother's stolen money?

"I want an answer, whoever you are. The Identdetector doesn't lie. Your name is Erec Rex, is it not?"

Erec nodded. His voice seemed frozen.

"Why are you called that?"

What kind of a question was that? Erec wanted to ask why anybody has the name they were given, but it didn't seem right to be smart with a queen. He shrugged, heart still pounding.

"Did you change your name to Erec Rex? Did you think if you called yourself Erec Rex you would win the contests?"

Erec again shook his head. The more she said his name, the more uncomfortable he became. What was she talking about? Did she think he was a criminal, like his infamous adopted mother?

"Where are you from?"

Erec hesitated. Should he lie to the queen? Then again, dare he tell the truth? "Americorth South." Erec hoped she didn't ask for details.

Queen Posey's expression softened. "Maybe you were named after the Erec Rex from Alypium. Is that so?"

Erec shrugged. It seemed like as good an excuse as any. He wasn't the Erec Rex they knew, only some kid named after him. "Yes. I think so."

The queen frowned. "But you changed shape, didn't you? Who changed your looks—or did you do it yourself?"

Erec stared at her, mouth open. How could he answer a question like that? "I really don't know. I don't remember what happened."

Queen Posey looked at him skeptically. "Obviously you can't be *the* Erec Rex." She sighed. "I hear there is another boy here too, who claims he used to be Erec Rex or something ridiculous like that. I think you are all trying to get special attention. Or you are psyching each other out to win." She looked reproachful. "Something bothers me about you, though. Well, I'll keep my eye on you. If you need anything, come to me."

Erec nodded, thinking that she would be the last person he would come to for help. He was lucky she was letting him stay there at all. He stammered, "Um . . . uh . . . your highness?"

"Yes?" Her voice was sharp.

"Did you know Erec Rex?"

She rolled her eyes. "Obviously." She pointed at him with a sly smile. "The real Erec Rex would know that, wouldn't he? I don't know why I was thinking . . . How old are you?"

"Twelve."

"Yes. The real Erec Rex would be thirteen." She looked satisfied.

"Your highness? I like to go by Rick Ross."

The queen was puzzled. "Rick Ross. Whatever." She pointed her scepter at him and he appeared back in the castle where she had found him. The chair he had been sitting in was gone, so he fell onto the floor in the hallway.

He found Bethany by the fountains. She ran, grinning, when she saw him. "I thought you were a goner. Wow, am I glad you're back. What happened?"

THE DRAGON'S EYE

"I don't get what she's thinking. She wanted to know who changed my appearance, and if I thought I'd win the contests if my name was Erec Rex. She must think I am a hardened criminal because of my mom. And she said another boy is running around saying he *used* to be Erec Rex."

She clapped her hands together. "Now it makes sense. I heard there was a kid who said he used to be Erec Rex and that he lost the first contest. I thought someone was talking about you. I didn't want to tell you because they said that kid was crazy."

Erec was still uneasy. "It was a close call. She asked where I was from. I had to say Americorth South, but what if she wanted details?"

"You lied? What if she finds out?"

His mother had told him to lie. His mother, who knew how to break into the castle treasury and Hecate Jekyll's storerooms. "See how easy it is to become a crook? I guess that's what happened to my mom. And now here I am, lying and stealing . . ."

"You stole something?"

"Think about it. Who knows who that money and the Sneakers really belong to?" The beautiful sunny skies and breathtaking scenery suddenly seemed dull. Erec had once taken pride in playing by the rules. "That's it. I'm going to talk to her right now."

Nobody was in Erec's room except his dog, who licked his knee and jumped up and down for a treat. Bethany stood guard by his door, partly because she could not wait to hear what Erec's mother had to say.

Erec placed the glasses over his eyes. His mother was taking a nap. "Mom," he yelled. "Mom!"

June jolted upright, looking wildly around, her hair streaming in every direction. "What . . . who . . . Erec?"

Erec waited for his mother to prop herself up in bed. "I need some answers. First of all, what did you do in Alypium? Exactly?"

"Erec, I told you we should go slow. It's too much—"

"No. That's it, Mom. Tell me now."

June fussed with her hair. "Okay, okay. I was ... the ... I took care of the royal triplets."

"The triplets who died?"

June raised her eyebrows. "You heard they died?"

"Everybody knows that here."

"Oh. Okay." June concentrated hard on her fingernails. "That settles that."

"Did you do something wrong? Like steal things?"

"Who me?" June's fingers fluttered to her chest. "Of course not."

"Who did the Sneakers belong to?" Erec asked.

"Why, me."

"And before you?"

"Just me." June became cross. "Did you talk to Hecate Jekyll yet?"

"No. I'm working on it, okay?" Erec said, annoyed. "It's been a long day, and I'm worn out. I'll try to get the ingredients after the second contest tomorrow." He figured she probably had been the triplets' nursemaid, but that there must be more to the story.

"Queen Posey talked to me today. She thinks there is no way I am Erec Rex from Alypium. I must be some kid named after him. And she asked about someone changing my looks. What was that all about?"

"Hmm?" June nervously studied her fingernails. "Are you sure you heard her right?"

"Yes!" Erec's annoyance grew. "Out with it, Mom. Something weird is going on. Kilroy and Queen Posey were staring at my pictures on the Identdetector machine. They said I looked different than I was supposed to."

June looked around the room as if hoping to find a way to change the subject.

"Mom. Tell me *now*."

"Okay. Fine. Erec, I had to change your looks when we escaped from Alypium. It was for your own protection."

"I don't get it. Who was after me?"

June didn't want to go on. "Erec, I wish you were here. This is the kind of thing I should tell you in person, with a cup of hot cocoa, not when you're alone in some dormitory."

"Go ahead. Please. It feels like you're here in person to me, anyway."

June sighed. "Thanatos Argus Baskania has it in for us. He's befuddled King Pluto, and I'm pretty sure that is why things are so messed up there now. He's been after you since you were a little boy. I had to hide you any way I could. I left your eyes the same, though." She had a pleading, apologetic look on her face.

Erec was struck silent. Then he exploded. "Baskania? The Crown Prince of Peace? The one who created the Kingdoms of the Keepers? The one who might be trying to take over Upper Earth? He's out to get *me*? You're not serious."

June nodded. "I am. Sorry. I know this must be upsetting."

Erec could not believe this. It was impossible. She must be lying to him again. "All right, whatever you say, Mom. I'll talk to you tomorrow."

"Are you sure you're okay?"

"Yeah. Too bad you left my eyes the same," he snapped. "It would be nice to have two working ones." Erec pulled off the glasses and put his head in his hands. She expected him to believe that the world-famous, incredibly rich Crown Prince had it in for him: a nobody kid who slept in a washing machine closet?

* * *

Erec stuffed his pockets with gold from the bag and gave handfuls to Bethany. "If I'm going to be a criminal, I might as well enjoy it. Let's walk my dog and Cutie Pie to the agora. I hear there is a great cloud cream and candy shop there. I'm buying a bathing suit, too."

Bethany looked excited. "I'll get shoes that don't hurt. Thanks, Erec."

"You ran that whole MONSTER race with shoes that were too small?"

Bethany nodded. "Uncle Earl never thinks my shoes are too small. If I can cram my feet in they're good enough."

"What about all the money you made at the newsstand?"

"Room and board." Bethany looked puzzled. "I keep wondering about what your mother said. She took care of the triplets before they died, and now she's in hiding, right?"

Erec's face turned dark. "You're not saying she killed them, I hope. She may be a lot of things, but she's no murderer."

"No, but what if something bad happened while she was watching them?" Another idea came to her, and she asked, "Erec, she changed your looks. Could you be one of the triplets?"

Erec shook his head. "I remember my lousy father a little from before I was adopted. Plus, I always have the same nightmare about him. He was no King Piter. Plus, the triplets would be thirteen now. I'm twelve." Just then he remembered, "The twins are thirteen, though . . ."

"Twins?"

Erec's heart dropped. Sammy and Danny. Thirteen-year-old twins. They must be from Alypium too. What if his mother had changed *their* looks? What if they were two of the triplets . . . that his mother had kidnapped? That would explain why she was on the run. And why she would be making up obviously fake stories like the Crown Prince of Peace being out to get him, to keep Erec from talking.

"I have a thirteen-year-old sister and brother, Sammy and Danny." Erec and Bethany stared at each other at this wild connection. "Nah," Erec shook his head. "Everyone knows the royal triplets were killed, right?"

Kids crowded behind the maze the morning of the second contest. Spartacus Kilroy blew his whistle. "This is the Pro and Contest. It will be the only group contest. You will succeed by working as a team. It will show your skills in diplomacy, debate, logic, and judgment.

"As you know, we have had a few unfortunate accidents. Five of your friends were injured from the rhinoceros, and six from the, ahem, minotaur, so they are unable to compete today." He cleared his throat. "Two dropped out because they were . . . upset by the circumstances. There are now one hundred eighty-seven of you. There will be twenty groups: Ten will win.

"Each group will listen to three debates, with speakers presenting pros and cons. Discuss each case, then cast your votes. The groups of ten have a disadvantage. They may be split down the middle, then must sit until someone changes his or her mind. I apologize. Our original plan was for all twenty teams to have ten people each.

"There is a right and wrong answer to each question. The ten top-scoring groups win. If there is a tie, we will look at the times the ballots were turned in. Stoney Rayson drew up random groupings." Kilroy blew his whistle and a projection screen lit twenty lists of names. Erec found his name in group number one.

"Look, Erec—you're listed as Rick Ross. Oscar, Bethany—we're all together!" Jack whooped and gave high fives.

"Yeah, surprise, surprise." Bethany looked annoyed. "Look who else is on our list: Balor Stain, Damon Stain, Rock Rayson, Ward Gamin, and Bette Noir. Nine people—how lucky. I'm sure it was no coincidence Rock Rayson's dad made the groups." She smiled.

"Balor really thinks you're something with those glasses."

"And that all my friends must be something too."

"Of course. Why else would you hang out with us?" She turned to leave. "I want to change teams."

Oscar said, "Are you guys crazy? We're on a team with Rock Rayson. I wonder if I'll get to meet his dad. Maybe we'll get to be friends. I can go over for dinner and everything." He sighed. "Stoney Rayson."

Jack laughed, and Bethany gave in.

Their group met in the entryway to the north wing. Balor, Damon, Rock, Ward, and Bette, a slender girl with long black hair, were waiting for them. Oscar waved. "Hey, Rock. I'm Oscar. Your dad's my favorite springball player. Loved that great play the last game with Australiorth."

Rock yawned.

"All right, idiots," said Balor. "Our room is over here." Balor led them into a conference room with a long table and nine chairs. Everyone took a seat. "There aren't enough judges to be in each room, so I'm running the show here. I work the projector, I take the vote, I count them, and I hand in the score. Any questions go to me.

"You lucky stiffs"—Balor swung his finger at Bethany, Jack, and Oscar—"are in here because I wanted to get to know *you* better." He pointed at Erec. "I've never seen anyone flip off a silver ghost before. I couldn't even do that. So we're gonna have a little talk. I want to check out those glasses.

"Anyway, you're in the lucky room today. We're going to win first, so you all owe me. I got the answers to all three questions—only then they changed the last question this morning, so now we don't know one."

"Why did they change it?" Bette Noir asked.

"One of the movies quit yesterday."

Erec wondered what that meant. Balor got up, flicked the light switch, and turned on a projector. A film started on a screen at the front of the room. "I'm gonna show the movies, even though we have the answers, so there's no arguments later." He flicked a switch and the room darkened. Damon started humming "Mary Had a Little Lamb," until Balor told him to shut up.

The first film was ten minutes long but felt like half an hour. A man in a suit and tie stood behind a podium. He argued in a very dull manner that the "forgetful ones" in Upper Earth should be told about magic. "They have every right to know facts, and even try to relearn magic should they choose, in the name of equality and fairness. It is even suspected that there are small, remote regions in Upper Earth where magic was never really forgotten. These people are not killing each other any more than you and I."

"Wow," Erec said. "I wonder where that is."

The man in the movie cleared his throat. "Please do not interrupt," he said, unmistakably looking at Erec. "You may ask questions at the end of the film."

Erec looked at Bethany, and she looked back in shock. The man talked on, but Erec stared at the screen in wonder.

Balor turned on a second projector, which showed another movie next to the first one. A tall woman in a blue suit argued that people of Upper Earth were made to forget magic for a reason. The man in the first film was still on the screen, and watched her with arms crossed.

The woman wrinkled her pinched nose. "They do not have the capacity to understand much anymore. They would use magic for evil and kill each other off, just like they were starting to before." The man from the first movie rolled his eyes. The woman saw him and scowled, crossing her arms. Bethany argued with the woman but could not change her mind. The man in the first movie nodded and clapped after everything Bethany said.

Balor flicked on the light and narrowed his eyes at her. "So, we have little Miss Open-Minded in our group, do we? This question is a gimme, even if I didn't have the answers." He passed out slips of paper to vote.

Jack said, "There is no right and wrong here. This is being debated so much because nobody knows the right answer."

"Of course there is a right answer." Balor played with the bronze whistle around his neck. "The answer, if it's not obvious, is no. The bumbling idiot Losers should not be told about magic." He laughed, along with Damon, Rock, and Ward, who put checks on their papers and flung them back.

Bethany squeezed her pen, face red, and tossed her dark curls back. "You're wrong. People from Upper Earth are smart as anyone here. They have the right to know. What was all that garbage about not being able to understand magic? Hah! And killing each other? People can do that without magic if they want."

Bette exploded in shrill laughter. "Getta load of her! Whatcha got, relatives down there or somethin'?"

Ward winked at Bette and stretched his arms over his head. "Those Upper Earth folk are savages. They would just as soon kill you as look at you."

Jack looked worriedly at Erec and Bethany. "My family knows Upper Earth people who are great. You don't know what you are talking about."

Oscar put a check on his paper and handed it to Balor. Erec looked at Bethany. "We know the truth. Who cares what the right answer is supposed to be. We'll be outvoted, anyway."

Balor gleamed. "I'm glad you're getting the rules, Rick Ross. But I'm disappointed that you think we should help the poor Losers." He tilted his head with a fake sad look.

Erec and Bethany voted yes and passed in their ballots.

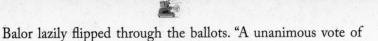

Balor lazily flipped through the ballots. "A unanimous vote of no—not to remind the stupid Losers about magic."

"Dum-dums," said Damon, nodding wisely.

Bethany threw down her pen.

The next short films showed two men dressed as generals debating whether to trust their nonhuman neighbors, or if it would be better to arm themselves to the hilt. Balor told everyone the right answer was to have large armies at the ready. Again, he counted a unanimous vote for his answer, despite Erec, Jack, and Bethany's marks against it.

The third film was a wider picture with many people in it. It was labeled "Ethiopia." A judge in long red robes held a diamond bracelet. "Two people were fighting over this. Neither is from here, and neither has proof of ownership. You decide who it belongs to."

A man in African garb stepped up to the left side of the film. "My name is Koorc. I am here visiting friends and family. What happened is simple. I bought the bracelet at home and brought it here to give to my mother on her birthday. I went out to find a box and paper to wrap it. I wasn't paying attention to where I was walking since I was admiring the bracelet, and I slipped on a patch of ice and fell. This woman saw the bracelet fly from my hand and tried to grab it from me."

The judge turned to the woman. "State your name and case."

The woman glared. "I'm Renwo Tneconni. This is ridiculous. Everyone knows women do not steal. It is not in our nature. We are honest and true. That is all I have to say."

The judge frowned. "You must tell what happened."

"Fine," Tneconni snapped. "The bracelet was given to me by an old boyfriend . . . who has since died . . . in a war."

The judge said, "There has been no war here in years."

"There has where I come from," Tneconni said. "I came to Ethiopia because my sister lives here. I have no money. Work is hard

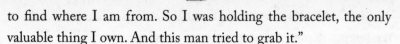

to find where I am from. So I was holding the bracelet, the only valuable thing I own. And this man tried to grab it."

Balor passed out the ballots. "Who did the bracelet belong to? Koorc? Tneconni?"

Rock said, "The man made more sense."

"I agree with Rock," said Oscar.

Ward nodded. "Yeah, she has a motive, too. She's dirt-poor."

Erec frowned. "Not every poor person is a thief."

Balor cracked up. "Practically."

Bethany spit out, "It belongs to the woman."

"Yeah, right," said Rock. "We know. Women aren't *capable* of stealing, right?"

"Her boyfriend died?" Balor cackled. "She probably killed him."

"The bracelet belongs to the woman." Bethany's face turned red.

"You're a girl." Balor laughed. "Of course you'd say that."

"Girl, girl, girl, girl," sang Damon, playing with the tassel on his floppy gray hat.

"What do you think, Bette?" Ward asked.

Bette smiled at Ward. "The woman is a thief."

"So, we're decided?" Balor asked.

Bethany stood. "If you'd all *shut up* and listen." Everyone stared. "The man said he slipped on ice. Not that you'd all know, but Ethiopia is in Upper Earth on the Equator, where it's always hot. That man was from somewhere else, and he messed up when he told that story. It's an obvious lie." Bethany sat in a huff and crossed her arms.

"She's right," Erec said.

"I'm with them," Jack said.

Balor bit his lip. "Fine. But if you're wrong, you'll be sorry. Not that we won't win anyway."

They checked off ballots and Balor said, "Unanimous. Bracelet belongs to Tneconni." The group followed him out.

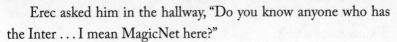

Erec asked him in the hallway, "Do you know anyone who has the Inter . . . I mean MagicNet here?"

Balor laughed. "I do, of course."

"Can I use it?"

"Sure. Come over tonight. And we'll talk about your glasses. Oh, wait a minute, not tonight." He grinned. "Wait a few days, then come use it."

Kilroy took Balor's answers and patted his floppy black hair. "First ones back. And, let's see . . . all three correct! You're winners." He winked. "Prizes will be given out at four."

Balor, Damon, Rock, and Ward high-fived and hooted. Balor looked knowingly at Damon. "I knew Ethiopia was in Upper Earth. It's in Europe."

Damon leaned forward, looking excited. "*My* ope?"

Oscar tried to corner Rock, asking about his father, but Rock dodged him. Erec and his friends went to the cafeteria for lunch.

Erec asked, "What's the big deal about reminding us about magic?"

Jack looked at Erec. "Ten years ago, King Piter was about to lift the spell so you'd all remember. A lot of people were upset about it. But then he got real sick, and his opponents took over. That's when President Inkle let Prince Baskania put the marks on your foreheads. They shut down the gateways between our worlds. Prince Baskania is working on a permanent spell so you all could never possibly remember magic."

"Prince Baskania, is that what he calls himself here? The multibillionaire who owns the Super A Team and too many corporations to count?" Erec shivered. So Thanatos Baskania really had a connection to this place. He thought about what his mother had said yesterday about Thanatos Baskania having it out for him, but it seemed ridiculous. If Baskania was busy trying to take over the world and keep Upper Earth from remembering magic, why would he care about Erec?

"His true followers call him the Sorcerer Prince. I don't know about the corporations you're talking about, but he does own the Super A Team. He's the most powerful sorcerer, and he's good friends with President Inkle. Most people around here think he saved the day, helping run things since King Piter's been sick."

"The most powerful sorcerer?" The idea sank in. No wonder Baskania had the Midas touch in the business world.

"He's ancient, spent centuries perfecting his magic. My dad says it warped him, made him sick for more power. That level of magic is so hard to attain, doing things like reading minds, warping time, seeing the Substance around us and understanding it. But it's not enough for him. They say he wants to do things even a scepter can't let you do, and he's working at it constantly. Create people out of nothing. Move the planets. Mind control." He shook his head. "Nuts, huh?"

At four o'clock Jack pointed to his watch. "Prize time, guys." They had been walking with Erec's dog and Cutie Pie through the flag gardens.

The prize pen behind the maze looked almost the same as the one with aniballs. Oscar saw Stoney Rayson walking away from the pen and rushed over. "Hi, Mr. Rayson, sir. I'm Oscar Felix. I'm friends with Rock. I was on his team today." Oscar reached out his hand, and Rayson nodded, ignoring it.

"Uh, hey!" Oscar shouted. "Are Rock and the guys getting prizes?"

Rayson shook his head. "I don't think so." He walked away.

Oscar called to Rayson's back, "Maybe we'll see each other later!"

Spartacus Kilroy stood in front of a large pen filled with white, glistening balls.

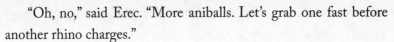

"Oh, no," said Erec. "More aniballs. Let's grab one fast before another rhino charges."

Bethany's eyes lit up. "Maybe I'll get a kitty friend for Cutie Pie. Or a hamster!"

"Lunch for Cutie Pie," said Erec. Bethany shot him a cross look.

Kilroy blew his whistle and everyone stopped talking. "Congratulations. There were ninety-three winners of the Pro and Contest. Let's hear it for the winners!"

Applause filled the air. Cutie Pie held her claws out and glared at the noisy kids. Erec's dog howled as if he had won himself. Erec thought he saw Cutie Pie give his dog the evil eye.

Kilroy blew his whistle again. "The next contest will be ten o'clock, Monday morning, here behind the maze. It is called the Tribaffleon. And, for a special treat, there will be a springball match between the Super A Team and Alypium in the agora on Saturday." The crowd burst into cheers.

Kilroy shouted, "I'll check off your names when you go into the prize pen. Everybody gets one inquizzle—only one. It will give a yes or no answer to any question you ask. But after one answer it pops. Think before you ask. This is a great opportunity. And don't take more than one."

Kids raced to check in and grab inquizzles. Some stood still as if they were afraid to talk. A boy grabbed one and said, "This is an inquizzle?" It vanished in a puff of yellow smoke and said, "Yes." He looked around, stunned, and then kicked the dirt and walked away.

Erec left his dog outside the pen with Cutie Pie. His inquizzle felt glassy and cool. White smoke drifted within the orb. What should he ask? Was his mother a criminal? He wasn't sure he wanted the answer. Where were Sammy and Danny? He wished he could get more than a yes or no. Would Hecate Jekyll have all the ingredients he would need for the formula? He would find that out soon enough.

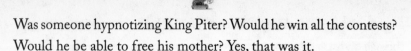

Was someone hypnotizing King Piter? Would he win all the contests? Would he be able to free his mother? Yes, that was it.

But then Erec stopped. He could not ask that. What if the answer was no? What would he do? How would he tell her? He couldn't ask. He had to go on believing he would get her out.

So what, then? An idea hit him, something he had almost forgotten with all of the other questions nagging him. He had always thought his birth mother was dead. June never mentioned her, even though she always said that his father was "alive and loves him." But recently when he asked, she balked. Was his birth mother alive too? Would he meet his father here?

Erec looked into the swirling mists of the inquizzle. "Is my birth mother . . . who gave birth to me . . . alive?"

The glasslike ball shattered in his hand, each shard melting into yellow smoke. "Yes."

She *was* alive! And she was probably here in Alypium, too. Erec did not have any memories of her. She must have left his father. And from what Erec remembered of his father, he didn't blame her for leaving. Only, why didn't she take Erec with her? Was she sick? Didn't she love him?

Bethany put her inquizzle down. "Your birth mother . . . who gave birth to you? Can you be more specific?"

"Leave me alone. What's your question going to be?"

"I'm afraid to ask . . . but I have to." She picked her inquizzle up. "Is Uncle Earl going to find me in Alypium?"

Her inquizzle exploded in yellow smoke. "Yes."

Bethany jerked back, horrified. Her fingers were frozen as if she still held the orb. "He can't make me go back. I'll just escape again. I know how to get here now." She sat, burying her face in Cutie Pie. "He *can't* take Cutie Pie away." Her voice was muffled from the cat fur. Cutie Pie growled as if she agreed.

Erec sat by Bethany. "It just said he'd find you, not get you and bring you back. Maybe he finds you and you escape, and then he never finds you again. Maybe he finds you here when you're seventy."

Bethany laughed unhappily, stroking Cutie Pie's fur. "I guess it was too much to hope that I'd never see him again. You know, he threw me birthday parties every year? I had to do all the work while the kids played. Then he'd sell my presents. He thought it was a great scheme."

Erec shuddered. "Don't worry. I'll make sure he'll never get you."

Oscar walked by. "I won't be one of the three final winners. At least, according to the stupid inquizzle. Who says they're right, anyway?"

Left and right, kids asked inquizzles if they would be final contest winners, black poofs and No's resounding through the air.

Jack walked over with a grin.

Oscar glared. "What? Don't tell me *you're* one of the three winners."

Jack shrugged. "Dunno. But I'm getting a new dog at home."

"When?" Bethany said, excited.

"I don't know." Jack's smile dimmed. "I hope it's before I'm eighteen."

They walked to the cafeteria for dinner with their fellow champions, many grumbling because they would not be final winners.

Cutie Pie pawed her fur. "Look," said Bethany. "I wonder why she's doing that."

Jack scratched his head in thought.

"I'm having fish tonight," said Erec. "Everything else is clouds and veggies."

"They're good, though," Bethany replied. She was rubbing her arms.

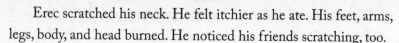

Erec scratched his neck. He felt itchier as he ate. His feet, arms, legs, body, and head burned. He noticed his friends scratching, too.

"Think we got into poison ivy?" Erec asked.

"What's that?" Oscar asked. "Some Loser plant?"

Bethany set down her water. "*Upper Earth* plant. I'll bring you some, Oscar. You can check it out up close and personal."

Oscar scratched his neck with one hand and his scalp with the other. "This is getting bad. I'm going to see Dr. Mumbai." He scratched both legs. "I can't even eat."

"Me too," said Bethany.

Jack and Erec nodded in agreement. They left their plates and ran to the castle. "Where is the royal hospital?" Erec asked.

A few other kids ran down the central hallway. "I bet I know where they're going," Bethany said. "Let's follow them." They ran past the west wing corridor where a smug-looking Ugry stood, pointing down the hallway. "Second left, end of the hall," he sang out with an eerie smile on his face.

Erec caught a sour smell as he ran past Ugry, and sneezed. They took the second left. Down the hallway, a crowd gathered around Dr. Mumbai, a tall woman with blond hair twirled into a bun. She looked at scalps, arms, and necks all around her with gloved hands.

"Attack fleas." Dr. Mumbai batted long eyelashes. "I have no idea how a brood got loose. They don't usually swarm in Alypium. Did these spread at the contests? I thought you all were in separate rooms."

"Unless it happened in the prize pen," said Erec. "Like the rhinoceros."

"Your prizes were infested? I guess that's possible." A show of hands confirmed that they all had won the second contest. "Well, everyone take a cup of napalmroid ointment and a sleeping pill. Cover your body, and come back tomorrow after I get more. For some reason my whole supply is missing. Luckily, I had ten spare tubs under the sink. I don't want to think about how bad you all would have been by the morning." She scooped ointment into plastic cups and handed them out.

They rubbed it on. "How long before this works?"

"You'll feel a little better tomorrow. It will take a few days before they're gone. Tonight will be rough so don't forget your sleeping pill. You'll need it."

They scratched all the way back to the dormitory. "I'm taking my sleeping pill now," Bethany said.

Erec's skin burned, but he could not stop scratching. He went to his room and took his sleeping pill. As he was drifting off to sleep, he wondered about the answer he got. His mother was alive.

He was thinking of how he would find her when he fell fast asleep.

Springball

EREC SLEPT PAST breakfast. He dressed slowly, exhausted from the sleeping pill and itchy, when he noticed his dog panting and scratching his dark gray and white fur. He looked like he had been up all night. Erec's heart dropped. "I forgot all about you. I'll get you something from Dr. Mumbai."

Erec ran to the royal hospital, where a crowd had formed, getting their morning dose of napalmroid. He grabbed cups for himself,

Bethany, Jack, and Oscar, then two more for his dog, and a sleeping pill coated in peanut butter. After Erec put napalmroid on himself and his dog, he spent the day in bed, itching and dozing. He could not even think of finding formula ingredients.

The next day was more bearable. Erec found Bethany in the cafeteria at lunch. She had deep scratches on her face and arms.

"It's my fault. I totally forgot about Cutie Pie. Luckily she . . . reminded me before I took my sleeping pill. She's still asleep."

Finally, they went to the castle kitchens, the ingredient list in Erec's pocket. Hecate Jekyll saw them and smiled. "Whadda ya need? More pomegranates?"

Erec pulled the list out. "Brownies would be nice. Maybe cupcakes." He had thought about how to ask for the ingredients. "I like to do experiments with different . . . things, kind of like a chemistry set. It's my hobby. Could I borrow some ingredients from you?"

"It depends what yer asking for. There's nothing I don't have . . . or can't get. I'm kind of a whiz at potions myself. That is what you're getting at, right?"

Erec nodded. "Have you heard of nitrowisherine?"

Jekyll laughed, delighted, her stiff nose high in the air and her eyes crinkling. "Oh, I see now what you're after, ya little menace. Pipe bombs aren't good enough for ya, huh? You need the big kaboom. What do your parents say about this pastime?"

"They're all for it." Erec suppressed a smile.

Jekyll flashed a huge grin. "I like them already. What else do you want?"

"Warthog essence?"

She winked. "Now you're *really* talking explosion. Now how can I be sure nobody will get hurt?"

"I'll be really careful," Erec said. "Do you have grain alcohol? Wolfsbane?"

Jekyll's brow knitted. "Grain alcohol . . . hmm." She suddenly looked stern. "I can't give alcohol to kids. Let me see that list." She grabbed the paper out of Erec's hand. Her eyes narrowed. "What is this?" Her stare felt like it pierced through his eye. "You have a glass eye," she said accusingly.

"So do you," Erec reminded her. He was confused. She was like him, then? Some woman in Alypium was his birth mother. Could it be her?

She sensed Erec's confusion, and a smile spread across her face. "I'm sorry for snapping." She folded Erec's list. He took it back as she tried to put it in her pocket. "All misunderstandings, I'm sure. Now I can't give you those ingredients. Way too dangerous for a nice young man like you. But I'll fix you both a big plate of cupcakes, brownies, and cookies. Did you two win the second contest? Come down with attack fleas like the rest of them?"

Bethany nodded. "Don't you think it's a little fishy that bad things keep happening in the prize pens?"

Jekyll nodded. "I've thought the same thing. Any ideas?"

Erec shrugged. "Balthazar Ugry gives me the creeps. I wouldn't put anything past him."

"Good thought," Jekyll said. "I'd pin any mischief on that one, myself. Any other thoughts?"

"It's a little strange Rock Rayson and his friends are so lucky," said Bethany. "They missed the rhino and the attack fleas. I wonder if Stoney Rayson is in on it somehow."

Jekyll disappeared into the kitchens and came back with a tray of treats. "Kids, keep your eyes open. I'm here if you need anyone to talk to. You can trust me."

Bethany pushed her chair against the sitting room door and sat, scratching her scalp. "I'll try not to listen."

"Go ahead." Erec sat on another chair, ready to put on his glasses. "I'll tell you everything anyway."

His mother was sitting on her bed, staring at her fingernails. "Mom?" Erec said quietly.

June dropped her book. "Erec?" She looked pale and worn.

"Is something wrong?"

"I'm tired. I miss you all. The twins are back and they're fine. Everyone's fine. You seem fine." She sighed. "And I'm a mouse in a trap. I mean, I'm really glad nobody needs me, it's just . . . nobody needs me." She looked sadder than Erec could remember.

"That's not true. It's terrible without you. I worry all the time."

June smiled sadly. "I'm not sure if that's better, really. I'm sorry. You just caught me in a mood. I'm fine. Except I'm stuck."

"Why don't they let you go?"

"Someone thinks I know more than I'm telling. I was dumb. I thought I had everything under control, moving a lot and erasing people's memories of us each time."

"You erased people's memories of us?" Erec paused. "Nobody remembers me from before we moved to New York . . . last week? My old friends? Is that why you never let me make long-distance calls? It wasn't the money, was it?" Fury rose in Erec. "And that's why nobody writes me back—ever?"

June looked like she was about to cry. "I'm so sorry. It was for your safety, really. Look at us now."

"Looks like it was for *your* safety, more like." Erec did not care anymore that she was upset. "By the way, my birth mother is alive."

June became pale. "How did you find out?"

"Don't worry. I didn't meet her. I asked an inquizzle. It was a prize for winning the second contest."

"Congratulations." June bit her lips.

"Don't you have anything to say about my birth mother?"

June shook her head.

"Well, that's a first." Erec wished he could slam a door and walk out, but he wasn't really in her room to begin with. "I have to go."

"Don't go, Erec. Not like this. I couldn't take it now. Tell me about the contest."

"Well, the strangest part is that all the winners came down with attack fleas. Last time the winners got attacked by a rhino—and a minotaur. It's getting so I'm afraid to win."

"That doesn't sound like a coincidence."

Erec heard Bethany shout, "Off!" and something crashed into him.

"Gotta go." He whisked the glasses off and saw that Bethany had flung a book at him. Some kids were entering the room.

"What happened?" a boy asked.

Bethany shrugged. "I thought I saw a mouse."

"So you threw that book at it?" He pointed.

"I lost my head, I guess."

The boy merely shrugged, not really interested.

After dinner, Erec laid in bed scratching and remembering his old friends who had forgotten him. His grief was not because of the messed-up Substance that had given him the heavy, sad feeling when he had first entered FES Station. No, he knew exactly whose fault this was.

The next day the itching was better, but Erec was still rubbing his leg when Jack burst into the room. "Springball's in an hour and a half. I'm grabbing lunch, then heading over to get good seats. You coming?"

They knocked on Bethany's door and found Oscar playing pool in the sitting room. Bags sat on the cafeteria tables, packed with apples, dried fruit, seeds, nuts, and sandwiches. The bread was thin and crunchy.

"What is this?" Erec asked.

"Dehydrated sprouted wheat berry bread," Oscar said sadly.

"Not bad, though," said Jack.

On the way to the springball match, Erec felt empty inside. All of his past friends had forgotten him. His only friends in the world were right here—until June made them forget too.

"How is springball played?" Bethany asked. "I saw headlines about it at the newsstand, but I could never figure it out."

Erec smiled, glad to think about something else. "Each team has a ball, and he is in play the whole game."

"He?"

"Yeah. The ball. They have to be good gymnasts, really agile."

"Wait . . . the balls are *people*?"

Erec nodded. "You didn't know that? Each ball tries to get in the other team's trap, or a hoop over the trap for extra points, and to stay out of their own trap. They wear thick, rounded padding that bounces, so they look like real balls with arms and legs. And they have two big springs: One sticks up from their heads and one out from their bottoms. They can bounce on them to get away.

"The Super A Team is so good they wear eye patches just to show they can win with only one eye. They're undefeated. It's hard to imagine, this group of amateurs has beaten every pro team for ten years straight. They're like pure magic."

Jack looked at him sideways. "You're kidding, right? They lose all the time. Look at 'em. Some are old. What they're really known for is *cheating*."

"Are you saying the Alypium team can beat the Super A Team at springball?"

"They could probably beat them at anything except posing for the camera. So could most of the Aorth teams."

"Wow," Erec said. "You must have amazing athletes here. I'm glad someone can beat them. The whole story about them is too much."

"What story?"

"Thanatos Baskania, the Crown Prince of Peace, is a corporate genius. He owns twenty huge conglomerates that stretch all over the world. Television, movies, oil, lumber, you name it. But he got kooky. And that's what too much money does. I guess, maybe too much magical power, too. He wanted everyone in Upper Earth to call him 'Crown Prince,' and he started a huge media blitz about how he's going to create the best springball team in the world—he's a big fan—and he's going to give each player a huge company to run. The television and newspapers ate it up.

"All the big springball teams in the world leagues thought their best players would be scooped. The players waited for tryouts, phone calls. Nothing. The Prince said he was finding players himself, but nobody knew how. The news went crazy; everyone wanted to know who would be picked. Finally the Prince said he had a team, but only one of them was a pro springball player—picked off the Miami Bounce. A lot of these guys didn't even look like athletes. Some were too old, like Rayson. There's no *way* that guy should be able to compete.

"Everyone laughed at first. But they play like demons and nobody can beat them. Baskania calls them the 'Team of Heroes.'

"It never stopped. Baskania got the American League to let them compete even though they're not a city team—paid 'em off, I'm sure. Then came all the movies, the fastaurants, comics, cards, figurines, toys. Three of them just got elected governor. I don't know how they have time for that *and* pro springball *and* being CEOs."

Jack looked stunned. He whispered, "Prince Baskania is making you think those guys are superheroes. They're all just regular athletes from the Kingdoms of the Keepers." He shook his head. "People here used to be terrified of the Sorcerer Prince, but now they think he's saved us from disaster. Since King Piter has been sick, he has 'helped' make decisions and run things. Everyone is desperate for a leader now."

Oscar's forehead wrinkled. "I didn't know he took his Super A Team to compete with the Losers. That doesn't seem fair."

Jack shook his head. "With communication shut down these last ten years with Upper Earth, I doubt anyone knows."

Cliff Arena hung over a sharp drop in the mountain at the edge of the agora. The part of the arena suspended over the cliff had no seats, only a solid glass wall, giving a spectacular view of the mountain range and the feeling that the entire arena sat in thin air. Erec, Bethany, Oscar, and Jack found great seats near the midfield line.

"This doesn't look right," Erec said. "Usually, the spectators look down into the arena. It's a huge pit with solid walls for the ball to bounce off. This playing floor is at our level. The balls will fly into the crowd."

"There's a force field around the oval," Jack said. "We get a better view this way."

The field otherwise looked about the same: an eighty-yard by fifty-yard oval with a midfield line down its center and four starting circles in each corner. Ramps, holes, nets, and small walls randomly scattered over the field. A large "trap" sat at each end, and over each hung a huge net eight feet off the ground.

Erec could not believe he might see someone actually beat the Super A Team. It was even more unthinkable that he was here at all, with fantastic seats. Erec spotted Olive Umpee sitting between Spartacus Kilroy and Balthazar Ugry several rows ahead. Kilroy and Umpee scratched continuously.

"Doesn't it seem strange that Ugry isn't scratching?" Erec asked.

"He must have done something to protect himself at the prize pen. What do you think?"

Jack looked stunned. "Why would he do that? You're not meaning that he planted the fleas, are you? He's here to help us."

Bethany rolled her eyes. "Help us into an early grave. Just the same, I wonder if Rayson had something to do with it. Where do you think Rock and his friends are getting all the answers to the contests? And they're never around when the winners are getting attacked by one thing or another."

Erec said, "Maybe Rayson is just helping his son, and Ugry is doing all the bad things."

"Rayson has a motive: scare other kids away so his son will win. I wonder what will happen to the next contest winners."

Oscar said, "You can't scare me away that easy. I'm more scared by what my dad would think if I lost." He scratched his legs. "Some idiots are quitting because their inquizzles said they would lose. I don't believe those things, anyway. Nobody's shown *me* proof they work."

Bethany smiled. "You're completely right. Mine was probably wrong too. Hey, before the game starts, fill me in on the rules."

"The balls try to get into the other team's traps and hoops and stay out of their own. A batter follows them around with a big rubber club to knock them loose if the other team gets them. The trapper guards the trap and the hoop with his body or a huge racket. Three points for getting your ball in the other team's trap, six for getting him in their hoop, five for getting the *other* team's ball in their trap, and ten for getting him in their hoop."

"Why are there more points for scoring with the opposing ball?"

"Their ball is fighting against you. There are three guardians on defense and four bouncers on offense."

"This'll be an easy win for Alypium," Jack said. "They just won the Dragon Cup in April."

Erec laughed. "On Upper Earth we call the championship the Big Spring."

"Star Wellcandle is the hot player now," Jack said. "He's only played a year, but he's the top scorer. His magical gift is perfect: He gets his wishes. It's hard to get a ball by him—you have to sneak it around. Of course, he's not allowed to wish for goal after goal, but he can wish for plays to go his way. Guy's amazing."

"I can't imagine getting everything I wished for," Bethany said. "What a dream."

"Yeah, but not for those around him," Jack said. "People feel sorry for his wife. She seems happy, but she's unrecognizable. Each year she gets taller, nicer, more understanding, and funnier. Her nose gets smaller, her eyes get bigger, and her hair color changes every week."

The lights went off and sparkles of color filled the stadium. An announcer's voice boomed. "*Wel*come to the special, off-season springball challenge between the Alypium Sky and the Super A Team, brought to you by the Castle Alypium, Flying Donkey Nectar, and Micro Cell Phones—get them while you're young!" An unseen band blared peppy music.

"That's Barnum Gong," Jack whispered. "He announces Alypium's games."

Spotlights zoomed, leaving fans and swirls of light in the darkness. Barnum Gong's voice rang. "And, now, without further ado, the Super A Team!" The crowd shouted with cheers and a few hisses as the players wearing red and black, with black eye patches, ran onto the field in beams of light.

"Robert Burr, ball; Mel Timan, guardian; Tom Fan, bouncer; John Arrete, trapper; Count Araignee, bouncer; Gog Magnon, batter; Franklin Stein, guardian; 'Mighty' Joe Liath, guardian; Rich 'Stoney'

Rayson, bouncer; and Rock Yettas, bouncer." The applause was wild.

"And now," boomed Barnum Gong, "our home team, the Alypium Sky!" The crowd roared like mad when Star Wellcandle ran out in his blue and white uniform. He looked smallish and distracted, not your typical athlete.

When Gong called out, "Pi Cleary, bouncer," Jack said, "He has a mathematical gift; he can figure out arcs and trajectories. He can throw a ball at just the right angle to get it in the hoop, or bounce it off its spring and make a perfect pass."

The lights came on. Robert Burr, in huge, round red padding, and the white Alypium ball opened with the head-off. Erec laughed. As many times as he had seen springball, it was still funny to see the giant balls with arms, legs, and a head sticking out. The balls ran and leapt off springy ramps, flying at each other headfirst. When the big springs sticking from their heads collided, they flew back toward their opposing teams.

"I love when their springs get stuck," said Erec. "It's chaos."

The springball game seemed more fast and wild than usual. If the balls weren't so big they would have been hard to follow. Bethany laughed, pointing. The little bits of arms and legs that were sticking out of the giant Alypium ball waved frantically as two Super A Team players ran with him down the field. He managed to break free and bounced off his spring to the other side of the field. But he didn't get far before someone kicked him toward the stands, limbs wagging and mouth open. A few audience members flinched as the giant ball flew at them spring first, until he hit the force field.

Batters ran around swinging rubber clubs, knocking balls out of players' arms. Mighty Joe Liath and Stoney Rayson guarded Star Wellcandle by blocking his view of the game. He must have wished them away, for a moment later they were flat on their backs. When an Alypium player kicked Burr, the Super A Team ball with a hooked nose and shaved head, into the trap, a whistle blew.

"And a score!" shouted Barnum Gong. "Three points for Alypium, red ball in the red trap."

"Well, now I've seen it all," Erec said. "I thought the Super A Team could never lose a point." He frowned. "The Alypium ball looks too big. I can't imagine he'd weigh in."

"Weigh in?" asked Jack. "Your balls weigh in?"

"Of course," said Erec. "They have to be under one hundred thirty pounds in full gear or they'd smash people."

Jack shrugged. "That wouldn't work here. It's too easy to find players who could levitate and trick the scales."

Robert Burr looked angry and spit. The players walked to their starting positions for the next head-off. The three guardians on each team lined up between the starting circles and the four bouncers along the midfield line. The whistle blew and the balls bounced off their springboards for a clean head-off.

"Look!" Erec shouted. "Araignee's flying! Like in the movies!" With the excitement of the game, Erec had forgotten the Super A Team had magical powers.

Jack looked at him funny. "He has been the whole game. It's his gift. Nobody knows how he got it, though. He's not from a flying family."

"No *wonder* they always win in Upper Earth." In an instant, Erec's opinion of the Super A Team fell. They were cheaters, not heroes. "So, Tom Fan really can pass through walls? Burr can defy gravity? The Count can really fly, and turn into a bat? And Franklin Stein can breathe life into deadly contraptions? Is anything made up?"

Jack shook his head. "They're only supposed to use their own magical gifts, not anything store-bought. The A Team got busted once for using a trap that moved to keep balls out."

Erec could not believe it. For the past ten years on Upper Earth people said traps in Super A Team games looked like they moved to keep balls out. They thought it was because Trapper John Arrete's speed made people dizzy.

The Alypium Sky easily outplayed the Super A Team. They won thirty-six to twelve, with a final great play by the Alypium team called the Tet Offensive. Every member of the Alypium Sky dropped their positions and rushed ahead of their ball onto the opposing side, as allowed with the play, tackling everyone in sight.

Erec couldn't wipe the grin off his face. Kids poured into the agora, buying nectar cones, going to Sky High Candy for spun sugar birds and honeycomb, browsing the pet store, and just wandering under the soaring mountains, eagles, and blue skies.

While Jack and Oscar went to get cloud creams, Erec said to Bethany, "I want you to try really hard to remember me."

"What are you talking about?" Bethany asked Erec.

A cloud passed over the sun. "I found out my dear mother erased my old friends' memories of me. Not just my friends—everyone who knew me before we moved to New York last week. Isn't that great? So, I figure you're next. I'll get her out, we'll go back to our tiny apartment in New York, where we can't afford to live, and everyone here will forget I ever existed. You'll probably have great memories of walking your cat and exploring the castle by yourself."

"Why would she do that?"

Erec slumped. "She says it was for my protection. I'm starting to wonder if it was for hers. She's the one they captured, not me. And she didn't seem too happy that I found out my birth mother is alive. Maybe my birth mother will take me back. This one ruined my life." He thought about Hecate Jekyll and her one eye. Who knows? Maybe she was his real mother.

THE DRAGON'S EYE

"You're just mad."

"I am mad. I was going to get gunpowder in the armory today. Maybe I'll walk my dog and enjoy the sunshine instead."

"Let's compromise. We'll hang out with our pets, then check out the armory after dinner."

Erec shrugged. "It's a deal, but only if we get cloud cream sundaes first."

CHAPTER TWELVE

The MagicNet

INNER WAS WILD pheasants, quinoa cakes, wild berries, nuts, a shredded vegetable salad, cold raspberry soup, and barbecued duck. Erec was surprised how much he liked it. He wondered if his taste was changing since he'd been here.

After cherub puffs and divinity, Erec and Bethany climbed into the castle. Erec wore his Sneakers, and the vanishing caps were in their pockets.

"I guess we can't just ask where the armory is," Erec said.

Bethany stopped a maid in the hallway. "Excuse me, is there a map of the castle?"

"A map?" The maid was amused. "Nobody who *should* be wandering would need a map, now, would they?"

"What kinds of things are in the different wings? I know the west wing is the king's quarters, throne room, and state rooms. What's in the south wing?"

"Too much to list off," said the maid. "Now on with you, I've work to do."

"Is there a library?" asked Bethany.

"Sure, in the east wing."

"A ballroom?"

"Several, of course . . ."

"Is there a throne room?"

"You said yerself it's in the west wing. Now let me go."

"An armory? Is there an armory?"

"Of course there's an armory."

"Where is that?"

The maid growled, "The south wing. That's enough."

"End of the south wing, right?"

"Of course." She walked away, grumbling, and Bethany winked at Erec.

"Good work."

They headed for the south wing. At the end were tall, inlaid mahogany doors, around fifteen feet high. They pulled them open and went into a short corridor. Two oak doors bore signs saying CONVENTIONAL ARMORY and MAGICAL ARMORY. Broken pieces of a suit of armor were scattered before the doors.

A stern voice called, "Who goes there?"

Erec and Bethany glanced around. Nobody seemed to be there.

"Who goes there?" Louder now, the voice sounded almost desperate.

"Um, Rick Ross and Bethany Evirly," Erec said.

"Password?"

"I . . . don't know."

"Then you must leave." The voice did not sound like one to be trifled with.

"Look." Bethany pointed at the head of the suit of armor. "It's talking."

The empty metal headpiece held still as if it did not want to be discovered. "Hello?" Erec asked. There was no answer.

Erec slowly reached for the door to the conventional armory, and the armor head swirled to face him. "Stop! You may not go in." A metal hand brandished a sword.

"We just want a peek." Bethany reached for the door. Several metal parts rustled on the floor, but the only piece that could move well was the hand not clutching the sword. It shuffled on its fingers to Bethany, grabbed her ankle, and squeezed.

Bethany screamed and kicked, but the hand held tight. Erec tried to pry it off.

"It hurts." Bethany stamped her foot and pulled at the hand.

"I'll let go when you leave." The head seemed suddenly cheered. A few moments later, though, when neither Erec nor Bethany left, the other hand flung its sword at Erec. The sword fell with a clatter a few feet from the hand, which scuttled to grab it and throw it again.

Erec picked up the sword and kicked the other hand into the corner. He raised the sword to whack the metal hand off Bethany's leg.

"No!" She whisked her leg away. "Are you crazy?"

"All right. Try this." Erec slid the sword between her ankle and the metal fingers and then yanked. A few fingertips flew from the hand.

"That's better." Bethany sighed. "Try again." Erec slid the sword back and chopped the fingers off with a sharp jerk. The hand fell off Bethany's ankle, which was now red with a long cut.

"Sorry." Erec kicked away the other hand, which had sneakily grabbed the sword and was inching back toward them.

"I'm fine. Let's go."

"You ruined my hand," cried the head. Bethany and Erec opened the door to the conventional armory. "Get out of there!" shouted the head. "Don't think I'm not coming after you. When I get you, you'll be sorry." Erec rolled his eyes.

The armory was humongous and nearly empty, save a few missiles and mortars. A large tank and several armored personnel carriers stood in what looked like an enclosed yard in back. Markings on the ground made it look like many others had been around them.

"Look at all the empty shelves and spaces," said Bethany. "It looks like there was just a war and they haven't restocked yet."

"My mom said the armory is just here in case of an emergency."

"Well, it looks to me like there's a lot missing."

Several missiles the size of small trucks lined the walls. Most of the empty spots near them had big skid marks where others had been. "Hey, over here." Bethany waved. Huge burlap bags marked "gunpowder" lay near piles of flak jackets and a few cannons.

"Oh, no. I forgot a bag," said Erec.

"Well, we have pockets," said Bethany. "How much do we need?"

"Two cups." They took the vanishing caps out and stuffed their pockets with gunpowder. Their hands and clothes became filthy.

"Is there a sink here?" Bethany wiped her hands on the burlap bag.

The mangled suit of armor yelled, and the door burst open. Erec and Bethany dove behind a pile of flak jackets, pulling a few over their heads. Erec put his vanishing cap on and disappeared, dirt and all.

Footsteps approached. Two people were talking. A hoarse whisper said, "Take the rest of the sidearms. Don't forget the racks of semiautomatics. We're good on assault rifles and LAW rockets. Over there, the grenades and land mines, grab all those, too. I've taken all we need from the magical armory. As soon as our three win the contests and get those scepters, we'll have all we need. We'll lay siege to Alypium first, then Aorth, and finally Ashona. With those scepters, nothing can stop us."

A familiar voice whined, "You promise Rock will be one of the winners?"

Bethany shot a look at where Erec should be, in front of a dirty spot on the wall. Rayson!

"Of course," the whisper hissed.

"And what if the stone doesn't scream?" Rayson asked.

"Who cares if the stone screams," the whisper replied. "People will be so glad to have new kings, nobody will notice. Just do your part and everything will go as planned. When the Sorcerer Prince gets those scepters, we'll be unstoppable."

"What about Ward Gamin?" Rayson's voice boomed, even when he was trying to be quiet.

"I'll get rid of him before the final contest. Don't worry."

"What if they don't win the fourth contest? We don't have that one under control."

"They will win." The whisper sounded impatient. Suddenly, an ear-shattering howl ripped through the room, sounding like a cross between a mating banshee and an angry werewolf. Erec flattened against the wall and held his breath.

The whisperer sounded breathless. "Get to work. I'm needed elsewhere."

Quiet footsteps drifted away, apparently leaving Rayson bumbling through the sidearm brackets. Erec peeked around the flak jackets and saw Rayson tossing revolvers, pistols, and shells into what must have been an invisible bag.

Bethany pulled Erec back. "What if he can see you with the cap on, like Ugry?" she whispered.

Rayson hummed tunelessly. The small arms clattered as he threw them into his bag. The noise got closer. "Let's see, I'll come back for this. What's in here?" Smaller clunks echoed into what must have been a full bag. "What's this, gunpowder? What a mess. Well, lifting spell for you." Rayson sounded a foot away. A thick blanket fell over the heavy gunpowder bags next to them and then disappeared, the bags disappearing under it. Erec could feel the edge of the blanket lift.

"Hmm." Rayson was right in front of them. "Flak jackets." He threw a few into his sack. Erec's heart sank. He and Bethany shrank lower behind the pile. Bethany looked sadly alone . . . unless Rayson could see Erec with the cap on.

Erec stamped a foot hard on the floor. A clatter arose in the hallway.

"Shoot." Rayson went still. Erec banged with both feet and more noise erupted outside the door. Rayson ran out, empty-handed.

"Quick, put your cap on," Erec said. "Let's go."

"If we're seen wearing them it's all over."

"If Rayson knows we heard him in here, we're *dead*."

Bethany put the cap on. As they ran to the door, Erec held Bethany's sleeve to know where she was. He stomped heavily, making noise down the hall and in the magical armory. Rayson was nowhere to be seen. "Careful," Bethany whispered. "He could be anywhere. He could be invisible."

In the entryway, the chopped armor shouted, "I know you're here!" Alarmed, they ran into the south wing. Up the hallway, they heard a loud "Oof." Rayson stood before Balthazar Ugry, looking like he had crashed into him.

Rayson was talking to Ugry, pointing to where they must have heard clatter from Erec's Sneakers. Erec and Bethany ran down a side hall and whisked their caps off.

"In here," Erec said, and they dashed into the nearest room. Both of them flew hard into the wall to their right.

"Ouch. What is this, some weird magnetic wall?" Bethany tried to pry herself off.

Erec sat on the wall, having already been through this. "It's one of the rooms that didn't change gravity." His good eye adjusted to the darkness. A pool table hung from the middle of the floor. It must have been nailed down. Everything else, the cues, balls, tables, and games that were on shelves around the room were in piles around them on the wall.

"How do we get out of here?" Bethany stood on the wall and jumped to reach the doorway, unsuccessfully.

"There's no hurry," said Erec. "Let's wait for Ugry and Rayson to leave. Surprised to see Ugry here? You think that was him whispering in the armory?"

Bethany shrugged. "A whisper is a whisper. But I'll bet it was him. Did you hear him? He wants the scepters, whatever they are, and then he'll destroy and conquer everything!"

"The scepters are what King Pluto and Queen Posey carry," said Erec. "I'll bet King Piter has one somewhere. They must be powerful. We better tell someone about this . . . only *who*?"

"We should probably tell Queen Posey. But let's start with your mom. At least we can trust her."

"Can we?" Erec said bitterly. "She'll just delete me from

everyone's memory. Then Ugry will take over with Rayson's help, right?"

"Cut it out. She was just protecting you."

"Yeah, right. Anyway, we're stuck here right now. I guess I'll tell her. Do you mind?"

"Of course not."

Erec put the glasses on, and he found his mother was writing. "Mom?"

June's eyes flicked up. "Erec? Oh, good. I was just writing a letter to your brothers and sisters."

"I got gunpowder."

"How did you? I didn't give you the password yet."

"I didn't need a password. The suit of armor was all chopped up. He still wanted to fight me, though."

"Chopped up!" June sat straight on the rocking chair. "Impossible! That was made by Vulcan himself to guard the armory. Nobody could destroy it." Her forehead creased with worry lines. "Someone pretty powerful is behind all this."

"Mom, I was even able to cut a few fingers off the armor."

"Once it's severed, its strength is lost. But . . . why would you do that?"

"Forget that. The armory was looted. Almost everything was gone. And two people came in. One was Stoney Rayson, if you can believe it, and I couldn't tell who the other was, but I think it was Ugry. They're planning on taking over Alypium, Aorth, and Ashona. They said when certain kids won the contests, Rock Rayson being one of them, they would have the scepters and then they would be unstoppable."

June put her hand over her mouth. "Tell King Piter. He has to know about this."

"Mom. King Piter is no help. Who else can I tell?"

June pursed her lips and stared at the ceiling. She pounded her bed. "I don't know. Erec, *you* need to win the contests. I know you can. That would ruin their plan . . . whoever's plan it is."

"Thanks for the confidence, but—"

"No. You can do it. And try to find King Piter's scepter. It's very powerful. Maybe you could get it somehow and fix him with it."

"King Piter doesn't carry a scepter."

"What? He would never let it out of his sight." She stood up and started pacing the room. "This isn't good. Try to find it. I'd warn Queen Posey about the armory . . . but we don't know who she's listening to." June shook her head. "Have you talked to Hecate Jekyll about the other ingredients?"

"It's no go. She looked like she might give me some, but when I mentioned grain alcohol, she changed her mind."

"It's okay, it's not her fault. I'll tell you how to break into her storerooms. It's not hard, just don't be seen. In the back of the kitchens there is a round metal plate in the floor, inscribed with an eye. Whisper into it . . . hmm, let's see. She used a silly phrase. Oh, yes. 'One eye sees all.' The plate will move and under it will be a hole with a ladder into the storerooms. Everything is alphabetized.

"Put the ingredients in a glass jar, but don't drop it. You could blow up the east wing. Bring it straight to your room and hide it somewhere safe." She put her head in her hands. "I can't believe I'm asking you to get explosives. I must be crazy."

"Don't worry, Mom. I'll be careful."

June sighed. "Have you found someone with the MagicNet to get the eagle feather and lion hairs?"

"Yes, some boys have it here."

"Good. And the horseshoe?"

"The boys have horses."

"Great." She looked relieved. "When is the third contest?"

"Monday. I'll get the ingredients from the storeroom tomorrow."

"Be careful," June said. "There's a full moon tomorrow night."

"Does that matter?"

June shrugged. "Probably not. Funny things sometimes happen, though."

"Mom, how many people can see me when my vanishing cap is on?"

"You have a vanishing cap? Perfect. Nobody could see you with it on."

"Nobody? Ugry can."

"Balthazar? He doesn't have that kind of power. It would be an unusual power, anyway."

"But he can." Erec sighed. "I better go. I'll check in later."

Erec took his glasses off. "Ugry's powers must have grown since my mother lived here."

"He's getting more evil," said Bethany. "We better warn Queen Posey about his plans."

"You don't know her. She's really powerful. My mom's not sure what she's up to. Plus, she's suspicious of me because of that dumb Identdetector."

"Well, I don't see that we have a choice," Bethany said. "Someone that can *do* something has to know about this." She stood on the wall, jumped over the pool cues, and balanced on the built-in wooden bookshelves.

"True. But how do you suggest we tell her? 'Um, Queen Posey, while we were hiding in the armory stealing gunpowder, we overheard Ugry and Rayson plotting.'"

Bethany walked on the bookshelves like they were balance beams. "No. Just say, 'Queen Posey—'" In an instant, a torrent of water dumped from the air onto Bethany. She slipped and fell onto the bookcases. The downpour continued, as if from a tidal wave. Bethany coughed and sputtered under the torrents, looking around desperately.

Water splattered Erec and started to fill the room, covering his shoes. For some reason, it only poured on Bethany. Erec looked for a source, and was surprised to see it was the pool table top. In fact, the entire green surface of the pool table was replaced by water, endless water, falling straight on Bethany.

Erec reached in to grab her from the avalanche, but her foot was caught. Her hand covered her face, but water flew from all directions. Erec hoped she could breathe. He yanked until her foot pulled loose. In an instant the water stopped. The pool table's surface was flat and green.

Bethany sat, coughing, on the edge of a bookcase. The water in the room was up to their knees. "Did . . . *she* do that to me?" Her eyes were red and a little more water poured from them. "A piece of the ocean came down out of nowhere."

"Not out of nowhere." Erec pointed at the pool table hanging on what used to be the floor, but now functioned as a wall, over Bethany. "What made it start and stop, though?"

Bethany looked up. "It started when I tripped on a bookshelf, and it fell in. My shoe got stuck. Then it stopped when I got out. Maybe the shelf flipped back again."

"Huh?"

"That's exactly when it started." Bethany crawled over the wooden shelves, pulling on boards near where she fell. Suddenly, a bathtub-sized gush dropped on her and then immediately stopped. "I found it! Look—there are wavy lines on the wood behind this shelf. It looks like a water symbol, marking this spot. This little shelf folds right up then back again." She sat down. "Only, why in the world would someone want something like *this* here? Look, the room is ruined."

"Maybe it worked differently before the castle was on its side. The water might not have dumped out."

Bethany stared up at the pool table, shivering. Her pockets were black from gunpowder. They stacked card tables on chairs and climbed from the room.

"I hope the mess won't ruin the walls," Bethany said.

Erec shrugged at the huge mess. "Someone will probably fix it with a spell."

They trudged back to the dormitories leaving a trail of water behind them.

Bethany was happily eating ambrosia in the cafeteria with Jack when Erec came to breakfast the next morning. When Jack went for seconds, Erec whispered, "I had enough gunpowder, luckily. Was yours—"

"Ruined."

Balor and Damon Stain were sitting across the room with Rock Rayson and Ward Gamin. "I'll be back." Erec walked over to them.

"Look who's here." Balor laughed. "We're slumming today. You actually eat this stuff?" He pointed at a mound of ambrosia.

Erec shrugged. "Can I use your MagicNet today?"

"Yeah, let's go now. I'm outta here." Balor shoved his tray forward, ambrosia and nectar untouched. "We'll get room service. C'mon." Damon, Ward, and Rock stood, grumbling. Balor looked at Erec. "You got money? 'Cause you're not bumming any off me."

"Shoot, no," said Erec. "Wait here. I'll be right back."

"Hear that, boys?" Balor grinned. "Old one-eye has to go get money from his little dorm cell." He grinned at Erec. "We'll walk slow. If you catch up, you can come."

Erec swallowed his anger and ran to his dorm room, where he

stuffed his pockets with gold, silver, and bronze. When he tore back, Balor and his friends were climbing into the castle. Erec followed them to the south wing. He wished he had a charge card so he could buy things on the computer. Maybe he could use Balor's and pay him back with the gold.

"Come see where the big boys live," said Balor. "Guest quarters on the second floor. The whole Super A Team stayed here last night. We had dinner with them. A real feast," he said, smirking. They climbed to an ornate hallway with chandeliers and plush plum carpeting.

"Did you hear the game room flooded yesterday?" Ward asked. "Real mess. All King Piter's fault, I'm sure. This place is in rotten shape."

Erec winced. "Did they get it cleaned up?"

"Why wouldn't they?" Ward said nastily. Erec had the urge to warn him that he better not get too comfy. His friends were supposed to win the scepters, and he would be "gotten rid of."

Balor swung around. "I have a great idea. Fair trade. You use my MagicNet, and I get to try out those glasses of yours."

Erec's hand flew to the glasses hanging on his chest. He remembered his mother said nobody could take them off of him. He hoped she was right. "Well, first I'll use the MagicNet, and then you can try to take these off me. If you can take them, you can try them on."

"Excellent." Balor seemed satisfied. "I always like a challenge." They entered a huge, plush room with an eight-foot screen set into one wall. The beds looked twice as big and fluffy as the ones in the dormitories. Low, foam-stuffed chairs with joysticks on their arms sat around the screen for playing video games. A maid was straightening the room.

"Out, servant. *Out*!" Balor roared at the maid. "Can't you see we're here?" She looked flustered and apologized several times as she ran out the door. Balor laughed. "They're like deer in the headlights."

Ward rolled his eyes. Damon stared dumbly at the screen, goofy gray stocking cap still on his head. "I wanna play Jackknife," he said. "Let's play Jackknife."

"All in good time, Damon. First our new friend here wants to get on the MagicNet." Balor snapped his fingers. His and Damon's names appeared on the large screen and the room darkened slightly.

Damon mumbled, ". . . Jackknife . . ."

"Do you know your site, or do you want to do a search?" Balor asked.

It looked like all four of them were going to watch. Erec hoped he could hide that he'd never used the MagicNet before. "I'll search." Erec put his hands in his pockets, trying to look casual, but his pockets were so full of coins they stuck out stiffly.

"Search," Balor called out and snapped his fingers.

A young woman's face with dark hair pulled in a tight bun, appeared. "Yes?" She looked out from the screen.

Balor nodded toward Erec, opening a hand in his direction. The woman on the screen looked impatient. "I need three lion hairs," Erec said.

"Lion hairs." The woman nodded briskly and the screen split into eight boxes, a different person framed in each. A box at the bottom of the screen said, "Next eight of forty-six."

Balor crossed his arms and tilted his head, obviously interested. "Eight on one all right?"

"Uh-huh," said Erec. From each box a person shouted, pedaling their wares, except in one of the lower boxes, where a woman with long gray hair and a tall feathered hat was sound asleep.

A woman's face with a black pointed hat and a crooked nose nearly filled screen one. She waved a few brown hairs toward Erec. "These'll do ya. Straight from the jungles of Kenya. Only eight shires, but for you, seven shires and five gands." She winked at Erec.

A thin man with a slick mustache in the box next to her jingled a small bag before the screen. "Alpha lion's mane hairs. Best you can buy. One gold ring. You won't do any better."

Everyone was talking at once. Erec glanced at Balor, who watched him expectantly. If only he knew how to do this. The woman with the pointed hat produced a little jar and rattled it. "Tiger claws ... eagle talons ... I've got it all."

Erec heard one of the vendors shout the word "certified." He wished he knew who was reputable. "Which of you are . . . certified?"

Most of the screen vendors immediately whisked papers in front of their faces. The others appeared to be searching madly around them but finally gave up and shrugged. Erec pointed at the screen numbered five, one that had a certificate, whatever that was worth. "Number five, how much?"

The young, dark-skinned man on screen five straightened up and held a small vial. "For three certified lion hairs I can give you a deal for nine silver shires. Of course, it would usually cost a ring and several shires—"

"Lion's mane?"

"Of course." He looked insulted.

"Do you have an eagle feather?" Erec asked. "Certified?"

The man searched around himself frantically and then pulled an envelope from somewhere. "Pure ostrich tail feathers."

"I need an eagle feather," Erec said.

Several hands waved long brown and white feathers before

them. "Right here!" "Over here! Genuine eagle feather! Only the finest."

Erec pointed to the woman with the pointed hat. "Number one. Is your eagle feather certified?"

"Of course." She wore a smug grin.

"How much?"

Her eyes darted to the side. "One gold ring and six shires."

Immediately her competitors started shouting, "One ring, two shires." "One ring, even!"

"Oh, all right," the woman with the pointed hat huffed. "One ring, one shire, five gands."

Erec said, "Okay, then."

"Aren't you even going to ask where they sell from? I only see two company names listed," Balor said.

Erec noticed for the first time that two vendors had a small box at the tops of their screens, one saying "Potion Portions," and the other saying "The Beastiary." Why bother asking what companies they were with? Erec would not have heard of them anyway. A few vendors shouted out names in response to Balor, others ignored him.

"Have any recommendations?" Erec asked Balor.

Balor shrugged. "You're right. They're all sleazy little off-brand shops anyway. It's okay. We know where they live." He narrowed his eyes. "You can't imagine what we did to a vendor who cheated us once."

A few vendors shrank back and looked like they were changing their minds about the sale. Quickly, Erec said, "Eagle feather— number one. Lion hairs—number five."

The woman and man in one and five smiled brightly, and the rest of the vendors left their screens, grumbling. Erec waited for them to ask how they should bill him.

"Well," said Balor, "go pay them, already. You're not expecting me to foot the bill." He laughed and looked at his friends, eyebrows up.

Erec had no clue how to proceed. Everyone was watching him, waiting. Go pay them. What did that mean?

"It's okay, boy," said the woman in the pointed hat. "Why, he's just had a bad experience, that's all. It happens to all of us. Someone grabbed me by the throat once. If I didn't have help here I could've had my head pulled through, and that would've been it for me." She shuddered.

"Oh, that'll calm him down, all right," said the man in square five. "Come here, boy. It's okay." Erec walked to screen five, while Balor and his friends snickered. The man's hand with the vial of lion hairs stuck through the screen into the room. Erec stared at it in shock. The hand looked as real as his own.

Erec reached into a pocket and counted out nine silver coins. "Is this right?"

The man looked kindly at Erec. "A little slow, are you? Yes, that's fine." He took the silver coins and gave the vial to Erec. "Do you want a receipt?"

"No, thanks." Erec found a gold coin with a hole, hoping that was a gold ring, and another silver coin. He held it out to the woman.

She looked at him critically. "I'm not going any lower. I need five gands as well."

There was only one other type of coin in Erec's pocket, a bronze-colored coin. Erec counted five.

"That's a good boy." The woman took the coins and handed Erec a long white eagle feather with a black tip in a plastic bag, followed by a certificate.

Erec turned to see Balor's smirk. "Afraid of the mean old vendors, are you?" Damon laughed in huge guffaws.

"That's a good boy," snickered Ward. Rock laughed, pointing at Erec.

"What are the lion hairs and eagle feather for?" Balor asked. "A courage potion?"

"No, just a hobby."

"Aah. He has a hobby, boys. What are you using them for?"

"Making explosions."

"Ooh. Very interesting. We like to do that sometimes too," Balor said.

"Yeah," said Rock. "We may need your recipe . . . *soon*."

"Good point, Rock old man," Balor said. "What's the recipe?"

Erec figured it wouldn't hurt to mention a few ingredients. "Eagle feather, lion hairs, nitrowisherine, a little warthog essence . . . and five crumbled leaves."

"*Leaves*? What kind?" Rock asked.

"Oak."

"And you swear by this?" Balor asked.

"Not at all," Erec said. "I'm just trying it out."

"Ward, write those down," Balor said. "What are you going to blast?"

Erec shrugged. "I don't know yet." He walked to the door.

"Wait a minute," Balor said. "I think you're forgetting something. You owe me a little thing around your neck."

Erec turned. "Oh, yeah. Three tries to get it off, then I'm going."

Balor rubbed his hands together. He pointed a remote control at Erec and pressed a button. "Akamptos."

Erec suddenly felt cool and tight all over. It was hard to breathe. He tried to speak, but his mouth wouldn't move. In fact, he couldn't move at all. He was frozen stiff, feather and vial still in his hands. If someone poked his shoulder, he would have fallen flat onto his back.

Balor swaggered to Erec. "I hope you didn't think you could strong-arm *me*, son of the great sorcerer Mauvis Stain." He lifted the glasses from Erec's chest. "Maybe for all the effort I'll have to keep these." Balor tried to pull them over his head, but they stopped, immovable, at his chin. He yanked and pulled, but they would not budge.

"Very tricky, Rick Ross." Balor did not sound happy. He pushed his remote-control button. "Aeiro." The glasses rose off Erec's chest, but they hit the same barrier at his chin. Balor's eyes blazed. He pushed harder and then stopped.

Balor paced, stroking his chin. "Ideas, boys? Hmm . . . maybe gravity will do it." He pushed his remote control button again. "Aeiro. Anastrepho."

The ground slipped from under Erec's feet and the room started to rotate around him. The floor slid by to one side. Erec's stomach lurched. He wondered if he could throw up, since he was still frozen. Soon he hung upside down in the air, his glasses hanging at chin level. Damon pounded on them, to no avail.

Balor said, "I suppose we could cut his head off. That might work."

Damon giggled. "Let's do it. Cut it off."

Ward smacked his forehead and plopped into a chair. Rock looked around the room. "How should we do it?"

"We can all keep a secret here, right?" Balor asked. "I'm starting to want those glasses even more." He pushed his remote control. "Apotemno."

A searing heat lurched through Erec's neck. It grew until his skin burned, and then it faded. Balor kicked a chair across the room.

Damon pulled a knife from his drawer. "I'll do it. I'll do it." He swung the knife at Erec's ankle. The blade dug into Erec's skin, causing him to cry out in pain. Damon pushed harder into Erec's ankle, and sang, "I am cutting off his head, off his head, off his head. Brother is a little lamb . . ."

"You bonehead," Balor said. "That's his foot."

Damon looked at Erec carefully and turned his head upside down. Then he swung with all his might. The knife stopped within an inch of Erec's neck. Damon swung again and again, but an invisible wall kept stopping him.

"He tricked us," Balor spat. "Leave him hanging." The four boys left the room.

Erec was sure they would never let him down. They would probably keep trying to get the glasses until he starved or bled to death from his ankle.

Blood pounded into his head. It was hard to breathe. At this rate they'd have the glasses soon because Erec was sure he wouldn't last long. When he wasn't thinking about dying upside down, he wondered about the explosive Balor was planning. He had a bad feeling about that, too.

After the longest ten minutes of Erec's life, Ward came back into the room. He pointed a remote control at Erec. "Anapalin."

Erec felt the room turn, gravity pulling at his side, then, finally, his feet. He took a deep breath and found he could move.

"Get out of here, idiot," Ward said. "I don't want you making the room stink. I like to hang out in here."

"Thanks." Erec went to the door and rested his hand on the knob. He looked back to see Ward glaring at him. He wanted to pay him back, somehow. "Be careful, Ward. There's a plan to get rid of you so your friends will win the contests and you won't."

Ward gaped at him in shock. "You jealous ingrate. I know who my friends are. You just want us to fight and destroy each other so *you* can win."

Erec merely shook his head. He'd tried to warn the guy.

He went to the royal hospital to get his ankle bandaged, saying that he tripped on a sharp rock. Once he was back in his room, he put the eagle feather and lion hairs in a drawer with the drying gunpowder. Now for the storerooms. He only hoped his mother remembered the right password.

Bethany was about to leave when Erec came into the cafeteria for lunch. "You look awful. Did you use Balor's MagicNet?"

"Uh-huh." Erec told her what had happened. "I'm taking it easy this afternoon. Nighttime is better to go raid the storeroom anyway, right? Less people."

"There's a band playing in the agora tonight. A lot of kids are going. Maybe the kitchens will clear out too."

CHAPTER THIRTEEN
The Tribaffleon

THE FULL MOON shone down on the band, Medusa, as they strummed electric guitars and thumped around on the open-air stage in the agora. Erec and Bethany stayed for the first songs, "Born to Be Styled" and "Poppa Was a Stone." They ate some imported chocolate rain from a place called Cinnalim, but they had to spit out the occasional bugs that were mixed in.

When it grew dark, they strolled casually to the castle kitchens.

They were nearly empty, with some lights off. A few maids and cooks scuttled through, getting their bags. Bethany asked a cook if Hecate Jekyll was coming back.

"In an hour or so. Can I get you something?"

"No, thanks." Bethany smiled like a little angel and the cook walked off. "Okay, let's get to work." They searched the back of the kitchens, looking under racks and bags of flour. "Look! Here it is." Bethany pointed at a round plaque, about three feet wide, on the floor. A closed eye was carved into it. "That's got to weigh"—she closed her eyes—"sixty-eight pounds, judging the diameter and cubic weight of iron."

Erec's eyes widened in shock. "How do you know that?"

Bethany blushed. "I just like math."

He whispered into the plaque, "One eye sees all."

In an instant, the carved eye opened wide, and the thick metal slid across the floor. Under it, a ladder led into a lit pit. Erec pulled the ingredient list from his pocket and put his vanishing cap on. Ugry would kick him out if he saw him wearing it, but if he was caught in the storeroom, it was all over anyway.

"I'll wait up here," Bethany said. "If someone's coming, I'll . . . drop this salt shaker down the hole."

Erec climbed down the long ladder into a narrow room. He hoped the plaque would not shut over his head. Everything imaginable was packed on shelves in bags, jars, and vials, with labels like "dried toad skin," "mouse antlers," "cricket breath," and "eye of newt."

Wolfsbane was easy to find in the *W* section. Erec stuffed six big handfuls of the torn rounded leaves and yellow flowers into the bag he brought. On a nearby shelf he saw a glass jar in the shape of a woman, labeled "spirits." Curiosity got the better of him. He unscrewed its lid, which flew from his hands. Four white, vaporous figures shot from the jar, each thanking Erec profusely before they flew away and vanished. Erec put it back carefully. Somebody would not be happy about that. Still, it seemed better that they were free.

He found the grain alcohol, but he realized he forgot to bring a glass jar. Instead, he poured it into a bag, tied the top, and set it down. The nitrowisherine was in a dark, round glass jar. Rancid-smelling gas steamed from the top. He carefully put one drop into a plastic bag.

The liquid sizzled through the plastic and fell to the floor. The room shook with a loud explosion. Erec was thrown onto the shelves behind him. His ribs hurt, but somehow no jars fell off and broke. He supposed a spell protected them.

Erec wished he had brought three glass jars. All of a sudden, three glass jars appeared on the floor. How the heck did that happen?

Bethany stuck her head down the hole. "Are you okay? I heard a little noise and the ground shook."

"A little noise? It was a blast," Erec said. "The storeroom must be soundproofed."

"What happened?"

"The nitrowisherine burned through the bag and exploded. Then I wished I had brought glass jars and they appeared. I think this stuff gave me my wish!"

"Drop another drop on the floor when you're done, and wish us safely back in the dormitory," said Bethany.

"Good idea. I wish I could get out of here now." Erec counted ten drops of nitrowisherine into a glass jar, five drops of warthog essence into another, and poured the grain alcohol from the now seriously leaking bag into the third. He grabbed the jars and the bag of wolfsbane and dropped a droplet of nitrowisherine on the floor.

The blast threw him back into the shelves and rang in his ears. "I wish Bethany and I were back in the dormitory with our ingredients, and the plaque was back in place."

In a flash Erec was in the dormitory entrance with Bethany, his bag, and three jars. He grinned. "I should have gotten more of that stuff." He grabbed the bag and a jar, and Bethany took the other two.

They found Oscar panting heavily outside of their room, his back on the door. Jack stood next to him looking stunned.

"What's up?" Erec asked.

The fear in Oscar's eyes changed to an angry squint. "Oh, nothing. It's just your dog, Erec. I think you need to have a talk with him. He's gotten a little out of hand today."

Erec heard a gurgling, panting growl. He opened the door.

"No! Don't go in there!" Jack shouted, but Erec was already inside. His dog had grown to twice his regular size. He stood on his hind legs, so he was taller than Erec. Erec recognized his gold collar and blue eyes, but otherwise he looked completely different—bulging muscles, a crazed look in his eye, and a frothing mouth with huge fangs.

The beast backed away from Erec, whining, into the corner of the room. Erec had never seen his dog look afraid, and it was odder now that he looked so fierce. When he came closer, the now hideous dog winced.

"It's okay, boy. I know. You're sick or something, right?"

Jack said, "Erec, be careful. He's a wenwolf. It's the full moon."

The moon gleamed in from the window. Erec stepped closer and the wenwolf yelped, pawing at the air to keep Erec away.

"We have to get you out of here." Erec looked around. The sheets were shredded. Scratch marks covered the walls and door. Erec reached to grab his wolf dog's collar, but his head dove into the corner. It sounded like he was crying.

Oscar and Jack watched in shock. "I don't get it," Oscar said. "When I walked in, he tried to kill me. I barely escaped."

Jack shook his head. "He's crying, 'Go away.' Poor thing. He must be ashamed for you to see him like this."

Bethany's arms were crossed, a twisted smile on her face. "Erec, you better come out here, and bring your bag."

"What is it?" He shut the door.

"You three take our room tonight. Melody and I can bunk with friends down the hall. The dog will be fine in the morning."

"That dog needs to be destroyed," said Oscar. "He lunged at me. If I hadn't left the door open for Jack—"

"No," said Bethany. "It's Erec's pet. You can't tell on him. We'll keep him tied up somewhere for the next full moon. The contests should be over by then anyhow. Just think, wouldn't it be great to have your own wenwolf? He could be . . . useful."

Oscar shrugged and mumbled to himself.

As they walked, Bethany whispered, "The reason he didn't attack you was *not* because you're his master. Think about what you were holding." She pointed to the bag stuffed with wolfsbane.

Wenwolf, Erec thought. Wolfsbane. This place got crazier every day he was here.

The next morning Erec's room was a mess. His dog, now his usual self, was asleep on the floor, tangled in a sheet. Erec rubbed his head. "Rest up, Wolfboy." It seemed like a good name now. He cleaned the room and changed for the third contest.

The crowd behind the maze was smaller now. Other kids gathered nearby to watch.

The wind tousled Spartacus Kilroy's light brown hair and blue cape. Umpee checked Erec off—"Rick Ross"—and stuck the number seventy-five on his back.

Kilroy blew his whistle. "There should be ninety-three of you, but we only have eighty today, so there will be just forty winners. I hear a few were discouraged because their inquizzles said they would not be final winners." He looked disturbed by this thought. "That was not the intention of that prize. A few others were upset by things that happened to the winners and have dropped out." He shook his head. "I want to assure you, the judges are aware of the situation. You will be perfectly safe from here out."

Erec was happy that Ugry was nowhere in sight. At least he felt safe for the moment.

"The third contest," continued Kilroy, "is the Tribaffleon. It is made up of three parts, with separate scores. We will start with the sword pull. I do not expect many to accomplish this. Perhaps none will. But if you do it, you will get a hundred points.

"Next is a timed race. You must ride a creature across a track. To make this more difficult, and in some cases safer, the creatures are babies. Since there are eighty of you, the first across the line will get eighty points, then seventy-nine, down to one.

"The final part is individually judged." Kilroy held up a rippled, uneven urn, riddled with pockmarks. It looked like it was molded from black mud. "This is a nocked urn, made just for our contest. Each of you will draw a paper from it. It will give you a specific test that will use your inborn magical gifts. Don't worry. If you are afraid you have not inherited anything, the nocked urn *will* discover something in you, even if it is small. You will be observed and scored from zero to one hundred."

Erec wondered what the nocked urn would find that he could do. Eat? Sleep? Tame crazy dogs?

The crowd followed Olive Umpee to form lines behind four stone anvils. Umpee and Rayson counted twenty kids to a line. Balor and his friends were at the end of the line on the right so Erec swerved to the left.

Stoney Rayson clapped his hand onto Erec's and Bethany's

shoulders, and steered them to the right behind Rock. "Nice glasses, kid." He winked. A girl lined up behind Bethany, and Rayson said, "That's twenty. The lines are full."

Balor turned around. A slick smile spread over his face. "This is your lucky day, Rick Ross. You're in the winning line. That's good. I want to keep you around here a while longer."

Erec remembered hanging upside down in the air, Balor and Damon trying to chop his head off. He gritted his teeth, but he didn't reply.

Rayson said, "These stones will release their swords only into the hands of a worthy king or queen. They are from the druids of Ireland—top-quality spells."

Erec watched as kids yanked and pulled until they were blue. The going was slow: Everyone thought one more hard pull might do it. Nobody was getting the swords out.

When it was Balor's turn, he pulled a remote control from his pocket and mumbled something. It grew a point, and small metal spikes shot from its sides. He slid it down the back of the sword. Stoney Rayson's arm slipped around Olive Umpee, and he turned her so they were facing away, Rayson pointing in the distance.

Balor's remote control shook, and bits of stone flew in all directions. One hit the boy at the next stone in the forehead. Balor stopped and waved to him. "Sorry. I think I'm getting it here."

The boy turned away and pulled harder, not to be outdone. Balor dug deeper into the rock, splitting it nearly in two. Finally, he yanked the sword from the broken stone. The remote control changed back and Balor slid it in his pocket. He waved the sword triumphantly over his head.

"Did you see that?" Bethany whispered. "We should turn him in."

"Rayson's the judge. Little luck we'd have," Erec said.

Rayson charged over. "A winner! Balor Stain! A young man worthy to be king! Great job, boy." He marked a score on his list. Balor slid the sword into the stone and sauntered away.

Damon walked up next, and in one yank pulled the loose sword out. He held it over his head with a goofy grin and did a dance. "Another winner," Rayson shouted. "Of course, another one of the Stain triplets. Equally worthy."

Ward faked pulling for a while before he easily slid the sword free. Rayson sounded shocked. "Another winner? Well, birds of a feather . . ."

Rock gave a few fake pulls and lifted the sword high. His father made a big fuss. "And look at that. I guess hero lines run in the family, eh? My Rock, a worthy king . . ."

Erec was next. He tugged gently and the sword slid from the broken anvil. It looked like the stone opened a bit wider as he pulled. He held it up.

Rayson smiled. "Name?"

"Rick Ross." Rayson nodded as Erec put the sword back. Bethany and the girl after her pulled it out as well, with envious looks from the other kids.

In the east lawn, a pen overflowed with baby animals of all types. They were mostly strange creatures Erec had never seen. Rayson joined Kilroy in handing creatures to each kid.

Kilroy grabbed what looked like three one-eyed horses held together by a bar. "Triclops." He handed the bar to Erec. "Oh, hi. Good luck."

The leathery skin coating the bar blended with the skin of the three horses. They moved in tandem around the bar: one leaping up, back legs on the ground, one in midair, and one landing, front legs on the ground, at all times, like a carousel.

Bethany was given a mynaraptor, a huge bird that looked like an enormous duck with fat ostrich legs and a sharp beak. It was the perfect size for her to ride, her feet sticking out over its broad back. The bird talked nonstop. "And when I was born, that was a month ago, there was a giant hailstorm. My momma says that makes me special. I know a lot for only being here a month. My momma says I'm very smart . . ." Bethany patted its downy head, unable to get a word in edgewise.

Balor Stain and Rock Rayson sat atop white winged horses. Damon and Ward rode funny creatures that looked like waist-high ants. Pincers waved around their crablike heads, sharp teeth filled their round mouths, and an eye stared from the center of their faces.

"Ginglehoffers!" Bethany laughed. "I can't imagine they'll control those." A few other kids had baby ginglehoffers as well, quickly discovering they had to be held by their heads or they would bite.

Everybody lined up with their baby animals. Bethany's bird was still talking: ". . . and that's why I like tulips better than roses. My great-grand aunt was named Tulip. She was famous for her fish recipes. Her husband Borick was friends with some of King Piter's plants . . ."

Oscar sat on a huge rabbit, holding its floppy ears. He laughed at a girl sitting cross-legged on a plodding tortoise.

The race was a straight shot, a third of a mile to the finish line. Kilroy blew his whistle. Balor and Rock cantered by on their white horses, which took wing and were at the finish line almost immediately. Damon and Ward were close behind. They held marshmallows on fishing lines in front of the ginglehoffers' faces. Erec shook his head. Of course they would be perfectly prepared. The ginglehoffer in the MONSTER race loved marshmallows.

Erec sat on the middle horse body and shouted, "Go," kicking its sides. The three-part animal slowly loped onto the field. Each horse stayed in the air an amazingly long time between its funny galloping steps. Erec felt like he was on a merry-go-round, but at least he moved forward.

All around, animals ran in circles or didn't move at all. A few walked back toward the starting line. Some kids were thrown and were left sitting in the dirt searching for their creatures. Oscar, on the huge baby rabbit, hopped wildly around the field, stopping here and there at patches of clover. The girl on the tortoise plodded slowly past him.

Bethany was engaged in deep conversation with her bird. They had not moved from the starting line. Erec shouted, "Go! Faster!" into the ears of his triclops and slapped its side. It moved a little faster. At least it was going in the right direction.

After he was almost across the field, he looked back to see Bethany and her mynaraptor still at the starting line, the great bird talking nonstop. All of a sudden, it spread its wings and flew over the field. At the finish line she slid off its back and grabbed it by the head, pulling it down to land. Erec crossed the line after her.

Umpee marked their names. "Bethany Evirly, twenty-two. Rick Ross, twenty-three." The girl on the tortoise came in soon after.

Jack, pale and greenish, fell off of his Dervish Toad, which happened to spin across the finish line. He looked like he might throw up. The toad had whirled so fast around the field it had been hard to see him. After Jack fell off, the Dervish Toad continued its wild ride onto the track, knocking kids off their animals.

Oscar's rabbit sat in a clover patch, midfield. He was trying to drag it by the ears without much luck. "What happened with your mynaraptor?" Erec asked.

"It wouldn't shut up. I begged and yelled at it, but it kept babbling."

"How did you get it to fly?"

Bethany rolled her eyes. "It kept talking about how it knew

everything about the castle, the king, Alypium ... Imagine, it was just a baby! I finally said, 'I bet you don't know about that clock tower.' It somehow heard me, and went on with crazy stories about the clock tower, probably made up. So I said, 'I bet you can't fly there.' And it did! It would have kept going if I hadn't jumped off and pulled its head down.

"That bird said the king has 'plants'—spies, I guess—and that Balthazar Ugry has been trying for years to figure out how to get the plants to talk to *him* now that King Piter is sick. But then it said Ugry was a decent man and talked about pink potatoes and how it would eventually grow twenty feet tall. I don't think it knows up from down."

A line formed at the nocked urn. Only two contestants could be tested at once, they were told. Melody was next in line. Her tight black hair curled around the warm, deep brown skin of her face. She drew a card from the green vapor in the urn.

"Play a song," she read. She sat in the grass, a smile sliding across face, and slid her top leg over the lower one. As she did, a beautiful melody filled the air. The sound was like a violin, but deeper, with sadness and happiness woven into the music. The crowd hushed, enchanted. When it seemed it could be no more perfect, Melody rubbed her forearms together. A new, strange, sweet sound, like an oboe, joined the other to make the most beautiful refrain Erec had ever heard. She popped her lips open and shut, adding sparkling percussion, and occasionally tilted her head in a chord flourish.

Bethany had tears in her eyes when the song ended. "Oh, Melody . . . I didn't know you could do that." Melody shrugged shyly. Spartacus Kilroy and Queen Posey gave her a score of ninety-eight.

A boy had to leap over a fountain, but he splashed in at the back and got a score of sixty-five. A girl was told to read Queen Posey's mind. The queen conjured a book from the air, and the girl recited the words she read, but then went deeper and said, "How much longer will this drag on? I can't sleep well here . . . What? This girl is getting into my thoughts. Stop! Enough!" The last word, "Enough!" was shouted by the girl and the queen at the same time.

Erec wondered what Balor's gift was. Hanging people upside down and trying to kill them?

When Bethany reached into the smoking nocked urn, a roll of paper came out instead of a slip. It was so long, she looked like a magician pulling reels of tissue from a hat. Queen Posey and Spartacus Kilroy looked at each other in amazement. Bethany read from the top: "Break the code." Strings of numbers filled the scroll.

Erec's heart sank. How could she ever do it? Bethany sat on the grass and smoothed the paper on the ground, gazing at it. A faint smile grew into a look of delight as she pored over the numbers. Then she laughed and held the paper up. As if in plain English, she read:

DEEP IN THE GROUSY FOREST DEN,

SYRINX, A TREE NYMPH, STAYED AWAY FROM MEN,

ONLY WANDERING FROM SLITHERY CAVE,

TO TEND HER TREES, WITH SPIRIT BRAVE.

SHE CAREFULLY CREPT UNDER COVER OF TREES,

TO HIDE FROM PAN, WHO WANTED TO PLEASE.

FOR THE LOVE OF THIS CREATURE SHE COULD NOT BEAR,

WITH HIS WILD WAYS, HORNS, AND GOATY HAIR.

BUT ALAS, PAN FOUND HER, HE HAD WON,

WITH HELP FROM HELIOS, THE SUN.

SYRINX SAW PAN, IN A FLASH SHE FLED.

HE CHASED HER TO THE RIVER BED.

SHE WAS CORNERED BY A RIVER THAT RACED WITH SPEED,

SO SHE TURNED HERSELF INTO A REED.

BUT AFTER A CRY AND A SLEEP THAT WAS LONG,

PAN HEARD SYRINX SING A SONG.

THE REEDS WHISTLED HER LOVE FOR HIM BECAUSE,

AFTER SHE CHANGED, SHE SAW PAN AS HE WAS.

HIS LOOKS DIDN'T MATTER, HIS HEART SHOWED THROUGH,

AS HER BEAUTY HAD CHANGED. NOW PLANT WISHED TO WOO.

PAN GATHERED THE REEDS AND CUT STALKS WITH LOVE,

HE MADE THE FIRST PAN PIPES, WHICH SANG LIKE A DOVE.

Bethany grinned. Kilroy clapped. "Fantastic! Outstanding! Excellent gift."

Queen Posey looked skeptical. "How do we know she didn't make that up? Or recite it from memory?"

Bethany skipped over, holding the paper. "It's easy. Each line is separated by a sequence of ten numbers. See? After the first line is one, four, nine, sixteen, twenty-five, thirty-six . . . the squares of one through ten. After the second line, *those* numbers are squared, see? One, sixteen, eighty-one, two hundred fifty-six. After the third line, those ten numbers are squared: one, two hundred fifty-six, six thousand five hundred sixty-one. Then in the first line of poetry, all of the letters are in relation to the letter A, except squared. A is zero, B is one, C is four, D is nine, C is sixteen. In the second line, it's all in relation to B, except cubed. A is negative one, B is zero, C is one, D is eight, E is twenty-seven. It's so great. I love this stuff. Then—"

Queen Posey cleared her throat. "I think that is enough." She suppressed a smile. "You are quite the mathematician. Have you had seer training yet?"

"Seer training?" Bethany said, puzzled.

"Of course, my dear. With your skills, you'll be a fine seer someday. In fact, the only person I've met as excited about codes and numbers was Ruth Cleary, King Piter's old AdviSeer. Maybe

you'll work in my court someday. With your skills, you'll go far."
She glanced at Kilroy, who turned red.

"AdviSeer Kilroy, you can read codes?" asked Bethany. "Are you
a seer?"

Kilroy stared at his feet. "No, never clicked, actually. King Piter
was very kind to hire me anyway."

Bethany scored one hundred points. Melody ran over and gave
her a hug. "How can you do that so fast?"

"It's hard to explain. Each number looks like a swirling color
to me. They're all different . . ." Bethany and Melody walked to the
hillside with the others.

Unfortunately, the girl judged by Ugry and King Pluto had
just finished making a flower grow. Erec wanted to be judged by
Kilroy and the queen, but King Pluto waved him over.

Ugry glared stonily as Erec reached into the nocked urn. He
was surprised how cold the green smoke was. He wiggled his
fingers and a warm slip of paper appeared. Erec read aloud, "You
will know what to do."

King Pluto leaned on his scepter, a patient smile on his face.
Ugry's cold stare was so intense, Erec felt he was looking right
through him. A bitter smell crept into Erec's nose. The king cleared
his throat. "Well, go ahead, boy."

What was he supposed to do? Announce Ugry's plans to take
over, and expose his treachery with the rhinoceros, the minotaur,
and the attack fleas? Then again, King Pluto might be in on
it as well, with his mother in Pluto's dungeon. So who was he
announcing it to? That is, unless his mother was a criminal.

Suddenly, midthought, a cloudlike, unreal feeling hit Erec. His
head spun and his stomach did the tango. Not now! He had to
stay in control, not be forced to do something. Especially now.
Dizziness made him stumble.

A moment later, the cloudy thought arrived as usual: facts, a command. *Look up. A huge boulder is dropping over your heads. Destroy it yourself with King Pluto's scepter or you will be killed in seconds.*

Erec shook with anger and fear. There was no fighting this one. He pointed over King Pluto's shoulder. "Look!" The terror and excitement in his voice were real. Pluto glanced back. Erec dove at the jeweled, golden scepter, knocking the king over. He landed on his back, scepter up, under the growing shadow of the boulder.

The scepter was warm. It quivered. "Who are *you*?" A voice ringing in Erec's head seemed to come from the scepter. "Well, I hope you know what you're doing."

Erec shouted, "Explode!" The scepter shook. Surges of electricity coursed through his body and out through the scepter. It felt like he was holding a thundercloud. He wondered if he could keep holding on, but he knew he had to. His chest, arms, and the scepter became as one. It seemed that he would burst apart.

A jet of blinding light rocketed through the shaft of the scepter. It struck the boulder, smashing it into fragments. As pebbles rained down all around them, Erec collapsed in the grass.

King Pluto's mouth hung open in shock. "Thank you." He glanced up, as if expecting another boulder to fall. "You know, you could have just asked *me* to take care of the boulder." He brushed himself off and winked. "But I guess that wouldn't be much of a test. You must be an incredibly powerful boy." Pluto picked up his scepter and examined it. "I'm supposed to be the only one able to use this." He checked the score sheets. "Your name is Rick Ross?"

Ugry's expression narrowed into deep suspicion. A cold chill ran through Erec when their eyes met. "I'm not sure what gift he actually showed. Stealing?"

King Pluto said, "Well, he knew the boulder was coming before anyone and knew what to do. And he also used my scepter. That's two gifts, I think. Score one hundred, right, Balthazar?"

Ugry nodded sourly. Erec backed away, stomach twisting. What had he just done? He had grabbed a king's scepter and shot an incredible bolt of energy from it. Maybe he really was fit to rule this strange land.

CHAPTER FOURTEEN
Swamp Gas

FORTY WINNERS' NAMES were posted behind the maze, Erec, Bethany, Melody, and Jack among them. Along with, of course, Balor, Damon, Rock, and Ward. Finding he had lost, Oscar threw an empty bottle of Flying Donkey Nectar against a signpost. "Stupid contest," he muttered, walking away. "Who would want to waste their time being king, anyway?"

Jack caught up with him. "It's all right, bud. None of us here will win in the end. It's all for fun, really."

Oscar's eyes were red, and he wiped them with the back of his hand. "Tell that to my dad. I can't go home now. He'll hate me. He's been talking about me winning this for months—that is, the few times I've been back from boarding school. He's already mad I haven't gotten the basics in sorcery apprenticing."

Jack comforted him as they walked away. "Just stay awhile. We'll tell him you lost at the very end."

After eating, Erec felt better. The more he thought about the scepter, the frightening, painful surges of electricity began to seem like nothing. Only the memory of its fantastic power remained. He wanted to feel it again. Maybe if he won the contests he could have his own.

Kilroy nervously handed out prizes while Ugry and King Pluto stood nearby. "The next contest is the Sea Search, Thursday morning at ten behind the maze. Queen Posey says you may bring a magical item."

"Is it worth taking a prize?" Bethany stood on her toes to see what they were. "If not fleas, what next?" Other winners seemed to be thinking the same thing. A few refused prizes and walked away.

Kilroy held up something that looked like a flashlight and turned it on. "I've checked these out. No fleas. These are Magiclights. Hard to see here in daylight, but these beauties put out a ray of light that will stay. When you turn it somewhere else, light stays there, too. You can color a whole room with light, and it stays lit until you flip the switch off. They're great for writing words in the dark; you can leave messages for friends." He moved it in an arc and a fan of light hung in the air.

Erec took one, curious about the thing. "Do they need batteries?"

Kilroy laughed. "That's funny. Isn't that a Loser thing? A bulb that light shines from?"

The Magiclight looked fine. No fleas or dangerous animals

around. Erec had a funny feeling he would be needing it.

Wolfboy jumped on Erec when he got back. After petting him, Erec switched on the Magiclight and wrote his name in the air. It hung there, glowing. Erec drew a circle around it and turned off the switch. The light disappeared at once. He put it with his Sneakers and money under his bed.

At dinner Bethany said, "When should we tell Queen Posey about Ugry's plot?"

Something had changed Erec's mind about telling Queen Posey, but he wasn't sure what. It seemed like a mistake. "She wouldn't believe us. I can tell she doesn't trust me."

"I'll tell her, then," said Bethany. "Somebody has to."

"Then what will she do? Confront Ugry? He'll deny everything and we'll get thrown out, or worse. Or maybe she'll tell King Pluto, and then we're in bigger trouble."

"I'll take that chance," Bethany insisted. "How can you let this whole world get destroyed by Ugry just to protect yourself? I thought you agreed with me."

"I don't know." Erec tried to think of a good reason but couldn't. "All I know is my mom said I could stop Ugry by winning myself. That would ruin his plans. I'd have one of the scepters." Wondrous thoughts filled Erec's mind: the power, the perfection, the magic at his fingertips. The boulder exploding into crumbling pebbles at his command. Yes, having his own scepter was the answer.

That was it. The scepter. Something about using it today had changed his mind. He wanted to solve the problem on his own. Who needed a corrupt king or untrustworthy queen to help? The power he commanded earlier had been *his*, he was sure, with some help, of course. Hadn't King Pluto said he was powerful? He could do it alone.

"Well," said Bethany, "*if* you could win all the contests, and you actually did get a scepter, it would still leave them with two—probably enough to do an awful lot of damage. That's saying, of course, that you beat Balor, Damon, Ward, and Rock, on top of all of their cheating." Bethany crossed her arms, unhappy he had changed his mind.

She was right. But still Erec wanted that scepter. "We can tell Queen Posey later, as soon as we lose," he said. "Maybe by then we'll know who to trust. Ugry's not doing anything until the contests are over."

"Except unloading the entire armory with Rich Rayson."

"That's already done," Erec said.

"Well, who knows what else they're doing! The queen might need time to get ready to fight back."

"I bet she'd go right to King Pluto. Why wouldn't she? And he might be in on it."

Bethany considered that possibility. "Kilroy seems like a good guy. We could tell him."

"Yeah. Or maybe Hecate Jekyll."

"She's nice, but she's only the head cook. She probably couldn't do much."

Erec shrugged. "I have to get the horseshoe tonight. It's the last thing I need for the formula. I'm going to take one from Balor's aniball horse. You want to come?"

"I do, but Melody promised me a concert after dinner. Can you wait?"

"Sure. Knock when you're ready."

It was dark when Erec and Bethany set out for the stables. He hoped the aniball horses would be there, or any horses. The door was ajar and lights were on. Straw covered the floor, and unusual animals strolled through pens, a few tethered to the walls.

Erec heard voices and laughter. He ducked, crouching behind the open door. Balor and Damon Stain were inside with Rock Rayson and Ward Gamin.

Balor was laughing. "These beauties are fit for kings. Imagine, flying our dragon horses, fire blasting from their nostrils, burning up everyone against us, waving our scepters . . ."

Rock's voice was solemn. "Yeah, except one of us won't be king. There can only be three. I wonder which three."

"Whoever's the best." Ward's voice sounded confident.

"Put on that goofy coat of yours and take a walk," Balor said. "I personally don't care, since I know I'll be king. Anyway, the fourth can be my AdviSeer."

Rock said, "My dad said the kings can't keep the scepters. The big guy gets them, and he'll be in charge over us."

"That's what *he* thinks," said Balor. "But how's he going to take them from us?"

"By magic," said Rock. "Because he can. Plus, he has the whole armory and powerful friends."

Balor sounded annoyed. "I'd like to try him one on one. Then we'd see. But all in good time. Right, boys? Anyway, only kings or queens can use their own scepters. So maybe he won't be able to use them after we get them."

Ward said, "Well, *some* people can use them even if they aren't kings. If they're powerful enough. Did you see that Rick Ross kid use King Pluto's scepter today?"

"He thinks he's hot stuff, using the scepter, escaping my trap, keeping his glasses from me. It's about time we paid him back. I hope he gets a good night's sleep tonight, right?" Balor laughed, and his friends joined him. "Let's go."

Erec and Bethany jumped behind a bush as the four boys left the stable and flipped the lights off. When their footsteps were long gone, they crept inside.

"Leave the light off. Someone could see." Erec turned his Magiclight on and waved it, making broad fans of light that hung in the air.

"Wow. That's beautiful." Bethany took it and drew shapes in the darkness. When animals walked through the rings and stripes, it looked like funny spotlights were on them.

Bethany filled the air around the four black horses with light. Smoke came from their nostrils. One reared slightly on its hind legs, and two blue-black shimmering, scaled wings flew open.

"Do those things even wear horseshoes?" Bethany asked. She shone light on their feet. Dark purple, shimmering scales covered their lower legs and deep silver glowed under their hooves. "I wouldn't want to pry one of those off. We could get fried."

She spread a fan of light around the stable. White-winged horses filled the pens, but none of them wore shoes. A tool that looked like a stretched hammer sat near a stack of horseshoes that gleamed the same deep silver. "This must be how they put them on," Erec said. "I could pull out nails with that end."

"Why don't you take one of these?" Bethany picked up a horseshoe from the pile.

"It has to be a used one." Erec walked to one of the big black horses. It tossed its mane, eyes glowing red. Small jets of flame flashed from its nose. Erec spoke softly. "It's okay. I'm just going to take a shoe off. It won't hurt. Let's see that foot."

Flames shot from the horse's nostrils. Its wings flashed open, and it lightly kicked Erec's chest. Erec flew back, winded, onto the straw. He caught his breath and tried another horse. "It's okay, boy. I just need one shoe. Give me your foot. Real easy . . ."

The horse streamed fire, singeing Erec's fingers. He had the feeling it could easily have burned him to a crisp. The horses seemed to be deciding what to do with him.

"Can't you get one of those 'cloudy thoughts'?" Bethany asked.

"I can't make them happen," said Erec. "That's the problem.

They control me, I don't control them. They usually come when someone's in danger."

All four horses were watching Erec now with glowing red eyes. Two of their faces were in the dark, and Erec could see only their burning eyes in the blackness. His breath caught, and again he had the feeling they could destroy him in an instant.

"Balor sent me," Erec said. "He was just here, but he forgot to get a horseshoe for something he's making."

The horse in front looked at the other ones. He touched a front foot with a back foot and flung a silvery shoe near Erec.

Erec picked it up and backed away. "Good boy. Balor will be happy."

Bethany switched off the Magiclight and the room fell into darkness except for eight glowing red eyes. Erec and Bethany scrambled from the stable. "These aniball animals are something else," Bethany said. "I hope dragon horses can't talk."

Erec tried not to laugh. "It's okay. Balor can't hate me any more than he already does."

By the time Erec got back, it was around midnight. Jack and Oscar were asleep. He put the horseshoe under his bed. In the morning he would find out how to mix the formula.

As he brushed his teeth, the mirror blurred. It had been a long day. He felt dizzy, and the room started to spin. Erec wondered if he was sick but then he got the sinking feeling that he was having another cloudy thought.

Not twice in one day. A war dance in his stomach whipped into a frenzy, putting his insides in full attack mode.

Then it hit him. Something terrible was happening. *In the air. Not poison, but a gas that would make everyone very sick.* He dropped his toothbrush and looked out his window. A thick bed of shrubbery ran along the building.

Erec ran down the hall and pounded on Franz Bugga's door. They had learned today that Franz's magical gift let him morph objects. The cloudy thought said Franz had to change the shrubs outside into rubber, so when Erec pushed people out the windows—

Wait! Erec stopped pounding. Pushing people out the windows? That was crazy. He stood still, hands shaking with the urge to wake Franz. How could he let himself do this? Then again, what if he didn't?

Franz opened the door, hair rumpled. "What's going on?"

Erec could not stop himself. "You have to make the shrubbery rubbery."

Franz looked annoyed. "What are you talking about?"

"Change it. Make it into big, bouncy, rubber. We have to jump. Poisonous gas is coming in."

"Yeah, right. You had a nightmare."

Without warning, Erec grabbed a crystal cricket off a shelf. "I'll smash it," he threatened.

"No! That's my grandfather's good-luck charm. Put it down."

"Do it."

Franz shook his head, but he went along. "If I get kicked out for this . . ." He opened his window and changed the bushes along the dormitory into a huge, air-filled rubber cushion.

Erec shoved Franz out the window, yelling, "Don't change them back," as he fell.

Erec ran down to the second floor, knocking on doors and shoving people out their windows. He shoved Oscar out asleep; he would have put up a fight if he was awake. Oscar's eyes opened in midair in wild confusion. Wolfboy sailed after him.

Once Erec woke Jack, he followed Erec down the hallway, helping him. "You better be right, buddy, or we're in for it."

They flew from door to door along the second floor, pounding and screaming "Get out!" Boys stuck their heads through doorways, confused, and Jack and Erec threw them out their windows. Erec felt like a springball player, shoving kicking balls through traps. They cleared the second floor, then the third. The element of surprise worked well for them. People were flying through the air before they knew what hit them.

On the fourth floor, Erec finally pushed Jack out a window, saying "Thanks!" It was getting too dangerous. Bethany watched him toss Melody out in shock. "Poisonous gas is coming in. Sorry," he explained to Bethany as he threw her out too.

Black swirled in the air near Erec's feet. Soon it was up to his knees. The smoke was rising; the first three floors must have been filled by now. Black vapor flowed through the staircase.

By the time he reached the fifth and final girls' floor, black mist swirled around his waist. On the plus side, it was very easy to convince the girls to jump.

The gas stung his eyes. Erec moved slower and felt like throwing up. The gas reached his face as he knocked on the last doors. His head spun. Was he going to make it?

He lurched toward an open door. The room was spinning. Two girls saw him and screamed. Or maybe they saw the gas. He pushed them toward their windows and tripped, spinning into blackness.

A thin sliver of light appeared in the darkness. Erec's good eye opened and the sliver grew until the light was blinding. Moaning, he shut his eyes.

"Look," a woman murmured. "Our hero is coming back." Erec opened his eyes and saw a very fuzzy Dr. Mumbai leaning over him. Behind her, Bethany, Jack, Oscar, Hecate Jekyll, and some kids all smiled.

Bethany ran to Erec, face twisted. "Are you okay?" He nodded, though he wasn't sure yet. "You saved almost everyone. How did you know?"

Erec shrugged, painfully. At least he wasn't breathing that poisonous air anymore.

Hecate Jekyll said, "Thank you, Rick Ross. You are just full of surprises." She turned to the doctor. "I'm sorry, but I think it's getting too dangerous here. Everyone should just go home. To heck with these stupid contests."

With great effort, Erec found his voice. "How long was I out?" He pulled an oxygen mask off his face.

Dr. Mumbai smiled. "Most of the day. It's four in the afternoon." Erec immediately remembered the blasting formula ingredients under his bed. He had to talk to his mother. In a panic, he felt his chest. His glasses were still there.

"Is everyone okay?" Erec asked.

"Pretty much. Only sixteen kids breathed the swamp gas, thanks to you. Oh, and one boy sprained his ankle falling from the window." She added, with an edge to her voice, "What is your gift, telling the future? Where are you from?"

Everyone leaned closer. "Americorth South," he whispered. He felt incredibly tired. Plus, he didn't want to tell them about his gift, although he knew his cloudy thoughts were exactly that. They seemed too personal to talk about. "Did anybody . . . die?"

"Heavens, no," said Dr. Mumbai. "Swamp gas is only fatal if you sleep long enough to starve to death. It can knock you out for days. If everybody breathed it in, nobody could report it. By the time anyone saw it, it would have been too late to make it down the stairs. There's no telling how long everyone would have lain there breathing it in. But you all could have missed the next contest. Maybe the kitchen staff would have figured out something was wrong at breakfast."

"Who did it?" Erec asked, sounding like he had gravel in his throat.

"We think it was a prank. Probably some kids who lost the last contest," Dr. Mumbai said.

Bethany rolled her eyes. "Or the same people who sabotaged us after the other contests."

Dr. Mumbai looked concerned. "Don't you think that's a little . . . paranoid?"

"I would believe it," said Hecate Jekyll. "Something's afoul. I worry something . . . worse could happen if everyone's not careful. Who knows what vicious person is behind this? Anyone who stays here is a fool. Better to be alive than trying to be king or queen." She marched to the door. "I better start King Piter's dinner."

Dr. Mumbai smiled patiently as the cook left. "She shouldn't worry you. I'm sure we'll catch the culprits soon. Anyway, this boy needs sleep. Time to clear out."

Erec lifted his head. "I'm fine. I want to go to my room."

Dr. Mumbai put her hands on her hips. "The dormitories are being aired out for three more hours, mister. And you're sleeping *here* tonight, where I can keep my eye on you."

Erec sighed, exhausted. If the place was being aired out, that meant no one would find his ingredients. He knew, though, he'd have to mix them as soon as possible. Whoever was trying to poison the contestants had to be stopped.

CHAPTER FIFTEEN
A Bubbling Brew

EREC AWOKE IN the morning and pulled his curtains
back. "Can I go now?"

Dr. Mumbai checked his temperature and pulse
and listened to his chest. "All right, hero. First, though,
eat some breakfast. You should be hungry."

Erec stood, legs weak. "Today's Wednesday?" Dr. Mumbai nodded.
"Will I have my strength back for the fourth contest tomorrow?"

"I suspect you'll be fine after a little nectar and ambrosia."

Erec felt much better after eating three times as much as usual. Once he was back at the dormitory, he fed and played with Wolfboy until Oscar and Jack were gone, and then he looked under his bed. The formula ingredients seemed okay.

Quietly, he pushed a chair against his door. Then he put his glasses on. His mother was sitting in her rocking chair. "Mom?" he whispered.

As usual, June jumped. "Erec? I've been so worried about you."

He noticed puffy dark circles under her eyes. "Are you okay?"

"I'm fine. Just tired of being here, that's all. Did you get any more ingredients?"

"I got all of them. The used horseshoe is from a dragon horse. Is that okay?"

June looked surprised. "Even better. But how did you get it?"

"I lied to it." No use worrying her about Balor. "So, what do I do now?"

She was pleased with him, he could tell. "Get a big glass jar," she said. "That will work as well as digging a pit. Put all the ingredients together at midnight, carefully, at a crossroads in the agora or in town. Make sure nobody sees you.

"Put the nitrowisherine in last, and wish out loud to blast me free. Stir it, then close your eyes, wave your hands over it, and chant, 'Bubwa, bubwa toiwet twubwa. Codewon boon ad codewon bubwa.' Carry it back *carefully*. It will be very powerful."

Erec wrote the chant with her help. "How do I measure three cups of grain alcohol?"

"It doesn't have to be exact. Cup your hands; that will be close enough. A heaping handful is about a cup of gunpowder or wolfsbane."

Erec told his mother about the swamp gas, and she shook her head. "I can't wait to get out of here. The formula needs to brew for

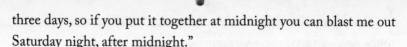

three days, so if you put it together at midnight you can blast me out Saturday night, after midnight."

"Three more days, then you're out, Mom!"

She looked upset. "I'm sorry about erasing everyone's memory of you. It was wrong. I just didn't know what to do." She sniffed. "I was afraid you weren't coming back."

Erec felt sorry he had ever been angry at her. "It's okay, Mom. I'm not mad anymore. Just don't do it to my friends from Alypium, okay?"

June's face relaxed. "I promise. How are the contests going?"

"Fine. The fourth one is tomorrow. It's Queen Posey's Sea Search."

"You'll do great. Tell me all about it."

Erec and Bethany walked with Wolfboy and Cutie Pie into the gardens. Cutie Pie chased the leaping lizards, howling and screeching as they got away.

Bethany frowned. "We can't wait much longer. I'll tell Queen Posey about Ugry with or without you."

Erec didn't want to talk about it, even if Queen Posey could help. What if she called the contests off? He would never win a scepter. Its feeling of power had stayed with him, deep down. When he realized what he was thinking, though, he was ashamed.

Still, Queen Posey would tell somebody else about the armory, very possibly King Pluto. Ugry would find out, and Erec and Bethany would be goners. "Bethany, think it through. King Pluto would know we knew."

"Maybe he's a good guy. We have no proof he's helping Ugry."

"Except for the small fact that my mother is in his dungeon." Erec kicked a clump of spinning daisies, and their bright tops whirled into the air.

Bethany rubbed Wolfboy's head. "Um . . . didn't you wonder the other day if maybe she was there because she had done something wrong? Didn't you think maybe she stole money? Or tried to kidnap the triplets?"

Of course. Erec wondered at himself. He obviously didn't want to think about it, but there it was. He did not know how his mother figured into things. Of course she *said* she was innocent and Erec wanted to believe her. But still, why would King Pluto want to destroy his own kingdom? Maybe he wasn't helping Ugry after all.

"Okay," he said. "Let's tell Queen Posey after the contest tomorrow. I guess it's our only choice." At least they would get to do one more contest before being thrown out of Alypium . . . or worse.

Only forty kids were left out of the original six hundred. Winning was starting to feel really possible. And maybe, even if Queen Posey found out about the armory, the contests would still go on and Erec could win a scepter. If only he could feel that power again! To use it at will and command all that magic. To be king. To right all wrongs and stop the Ugrys and the Raysons. And maybe even hang Balor upside down in the air. Yes, that too.

"My mom says someone might be hiding King Piter's scepter. If we found it, maybe I could use it to help us."

"Nobody can use his scepter except him, remember?"

"But I could. I used King Pluto's."

"That doesn't mean you could use King Piter's."

"Ugry must be able to since he wants them all."

"Maybe he can only use them after they're given to the next kings," said Bethany. "Maybe they have spells on them now. Who knows?"

"I still think we should look for it. It might help us find out who is hypnotizing the king."

Cutie Pie leapt on Bethany's shoulder and whispered in her ear, a paw in front of her mouth. Bethany giggled. "She's talking again." Cutie Pie whispered more. "She saw some boys making bombs behind the bushes. Let's go see."

They peeked through the shrubs. Balor, Damon, Rock, and Ward were mixing ingredients and setting off small explosions.

"This won't be enough," Rock complained.

"It will when it's magnified by a thousand," said Balor.

Erec and Bethany turned to each other. What were they planning? Cutie Pie stalked back toward the fountains, tail high.

After lunch, Erec and Bethany went to the west wing. Erec had his Sneakers on, and they had vanishing caps in their pockets. "You should stay out here," Erec said. "No need for both of us to risk getting caught. You can distract Ugry if he comes by."

"You know," Bethany said, "if Ugry sees you, Kilroy won't help you this time."

Erec nodded because he knew she was right.

"I hope you find the scepter."

"Me too."

Erec put on his vanishing cap and darted past the guard. He had already decided what to say. If he saw Ugry he would whip the cap off and pretend he had been looking for him to tell him about Balor's bomb.

Running was smooth and noiseless with the Sneakers. They only sent sound elsewhere if Erec stamped hard. He was glad when he spotted Kilroy walking down a hallway with coffee and cookies on a tray. He would probably lead the way to King Piter.

As he came closer, Kilroy tripped, and coffee splashed over the mug onto the tray. The splashed liquid hissed, and smoke rose, smelling like rotten eggs. Was that what they were serving to the king? Kilroy went into a room, and Erec darted in after him. King Piter was sitting in front of a crackling fire on an ornate, cushioned chair. His long gray hair and white beard hung limp around his face. He looked up, confused.

"It's okay, King Piter," Kilroy said. "Drink your coffee. You will feel better, I promise." The king made a face. "Now, your majesty," said Kilroy. "Be a big boy. Drink up." The king shook his head. Kilroy reached, but before he could take the cup the king tipped it over. Coffee spilled all over the floor with a loud hiss, black smoke rising into the air. The smell was so horrible that Erec held his breath. He held back a cough so Kilroy wouldn't hear him.

Kilroy's face turned red. He smashed the cup into the fireplace. "Don't move. I'll be back with more coffee. You will drink it, even if I have to use the funnel." He stormed from the room and slammed the door.

A faint smile appeared on the king's face. When Erec realized nobody else was there, he coughed until he could breathe again. King Piter looked like he might fall asleep any minute.

Erec pulled off his cap. "King Piter?"

The king did not look surprised that Erec materialized before his eyes. Then again, he did not look awake enough to be surprised. He smiled lazily.

"King Piter, where is your scepter?"

The king raised his eyebrows and looked around as if he wasn't sure where he'd left it.

"Did somebody take it?"

The king looked around some more and relaxed into his chair, eyes half-closed.

"King Piter?" The king opened one eye. "I wouldn't drink that coffee if I were you." The king nodded and fell right to sleep.

Erec searched the room. No scepter. He looked in the broom closet and bathroom. Nothing. He put his cap on and snuck out of the room, shutting the door behind him.

Hallways upon hallways stretched through the west wing. How would Erec ever find something hidden there? He wasn't sure where to start.

Big double doors at the end of a hallway towered over others. That looked like a promising place to look. Erec slipped through the doors.

The room was massive. At the far end was a magnificent gold throne that stretched halfway to the thirty-foot ceiling. Gems studded its arms and back. In the center of its high back sat an enormous, round diamond, the size of an extra-large pizza. Ornate carvings and pearl inlays swirled in a language Erec had never seen.

A long, empty groove ran along the right arm. Erec had the feeling that the scepter fit into it perfectly. At the base of the throne was a big, rough, jagged stone. It looked oddly out of place amid the finery.

Yet the room was empty except for some humongous chandeliers, ornate draperies and tapestries, and pictures of kings and queens on the walls. The scepter wasn't there. Erec snuck out of the throne room, disappointed. He passed the Port-O-Door by the closet where he had found the sneakers. After looking through a few sitting rooms he gave up.

Back out of the west wing, Erec told Bethany about the strange coffee. She became upset. "Kilroy is poisoning the king. Maybe it was *him* whispering to Rayson in the armory."

"Are you kidding?" Erec asked. "Ugry hates the kids. I think he's trying to scare us away—now with swamp gas—so only Damon and his friends are left to win and he'll get the scepters. Kilroy seems like a good guy."

"We have no proof he's a good guy."

"He helped us when Ugry tried to send us home, when he caught us in the west wing."

Bethany did not look impressed. "Remember when we saw the men putting the minotaur in the maze?"

THE DRAGON'S EYE

"Yeah."

"Well, they said the king's AdviSeer told them to put it there. Kilroy is King Piter's AdviSeer, just like Ugry. Maybe it was him."

Erec shook his head. "I don't think so. Kilroy is so . . . nice." He shrugged. "I don't think I'll ever find the scepter here. It's probably locked in Ugry's safe." Erec stomped his foot in anger, making a crashing noise down the hallway in the west wing. The guard jumped and looked behind him, his remote control out. Bethany rolled her eyes.

"It doesn't matter," Erec said. "I still have my mother's ingredients."

Erec met Bethany at eleven-thirty that night by the dormitory entrance. They walked to the agora, carrying the formula ingredients and an extra glass jar. The night was quiet. A few people flew by on white winged horses, and others soared alone.

They walked down small, dark streets scattered with homes and pine groves, staying as far from other people as they could. The houses looked small in the dark, like log cabins.

"I wish I had a watch," Erec said. "How will we know when it's midnight?"

The answer came when a clock tower banged out twelve gonglike tones. They were at the crossroads of two small streets, where they were completely surrounded by trees, except for one small house far from the road.

"Do we put it together in the middle of the road?" Bethany asked.

"It couldn't hurt," Erec said. He had never seen cars in Alypium, only occasional buses, winged horses, and doors that appeared from nowhere. They put the wide-mouthed glass jar in the middle of the crossroads. Erec pulled out his list.

"Four handfuls of wolfsbane." He grabbed four clumps of the

fibrous roots, tore them up a bit, and stuffed them in the jar. "Two cups of gunpowder." He dumped two heaping handfuls onto the wolfsbane. "Three cups of grain alcohol." Bethany poured three times to fill Erec's cupped hands.

Erec found a stick and stirred the gunpowder and leaves into the clear liquid until it was thick and black. "Five drops of warthog essence." Erec carefully poured in the five drops he had measured in the storeroom. When it hit the liquid, there was a loud cracking sound and then a hiss. The liquid started to swirl in the jar.

"One eagle feather." Erec dropped the feather in, and it disappeared into the swirling mixture. "Three lion hairs." He carefully opened the vial and dropped in the three spiky brown hairs. A loud growl erupted as they churned in. "One used horseshoe." The dragon horse's shoe barely fit through the top and fell in with a splash. Foam and bubbles erupted through the formula. Hot steam shot from the opening.

Erec carefully picked up the nitrowisherine. "After this goes in, I'm supposed to wish for this to blast my mother free. Maybe you should wish too." Each drop that fell in sounded like a distant explosion as it hit the bubbling, swirling liquid. Erec closed his eyes and said, "I wish this formula will blast my mother free from her force field." Bethany repeated his words, saying, "his mother."

Erec stirred the bubbling brew and read from his paper. "Bubwa, bubwa toiwet twubwa. Codewon boon ad codewon bubwa."

A loud, hot blast pushed Erec and Bethany back. The jar flew into the air, landing on its bottom without spilling.

Lights switched on in the small house on the hill. Erec put a lid on the jar, picked it up carefully, and walked fast with Bethany back to the dormitories.

Erec slid the jar under his bed. If it got knocked over the whole dormitory would explode. He woke Wolfboy. "Look, boy. Nobody can touch this, okay? Guard it. It could blow us all up."

Wolfboy panted, tongue out. He turned in circles, dropped to the floor by Erec's bed, and fell asleep.

Erec didn't want to risk talking to his mother with Oscar and Jack in his room, even if they were asleep. He went to the bathroom, knowing it would be empty this late at night. He stood against the door, ready to take his glasses off if he felt it move.

"Mom, wake up," Erec whispered. June murmured in her sleep and turned over. "Wake up!"

She lifted her head. "Erec?"

"Sorry. I just wanted to tell you I made the blasting formula."

June smiled. "Great! Oh, I can't wait to get out of here. I think the easiest way here is through a Port-O-Door. I just wish King Piter could take care of things and get me out of here. Did you ever get an idea where his scepter is?"

"No," said Erec. "It could be anywhere."

"Did you look in the throne room?" June asked.

"I did. What's that big rock by the throne?"

June smiled. "That's the Lia Fail. Legend says the stone will shriek at the crowning of a rightful king. Of course, I was too young to remember Piter, Posey, and Pluto's ceremony, but my parents say it screamed three times that day. You'd better get to sleep. Good luck with the contest tomorrow."

Erec took the glasses off and fell asleep as soon as his head hit the pillow.

CHAPTER SIXTEEN
The Sea Search

A SMALL GROUP GATHERED behind the maze for the fourth contest. Kilroy looked disappointed by the turnout. "Only thirty-four today? Where are the other six?"

They had decided to go home after the swamp gas incident. A lot of spectators had left as well.

Ugry stood to the side. He looked paler than usual, the crease down his forehead seemed deeper, and he wore a particularly sour expression. Bethany whispered, "Remember, Rayson said they couldn't cheat at this one."

Kilroy cleared his throat. "These last three contests are special. A king or queen planned each one. This is Queen Posey's, the Sea Search. The next contest was planned by King Pluto, and the final one by King Piter."

Erec had the feeling that King Piter wasn't up to planning the final contest. He wondered if Kilroy had done it himself. Kids had brought magical items, as the queen allowed, many brandishing remote controls. Sneakers and Magiclights didn't seem like a help underwater, but Erec and Bethany had vanishing caps in their pockets. Hopefully Ugry wouldn't notice if they used them.

Queen Posey drew a circle of water around the competitors, herself, and Kilroy. In a flash, everybody was standing on a deserted beach. Cliffs overhung the water. Ugry followed a moment later.

Kilroy's good humor seemed to be back. "This will be great. You'll get to see ocean life up close! No masks or fins. Queen Posey will let you all breathe underwater. Your job is to find a hidden treasure chest. The fish and water sprites know where it is, as well as a few merfolk, if you happen to see one.

"You may *not* use magic to harm any sea creatures. The first twenty back with treasure from the chest will win."

Queen Posey said, "Hold hands in a circle." After some grumbling and shuffling, a circle was formed.

Erec reached for the hand next to him and was sorry to see that it was attached to Balor Stain. A slick smile spread across Balor's face. "Good luck, one-eye." Balor's cold hand clenched his until his fingers hurt.

The queen said, "Take a deep breath and go under. I will put a charm on you. It will let you breathe under the water, and also a few surprises, too. Do not come up until you are finished. Once you rise above the water, the spell will break."

Erec plunged under the water, shaking from the cold. Kids looked at each other under the water, cheeks full of air, wondering if they could let go of one another's hands. Erec wondered if the charm was working. He still felt cold and was more and more hungry for air. Everyone was looking around wildly. Erec wasn't sure which was worse—taking a breath of water or coming to the surface and blowing his chances.

Balor smiled, still gripping his hand. He looked like he was comfortably breathing the water. Erec's lungs burned. Some kids coughed under water. A few rose to the surface, more worried about drowning than losing.

Erec had to breathe. He sucked in water, prepared to choke. The liquid felt like cold air, so he automatically pulled in a deep breath. His chest stung, but he breathed fast and deep until he caught his breath, and then coughed as his body adjusted.

The ring of kids scattered. Erec let go of Bethany's hand. He tried to shake free from Balor's, but Balor gripped his hand harder and pushed him toward the surface.

Erec kicked the water, fighting his way back down. His left leg splashed into the air. He wondered if Queen Posey's spell would be undone, but, thankfully, he could still breathe water. He was sure if his head surfaced, he would lose. Balor grabbed his glasses, as if he might be able to take them underwater. Still he could not pull them higher than Erec's chin.

Erec twisted out of his grasp, but Balor grabbed his ankle and pushed him back to the surface. His icy blue eyes gleamed with hate. Erec's eyes met his and anger filled him. So what if Balor was powerful enough to hang him upside down in the air? Erec was not going to be afraid of an obnoxious bully. He remembered Balor picking on the maid in his room, making fun of Bethany, even bullying his own friends.

Erec snarled and dove at Balor, grabbing his neck. His legs pounded the water as he drove Balor down. Balor pulled a remote control from his pocket, but Erec grabbed it from his hand and snapped it in two against a rock. The pieces drifted into the coral reef below.

Balor's pale blue eyes widened in shock. "I'll get you, Rick Ross. You wait." His words were surprisingly clear in the water. Balor swam to his friends waiting nearby.

Erec hoped the fight with Balor didn't put him behind in the contest. Some kids, he saw, had gone through the surface and were still bobbing at the top. He found Bethany searching through the coral spikes that towered up from the reef. She laughed, and it sounded like bubbles. "You showed him. Maybe he'll lose now."

"He'll probably steal a remote control from a friend."

She did a somersault in the water. "I feel like I've swam my whole life. Maybe that was part of Queen Posey's spell."

The colors of the reef were spectacular. The coral glowed in yellows, pinks, and pale greens. Bright yellow fish with black stripes darted in and out of waving seaweed. Thin white fish that Erec could almost see through swam in huge schools around the coral beds. An eel darted under an anemone.

Kids overturned loose coral, dug the sand around the reef, and shuffled plant leaves. Nobody seemed to be finding anything. There was a lot of noise, which seemed odd. In fact, the reef sounded like a shopping mall at Christmastime.

A crowd gathered around Jack, who had the gift of speaking to animals. A large fish whispered into his ear about swimming conditions but would not say a word about the treasure.

The water was pleasant and warm from the sunshine. Although swimming felt nice, nobody was having any luck. Erec wondered why the kids with remote controls couldn't make the treasure appear.

Maybe they had to know what it looked like first or where it was.

"I'm hungry," Bethany said.

"Do you like sushi?" Erec laughed.

Just then, angry shouts and curses filled the water. The fish around Erec darted away.

Erec realized what had happened. The talking had been from the fish themselves. Understanding fish must have been one of Queen Posey's surprises.

Others were catching on too. A group gathered around a blue fish with yellow fins. Bethany found a school of orange and yellow striped fish diving through holes in the reef. "Um, excuse me? Fishies?" she said.

Seven beaked noses pointed at her. "She can talk!" one squeaked. "Amazing!" The fish swam uncomfortably close to Erec and Bethany's faces.

"Have you seen any treasure chests around?" Erec asked.

Seven voices babbled at once. "Do you have food?" "He can talk!" "Food? Food?" "Food!"

They swam closer, almost touching Erec's face, shouting, "Food? Food?" until one nipped Erec's nose. Erec swam away, his feet kicking at fish in all directions.

Melody swam away from a silvery fish, her brown legs kicking her closer to Erec and Bethany. She shook her head. "It just talks about what it likes to eat, which smaller fish, worms. Maybe it'll tell us more if we feed it."

Kids scoured the reef floor for fish food, yet smaller fish were impossible to grab, and no worms were in sight. Erec turned his face from side to side so he wouldn't miss anything with his one good eye.

Schools of fish swarmed around Balor, Damon, Ward, and Rock, whose hands overflowed with fish food at the edge of the reef. When the food was gone, Balor pointed a remote control at their hands, and they filled again. The four were hard to see through the swarming mass. Different fish swam by their ears as if telling them something.

Soon, Balor and his friends dove below the reef, where it dropped off into the ocean. Some kids followed them. Other kids with remote controls made fish food and feeding frenzies. Soon fish whispered in their ears as well.

Erec got close enough to a fish feast that some of the fish must have thought he was feeding them too. A yellow fish that looked huge from the side, but very thin from the front, swam to his ear. "Dive deep under the reef. The water sprites might help you."

By that time most of the kids had followed Balor and his friends under the reef. Balor seemed to be winning even without his usual outside help.

The water was dark under the reef. A few sunny rays streamed through holes in the coral like spotlights. The water was colder, but Erec still felt comfortable. He was surprised how deep the water was. Long caverns shot under the coral. A cold, slimy hand touched his arm and he jumped . . . but it was only seaweed reaching from the reef. In the shadows Erec could see kids searching, but he saw nothing that looked like a water sprite, whatever that was.

Gold flashed nearby. Hoping it was the treasure, Erec dove after it. A shining gold circle or coin sparkled through the water ahead of him. It was just out of reach. If only he got a little closer, he could grab it. Erec followed it into a deep underwater cave.

He looked back, wondering if he was going too deep, but the flash of gold glinted from the corner of his eye. It was irresistible. Erec followed it deeper, forgetting his worries. Something told him the gold meant treasure. Maybe not just for this contest, but other treasure beyond his wildest dreams.

Before he rounded a corner, something yanked his foot, jerking him backward. Confused, he turned to see Bethany tugging him.

"What are you doing?" Bethany said, upset. Erec wondered what was wrong with her. He felt a little confused. The gold glittered in the corner of his eye, and he turned to follow it. Of course: She was jealous because he'd found the treasure.

She yanked his foot harder. "Are you crazy? Let's get out of here!"

Erec tried to kick her away, but Bethany seemed possessed. Sure she wanted the treasure for herself, he struggled, but Bethany had a grip on some coral, and yanked him from the glinting gold. He twisted and kicked some more, until Bethany pinched him hard on the leg.

"Oww. Why did you do that?"

"Because you're *bewitched*! You're following an ugly sea monster into its cave!"

Erec turned in horror to see a huge black shape with tentacles waving where his gold glint was, slinking deeper into the rocks. He gritted his teeth. "Ugh. Thanks." He hoped it was too dark for Bethany to see how red his face was.

Deep caverns shot under the murky coral of the reef. A dozen water sprites, in dresses of woven algae, darted through the water. They were smaller than Erec but could have been any age. Long seaweedlike hair of blues and greens waved over their pale blue skin, but their eyes sparkled and their faces lit with laughter, especially when they were teasing the kids. Swimming close, they acted like they had something to say, but dove away laughing. They hid in rocks and coral, springing out in front of unsuspecting souls to make them jump. It seemed they never stopped giggling. Catching a water sprite seemed impossible. The harder Erec tried, the faster they slipped away, taunting and laughing. Bethany and Melody cornered one against some coral. They lunged, and she shot straight down, letting them crash into each other, bumping heads. Sprites spun like otters, grabbing the hands of contestants before diving away, laughing. The kids bargained and pleaded for the sprites to tell them where the treasure was, but the sprites seemed to think the whole matter was a joke.

A sprite wrapped a thin blue arm around Erec and Bethany's shoulders. "Have fun with the sea monster?" she asked. "Did you think you were going to get rich?" Her voice tinkled like bells.

Erec eyed her sourly. "I bet *you* know where the treasure is."

The sprite giggled. "Of course. But you never will." She looked away, ready to go tease someone else.

Bethany said, "Tell us. We want to win this . . . before some bad kids do."

The sprite threw her a sharp look. "Why *should* I?" She swam away.

Erec shook his head. This seemed hopeless. Bethany stared into the ocean, brows knit. A smile started to curl on her lips. Erec looked toward where she stared, but nothing was there. He wondered if a sea monster was putting her under a spell.

She flashed him a grin. "I've got it! She gave us a clue—"

Before she could finish, high-pitched shrieks filled their ears. Not far away, a water sprite was bound tight with thick ropelike seaweed. Balor pointed a remote control at her and the seaweed tightened with a jerk. The sprite screamed in pain. Her angry friends tried tugging the seaweed off her without success.

Balor cackled. "Who's laughing now?" The sprite stuck her lip out and struggled against her chains. "It's okay, water lily, just tell old Balor here where the treasure is and you're free as a fish."

The water sprite looked steaming mad. She nodded for him to come closer and whispered in his ear.

Balor laughed with glee and swam off into a tunnel hidden by seaweed, leaving her trapped in her seaweed prison. Damon gave her flowing blue hair a tug as he swam by.

"You idiots." Ward aimed his remote and set the sprite free. He pointed at the sprite. "Next time don't play stupid games with me and my friends." He disappeared into the tunnel after Balor, Damon, and Rock.

The water sprite dusted herself off with a good-riddance look on her face. She had red marks on her arms and legs.

Eight or nine kids followed Balor's friends into the tunnel. Erec asked Bethany, "What do you think? Should we follow them in?"

"No way. Those sprites aren't dumb. That one gave us a clue."

"What clue? Did I miss it?"

"When we asked her to tell us where the treasure was, she said, 'Why should I?' That was a great clue!"

Erec looked at her with an eyebrow raised. "You think so?"

Bethany crossed her arms. "What got the fish to help us?"

"Feeding them."

Bethany signaled *keep going* with her hands.

"We're playing charades now?"

Bethany rolled her eyes. "Okay. The fish helped us when we helped them. I think it's the same for the water sprites. We need to give *them* something so they'll help *us*."

Erec put out his hands and gestured all around. "And what can we give them? Seaweed? Water? We have no sprite food in our pockets."

Bethany grinned. "That's it! Great idea!" She whipped her vanishing cap from her pocket. "They'll like these, I bet. Maybe that's why we were allowed to take magical items here."

Erec was astounded. "You would give them your vanishing cap? They'll love it all right. They'll laugh and take it, and we'll be no better off than we were before."

"It's our only chance. I think that sprite wants us to win."

A few kids with remote controls took cues from Balor and were trying to poke or club the sprites, or even capture them. None had Balor's success, but the sprites grudgingly pointed them to the same tunnel. Others kids continued to beg and cajole without luck.

Erec had a funny feeling that Bethany was right. The sprites seemed too ready to point the annoying kids toward Balor's tunnel, and the other kids were getting nowhere. He pulled his vanishing cap from his pocket.

The sprites were no longer playful and laughing after Balor hurt their friend. They seemed less helpful, if possible, than before. Still, Bethany and Erec waved two sprites over. The sprites put their hands on their hips and looked at them expectantly.

Bethany waved her cap. "Watch." She put it on and disappeared, then reappeared with it in her hand. The sprites laughed in delight. "Do you want it?" A sprite grabbed it from her hand. Bethany signaled to Erec. "They deserve these after what they've gone through today anyway."

Erec held his cap out and the other sprite whisked it away. They put the caps on and vanished. "Oh well." Erec shrugged. "You're right. They deserve them. We had them long enough."

In a flash, the sprites reappeared, caps in hand. Over the next few minutes they disappeared and reappeared continuously. Then the pleased sprites beckoned them to follow as they dove deep under the coral.

The sprites plunged around a narrow bend and pointed up to a hole where twenty keys were embedded deep in rose coral. Words were chiseled above the keys. The sprites waved and swam away, putting on their caps and disappearing in a flash.

"I wonder where Balor's tunnel led. You don't think it led to the sea monster, do you?"

Bethany looked worried. "I'm sure Queen Posey wouldn't want anyone getting hurt. Contestants are supposed to be eliminated, not killed."

"Those water sprites were pretty mad, though. Maybe they have their own plan."

Words neatly engraved in the coral read, "Answer this riddle: Why can you always depend on the queen?" Below it were carved these words:

I TIDE MY SHOE, IT FITS ME WELL,
SO I'LL REEF THE EXPENSIVE THING ON,
BECAUSE I STUBBED MY UNDERTOW,
BUT NOW ALL MY SAND DOLLARS ARE GONE.

IT'S COLD TROUTSIDE AND YOU'RE HUNGRY, DEAR,
BUT, BEACH YOUR LIFE, WE'LL HAVE FUN.
BEFORE YOUR KINDNESS EBBS AWAY,
SHARE MY WARM FIRE AND CURRENT BUN.

ONLY YOUR FRIEND, NOT YOUR ANEMONE, WILL SAY:
YOUR UNDERWATER'S SHOWING OVER YOUR PANTS.
I SEA YOU WEAR RUFFLY BLUE ONES,
LIKE THE EMPEROR PENGUIN OF FRANCE.

WE WAVE HELLO, AND THEN GOOD-BYE,
ICE SEE YOU ARE ALMOST DONE.
GAZE UP TO THE TWINKLING, STARFISH SKY,
OR EELS YOU WON'T NOTICE—YOU'VE WON!

Erec stared in silence. How could he solve a puzzle from a crazy poem?

Bethany's eyebrows knit. "Five thousand, two hundred fifty six . . . no, that can't work. Ugh." She crossed her arms. "I've tried about every function. Nothing seems to work. Maybe if the letter A is a derivative of pi only when there are no other vowels in the word, then B could be related to the linear root of its integral—"

"Bethany, this can't be that complicated. I mean, everyone has to have a shot at this, right?"

She shrugged, looking disappointed.

Erec laughed. "It's pretty funny, actually: the 'ruffly blue underwater showing over your pants.' Each line has a play on words about the ocean. Look: tide, reef, undertow, sand dollars, trout, beach . . ."

Bethany grinned. "Ebbs, current, anemone, underwater, sea, Emperor Penguin, wave, ice, starfish, and eels. That's easy. The first letters spell out 'trust because wise.' That's why you can depend on Queen Posey. Trust her because she's wise."

With a creak, the coral wedged open. Two keys slid onto a ledge. They took the keys and swam through the hole into what looked like a room with coral walls, floor and ceiling. Sunlight streamed through so many holes above that it looked like a disco.

In the middle of the room sat a black chest with gold buckles. A thick yellow sea serpent with big eyes and sharp teeth was coiled on top of it. Its jaws were wide enough to snap off a hand. "I hope he's supposed to be here," Bethany whispered.

Erec and Bethany slowly approached the serpent. "We have keys," Bethany said.

The serpent hissed, "Put them in my mouth if you want the treasure."

Bethany's hand shook as she dropped the key into its jaws. He gulped and opened his mouth for Erec's key. "Uncle Earl doesn't seem so scary anymore," Bethany said with a laugh.

Erec dropped his key into its mouth from as far as he could. The serpent swallowed and slid off the chest. Inside the heavy lid were twenty black bags. Erec and Bethany each took one and shut the chest. The serpent slid back on top and hissed.

In the bags were six plastic packets and a note. "INSTAGILLS. Instructions: Choose a location on your body, three gills on each side. Place the marked edge of the packet against your skin and squeeze. Gill will permanently enter skin. It is advisable that the location not be covered with clothing to ensure ease of breathing. Must be done in water immediately. Instagills close automatically when out of water to allow for immediate lung breathing. Open each time you are in water. Guaranteed for life."

Erec looked at Bethany. "This is great. Where should we put them? On our face like Queen Posey?"

Bethany looked worried. "I hope they don't scar too much. I'll put mine on my back."

"They'll be covered up. What if you're in water someday with a shirt on? Like now? I'm putting mine on my wrists." Erec held a packet to his wrist and squeezed it. For a moment he felt a pinch, and then a gill in his wrist opened and shut. "Look at that!" Erec put three gills into each wrist and stared at them moving in the water.

Bethany held a packet in her hand with a disgusted look. "I don't really need these."

"Come on. They'll close on land. Just think: You'll be able to always explore underwater like this. You have to put them in."

Bethany cringed and squeezed a gill into her palm. "Ow!" She shook her wrist and put the rest in, three in each hand. "Do you think we'll always be able to understand the sea creatures?"

Apparently, the sea serpent had been listening. "Everyone knows humans can't talk. You'll be back to your dumb selves after the queen's spell wears off."

"That was nice," Bethany said to Erec.

"Let's go." He swam out of the hole with her behind him. They brought their empty bags to the surface.

All eyes turned to Erec and Bethany when they splashed to the surface. The six kids who had risen to the surface early had given up and were sitting by the shore. Erec looked at his wrists. The gills had closed and left thin black lines.

Immediately, he was starving and freezing. Bethany's teeth were chattering. As they walked to shore, Queen Posey rose. "You found the treasure?" She examined the gill lines on their wrists and hands. With a wink from Queen Posey, they became instantly dry. The front of Erec's hair was straighter and the back curlier after being wet for so long.

Kilroy clapped them on their backs. "The first two winners! You came in at a tie at four hours and fifteen minutes."

Four hours? No wonder they were hungry. Bethany saw a snack table on the beach and ran for it. Erec followed, realizing they had missed lunch. They gobbled down sandwiches, fruit, cookies, and nectar until they felt better.

He and Bethany waded in the water and then rested in the sand with the others while they waited. They practiced putting their hands and wrists under the water and breathing through their Instagills. It worked without effort.

After a few hours, it seemed like nobody else was coming back. "Maybe we should tell Queen Posey about the sea monster. What if they were eaten?" Bethany said. "And there is something else we need to tell her too." She looked knowingly at Erec.

"What?" Erec was ready to fall asleep in the sand. The sun was hot and it had been a long day.

"You know."

Erec waved off that idea. "Ugry is here. We can't tell her now."

"As soon as we can, then." Bethany talked to Queen Posey for a moment and came back to where Erec was sitting. "I told her the water sprites might have sent some kids to a sea monster, but she said they wouldn't hurt anybody. She said in an hour the time would be up, more winners or not."

Erec picked his head off the sand. "Then we'd be the only winners?"

"Uh-huh!" Bethany grinned.

"We'll be king and queen!" Erec whispered. "I wonder how they'll pick the third one. I bet they'll give it to Balor since Ugry wants him in," he said, glancing at Ugry across the sand. The sun hadn't touched his pale appearance.

"And we'll have two scepters, so Ugry won't be able to take over for sure," Bethany said. "I told the queen we had something important to tell her, in secret. She said we'd talk after the contest."

Erec let the cool water run over his toes while Bethany ate cookies and drew math formulas in the sand. She raced to see how much she could calculate before the waves washed her work away.

Erec's nose stung from sunburn. He wished he had a watch. It felt close to dinnertime.

Queen Posey threw the book she was reading into the air and it vanished. "That's it." She dove into the water and returned pulling a huge bamboo raft filled with contestants. Melody and Jack waved from it with glum looks on their faces. Balor and his friends were not among them.

Queen Posey dove again, this time returning with Balor and the kids who had followed him into the tunnel. They yawned, stretched, and rubbed their eyes as if waking from a deep sleep.

Balor's dream must have been a nightmare, for he was in a foul mood. "I'm not done. This isn't fair. I demand a rematch."

Queen Posey said to Kilroy, "These kids found the sirens." Kilroy

THE DRAGON'S EYE

counted fifteen in their group, who mostly dropped onto the sand to slowly wake up.

"What sirens? I didn't hear anything," Erec said.

Melody laughed. "Sirens are sea creatures that lull people to sleep with their songs. I guess those guys would have slept forever if Queen Posey hadn't rescued them."

Kilroy, Ugry, and Queen Posey discussed the results away from the kids. "This is it," Erec whispered. "It's you and me, King and Queen. I call Alypium."

"Forget it," she said, giggling. "You get Ashona. I can tell you liked it down there."

Ugry and Kilroy argued fiercely, and Queen Posey did not look happy. Erec snuck closer and heard Kilroy say, "I called King Piter on my cell." He held up his finger. "You know I'm the one he talks to." Queen Posey saw Erec and Bethany nearby and shooed them away. Ugry was in a rage.

Finally, Kilroy announced, "We have decided who will advance to the fifth contest." He glanced at the queen. "It was a very difficult decision. We have two definite winners." He gestured toward Erec and Bethany. "We have a group that found the sirens"—he held a paper in one hand—"and a group that didn't find anything." He held a sheet in his other hand. "It was a very . . . tough . . . choice, but the group who found the sirens will be admitted into the next contest because at least they found *something*."

There were groans and curses, as well as cheers and whoops. Jack flopped into the sand and Melody buried her face in her hands. It wasn't clear which of the judges had arranged this solution. All three looked upset.

Erec flew to Kilroy. "You can't let that group win. They were sent to the sirens because they were attacking the water sprites. They would have lost for sure if there was enough time."

Kilroy held up a hand. "I'm sorry. There will be no more discussion. I couldn't change this, believe me." Frowning, he looked at the queen and Ugry and then faced the group. "There will be seventeen of you in the fifth contest, which was devised by King Pluto. It's called the Under Mine. That will be in four days. Monday morning at ten, behind the maze."

Queen Posey drew a line of water in the sand around everyone, and suddenly they were all transported behind the maze. It was getting dark and Erec was hungry. He trudged to the cafeteria with Melody, Jack, and Bethany.

Jack shrugged. "It had to happen sometime. What are the odds I'd win? I'm just glad I got as far as I did."

"Me too," said Melody.

"It's not fair!" said Bethany. "You both should have won. Balor and his gang were sent to the sirens so they would lose."

Jack remained cheerful. "You two will just have to try even harder and win for us."

Bethany didn't see it that way, though. "Now we'll be competing against all the meanies with no morals who go around hurting water sprites." She stopped when she felt a hand on her shoulder. Queen Posey was behind them.

"You wanted to tell me something?" The queen looked tired, but Erec wasn't sure if that was because of the gill lines under her eyes. Melody and Jack waved and went into the dormitories.

Bethany nodded. "Erec and I were exploring the castle, and we wandered into the armory. It was almost empty. Then we heard voices and hid. Two people came in, and one definitely was Stoney Rayson. The other voice was harder to tell, but we think it was Balthazar Ugry. They were stealing weapons from the armories. They said when 'their three' won the contests, they would take the scepters and . . . what did they say . . . 'lay siege' to Alypium, Aorth, and Ashona."

Queen Posey shook her head. "That's crazy. I don't believe this kind of talk."

"Go look at the armory," said Bethany. "It's empty. We're telling the truth."

The queen didn't answer. In the silence Erec heard a faint hum from her scepter. He pointed at it. "Does it talk to you?" he asked.

Queen Posey looked up, surprised. "Yes, sometimes. Only when it has something to say."

Erec remembered King Pluto's scepter talking to him, although it was a little rude. "What is it saying now?"

She laughed with a twisted smile. "That you might be telling the truth." She looked hard at Erec, studying him now. "I don't know about you. It's strange. There's something about your eyes. Anyway, thank you for coming to me. I'll look into this immediately."

"Um, Queen Posey?" Erec said.

"Yes? What is it?"

"Do scepters talk to other people too?"

"No," she said. "Only the king or queen. Except in the coronation ceremony. They talk out loud then, if I remember correctly."

The queen wagged a finger and vanished. Erec and Bethany were left to wonder if she'd do anything, or if she could.

Erec said, "I hope she's not hooked up with Ugry."

CHAPTER SEVENTEEN
A Burl Wood Arm

IT WAS FRIDAY morning. The force field–blasting formula would be ready midnight tomorrow. Then the fifth contest, King Pluto's Under Mine, was soon after. Jack and Oscar were staying for the final contests. After they left for breakfast, Erec put on his glasses.

He found June sitting on her bed, crying.

"Mom? Are you okay?"

She quickly blotted her face with a handkerchief. "I'm fine. Of

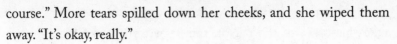

course." More tears spilled down her cheeks, and she wiped them away. "It's okay, really."

"What happened?"

"Nothing. I just . . . changed my mind, that's all. You can't come rescue me. It's too dangerous. I'll get out eventually . . . I'm sure. You have an important job *there*. How did the fourth contest go?"

"I won," he told her. "Mom, I don't understand. I'm coming Saturday at midnight."

"You can't."

"Of course I can. The blasting formula is brewing under my bed. There's a Port-O-Door in the west wing. You'll be out soon."

June laughed with red eyes. "I've been so stupid. I was so focused on getting out of here I put you in danger. Blasting solution under your bed. What if it got kicked over? Get rid of it, Erec. Forget saving me. It can't be done." June squeezed her eyes shut tight.

"But what about little Zoey, Trevor and Nell, and the twins?"

Tears poured from June's eyes, and she couldn't stop.

"Mom, I'm getting you out. You can't stop me."

June looked around in fear. "Please, Erec. Don't. I knew it would be difficult for you to get through the dungeons, but I just found out exactly how hard it would be. I should have figured King Pluto would have more than guards, bronze ghosts, and silver ghosts patrolling here, but that's all I ever saw. I just found out it's much worse."

"How much worse?"

June took a deep breath. "He has destroyers." Her voice fell to a whisper. "And shadow demons."

She looked so alone. Erec wished he were with her. "What are destroyers?"

"Hideous stone monsters that kill people."

"And shadow demons?"

June glanced around her room. "I happen to know a lot about

shadow demons. They can look like anything, but they like to take the shape of the person they're with. It's like looking in a mirror. They can read your worst fears like a brochure of your soul. Your doubts and misguided desires guide them into your mind. They talk to you, reason, make sense, but they connect with your shadow side. They loosen your resolve, steer you the wrong way. And when they win you over, they devour you, and you die. Any other questions?" June flopped back in her bed and put her arm over her eyes.

"Well," said Erec, "I just won't let them get to me. I'm pretty stubborn, you know."

June chuckled under her arm. "So am I. Forget it."

"No, really. I'm sure if I was prepared I could beat the shadow demons. I'm not letting you rot in there."

"Don't forget the destroyers, Erec. You'd be lucky to get far enough to see a shadow demon."

"There has to be a way to get through them," Erec said. "What can destroy stone? A jackhammer? A sandblaster?"

"There is a trick, but it can't be safe."

"What is it?"

"I don't know. I don't want you to get foolish ideas and try to come in here. You can help me better there. Win the next two contests. Become king and then get me out." She waved him away.

"What if I don't win? There's no guarantee."

"You have a good chance. I've seen you in tough situations. You usually know how to react."

"Good. Then I should be able to get you out of there. All I need is a little stubbornness."

June rolled over and sat up. "Stubborn you are. Do you really think I'll let you come here and risk your life?"

"It's not really your choice, is it? The formula is ready tomorrow night. I'm figuring out how to do it. I need a mother, and so do my brothers and sisters."

"Erec, you could die."

"I'll be fine, Mom. I've learned a lot here. I've rescued kids from swamp gas, fought a minotaur. I even used King Pluto's scepter to save everyone from a huge boulder. I can do it."

June covered her face with her hands. "Your life is more important than you know."

"Got it covered, Mom."

Bethany sat with Melody, Jack, and Oscar at lunch. Jack and Melody were in a surprisingly good mood for having just lost the Sea Search.

"Melody said she'd stay for the fifth contest, or as long as you and I are in," said Bethany.

"You were the only two who really won the fourth contest," said Jack. "You guys have *my* bet."

"We're down to seventeen," Bethany said. "Our odds are 17.647 percent—that's three out of seventeen. Not too bad."

Oscar shook his head. "Put your seat belts on. You have stiff competition."

"We'll see about that." Erec smiled. Things were going great. Why shouldn't he win the contests *and* blast his mother out of her dungeon? He beat Balor underwater and broke his remote control. Nothing would stop him now. Not even destroyers and shadow demons. Which reminded him, he had to find out more about what they could do.

After lunch, Erec and Bethany walked to the library. "Are you sure you want to go into Pluto's dungeons?" Bethany said. "They sound dangerous."

"I can't let my mother rot in that place. I just need to learn about destroyers and shadow demons. There has to be a way to get by them."

A wide spiral staircase ran up the many levels of the library tower. A librarian with wide granny glasses was happy to point them to the third floor, where the books on beasts were kept. "But the books must stay here."

They browsed through subheadings such as "Misunderstood Monsters" and "The Strange Animals of Upper Earth" until they found the section labeled "Dungeon Creatures." They carried armfuls of books to a table. Bethany picked up *The Total Loser's Guide to Escaping Dungeons*.

"There are sections about different famous dungeons. Listen: 'The outer dungeons in King Pluto's castles are famous for their acid rock walls. They melt whatever they touch, including flesh.'"

Erec took a breath. "Do the walls close in on people?"

"No. But this says destroyers live in them, and they come out of the walls."

She flipped pages. "Port-O-Doors will only go into the outer dungeons. Most prisoners are in the inner dungeons. The doors could open in the middle of an acid rock wall, or even into a destroyer's nook or a prisoner's cell, and anything there could come right through the door. You're supposed to try at least three locations before you pick one to walk through. And once you're in, finding the inner dungeons can be hard. The outer dungeons weave through the inner ones."

Erec looked through *In the Face of the Shadow Demons: A Survivor's Story*. It was a slow, dry book by a man who prepared his whole life to confront a shadow demon that blocked the way to his family's stolen fortune. The first chapters were about his strict diet and yoga training.

Bethany read *Destroying Destroyers: The Paper Chase*. Her face grew pale. "These things are disgusting. You don't want to do this, believe me."

"I have to, Bethany. It's my mom in there. What does it say?"

"Destroyers are made of stone, and their mouths drip with acid. They have no eyes or ears, but they have a strong sense of smell, which is harder to hide from. They live in the walls, but they come out when they smell anyone. Once they latch on to you, the acid eats through and digests you, leaving just your bones." She shivered.

"My mom said there was a trick to get by them."

Bethany flipped pages. "Paper. It seems pretty dangerous to me. You need lots of paper, cut into three-inch squares. A destroyer has a suction hole above its mouth. They continuously suck in air to smell what's around them. Paper can cover the hole. It confuses them. The smell overwhelms them, and they can't sense what's around them anymore."

"Doesn't the paper fall off?"

"No. The suction holds it there."

"Could something else work, like wood or plastic?"

Bethany read some more. "That could be too heavy and fall off, or crinkle and get sucked in."

"How do I get paper on their suction holes without them grabbing me?"

Bethany checked the book again. "The best way is with a wooden arm. You can reach them from far away."

"A what?"

"It says, 'wooden arms, the kind at your standard magic shop.'" She bit her lip. "You better get one soon so you'll have time to practice. You won't be able to make a single mistake."

Erec skimmed through chapters about consciousness-raising techniques and meditation sessions and finally put *In the Face of the Shadow Demons* down. He glanced through *Dungeons and Demons*, an equally dry book about self-awareness and internal motivation, and wondered what it had to do with dungeon monsters. He would have to find out what his mother knew about shadow demons, since she said she was something of an expert.

After hours of poring through books, learning a lot about destroyers and almost nothing about shadow demons, they walked Wolfboy and Cutie Pie to the agora. Cutie Pie had been quiet lately. Erec guessed there had been nobody to tell on. They bought the animals treats at the pet store, got nectar sundaes, and Erec bought loads of plain white paper.

Erec lay on the lawn by the fountains, watching Wolfboy chase butterflies. Bethany was asking kids where they could find a magic shop for the wooden arm. A shadow appeared over Erec. Behind him, King Pluto stood in a long ermine robe. It seemed he should be boiling hot, but he rubbed his arms, shivering.

Erec sat up. The king pounded his scepter into the dirt twice and two chairs sprang up. He sat on one and nodded for Erec to join him.

Erec's heart pounded. Queen Posey must have told him about the armory. He wondered if he was headed to King Pluto's dungeons sooner than he thought.

"Looking at my scepter? You were pretty impressive with the boulder the other day."

Erec shrugged.

"No, really. Not many people can use a king's scepter. Nobody, actually, except the king. You are quite an exceptional young man, aren't you, Erec Rex?"

Erec drew a sharp breath before he could stop himself. How did the king know his name? This was not good.

"Don't look so surprised," said the king, his voice oily. "It just took a tiny bit of research. You did sign yourself into Spartacus Kilroy's book as Erec Rex, did you not? You couldn't really be Erec Rex, could you? Then again, Posey told me about the interesting event with the Identdetector."

King Pluto leaned forward. "Let me see your eyes . . . ah, yes. Now tell me, where's your family?"

"Um . . ." Erec almost forgot his alibi. "Americorth South."

"Oh, interesting. Where in Americorth South? I go there all the time. I'd love to meet them."

Great. He was talking to the king of Aorth, trying to play off that he was from his kingdom. Erec's mother never mentioned parts of Americorth South. Erec thought he'd be safe and just say a street name, but he couldn't think of a good name. "Smith Street."

"Ah. The Ross family on Smith Street. What are their names?"

Erec wished he had thought up these details before. "Um, Sylvie and Scott." Friends of his mother's, the only names that sprang to mind.

"Sylvie and Scott Ross—or Rex?—on Smith Street. I'll call them tonight. I really should congratulate them on their outstanding son."

Erec stared between his knees at the grass. He could not believe how dumb he had been.

"Oh, by the way," said King Pluto, shivering, "Posey told me all about what you and your little friend overheard in the armory. I find it all *very* interesting. I told her I would take care of the situation immediately. Guess what I found out? The armory was being emptied for its annual cleaning!" King Pluto smiled at this innocent reason. "Rayson is a dunce. He makes up stories and even starts to believe them himself. Just ignore what he said. Everything is under control. Do you understand?"

Erec nodded quickly.

"Good. By the way, what were you doing in the armory?"

Erec cleared his throat. "Um . . . exploring, sir."

"Ah, yes. Exploring. Well, I wouldn't be caught exploring anywhere near the armory again if I were you. Someone might think you were the cause of any . . . trouble."

Erec nodded again.

"I'm glad we understand each other." The king winked. "It's really good to know that you are here, Erec." The king stood and waved his scepter. The chairs vanished, and Erec fell into the grass. "Time for a bath and a warm fire. This place is freezing." The sun shone hot on Erec's back, but he didn't say a word. "Good luck in the next contest."

It seemed that King Pluto was not sending him to the dungeons. At least not yet. Hopefully, when he found no Sylvie and Scott Ross on Smith Street, he wouldn't change his mind. But Erec had a funny feeling that the king wasn't expecting to find them.

As the day went on and King Pluto never reappeared, Erec felt more and more on top of the world. Nothing could go wrong now. Now that the weight was lifted off his back, he realized how worried he had been about Queen Posey telling King Pluto what they heard in the armory. It seemed silly now to even think the king would send him to the dungeons for overhearing a conversation.

Bethany wasn't happy, however. "It seems fishy. I wish Queen Posey were handling it herself. Should we talk to her again?"

"No! We did what we could. Let's not push our luck." Erec was sure a second visit from King Pluto would not go as well as the first. They walked through the castle gardens. Soon, Melody would be going shopping in the agora, so Erec could use their room to talk to his mother.

Erec felt a funny tingle on the right side of his face. It was barely noticeable, just a mild warmth, if anything. He glanced to his right. An intense gaze burned into his eyes. It seemed to penetrate into his mind, almost blinding him. The stare was so overwhelming he was not sure who it belonged to.

Erec finally focused on Spartacus Kilroy, who was carrying a tray of coffee and talking casually with Hecate Jekyll. Neither of them seemed to notice him. He shook his head. Maybe he had imagined it. A lot was going on in his mind today.

Bethany left Erec in her room. Melody was out. He put his glasses on. "Hi, Mom." June lay in bed, staring at the ceiling. "I bought a ton of paper at the agora."

"You did what?"

"Bought paper. I'll need it to get by the destroyers."

She put her head in her hand. "You don't understand, Erec. I can't lose you."

"And I can't lose you."

"How can I stop you from coming?"

"You can't. I'm fine. I've researched destroyers, and I'm going to practice and be ready before I come. I'm buying a wooden arm. I need you to tell me about the shadow demons, though. Will I run into one?"

"I'm sure if you came you would. They can sense what's happening around them."

"Are there many?"

"They work alone. Only one would approach you. If it won, you would die. If you defeated it, others would keep their distance because they know you won't cave in."

"So, how do I defeat one?"

June shook her head. "I need to think about this, Erec. You may not understand what you're getting yourself into."

Bethany went with Erec into town. Wolfboy and Cutie Pie tagged along. Medea's, a small, run-down magic shop with cracking deep red paint, sat on the edge of town. Before they walked inside, the door burst open. Balor, Damon, Rock, and Ward came out. Balor brandished a polished silver remote control.

"Well, look who's here." Balor grinned. "Rick Ross and his girlfriend. Rick *is* your name, isn't it?" The boys laughed. "I think you owe me a gold ring and three shires for this fine new remote control, seeing as how you broke mine in the last contest."

Erec wasn't scared of him anymore. "Forget it, Balor. That's the price you pay for trying to make me lose."

"Think you can't lose, Rick Erec Rex Ross?" He pointed his finger right in Erec's face. "Just wait until the next contest. You're history."

Erec shoved aside the finger. "Want this remote broken too, Balor?"

Balor narrowed his eyes at Erec and stuffed the remote into his pocket. "Just you wait." He walked down the street with his friends and stopped at the corner. The four stood there, looking at Erec and Bethany. Balor held his arm out, like he was staring at his watch.

"What are they up to?" Erec asked.

"I have an idea," Bethany said. "Cutie Pie can walk by them and she'll come back and tell me." She rubbed Cutie Pie's head. "It's great having a kitty that tells secrets." Cutie Pie jumped from her arms and slunk down the street toward the boys.

"Let's go in," Erec said.

Bethany looked to make sure Cutie Pie was okay and then screeched. "Let *go* of her!" She raced down the street. Balor was stuffing Cutie Pie into a bag and laughing.

"A cat that tells secrets is worth keeping," he shouted. He disappeared down a side street. By the time Bethany reached the corner, Balor and Cutie Pie were gone. Damon, Ward, and Rock were snickering.

"Trying to spy on us with a secret-telling cat?" Ward laughed.

Damon made a goofy face and said, "Blaaaah," with his tongue out.

Bethany ran back to Medea's, tears filling her eyes. "What if he hurts her?" The tears didn't fall, though. Instead, her face hardened with determination. "I'm getting her back if I have to break into his room." She sat in a corner with her arms crossed while Wolfboy nuzzled her feet.

The shop was small but packed with cases of remote controls, boxes of powders, vials of potions, and racks of magic clothing. Bright red and yellow tapestries covered the walls, rustling as though they hung in the wind. Tie-dyed cloths draped the ceiling. The lights that shone through them took on rainbow hues. In an opened box behind a glass case, a bloodshot, withered eye stared at Erec wherever he moved.

Erec jumped when a hand gripped his shoulder. It was an old woman with long white hair hanging loose. Her blue eyes sparkled through the wrinkles that made up her face. He wasn't sure if she was smiling or if that was just how her wrinkles hung.

The woman grabbed Erec's hand and studied his palm. "Oooh, it's you! It's about time," she said, giggling. "You're a tough one. Spirited. Nothing will keep you down. Just don't get too full of yourself. Be aware of who's around you. You must learn to trust others, but also which others to trust. The answers you need are without as well as within."

"Thanks," Erec said, uncomfortable. The woman kept staring at him. He wondered if she wanted money for the unasked advice, but then she shuffled behind the counter.

"Can I help you?"

"I need a wooden arm that can pick things up."

The woman nodded. "Of course. You'll need an arm with a good mind so it can help you."

She slid a finger over rows of wooden arms in a case, pulling out three as she went. They looked like jointed sticks with pincers on the end. A light-colored wooden arm bent easily in her hands. "Willow. Wise old wood. This'll have good reach. Flexible is good for your needs."

She lifted a darker arm. "This is a used one, from a crafty wizard, so it could help you the most. But he might have trained it to do odd things." She pushed it off to the side. "Of course, that one's far less expensive."

She lifted the third arm. It was black, with detailed carvings that looked like hieroglyphics down the side. "Egyptian burl wood. This one is specially charmed to protect its owner. Of course it's pricey, but it's made for life-or-death situations." She glanced at Erec. "It's a smart one, this arm, and worth the price if you need it."

Life-or-death sounded right to him. "I'll take it."

The old woman muttered an incantation in a singsong and the arm shivered. "Are you trained in the arts of magic, boy?"

Erec shook his head.

"Well then, we'll put a button at the end that will make it grip." She tapped on the arm. "You move the arm with gravity or by willing it."

Erec thanked her and paid four gold rings and five silver shires.

The woman glanced at Bethany, still on the stool looking as if she could murder someone. "What about you, dear? Is there anything I can do for you?"

"No, thanks."

"Are you *sure*, dear?"

Bethany's eyes widened. "Oh. Yes." She ran to the woman. "My cat was stolen. I need her back. Please."

A smile seemed to light beneath the wrinkles. "That's better." The woman studied Bethany's hand. "Oh my . . . *my*. Do you know how special you are?"

Bethany tried to smile back. The woman patted her palm. "You have great powers within you, my child. You have no idea. Learn to harness them. Those fears you have are childish. Let them go. You are much stronger than those you fear." The woman squeezed her hand and let go. Bethany stared, transfixed.

"It's okay, dear." A wrinkled hand patted Bethany's shoulder. "Let's talk about that cat."

Bethany was jolted from her reverie. "Her name is Cutie Pie. She was just stolen right before I came in here by the boy who bought the remote control."

"I see." The woman nodded. "What would you like me to do?"

"Bring Cutie Pie here now."

"Aah," the woman croaked. "If only that were possible. I cannot sell my services, only my goods. But there is one thing I can do. Would you like to see your cat?"

"Yes, please," Bethany said, excited. The woman opened a drawer and pulled out a large object covered in black cloth. She set it on the counter and pulled the cloth away, revealing a crystal ball. With a wave of her hand, vapors swirled within it. "Put your left hand on the ball." The old woman put her hand on the other side.

"Cherished crystal, from when the earth was young, show us this girl's cat . . . Say its name, child."

"Cutie Pie." The swirling mists formed into the image of a bag hanging from a hook on a wall. A hand shook in front of the bag, blood dripping from one of the fingers. Curses filled the air.

"Show us inside the bag," the woman whispered. The image changed, and there was Cutie Pie curled within a cloth sack. Someone had dropped cat food on top of her and she was eating it.

Balor Stain's voice echoed. "Stupid cat. You'll learn who your new master is or you'll stay in there. Forever. *I* want a cat that tells people's secrets, and you're *mine* now."

Cutie Pie did not seem concerned as she licked cat food off her paw. Bethany looked panicked. "What can we do? Can she hear us?"

"No, child. She can't hear us, and you can't make anything happen. But you could . . . suggest something to her."

"What? To bite Balor's hand off?" Bethany asked.

The woman cackled. "Looks like she's already tried that. Maybe something more practical. Say, for example, you give her the idea to escape. Maybe to use those sharp claws on that bag, hmm?"

"Oh, yes!" A smile lit Bethany's face.

"Go ahead. Tell her."

Bethany told Cutie Pie to use her claws to escape. The cat held up a paw and turned it, examining her claws, and then pushed her paw against the bag. The cloth was thick, but a claw popped through. She wiggled it until a tiny hole appeared.

The woman let go and the image disappeared. "Can we watch her more?"

The woman shook her head. "Too much is spying, even on your cat. Give her time, she'll come back."

"What if she can't get out? The fabric looks tough."

"I bet she will. If you don't see her in a week, come back."

"Can I come see her tomorrow?"

The woman cackled. "Patience, girl. You owe me a shire."

Bethany looked sheepishly at Erec. "I didn't bring any money."

He gave a handful of silver and gold to Bethany. "Keep it. It's as much yours as mine."

Bethany seemed calm as they walked into the evening light. "Did you hear what she said when she looked at my palm? It was like she was reading my mind."

"What, that you're so powerful?" he teased.

"No! She said my fears are childish, and I'm stronger than those I fear."

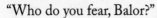

"Who do you fear, Balor?"

Bethany rolled her eyes. "My Uncle Earl. I've always been afraid to stand up to him. It was such a relief to escape him."

"Funny," Erec said, "she didn't seem right about my palm at all. That whole thing about trusting others. I have no idea what she was talking about."

Using the burl wood arm was awkward, but Erec soon was able to close the pincer hand with the button. Steering it was harder. The joint was flexible and moved in four directions. However it moved, gravity pulled the far limb down. If he twisted it, he could give it finer motions, but it wasn't easy. He let Jack and Oscar try it awhile, telling them it was a game. They weren't much better than he was. He picked up pieces of paper on his bed and practiced putting them on his pillow until he could barely hold his eyes open.

Saturday morning Erec woke with a start and grabbed the wooden arm from under his pillow. The formula was fine. Wolfboy guarded it by his bed. He had to practice with the arm. Jack and Oscar were out so he pulled a chair against the door and put his glasses on. His mother sat on her rocker, deep in thought.

"Mom?"

"Did you get a wooden arm?"

"Yup. Four gold rings and five silver shires."

June winced. "Boy, we could have used that money in Upper Earth."

"Well, we have it now, tons of it. We can get a house again, with our own rooms."

She nodded. "I've thought about it. I don't want you to come through these dungeons, now that I know what is in here. But it's important that I get out of here. If there was anyone else I could ask. But you are special, Erec. You can do this. Even though you have only one good eye, you have a better inner vision than most people. You'll have to be ready, though, by tonight."

Erec smiled. "So, how do I beat a shadow demon?"

"Resolve. You must know yourself and trust yourself. It will steer you off track, make you doubt, call to your worst feelings and emotions. They have great power over the shadow side of people. It is our other side, the goodness and trust in our nature, that can beat them. So, to defeat it, you must fill yourself with belief in your goals, yourself, your goodness. Then walk right through it. If you do, it will disappear. If you don't, you'll die."

"That's it? I just walk through it? You're kidding."

"Yes, but you need to be filled with hope, love, and belief to do it."

"And what if I'm not? What if I just run through it with a blank mind?"

"You won't be able to. To prepare, you must meditate. Sit alone. Concentrate on your belief in yourself, your purpose, who you are. Do you understand me?"

"Yes." Erec thought it interesting that his mother said he needed to believe in himself, and the old woman at Medea's said he needed to believe more in others . . . at least some others, whatever that meant.

"Shadow demons are among the worst thing you can run into. Don't underestimate them. If you don't have a respect for their power, you'd better not come."

"I do. I'll be fine."

"Check with me later. And don't forget to meditate, okay?"

Erec cut paper into squares and practiced putting them on the wall. It was slow going. Finally, he took the wooden arm and Wolfboy outside, grabbing a bottle of Flying Donkey Nectar from the cafeteria on the way.

Erec tried pulling blades of grass, which was much harder than putting paper on the wall. For fifteen minutes he reached for a leaf hanging from a low branch. Each time the pincers got close, gravity pulled and the hand fell.

"Can I have a try?" Bethany appeared behind Erec.

"It's hard." Erec handed her the arm. She looked it over, turning it various ways and playing with the button. Then, on her first try, she plucked the leaf that Erec could not reach.

"How did you do that?" Erec tried not to sound annoyed.

"I willed it there. Like the old woman said." She handed the arm back to Erec.

"How?"

"I just told it to, kind of." She shrugged.

Erec reached for a different leaf, but the hand crashed down.

"Focus. Move it in your mind."

Erec concentrated hard and the hand twitched a little before it dropped. "Ugh."

"You'll figure it out," said Bethany. "I'm going to buy treats for Cutie Pie, when she comes back. Want anything?"

"You aren't, by chance, going to Medea's to try to see Cutie Pie again?" Erec grinned.

Bethany suppressed a smile. "Well, that woman said I couldn't. But you never know, maybe somebody else is working there today!" She left, nearly running, for the agora.

Erec concentrated hard on the arm. He wished it was as easy to use as the scepter. He held it so the far limb drooped, and willed it as hard as he could to reach up. It waved a little. He tried harder, but each time it barely moved.

Erec felt like his head was about to burst. He held his breath and squeezed with all his might, trying to force magic from the arm. He aimed again for the leaf. This time the arm did not move at all.

All of a sudden, a leaping lizard flew at Erec's face. Without thinking, Erec swatted it away. But instead of his hand, it was the wooden arm that stretched easily through the air and sent the creature flying.

Erec stared at the arm. When it hit the lizard, he hadn't even tried to make it move. Well, not exactly. He just used it like it was his hand. Erec reached up the tree the same way that he swatted the lizard and grabbed a leaf. It was easy. He had been trying too hard.

He spent the rest of the morning reaching for leaves, plucking blades of grass, picking tiny bits of dirt from the fountains, scratching Wolfboy's ears, and moving paper all over the place. At one point he thought about meditating. It seemed silly. He knew who he was. Meditating wouldn't help as much as extra time practicing with the arm.

By afternoon, the wooden arm was like a third hand. Better, really. When he reached with it, no matter how fast, he never missed. Like the old woman said, it seemed to have a mind of its own.

CHAPTER EIGHTEEN

Shadow Demon Logic

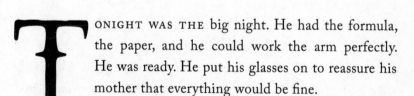

TONIGHT WAS THE big night. He had the formula, the paper, and he could work the arm perfectly. He was ready. He put his glasses on to reassure his mother that everything would be fine.

"Mom?"

She was lying in bed flipping through *Better Castles and Dungeons* magazine. She looked up with a smile. "I hope I see you tonight."

"The arm works *great*, Mom. It's so easy."

"Good. Have you been meditating?"

"Oh . . . yeah." Erec promised himself he would later.

June hesitated. "There's a password to get into the outer dungeons with a Port-O-Door, so only Pluto's staff can get in and out. My friend undercover here told me this week's password." She hesitated for a moment. "It's 'heat blister.' Erec, I trust you. You can do almost anything you try to do. Just don't be stupid. If things go wrong, turn back."

He didn't answer, and at last she continued. "King Pluto has castles under each continent: I'm in Americorth North. A code will be printed on the Port-O-Door. Memorize or write it down so you can open it from the inside. And make sure you remember *exactly* the way back to your Port-O-Door. That's crucial."

"Or I'm stuck in the dungeons forever."

June shuddered. "There is no forever here, Erec. You wouldn't last that long. The goal is to be quick and decisive. In and out, okay?"

"Okay, Mom."

"The inner dungeon has concrete hallways that open up in front of the prison cells. You'll see me. The cells are clear force fields hanging in air. I'll get rid of my inside scenery before midnight so I can see you, too.

"Don't forget, you might run into a prison guard or a bronze or silver ghost. The ghosts can't touch you, but a prison guard could get in the way. Use your Sneakers to distract them. Hopefully they'll be asleep." She sighed at all the obstacles he would face. "Thanks for rescuing me. I love you, Erec."

"I love you, too. How do I use the formula to get you out?"

"It's easy. Put it by my cell and say, 'Suntribo,' and then run. You'll have thirty seconds before it blasts. If you drop or throw it,

THE DRAGON'S EYE

it will explode right away, and you could get hurt."

"Hold on." He wrote "Suntribo" on a piece of paper and taped it to the jar.

"Don't forget to bring your paper pieces and wooden arm tonight with the formula."

Erec practiced with his arm the rest of the day. When he concentrated, he felt twinges of sadness and discord around him: the Substance. Focusing seemed to make him more aware of it.

Before dinner he tried meditating under a tree. He thought about believing in himself, but his mind kept wandering to food. Maybe he should try after he ate, but it seemed silly. He knew who he was. At least, enough to walk through a shadow demon.

He knocked on Bethany's door on the way to dinner. "Did you see Cutie Pie in the crystal ball?"

"No. The old woman was there again. I found out she *is* Medea. Before she shooed me away, she winked and told me that Cutie Pie was fine and I needed to give her more time. Did you figure the wooden arm out?"

"Finally. It's easy now."

"Too bad we gave up the vanishing caps. Of course, the destroyers find you by smell."

"And the shadow demons just sense you're there somehow."

"I guess gills won't help much in the dungeons." Bethany sighed. "I can't wait to meet your mom. I bet she'll figure out what's wrong with King Piter. Maybe she'll get to the bottom of what happened at the armory."

"That could send her right back into the dungeons," he pointed out. "She'll have to go home to my brothers and sisters." He added darkly, "We'll have to move again, to hide from whoever caught her."

Bethany saw that he was nervous. "Do you want me to distract the guard at the gate tonight so you can sneak through?"

"Sure," he said, glad she was coming. "I'm going close to midnight."

They walked through the gardens late after dinner. Erec worked his wooden arm continuously, picking up rocks, stones, and flowers to burn off his nervous energy. He kept putting leaves on Bethany's nose.

"Cut it out!"

"I'm sorry. It's just really good practice."

They played a game of tag, where Bethany ran and Erec tried to put paper on her nose with the wooden arm. That calmed him down quite a bit. Then they talked about how to hide his mother once she was free.

At a quarter to midnight, they went inside. Erec put on his Sneakers and took a big pile of cut paper in a plastic bag with a pen. He wore long pants and a jacket, to protect him from dripping acid rock, and tucked his burl wood arm under his right arm. He slid the glass jar of blasting formula from under his bed and patted Wolfboy on the head.

Erec held the jar carefully. If he dropped it, he would not see his mother . . . or live to see anyone at all. He wished he had practiced using his wooden arm while holding a jar, but it was too late now.

At the west wing, the guard at the rope looked half asleep. He held a remote control limply at his side. Nobody else was in sight.

"Good luck. See you in the morning." Bethany walked up to the guard while Erec slipped into a shadow by the corner. The guard looked confused as she asked him a series of pointless questions like "When will the castle turn onto its other side?"

Erec slipped under the rope while the guard was turned away and stole noiselessly down the hall. If a maid saw him, he would say he was looking for Spartacus Kilroy because he felt sick. He knew it didn't make sense, but he hoped she would feel sorry for him and let him go.

The Sneakers let him run fast, silently, and smoothly so the formula did not bounce in the jar. He slowed at corners so he would not have to stop suddenly and disturb it. The halls seemed empty.

Erec turned another corner, only to find Balthazar Ugry standing at the end of the long hallway. His eyes narrowed. A chill filled Erec as his gaze connected with Ugry's.

Ugry soared toward Erec.

Running blindly, Erec darted down one side hall and then another. At least Ugry wouldn't be able to hear his footsteps.

For some reason, Erec could not hear Ugry's footsteps either. Maybe he was too far to hear. But he knew Ugry was following him. He peered around a corner, and it was empty. Cautiously, he walked down the hallway, stomping his feet to throw sound down another corridor.

It seemed to work. For a while there was no sign of Ugry. Then he heard a growl. "He won't get far. Just wait until I get my hands on him." Erec ducked into a darkened doorway, shivering. It occurred to him that Ugry might be invisible.

Erec didn't hear anything for a long while. He snuck back down the hallway. Right before he turned the last corner, he saw Ugry's back at the other end of a long hallway. He stamped his feet and darted toward the Port-O-Door, hoping Ugry did not see him.

The doorknob turned easily, and Erec stepped into darkness. When he shut the door behind him, the small vestibule lit up. At the top of the screen, under PORT-O-DOOR, was written PASSWORD: 125709. Erec scribbled the numbers on a piece of paper and stuffed it into his pocket.

The screen split into four sections labeled ALYPIUM in white, ASHONA in blue, AORTH in red, and OTHERNESS in Yellow. Erec grabbed the pointer and touched AORTH. The screen divided into seven red sections: AMERICORTH NORTH, AMERICORTH SOUTH, EURORTH, ASIAORTH, AUSTRALIAORTH, AFRICORTH, and AUNT ARCTICORTH. Erec touched AMERICORTH NORTH, and the screen showed a rough map.

Erec had a feeling that Ugry was close by. He touched a dot in the middle of the map labeled KING PLUTO'S CASTLE. An outline of the castle appeared, with lines dividing it into floors. Most said ACCESS RESTRICTED, except for a small part of the ground floor and the dungeons. He poked the bottom layer, DUNGEONS.

An overhead drawing of the dungeons popped onto the screen. The areas were not labeled. Erec touched the exact center of the dungeon with the pointer. A sign on the screen said ACCESS RESTRICTED. He tried a few spots close to it, again with no luck.

Ugry's voice was close through the door. "If he thinks he can get away . . ."

Erec's breath caught. Compared to Ugry, the monsters of the dungeon seemed like nothing. He moved the pointer slightly from the center, working as fast as he could. He had a feeling that Ugry would burst in at any moment. Finally the screen said LOCK, and he typed in the password "heat blister" and heard the doorknob click.

Erec opened the door and a blast of heat burst in. The hallway glistened with red rock walls coated with wet slime. A bitter smell filled the air. Bethany had said to try several areas before going in, but Ugry was too close. This spot seemed as good as any.

Erec stepped through the door and shut it behind him. Despite the awful smell and the heat, Erec was relieved to be far away from Ugry. He was now far across the world . . . and so close to his mother. His wooden arm was in his right hand, a stack of cut paper in his left, and his left arm wrapped around the glass jar of blasting formula. He was armed and ready.

He walked down the hallway, careful to remember which way he was going. The red walls oozed with acid. He turned the corner and almost walked into a skeleton holding a pair of scissors. His heart leapt into his throat. For a moment he thought it was a destroyer.

Holding paper in his wooden hand, Erec carefully walked around the skeleton. His blood raced with excitement and fear. The bubbling, dripping walls turned his stomach. A huge red droplet slunk down nearby and hit the floor with a crackle. Tiny red drops spattered everywhere. Steam hissed as one landed on Erec's jacket. It left a perfectly round hole in his sleeve.

Erec wondered why his mother hadn't warned him that the dungeons were excruciatingly hot. Didn't she know? Soon, he left his jacket on the floor, even though his arms were unprotected. He held the jar tight. He hoped he wasn't so sweaty it would slip through his arms.

The sound of his own panting filled his ears. He turned again at the end of the hallway. Then he heard a hiss. He looked behind him.

Something bulged out from the wall. The gloppy red rock seemed to be taking on a life of its own, forming into something like a head, and then, more clearly, a hand. Shoulders and arms thrust from the rock with a wet smacking sound.

A blank stone head swung toward Erec. There was a black hole where the middle of the face should have been. Below it, red fluid dripped from a larger opening. It ran onto the thing's stony chest. It looked like living, moving rock.

Erec stared at the destroyer. He remembered how they attached their acid mouths, digesting people before they devoured them.

He froze at the awful sight. His heart pounded hard enough to burst through his chest. The thought of running up

to the indestructible creature with a long arm and paper seemed ridiculous.

The creature emerged with a thud. It stomped toward Erec, shaking the floor. Erec sprang into motion and darted away. He ran to the end of the hallway.

The creature swiftly overtook him. Erec's breath jerked in spurts, but he was barely aware of it. He flew around the corner and then stopped.

It was strike first or be eaten. With one swift motion he stretched his burl wood arm as far around the corner as it could go. As soon as the destroyer was in reach, he put paper over the thing's suction hole.

It stuck. The tiny corner of paper that touched its mouth hole sizzled away.

Erec darted back around the corner. The destroyer continued forward, arms out in front, but slower. It looked silly and grotesque at the same time, paper held onto its nose in an eternal sniff. The thing walked straight into the wall, where it sucked back in with a pop.

Before Erec could catch his breath, two more destroyers emerged from a wall in front of him, faceless heads swinging toward him.

Erec's heart and lungs were running at hyper speed, pounding and panting wildly. He tried to focus. His body told him to run, but they would easily outrun him. He grabbed paper with his wooden hand and took a step, shaking, toward the closest destroyer. As soon as it was within reach, he popped paper over its nose hole, avoiding its broad arms by reaching high and letting the wooden arm arc down. He dashed away.

The destroyer turned its head wildly, swinging and hitting walls. Finally it stumbled onto the floor. The blind creature must have needed smell to tell it where the walls were. Without smell, it was in a blank void.

The other destroyer pounded down the corridor toward Erec. Roughly it shoved the confused destroyer out of its way. Erec was ready with paper. The wooden arm worked like a charm. In a moment the baffled creature was attacking the other destroyer. Soon they jostled back into the walls.

Right then another destroyer appeared behind him. Erec reached high on his toes to paper it and then darted down the hallway. He was amazed that he had not had a cloudy thought. They seemed to come to him in far less dangerous situations than this. Maybe it was because he already knew what to do. But it would be nice to know which hallway to take. Erec was amazed that for the first time in his life he actually *wanted* a cloudy thought.

A destroyer turned the corner right in front of him. He jumped back and reached it with paper just in time. Behind him, two more appeared. Erec ran back and papered the closer one, but it continued to walk in his direction. He ran to the middle of the hallway, but he was stuck between two of the stony goliaths walking right toward each other.

Erec dropped to the floor, careful not to jiggle the formula, and looked wildly around. The two destroyers continued straight toward him, even though they couldn't smell him. He was about to become part of a terrible sandwich.

In wild fear, he crawled in the direction he was first headed. The destroyer strode toward him, but did not reach down to him. He scrambled between its legs, tripping it.

The thing spun and hit the wall. The other one tripped over it. Both tussled on the stone floor, confused. In the meantime, Erec took off.

At the end of the hallway, four more destroyers sucked out of the walls, one in front and three behind him. These were closer than before. Erec worked quickly with paper on the closest two and then waited, trapped between them. He squeezed the glass jar to his chest.

The two destroyers that still had their smell pushed the other one toward Erec. He had an urge to splash the formula on them, but he would probably end up blasting himself to pieces. He wondered with a sick feeling if he would ever find the inner dungeons or if he was trapped with these monsters forever.

The destroyers came dangerously close. Erec crouched, ready to crawl past one's legs, but then it stumbled, disappearing, into a wall. He ran down the hallway, thankful that his magic Sneakers made his shaky strides steady. The two uncovered destroyers behind him pushed past and tore after him.

Before Erec reached the end of the hallway, a bunch more squeezed from the wall behind him, at least five. He was sure that, sweating and panting, he was a flashing neon billboard by now to their sense of smell. He didn't stop but rounded the corner and saw an amazing sight.

The hallway ahead of him was filled with destroyers, lumbering toward him with outstretched arms and dripping mouths. And behind them, at the end of the hallway, bright light gleamed. The inner dungeons.

Erec felt so close, but the disgusting stone zombies surrounded him. He would never make it. He reached with his wooden arm, unsure which way to point it first, when his head started to spin. It was the heat and the smell. He was fainting. Either the jar would drop or he would be devoured by acid. Either way he would certainly die. He grabbed the jar tighter as the creatures approached.

Then the fog in Erec's head melted. He was having a cloudy thought, different from any other. His stomach felt fine. The dizzy feeling was much shorter, possibly because he would die if it lasted longer, and his determination was stronger than he had ever known it to be. He felt as if his strength had doubled.

Instead of fighting the cloudy thought, he became one with it. For once, it felt like his own will in action, not something outside of himself. Maybe because he knew he would die without it or because he had learned to believe, a little, in magic and in himself.

When the cloudy thought took hold, Erec flung paper onto the suction holes of three nearby destroyers. He dropped to his knees, cradling the jar, and ducked under a confused destroyer's leg. It tipped into the crowd behind it. Erec came up with paper outstretched, covered another nose hole, and crouched, using the papered one to knock several more down behind it.

The light at the end of the tunnel approached. Four more destroyers were in the way, close together and drooling red. Erec put paper on the closest and stepped back. Another butted by it, and he reached it with paper as well. The two confused destroyers were pushed closer by the two behind them. They fell to the floor.

Erec stepped onto the back of a destroyer. He put paper on the third one and leapt into it, kicking its chest, and shoving it into the fourth. He ran over them, but the fourth one reached up and grabbed his wooden arm, snapping it in two.

Erec stumbled backward. The destroyer got up, towering over him. His wooden arm was his only protection, and now it was gone. He ran for the light, but the destroyer was faster.

The entrance to the inner dungeons was in front of him, and he flung himself through. He squeezed his eyes shut, expecting to be clobbered and sizzled with acid at any moment.

Nothing happened.

Erec opened his eyes. The destroyer drooled and pawed the air at the entryway to the inner dungeons. Apparently it could not enter the well-lit, concrete hallways.

Erec carefully tested a white wall to assure himself there was no acid. It felt fine. He walked around a corner to get out of sight of the destroyer and collapsed against the wall in a heap. He set the jar on the floor, slid down, and rested his head on his knees. All he could think was, *I am here.*

Sweat coated him and, even in the heat, he started to shiver. He sat for a long time until his breathing slowed, and he felt better. For the first time, he had not been sick after a cloudy thought. He wondered why.

The burl wood arm was gone, but he was close to his mother and he had the blasting formula. He hoped she knew a better way out, because it would be impossible to go back to the Port-O-Door.

The hallways were well lit but empty, probably because it was the middle of the night. The prospect of coming up against an armed guard seemed like nothing after what Erec had gone through. And a shadow demon . . . well, he just had to walk through it.

Every now and then a part of the wall would be gone and a clear, floating room would hang suspended in its place. Erec could see right into each cell. Their gleaming, shining walls were made of the force field material. He wondered if most of the inhabitants put up what looked like a room inside, like his mother did, so they wouldn't have to see the dungeons. A tentacled creature lifted an eye and watched him walk by.

Most people and creatures were asleep. His mother had said she would be waiting by the edge of her cell. He walked through hallway after hallway with no luck. Finally, around a corner in a gap in the wall, there she was.

June jumped up and down, waving wildly and cheering. Erec could not hear a word she said. He walked to the edge of her cell.

Suddenly, someone behind him cleared his throat. Erec glanced up the hallway. There he saw himself in a full-length mirror. But his image moved as he held still. He froze. The boy who looked exactly like him walked toward him.

THE DRAGON'S EYE

"Now," said the boy in Erec's own voice, "you didn't think I'd let you just walk right in and out of here, did you?"

Erec stared, mouth open. It was stranger than he could believe, watching himself walking around and saying weird things. This was obviously a—

"That's right," the boy who looked like Erec said. "I am a shadow demon. And you are Erec Rex, confused and misguided boy who thinks he is here to save his mother. When really it's *me* who is here to save *you*."

Erec really did feel confused, listening to this thing that looked like himself.

"You think you can take that incredibly strong formula and blast your poor mother out. Do you know what would happen to her if you did that?"

Erec looked at himself suspiciously. "She'd get out."

The shadow demon that looked like Erec sighed. "She would die from the explosion. And then I would have to kill you for breaking a prisoner out of here. I really don't want to have to kill you. What a future you have! Stop and think, Erec. Do you know how strong that formula is?"

Erec remembered the huge explosion in Hecate Jekyll's storerooms from dropping one drop of nitrowisherine alone.

"That's right," said the shadow demon. "Do you want to kill your mother, Erec? That's what that stuff would do." He pointed at the jar.

Erec reminded himself what his mother had said about the shadow demon trying to steer him off course. All he had to do was walk right through it. That easy.

Yet when Erec took a few steps toward the shadow demon, it took the form of a destroyer with a gaping, acid-dripping mouth. Erec backed away and gasped. The shadow demon instantly changed shape again to look like Erec. "I really wouldn't recommend coming any closer," he said. "You don't know how easy it is for me to kill you." He laughed, an innocent boy's laugh.

"Your mother is sadly misinformed. She got her information about shadow demons from gossip magazines. We're very misunderstood. But that old myth about walking through us is the worst. That's the way you *die*. Try it if you like." The shadow demon changed shape back into a destroyer, but this time with a swaying cobra's head coming from its stomach. Erec backed away without thinking. Again the shadow demon took on Erec's features.

"I'm not saying there is anything wrong with your mother. She's very sweet, actually. But she's of no use here. Won't talk. We're letting her go in two days. So you just need to go back and wait. That way you'll both be together soon, right?"

Erec glanced at his mother. She obviously could not hear their conversation. She was gesturing wildly for him to run at the shadow demon.

"See, there she goes again," Erec's image calmly said. "She means well. But this isn't the first time she's been wrong, is it? I mean, she didn't even know how hot the dungeons were, did she? Her little cell is cool enough. She doesn't know what it's like out here. Or . . . did she warn you about the heat?"

Erec wished she had. "It's okay." The shadow demon sighed. "She loves you. But she'll never understand you. She has you all caught up in this insane rescue mission, but you have more important things to think about. Like that scepter. King Pluto's scepter. You used it, Erec. That takes incredible power. And you felt it, didn't you?"

Erec nodded. He did feel that power . . . could almost feel it now.

"You're ready for it, Erec. And you're *so* close. Only two more contests. Then one of them is yours. And why only one? Maybe two? All three? Who else can use them like you?"

Erec pictured the scepter in his hands so vividly he felt it, mouth watering. Then he remembered where he was and why he was there. The shadow demon seemed able to steer his thoughts so easily. Well, he wouldn't let it. His mother had warned him . . .

The boy who looked like Erec shook his head and laughed. "Do I look like an evil murderer to you? Wouldn't I have killed you by now?"

Erec looked at his mother, who was now standing limply in her cell. She said to just run through it. Maybe she was right.

The shadow demon said, "Do you think King Pluto is so evil he has ruthless killers patrolling down here? I'm here to keep order. I really don't want to kill you or to clean up the mess of your mother that blasting formula would make, so I'd advise you to go now. Go and get that scepter, be with your new friends, show those Stain boys who's boss."

Erec's head spun. If he ran into the shadow demon he could be killed, and he might blast his mother with the formula. But his mother had said that if you don't walk through the demon, and it melts your resolve, then you become its chocolate soda.

Erec's mirror image grew more serious. "I didn't want to have to bring this up . . . bad feelings and all . . . but it looks like I have to. Do you know *why* your mother is a prisoner?"

Erec shook his head. Against his better judgment, he really wanted an answer.

"Pretty strange she didn't tell you herself, huh? But why would she? She's a criminal, Erec. You were right when you suspected she stole that money and the Sneakers. But there was more. Much more.

"Your mother is not to be trusted. She tried to kill the royal triplets almost ten years ago. Just snapped. Went crazy. She ended up kidnapping two of them, your brother and sister Danny and Sammy. But don't be angry at her, Erec. She's really not evil. Just confused, crazy maybe."

Erec's head was swimming. All of his doubts were coming to the surface.

"You always knew she was a little off-target, didn't you? All those times growing up when she talked about 'magic this, magic that.' Ridiculous."

His old feelings of embarrassment surfaced. He had tried to tell her he was too old for those dumb stories, she just wouldn't listen.

"And then there is that small incident of erasing everybody's memory of you. How does that feel? Did you know that nobody from your class in school last year remembers you at all? That's right. Did she really say she wouldn't do it again?" He shook his head and clucked his tongue. "She can't help it. Don't blame her. She thinks she knows what she's doing . . . really. Just don't do anything *stupid* now because she told you the wrong thing."

Erec stared at the glass jar in his hands. He felt ridiculous. What was he thinking coming here? "Can I put my glasses on and talk to her before I go?"

Erec's image smiled. "Take your time. But remember, she's a little unstable. You'll have to break it to her easy that you're leaving. Tell her we're letting her out in two days. But be kind, she's *very* confused."

Erec put the glasses on and he was back in the room with his mother. Instead of looking at him, she stared through the now clear wall at what looked like two versions of Erec, one walking slowly toward the other that had glasses on. He stared at the two images of himself, transfixed.

"Take those off," she screamed. "Get out of here! He's coming to kill you!"

"Mom, he's not killing me," Erec said. "You're getting out in two days. I don't need to blast you out."

"Erec, he's lying," June cried. "Take the glasses off *now*! *Walk through him!*"

"Mom, it's okay. Really."

"Erec! Listen to *me*. Don't believe the shadow demon!"

Erec looked through the clear force field of his mother's cell. One version of himself was now swiftly approaching the other. It was strange, mesmerizing, to be one place and watching two of yourselves through a big window.

June screamed, jolting Erec into alertness. The shadow demon grew, changing into a hideous beast with long fangs. The beast opened its jaws wide over Erec.

Erec yanked the glasses off just in time. The beast's mouth was closing over him. He tried to run, but was frozen where he stood. Something strange sank into him. Not teeth, exactly. He felt lighter, as if he was disappearing.

Erec was lifting from the ground. Despair filled the last bits of his consciousness. He had lost. He believed the shadow demon. In a burst of anger and hope, he flung the glass jar of blasting formula at his mother's cell.

A white-hot, fiery explosion pushed him into the air. He couldn't see the shadow demon's jaws, but they were still there as his body crashed against the dungeon wall.

Everything began to fade. In a gray mist he heard a woman cry. A soft swoosh of cloth fell around his body and face. He fell into blackness.

CHAPTER NINETEEN

Really, Really You

A FTER THE DARKNESS, the dreams started. Erec was chased by himself, and the self that chased him split in two, then four. Soon hundreds of Erecs were everywhere, trying to kill him. His mother floated overhead, shouting advice. He tried to throw her the jar, but it exploded in the air. He grabbed a scepter to save them, but it wouldn't work. All was lost.

He woke up dizzy and sweating. Nothing looked familiar. He

heard voices but didn't know whose they were. Everything was white. When he tried to move, his hand stung, and he saw a tube there. A sheet covered him, and under he wore a white hospital gown.

A familiar voice said, "No, I just ate lunch. Thanks." Then, in a moment, Bethany was looking down at him. How could she be here? Where was he? He wondered if he was dead or having a dying vision.

"You're awake!" Bethany shouted. "He's awake!"

Dr. Mumbai was there in a flash. "Erec?" She took his pulse and listened with her stethoscope. "What happened to you last night? Did someone kidnap you?" She looked upset.

Erec shook his head. Every muscle ached when he moved. It seemed incredible, but here he was in the royal hospital in the castle. Could his mother have managed to send him here?

"You could have *died* last night. Thank goodness somebody brought you in. I had to use the cardiorestarter to get your heart on track. What happened?" Dr. Mumbai crossed her thin arms.

Erec shrugged. "I don't know."

"Bethany says you might have been sleepwalking. Is that what happened?"

"I think so," Erec looked at Bethany, thanking her in his mind for coming up with a great cover, as usual. "Who brought me here?"

"Great question. Someone put you here in the middle of the night and woke me up with this." She held up a scrawled note reading, "You have a new patient. Rick Ross needs you immediately." It was not signed.

"Did you see who left the note?" Erec was short of breath.

"No. I felt a jab and it dropped into my hand. By the time I turned around, whoever left it was gone." Dr. Mumbai was bewildered. "And then there you were, white and clammy, barely breathing. Your heart was racing and your pressure was dropping fast.

"You were in shock, and I have no idea why. There was no evidence of injury. I ran six liters of fluid in and gave you Normotension. Your blood pressure stabilized, but you stayed unconscious. Every now and then you got a terrified look on your face." She touched his cheek. "I thought I was too late."

Erec pulled himself up slowly, which made him dizzier. "Can I go?"

"Absolutely not. You will rest here for a few days at least so I can watch over you. And those glasses! I couldn't get them off last night. They really could have gotten in the way if you needed surgery."

"But the fifth contest is tomorrow morning," Bethany said.

"That's too bad." Dr. Mumbai checked her watch. "I'll be back later with more Normotension. You lucked out, kid."

Erec dropped back onto his bed. When the doctor was out of earshot, Bethany whispered, "What happened?"

Erec squeezed his eyes shut. "I failed," he said hoarsely.

Bethany looked worried. "Tell me everything."

Erec glared at her. "That's it. I failed. I'm a big loser. My mother told me exactly what to do, and I couldn't do the simplest thing. I decided to believe a shadow demon rather than my own mother. And then it was killing me. I should have died."

Bethany stared at him. "Who brought you here?"

"I have no idea." Erec put an arm over his face, wanting to block out the entire memory.

"Don't worry. Rest up. I'll sneak you out of here tomorrow morning. Eat lots of ambrosia. That stuff's like chicken soup—"

"Butt out, Bethany," Erec interrupted. "I think you've helped me enough."

Bethany's chin puckered. She said quietly, "I just thought—"

"That's the problem," Erec said. "You think too much—of me. I'll never live up to your standards, or my mother's, or anyone's. I couldn't have even won the fourth contest without your help. I'll never win the fifth. You go. You're obviously a queen-to-be. Leave me alone."

"Erec . . ." Bethany's eyes were wide.

Erec scowled. "Just go away." Bethany left with a sniff, and Erec immediately felt terrible. He was really angry with himself. He dreaded putting his glasses on and facing his mother, but she must be worried sick. She might even think he was dead.

Then Erec's breath caught. What if something bad happened to his mother in the explosion? The shadow demon said she would die. What . . .

Erec bit his lip. He had to face what he had done. See if she was okay. He brought the glasses to his face but dropped them. Not now. He was too weak and tired and miserable to even imagine his mother hurt, or face her disappointment.

He closed his eyes. Soon he would get the nerve to check. He would have to.

Erec slid the curtain around his bed and pulled the sheets over his head for more privacy. His hands trembled as he brought the glasses to his face. The darkness changed to a very dim light. Erec looked around, not sure where he was.

He heard his mother sobbing. It looked like she was in a strange, dark kitchen. A refrigerator reflected the light of a flickering streetlamp outside. Amazingly, this was not King Pluto's dungeons. His mother sat, head collapsed on a table, wailing.

"Mom?"

June didn't hear him at first, so he said it louder. She jerked up, looking suspiciously into the air. "Erec?" Her eyes were red and her face was swollen.

"Mom, I'm *fine*. I'm fine, Mom. It's okay."

June burst into tears. "Am I imagining this?"

"No. It's really me. I don't know what happened last night. I'm so sorry I messed up, Mom. I was so stupid. It's just . . . that shadow demon really knew the right things to say."

June clutched a pillow to her chest. "Where are you?"

"I'm in the royal hospital in the castle. Dr. Mumbai said someone put me in a bed last night. I guess I didn't look so good. But I'm fine now."

June looked like she didn't trust Erec's voice. "Are you sure you're alive?"

Erec managed to laugh. "The way I'm aching, I'm too sure."

"I'm just imagining this," June wailed. "This can't be real."

"Maybe I'm imagining it too. I thought I was a goner. But Dr. Mumbai did a pretty good job, I guess. We have no idea who saved me."

June burst into laughter, tears rolling down her face. "Oh, thank God. It almost looked like . . . but it was too much to hope for."

"What?"

"It was so hard to see. You were lifting off the floor, getting pulled into the shadow demon. Something shimmering was coming out of you. Then there was the huge explosion, and it was hard to see you at all, but the shadow demon was still there. And then, something strange. A flash of black cloth. You soared away. It looked like it chased you with a roar. I had a moment of hope . . . but it seemed ridiculous. How could you have survived? Then I thought that was just the way the shadow demon works. It was so hard to tell."

A smile played across her face. "You did it, Erec. You got me out. You threw the formula at my cell, and it worked. So I did what I had to. I escaped into King Pluto's castle. Once I was out of the force field I could do a little magic, so I came home, grabbed the kids from their beds, and ran to a friend's apartment. They're all fine, Erec. They're sleeping."

June blotted her eyes. "Are you dead? I can't imagine someone saved you. Unless someone powerful . . . King Piter?" She sniffed. "Maybe he saved you. I am talking to you now, aren't I?"

"Yes."

June smiled broadly. "Yes. Here I am, talking to you now. I did see you get pulled from the shadow demon . . . You're *alive!*" June was now pacing the room, squeezing a kitchen towel, and jumping up and down. "You're alive! You're alive! I love you! You're *alive!*" She threw the towel in the air.

Erec couldn't help smiling.

"You better get your bottom in gear to win those next two contests. You're going to win that scepter and save Alypium!"

All of the aches he felt came back in a rush. "I could just come home."

She shook her head. "Come back now, and we stay in hiding forever. If you can use a scepter to help King Piter return to normal, we'll be protected. I know you can do it."

"You'd trust me after what I did?"

"Shadow demons are incredibly good at finding our weak spots. I should have known you weren't ready."

Warmth surged into Erec's arms and fingers. His mother clasped a teacup to her heart, singing, "It's really you, it's really, really you." Then she put it down. "The twins are acting a little strange, but I think they'll come around when things settle down. Anyway, don't use the glasses too much when I'm here. I don't know if somebody could trace them somehow and find us. They send waves through the Substance. We'll be moving soon. When you're ready to come home, put them on and I'll tell you where to go."

"Aren't you coming to help wake up King Piter?"

June laughed. "With King Pluto right there and whoever else has it in for me? Who would I help if I ended up back in the dungeons?

No, I'm counting on you." She looked into the air, hands clutched over her heart. "I'm sorry I didn't tell you more about where you were from, years ago. It would have been dangerous, but I should have figured out a way. What I'm trying to say is . . . it's my fault you didn't trust me more."

"Great. Because I have lots more questions."

June looked embarrassed. "Well, we'll see. When is the next contest?"

"In the morning."

"Get your rest." June grinned.

Erec took his glasses and the covers off and sat up. He flipped on the light by his bed. He called out, "Any ambrosia around here?"

Erec started to feel much better. Dr. Mumbai's gray cat with X-ray vision, Seeker, walked back and forth over him, looking again for internal injuries. There were none.

"Please can I go? I feel fine." He ignored his aching muscles.

"No. I need to keep my eye on you a few more days."

"But the fifth contest is tomorrow. I *have* to be in it."

Dr. Mumbai cocked an eyebrow at him. "I can't let you risk your life. We have no idea why your body went into shock. What if it happened again in the contest? You'd stress your system far more than just sleepwalking."

Bethany would have thought of a way to bust him out. Her feelings were probably still hurt or she'd have come back. Erec felt like an idiot. He pulled the covers over his head.

He had only disappeared for a minute when he heard someone come in the room. When he peeked out, Bethany was standing there with two tall nectar fizz sundaes.

"I'm sorry," Bethany said. "I can't imagine what you're going through. I shouldn't have been so—"

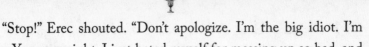

"Stop!" Erec shouted. "Don't apologize. I'm the big idiot. I'm sorry. You were right. I just hated myself for messing up so bad, and it all came out."

Erec sat up and a smile filled his face. "But it's okay now. It worked! My mom is free. She's with my brothers and sisters, and they're all fine. They're still on the run, so we have to win those scepters and help King Piter snap out of it. Then we can go home in style."

Bethany bounced up and down on her toes. One of the nectar fizz sundaes spilled onto her arm. "You did it!" She gave him a sundae and pulled a chair up.

Erec told her every detail about the dungeons. Bethany squealed when she heard about the destroyers coming from all sides. The awful adventure became fun to describe, especially from his safe hospital bed. They toasted their sundae glasses when Erec told how he threw the blasting formula at his mother's cell.

"I'll come back around eight tomorrow morning. We'll get you out of here for the contest," Bethany said. "It starts at ten."

"I'll try to be ready."

Erec awoke to the dim light of the hospital ward. The windows were shuttered. He had no idea what time it was. Bethany had not shown up, so maybe it was still early. If he only had bought a watch.

The room was quiet. A few kids were asleep, and a girl nearby read a magazine. Erec pulled the IV line from his hand. A few drops of blood ran over his skin. He slid his clothing on underneath the gown. His pants and shirt stunk of bitter dungeon odor and sweat. The smell made his stomach clench.

The IV machine started beeping. He rushed out of the open ward into the office. Only one door led into the castle, but it was locked. Erec rooted through a desk looking for keys, frantically throwing papers and files from drawers.

He heard giggling. He turned, and there stood the girl who had been reading a magazine. "There's a button on the wall," she said. "You can open the door that way."

"Thanks!" Erec raced over and pressed the button. The door popped open with a buzz.

"No . . . thank *you*. I'm Darla Will. You saved me from the swamp gas." She smiled.

"Do you know what time it is?"

Darla pointed to a clock hanging between bookcases. It read nine o'clock.

"Thanks," Erec said. "You really know your way around here." He wondered if Bethany had overslept.

"I'm here a lot." Darla bit her thumbnail.

"You sick a lot?"

She nodded. "That's my gift—a curse, really. If anybody gets sick or hurt around me, I get it too, only twenty-four hours earlier. I came in Friday night in terrible shape, probably with whatever happened to you on Saturday night. But my roommate brought me here before it got as bad."

"You had hypo-whatever shock?"

"I guess. I just felt sick and horrible, and my heart was pounding."

"Did you see who brought me here Saturday night?"

"No. I was asleep. Give me your gown. I'll make it look like you're still in bed. And I'll shut off the IV."

"Wow. Thanks, Darla."

"Good luck in the contests, Rick Ross!"

Erec raced through the castle. His muscles still ached, but he didn't care. He guessed he had time to shower and change and still get to the maze before ten.

After changing he pounded on Bethany's door. "Open up! It's time to conquer Alypium!"

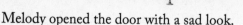

Melody opened the door with a sad look.

"What's wrong?" Erec asked.

"Bethany's gone."

"What do you mean?"

"Her Uncle Earl found her. They just left."

"No way." Desperation filled Erec. "Why would she *go* with him?"

"She seemed pretty afraid. He wasn't happy."

"Did he know the fifth contest was this morning?"

"He didn't care. He had some kind of magical chain so she could never walk farther than ten feet from the newsstand again."

"Did he say which way they were going?"

"He mentioned a Port-O-Door at Alypium station."

Erec ran. Between his Sneakers and his fears for Bethany, he had never run faster. He wasn't sure if they were taking a bus to the station, but he ran to the closest stop just in case.

There was Bethany. She looked defeated and lost next to the man he recognized from the newsstand, what seemed like eons ago. Like the first time, her Uncle Earl seemed familiar, in a terrible sort of way. Erec remembered everything Bethany had said about him, and he filled with anger and hate. Bethany would not get on that bus.

"Bethany." Erec ran to her as the bus pulled up. "Let's *go*." He grabbed her hand and tried to run.

She looked paralyzed with fear. Her uncle pulled out his remote control. "No, not again!" she cried.

"Come *on*, Bethany," Erec said, pulling her. Her uncle pointed the remote at her, and she lifted from the ground, howling in pain. Erec grabbed the remote control from his hand and smashed it into a rock. Coils and wires came out. Bethany dropped down. "Run!"

They ran into a wooded area near the castle, her uncle close behind. "Keep going," Erec said. "I'll meet you behind the maze. We still have time." Erec swung to face Earl Evirly. Earl was bigger and taller, but compared to a destroyer he looked like a mouse. Erec remembered toppling the stone giants into each other, and he charged, diving at Earl's knees, knocking him over like a bowling pin.

Earl howled and cursed, rubbing his legs. He reached in his pocket but then seemed to remember Erec had broken his remote control. "You thug . . . you're going to get it for this."

"Yeah, we'll see." A tangle of vines hung from a tree. Erec shook some loose.

Earl winced and rolled over. "I think you broke my leg, you hoodlum," he whined.

"You deserve it. Put your hands behind your back, or I'll break your other leg." Erec tied him tight to a tree with the vine and ran.

CHAPTER TWENTY

The Under Mine

ETHANY WAS BEHIND the maze with the fifteen kids put to sleep by the sirens in the fourth contest. Kilroy, Umpee, King Pluto, and Ugry stood to the side, Ugry glowering worse than ever. A small crowd sat by the maze, including Jack, Melody, and Oscar.

Erec realized that Ugry might pull him out of the contest. The last time they saw each other, Ugry had been wildly hunting for him in the west wing. He stepped behind some kids to hide from Ugry's view.

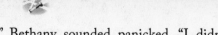

"Where's Uncle Earl?" Bethany sounded panicked. "I didn't know he had a remote control. He must have hidden it from me all this time."

"He's tied up in the woods."

She looked at him in shock. "We're in for it."

"I'm glad to see all seventeen of you made it to the fifth contest," Kilroy said.

Balor slid close to Erec. "Here's our friend, the hero, who likes to make explosions. You like explosions, Rick Ross?" Erec ignored him as Balor swaggered back to his friends.

Kilroy continued, "This contest is called the Under Mine. As you know, it was devised by King Pluto." The king smiled and nodded at the group, giving an extra nod when he met Erec's gaze.

"It's nice and simple," Kilroy continued. "You go down into a cave, find your way through the pathways and around the obstacles in the darkness, then out the other end. The first nine out will win."

Bethany said, "Our odds are fantastic. Over half of us will go to the last contest, and a third of those will win!"

"Which third, I wonder?" Erec looked at Balor, Damon, Rock, and Ward. Then he noticed what they were holding. "We should have brought our Magiclights," he whispered. "Other kids have theirs."

Kilroy led the group to a large pit in a field. Balor and his friends stood at the far end. Others followed them, figuring they must know something. Kilroy blew his whistle. "Go!"

Seventeen kids slid into the darkness. Magiclights flashed on. Balor, Damon, Rock, and Ward, lights on their hats, dashed up a mound of dirt and disappeared through a small hole. Only a few kept up and ran through after them. Everyone else clustered in that direction.

Magiclights flashed on and off, lighting up dozens of tunnels that led in different directions. Ramps went up and down, large rocks blocked passage entryways. The Under Mine made the castle maze look like a cakewalk. Erec and Bethany followed the light left by others, and searched for flashes in the distance. He could not imagine how difficult this would be if nobody had lights.

On the other side of the hole that Balor climbed through were just as many twisty passages and obstacles. Balor's group was long gone, so kids spread out to search, and it became even darker. Erec felt along a wall, blackness around him. He tried not to think about being lost in twisty caves in utter darkness. Everything felt like it was closing in. It helped to take deep breaths and concentrate on winning a scepter.

Bethany had a tight grip on the back of his shirt. "I'm not getting stuck here alone. Let's follow them." She pushed Erec toward three kids with Magiclights. "They have as much a chance of finding their way out as we do. More, I guess."

The Magiclight hanging in the air started disappearing as kids realized that others were benefiting from it. The caves got even darker. A boy ahead of them climbed up a large rock and through a hole in a low spot of the cave roof. Erec wondered if he upset something heavy up there, because a booming rumble sounded from above.

The walls and floor began to shake. A strange chorus of hoots and hollers erupted. Glowing bronze sheets of light sailed in from one of the tunnels. They cackled and shrieked, with eyes glowing like red coals, smashing Magiclights against rocks, whirling kids through the air. Erec realized they were bronze ghosts.

The bronze ghosts seemed to love chaos and destruction, for they laughed and whooped as they soared. A few kids thrown by the ghosts had hit their heads and looked hurt. Erec stood in front of Bethany, shielding her. At one point, a ghost dove at him, but before he touched Erec the ghost's hand froze in midair. The ghost grunted, and flew on to throw a boulder at other kids.

The glowing ghosts flew out another tunnel as fast as they had come in, leaving the room in utter darkness. Erec reached for Bethany's hand. They felt the walls for any openings left by the ghosts.

"It's okay," Bethany's voice shook. "Kilroy will realize that we're stuck. They'll get us out." Erec tried not to think what Ugry would do—probably plant a flower on the dirt over the cave and dust his hands.

The walls started to shake, much harder this time. Then there was a huge explosion. A wall blew into the cavern. The dirt roof fell in heaps. Rocks splattered through the blackness. With a thunderous rumble, the cavern filled with dirt from above.

Muffled screams came from all around. Bethany's hand yanked out of Erec's. He crouched in the blackness. "Bethany? Are you okay?"

He could hear her crying. "I'm stuck. I'm going to *die*. Ohhh, help me." Erec reached toward her voice. A huge rock sat on Bethany. She was panting as if she could barely breathe. Then Erec heard gurgling and her breath stopped. He felt and found her face was in a pool of water.

"Oh, no, you're not." Erec put Bethany's hand into the water, hoping her Instagills would work.

Then his head started to spin and he felt like he was floating. It was another cloudy thought, and he was never happier to have one. He focused deep within to put all of his energy into it.

It told him the way out. And more than that, it told him where to go to save those that could be saved. First he slid behind the large stone on Bethany, kicked away the rock wedged behind it, and shoved it off her.

She lay in silence, but he knew she was alive. He scooped her from the water and made his way over the wreckage to a boy with blood on his head lying in the dirt. "Up you go." Erec reached into the blackness and grabbed him under his arm, walking alongside him. Two more girls could walk once they were freed, and another boy was carried by the walking kids. As a group, they made it slowly through the rubble, through tunnels to the cave's exit.

Erec pushed Bethany out first, then climbed after her, pulling the others behind him. She deserved to win after what she had gone through.

Kilroy paced at the exit. "What's going on?" He stared at Bethany and the badly injured boy. "What happened? They need to get to the royal hospital, fast. I heard loud noises, but I couldn't get a hold of *anybody.*"

Erec saw Balor Stain grinning, and remembered he had been making explosives. Erec pointed. "He did it. They set off explosives in the caves before they got out. And bronze ghosts were down there. There are more kids stuck."

Kilroy looked shocked. "Balthazar and I thought something was wrong. Only seven of you came out before the noises started. There must be . . . four left. Balthazar just went in to see what was happening."

Erec shuddered, but Ugry appeared moments later with a girl, who was gasping for breath, floating under an arm of his cape. His eyes were slits and he looked monstrous. Erec shuddered when he saw him. "These *contestants* are going to the royal hospital," Ugry said.

Ugry waved his walking stick, and Erec, Bethany, and the others were suddenly lying in beds in front of a shocked Dr. Mumbai. "The cave fell in on us," Erec said. "Bethany and these two are really hurt."

Dr. Mumbai's hands dug into her hips. "And what were you doing there? Did risking your life to be in the contest help anything?"

"It helped us get out. He rescued us," said a girl.

"Yeah, and he won, too," said a boy.

Erec, for the first time, realized that he and Bethany had won. Kilroy had said that seven kids were out, and Bethany and Erec had been next. Bethany lay limp in her bed. Erec sat next to her. "You hear that, Bethany? You won. You're on your way to being Queen Bethany of Alypium."

Dr. Mumbai pushed everyone aside and took Bethany's pulse, feeling her breath with her hand.

"Step away." She looked at a girl whose leg was soaked in blood. "Everyone who can breathe, move down the ward." She pushed Bethany's bed near the boy who was bent over, moaning, and pulled curtains around them.

During the next hour, the other three kids stuck in the Under Mine appeared in various states in hospital beds. Every time the room cheered. None of them were as bad off as Bethany or the boy. Finally, Dr. Mumbai emerged. Everyone looked up. "They'll be fine. It looks like Bethany's Instagills saved her. Thank you, Erec."

Erec's body relaxed. The aches he felt that morning came back with a vengeance. Relieved that Bethany would live, he collapsed onto his bed with a grin.

Erec woke from a nightmare of crashing caves and destroyers. For a moment he forgot where he was and had no idea what time it was. He heard arguing. Bethany's Uncle Earl was telling Dr. Mumbai that Bethany needed to come home right away.

"Not on your life," Dr. Mumbai said. "*I'm* in charge here, although there seems to be a little confusion about that lately. She is in no shape to get up at all, let alone leave."

Earl flinched. "When can I take her, then?" he whined.

"When I okay it. It will be at least three or four days."

Earl stood over Bethany, arms crossed, like one might stand

over a lump of gold. Erec noticed a glint in Bethany's eye. Instead of looking afraid, she looked pleased, somehow, as if things were perfectly under control. Erec wondered why, because he had not yet figured out how to stop her from being carted away again.

Earl said, "Don't think you're keeping her here three more days. My newsstand is losing money every moment." Then he left.

Bethany's eyes narrowed. "Oh, boy. Will he be sorry." She coughed. "Wow. It hurts to breathe."

"Aren't you afraid of him?" Erec asked. "He probably bought a new remote control."

"Who cares?" Her voice was getting stronger. "After almost dying, being smashed under a huge rock in the pitch black, Earl and his tricks seem like nothing."

Erec thought of how *he* felt about Earl after having been trapped with acid-dripping destroyers, and he laughed.

"I was afraid of him since I was tiny. Well, I'm not his slave anymore."

Dr. Mumbai appeared with a big, green, gloppy spoonful for Bethany. She swallowed it bravely. Erec hoped she was right.

Spartacus Kilroy came into the royal hospital with a dazed look and a deep scratch on his cheek.

"Was that from the explosion?" Erec asked.

Kilroy's hand flew to his face. "Oh, this? No, it's nothing." He shook his head as if to clear his thoughts. "I want to thank you for your bravery in the Under Mine. You really helped these kids." He gestured around the room and smiled. "You won, you know that, right? And, even though we're all a little shook-up, I'm excited to tell you that the final contest will be tomorrow morning."

"What?" Bethany said. "Aren't there going to be investigations first? Find out who was responsible for the explosion and then kick them out?"

Kilroy shook his head. "Not my choice, anyway, but we need new rulers now more than ever. King Piter isn't doing us much good. It's time for new blood. Anyway, the sixth contest was recently changed. You're, uh, going to have to get something of value from a dragon's lair. We're taking you tomorrow morning."

"Perfect timing!" Erec smiled. "Bethany should be better by then."

"Bethany?" Kilroy looked confused. "You want to come?"

She nodded slowly. "Well, yeah,"

"She won too. She got out ahead of me."

"Yes, but you *took* her out. And her uncle is eager to get her home. She's been through enough."

"No! She's coming. Or I quit."

Bethany shook her head at Erec, while Kilroy looked at him strangely. "You're kidding, right? You'll go on without her. You wouldn't drop out now."

"Watch me."

Kilroy put his hands up. "Okay, okay. She can come. I'll pick you both up tomorrow morning . . . where . . . here?"

"Fine," Erec said, confused. "What about the other winners? Aren't they coming?"

"Oh, yeah. They're going to different dragon lairs, of course."

The door banged open, and Balthazar Ugry swept into the room. "You are not taking this boy to that dragon lair. You hear me, Kilroy?" Erec's breath caught. Ugry smelled worse than usual, almost bitter, like Pluto's dungeons. He looked terrifying.

Kilroy stared. "What, over your dead body?"

Ugry's voice thundered. "You do not amuse me. The boy stays."

"There's no reason for that."

"Really? I caught him pilfering in the king's chambers the other night. He's disqualified."

"Balthazar, not to doubt your word, but where's your proof?"

Ugry's eyes burned as he stared at Kilroy and then Erec. He turned and left without another word.

"Well," Kilroy said, "looks like he doesn't want you finding something."

"Hey," Bethany said, remembering something, "don't we get prizes for winning the fifth contest?"

Kilroy laughed. "I'm sorry. With all the commotion I entirely forgot. Here." He fumbled around in his pocket. "Why don't you take these." He handed Erec and Bethany each a small vial of gold glitter. "Heli powder. Dust a little on and you can fly for an hour." He winked. "Usually kids don't get to fly, so enjoy it. See you here tomorrow at ten. And don't worry about Balthazar."

After he left, Bethany asked, "Did it seem funny that he let me come tomorrow just because you said you wouldn't go without me? I thought he'd just say fine, we're both out."

"He's a good guy. He saw that it's only fair."

Erec and Bethany clinked their heli powder vials together. "Here's to the future king and queen!" Erec said.

"Three kids out of the last nine will win—that's one in three odds," said Bethany.

Erec had a bad feeling their odds were a little worse than one in three, with Balor Stain in the picture.

"Just think, if I become queen I can lock my Uncle Earl in a dungeon."

CHAPTER TWENTY-ONE
Aoquesth

THE NEXT MORNING Erec and Bethany were ready, Magiclights and heli powder vials tucked in their jacket pockets. Erec wore his Sneakers.

Kilroy showed up at the royal hospital a few minutes before ten, looking pale and worried. Erec noticed that he was not wearing his usual blue cape. King Pluto was with him, wearing a long, thick coat and a big grin.

"Who's taking the other seven kids?" Bethany asked.

"Other judges." Kilroy looked unhappy. "Let's go."

King Pluto raised his scepter and the four appeared at the mouth of a large, stone cave. Stoney Rayson was waiting there.

King Pluto smiled. "Erec is first. Here are the rules. A dragon in there is guarding something that you need to get. It's an eye . . . the dragon's eye. Use any means possible. Have you learned any magic? I could give you a remote control."

"I don't know that kind of magic," Erec said, feeling nervous. "I'm supposed to take an eye out of the dragon?"

"Oh, heavens, no." King Pluto laughed. "The eye isn't *in* the dragon. He's guarding it. Getting it might be . . . challenging. Cleverness is your best bet. Take your time. If a full day goes by, we'll send in . . . Bethany here to make sure you're okay. When you get the eye, bring it out, carefully, and hand it right to me. That would make you a winner. If you mess with it at all, try anything silly, you not only lose, but you go straight into my dungeons . . . and I think you know how bad that is. Understood?"

Erec nodded. He was amazed King Pluto knew he had freed his mother from the dungeons and he was still letting Erec compete.

"Then I get a turn?" Bethany asked.

The king threw her a withering look. "You're next."

Erec heard a sharp noise like a laugh and he looked back. Something moved behind some bushes. He wondered what it was but could not see anything unusual. He frowned. "Can I use your scepter?"

King Pluto cocked an eyebrow. "My scepter alone won't do the trick. The dragon is very powerful." He thought a moment. "If you absolutely need it, come back out and we'll see."

"What's the name of this contest?" Bethany asked.

King Pluto frowned. "I don't know. AdviSeer Kilroy, what would the name of this contest be?"

Kilroy's voice shook. "Good question. Since it's a new change, we didn't think up a name. I'd call it the Dragon's Eye."

Erec walked to the craggy rocks that formed the cave entrance. The passageway narrowed and got darker farther inside. Erec peered in, remembering the Under Mine caving in. He wondered if the dragon breathed fire. Could it burn him to a crisp? Should he be wearing heatproof armor? How in the world could he trick a dragon?

His imagination went wild as he thought of all the dragons he'd seen in books or movies. What would it look like? Maybe it would be as small as a dog. Yes, it must be harmless. He wouldn't be sent anywhere where he might die, would he? He turned on his Magiclight, filling the passageway with light.

Around a corner he heard a loud booming noise. As he got closer, he realized it was laughter. Wild, raucous laughter, coming from the dragon. The chortles were so earsplitting and deep that Erec realized this dragon was bigger than a dog. He slowed down but forced himself onward.

The dragon cackled, "Oh, this is keen. Really. They sent another one. Will you fools never stop trying to get the eye? How do you like to be done, lightly toasted or deep fried?"

Erec froze at the doorway and looked into a huge, rounded cavern. Light abounded from an unseen source. The cavern sparkled. Gems of all sizes and colors were fixed to the walls in wild patterns. Ruby-encrusted tabletops overflowed with stacks of gold bars and bowls of diamonds. In a corner, black leather chests brimmed with treasures.

Scepters and remote controls were neatly stacked alongside piles of magical items. Suits of armor, swords, chain mail, and shields, highly polished and gleaming, were artfully arranged. Some of the suits were posed in fighting positions, others lined in neat rows.

Erec had the feeling that the swords and armor were from grown men stupid enough to think they could fight a dragon and win. And here he was, a boy, with no armor, no remote control. If only Kilroy and King Pluto knew! They would never have sent him here.

The laughter died down. "Oh, I suppose you'll want me to give you some sort of test, hmm? A riddle? A game? Well, let's get on with it. I am a bit hungry. You'll never get it right . . . you can't. But dragons do like games, you know."

Erec's eye caught on something. There, hanging from a jeweled dagger in the wall, was a bright blue cape with a big white star and a tear in the side. Kilroy was here! Erec was stunned. They knew what they were sending him into. And it might be his death.

There was movement in the far corner of the cavern. A huge black nest of iron shavings and tree branches fused with melted gold, silver, and jewels gleamed from an immense alcove. A shiny, black, jointed wing unfolded and then closed again over a huge back. Glittering red and purple-black scales covered its body, and blood red spines grew down its back and tail. The beast's immense muscles rippled.

Erec was mesmerized, sure he was about to die, yet fascinated with the stunning creature that would kill him. Why anyone would try to harm one of these beautiful, powerful beasts was beyond him. The dragon was around twelve feet tall and twice as long, but it moved smoothly and gracefully. Steam gushed from its nostrils with each chuckle.

Its gaze met Erec's and the laughter stopped short. The dragon stared at him for a long time. One of its eyes glowed bright green, and the other was dim. Oddly, Erec's fear vanished. The dragon looked wise and beautiful, in a powerful, immense way.

"What a surprise," the dragon said. "But, then again, this *is* when your father said you would arrive. My, you look different."

"My father? You know me? We haven't met, have we?" Erec said.

"No, we have not met. But I've seen your picture. You look entirely different. Oh, pardon my manners. Let me introduce myself. I am Aoquesth, at your service. Please, don't worry. I won't hurt you. Come sit."

Erec took a deep breath, and walked stiffly into the cavern. For some crazy reason, he felt safe. And maybe, just maybe, he could get that eye.

He sat at an ornately carved onyx table close to the dragon. "It's *so* good to have company." The dragon sighed, resting on its haunches. "Ah." A long claw pointed at Erec's wrist. "Instagills. I have some too. The real kind. So handy, aren't they?"

Erec nodded stupidly. He couldn't stop staring at the magnificent creature whose black, jointed wings occasionally opened to an amazing span.

"I'm sure you can talk," the dragon continued. "Don't worry, I understand every language, just like dragon tongue is understood by all."

There was more silence as Erec gazed around the cavern in awe.

The dragon sighed. "I suppose I must ask you a riddle. It's one of my rules. But don't worry; I'll help you with it. Let's see. . . . Why is the world like a defective jigsaw puzzle?"

Nothing popped into Erec's mind, but he was quite nervous and it was hard to think.

"Take your time," the dragon said. "We'll come back to it later. Tea? Biscuit?" He swept a tin off a shelf. Erec shook his head.

"Let's play a game. Dragons love games. What do you like? Gin? Chess? Poker? Mancala? Senet?"

"I'm not good at chess, but I don't know the others." Erec wondered if getting the eye would hinge on a chess game that he would surely lose. "Is there a prize of some kind?"

"Good idea! The most precious prize of all. The only thing we can both give equally. Truth. The winner gets to ask a question, anything at all, and get a truthful answer. To the best of our knowledge, at least."

The dragon set a big amethyst chess board with inlaid marble on the table. The pieces were carved from diamonds and rubies in the rough.

"Would you like a drink? Root scotch? Whiskey? Firewater?"

"No, thanks."

"You go first," the dragon said. "The pieces are enchanted. You can empower them with your inner hopes and desires and fill them with energy. Then they will move on their own. If your aspirations are strong and worthy, they will make wise choices. The harder you want to win, the better they will play."

Erec thought this helped his odds. He was no chess master, but his hopes and desires were huge. He was so close to winning the eye and becoming king.

He looked at a piece and willed it to move like it was a hinged wooden arm. Nothing happened.

Aoquesth cleared his throat, a cross between rolling thunder and nails scraping a chalkboard. Erec's spine stiffened. "That won't work. If you want to move the pawn forward two spaces, just pick it up. Or, close your eyes and *want*. Want to win. Want to succeed. Then look at your pieces and implore them to move for you. It's your choice, really."

Erec stared. How did Aoquesth know his move?

"Oh, don't worry. I can't read your mind. That is, unless you really concentrate, like that."

Erec, feeling foolish, pushed a pawn ahead two spaces. The dragon snorted. One of his pawns sped forward on its own accord.

"How long have you lived here?" Erec asked.

"About five hundred years. My dear Nylyra died a century ago, so I've been quite alone." He sighed a plume of hot steam. "It's so good to play a nice game of chess with company. Recently I've been plagued with marauders, all after that darned eye. Well," he chuckled, "at least they're good snacks."

Erec realized this nice visit might come to a bad end yet, when Aoquesth discovered what he wanted. He looked at his pieces and thought about winning. Winning the contest. Winning the crown. Getting the scepter. Freeing his family from a lifetime of hiding. Freeing Bethany from her uncle. His mind swirled with need, and he pleaded with his chess pieces to win. His rough white diamond knight jumped ahead.

The dragon chuckled, one of his red knights jumping out. The game went on silently. Pawns hopped and bishops swept across the board. The dragon took a white castle, then another.

Erec concentrated. The next piece, a pawn, buzzed in Erec's mind. It willed him to move it with his own hand. He reached to touch it. It quivered with energy as he pushed it diagonally to take a red castle. Throughout the game, that pawn continued to need Erec's help, while the other pieces moved themselves.

"It's the Sicilian Dragon defense." Aoquesth winked. "Watch your queen. She's playing timid if you ask me."

Erec took a breath. His queen was in jeopardy. He focused harder on his dreams and protecting his queen, and she was soon safe. He accidentally knocked a red pawn off the board, into the pile. Aoquesth set a white one in its place. "But . . . that was your pawn," Erec said.

"No, I'm sure it was yours."

Erec was delighted when the pawn he had to push with his own hand moved into the seventh square. Another followed it, but that one was cornered by a red bishop. He couldn't lose it. He was so hopeful it or the other pawn would make it to the eighth square.

Focus. All of his rage and pain, his wishes and love, rushed out in a torrent. And out of the blue, his queen crashed out of nowhere to capture the red bishop. Aoquesth took a different pawn, and Erec pushed his pawn into the eighth square to become queen. He stared for a minute. "Checkmate."

"I've never seen *that* pawn promote and checkmate." Aoquesth drummed his claws on his stomach and leaned back. Erec hoped he wouldn't be angry and burn him to a crisp. "You win. Ask me anything you like."

Erec wanted to ask Aoquesth about the eye, but he was too curious about something else. "Why do I look different? What did I used to look like? An Identdetector said I changed too."

"That is really two questions. Dragons like rules, you see. I'll answer the first one. If you get the riddle right, with my help, then I'll answer your second question.

"Your mother changed your appearance, magically. She did it to protect you. Thanatos Argus Baskania was out to get you. You were in the way of his ultimate plans. When you were three, you moved into hiding. June changed your looks enough to disguise you, but she kept your eyes as they were . . . your eye, that is."

Erec choked. She had told him that herself, but he had not believed her. "But Baskania is the most powerful sorcerer in the world. He's trying to take over Upper Earth. He owns the Super A Team. What would he want with *me*?"

"That's a different question." Aoquesth's sigh heated the room. "You don't know much about yourself, do you?"

Erec shook his head rapidly. "What happened to my birth mother?"

"Now, that's a fourth question," the dragon told him. "Let's not get greedy. Have you thought of an answer to the riddle yet?"

He had forgotten it entirely. "What was it again?"

"Why is the world like a defective jigsaw puzzle?" Aoquesth stretched on the floor.

Erec's mind spun. If he could ever answer that riddle, it would not be in a cavern with a dragon. Aoquesth reached under a table piled with spun gold and silver, and slid a jigsaw puzzle in front of Erec. It was a silly puzzle: a picture of dragons flying with fairies. He pierced a puzzle piece with a talon and lifted it, tapping the empty space.

A piece missing from the world? A missing piece? Missing link? Erec hesitated, "A piece is missing?"

Aoquesth chuckled. "Close enough. Peace is missing. I'll count that as correct."

"So, do I win something?" Erec thought about the eye.

"Of course. Didn't I tell you I'd answer your next question?" Erec was disappointed, but he tried not to show it. "What did you look like? . . . Let's see, you were quite young. Your hair was wildly curly, almost white-blond. Your mother tried to turn it straight when she changed your looks, but part of it refused. Your face was wider. You were very tall and big for your age. Now you're . . . more average, but your strength is the same as it was."

Erec had no baby pictures from before age four. He thought about the rich, powerful loony, the "Crown Prince," wanting him dead. It seemed impossible. How would he have even heard of Erec? He would never have believed it before, although playing chess with a dragon did tend to make anything seem possible.

"I wish you would stay awhile." The dragon sighed. "It does get terribly boring here. Although I suppose it will be better when I no longer have to guard that eye."

Erec's head rose sharply. "Are you giving it to someone?"

"Yes, of course. You."

Erec was totally confused. "You're giving me the eye? The one

THE DRAGON'S EYE

you've been guarding, that people have died"—he gestured around the cavern at the empty suits of armor and tables of remote controls— "trying to get?"

Aoquesth laughed. "Those weren't *all* from idiots trying to get the eye. Some are quite old. But, yes, I'm giving it to you."

"Why?" Erec wondered if he should keep his mouth shut, take it and run, but he could not help asking. "Is it because I won at chess and got the riddle right?"

Aoquesth's voice softened. "You don't know? I'm giving you the eye because it's yours. You are the one I've been guarding it for, for the last ten years, Erec Rex. It is *your* eye."

Erec's hand flew to his glass eye. He felt dizzy. Nothing made sense.

Aoquesth blasted flames into an iron stove, and a kettle on top immediately whistled. He poured tea into a clean cup with a claw. "Have a sip. You know nothing at all, do you?"

Erec shook his head. The tea was spicy, and burned a little going down, but it helped him relax.

Aoquesth sighed smoke rings. "I'm afraid I'll have to break more of my rules today. Oh, my. Dragons and their rules. I had to help you with the riddle because I would have had to kill you if you got it wrong, a very old rule of mine. It's just not a good day when I have to break them.

"I will tell you the story of your eye. A while ago, your father...don't look so shocked; drink more tea... your father was on an expedition. He liked to keep a finger on the pulse of other lands. He caught me in a most unfortunate situation. I had stupidly flown through a tangle of trees with a fat elephant weighing me down, and my wing caught. It twisted in the branches and broke, leaving me tangled on the ground.

"Left alone, I'd have escaped before long. But I was still hurt when a group of men found me helpless. I was sure my life was over.

A dragon, you see, is priceless. Each of our scales is worth a fortune to humans, for medicines and potions. Our bones and claws are precious; even our blood brings riches. And above all that is the cave nearby filled with . . ." He nodded toward his humungous piles of treasure.

"Some of the men raised arrows and swords; your magic cannot kill us, you know. I tried to breathe fire at them, but I was so tangled I couldn't turn far enough. But your father is a remarkable man. He stopped the others from killing me, even helped untangle me. What's more, and even more embarrassing, I do believe he may have actually rescued me once before that as well." Aoquesth cleared his throat with a grating rasp.

"I owed him a debt of gratitude. He did not want treasure so I offered the best I had: my eye. Instead of keeping the power for himself, he chose to give it to you. You were too young at the time to use it, of course. But your eye was taken, as was mine. They were joined by the very best of sorcerer inventors, Heph Vulcan, for you to have on your fourteenth birthday.

"I suppose things never turn out as planned. You went into hiding. Your father knew the eye was not safe, so I agreed to guard it. I was starting to wonder if either of you would ever come get it. The number of fools who have wandered in here thinking they could waltz out with it was preposterous. And the measly amount of meat on men's bones made them barely worth the effort of the snack." He went into the alcove where his nest was and returned with a small black jar, setting it on the table before Erec.

"What should I do with it?"

"It's up to you. My part of the deal is done. Throw it away for all I care. But you'll probably want to keep it."

"But . . . I'm supposed to give it to King Pluto and . . . Spartacus Kilroy." Kilroy's cape dangled from the jeweled dagger. He had been here already . . . to try and get the eye? Erec began to wonder what would happen if he gave it to them. Would they take it and kill him?

Erec pointed. "The man who wore that cape . . . did he try to steal the eye?"

"I think he wanted to, but the moment he saw me he fled. I missed him, but he wasn't worth chasing. Far too bony."

"I'm supposed to give my eye to him, and they'll make me king."

Aoquesth laughed. "How feeble! You can't be that stupid!" He yawned with his huge, long mouth. "Tell them to shove off. The eye is yours. Now *you* have to protect it."

Erec would never get past King Pluto's scepter. That is, unless . . . "May I please leave the eye here for a few more minutes?"

The dragon looked surprised. "Make it fast. My time of guarding this thing is up, and none too soon."

Erec walked from the cave and saw Balor, Damon, and Rock scramble behind some bushes. Bethany was in a chair. She seemed stuck, struggling to get up. She shook her head wildly, mouthing, *No!*

Kilroy and King Pluto ran to Erec.

"Did you get it?" King Pluto asked. "Where is it?"

"Almost," Erec said. "I think I tricked the dragon. I answered a riddle and he was really surprised. Now he can't kill me. I just need the scepter, and I'm sure I can get it."

King Pluto's fist tightened around his scepter. "This is no toy," he protested. "Nobody should use this but me." His brows knit.

"But if I win the contest I'll get one, right?"

A crafty look crossed the king's eyes. "Of course. Silly me." His grip did not loosen. "You do know this won't protect you. Dragons have powerful magic. A scepter can't control them."

"Right. Or you would have gotten the eye yourself."

"Of course," said the king. Then his face darkened. "Not." He crossed his arms. "This is *your* contest, not mine. What was that dragon telling you?"

"He barely spoke." Erec shrugged. "Anyway, it's up to you. Do you want me to get the eye or not?"

King Pluto's face twisted into an angry half smile. He shoved the scepter at Erec. "You better bring this back *with* the eye or you and your family will wish you were dead."

A light, pleasant feeling came from the scepter. Words sounded in Erec's head. "Well, now what are you going to do?" It sounded scornful. "I can't destroy the dragon, you know."

Erec turned to Bethany, struggling to get out of her chair. He tilted the scepter slightly. "Release Bethany," he thought. Swirls of electricity ran through his body and down his arm, and then Bethany shot from the chair. Erec put a finger to his lips, and she sat back down.

"What is it?" King Pluto looked at Bethany, sitting innocently.

"She just needs to calm down," Erec said. He pulled the vial of heli powder from his pocket and held it up for Bethany to see. He shook it, mouthing, *Now.*

King Pluto strode forward. "What do you have there?"

"Just my prize from the last contest," Erec shouted as he ran into the cave.

Aoquesth was humming and rearranging remarkably huge jewels on an ornate table. The black jar with Erec's eye lay where he had left it.

"Thank you for waiting."

"You're welcome, Erec."

Erec picked up the jar and found it was warm. "Aoquesth? If I lost the chess game, what would you have asked me?"

The dragon snorted. "If you would use the eye for good or evil.

THE DRAGON'S EYE

It's your business. But I think you will use it for good, like your father would."

Erec wondered how surprised he would have been if Aoquesth asked that before he knew the eye was his. "Can you tell me how to get back to Alypium? I have a vial of heli powder that will let me fly an hour. Will that do it?"

"You'll need to fly three hours, high as you can, due east, straight from the mouth of my cave. You will pass over two seas. At the great mountains, you will see the giant bubble around Alypium from far off—seeing as you are acquainted with magic, that is."

"I'll never get that far." Erec held the small vial up.

Aoquesth sighed. "I suppose I could let you get caught by those pests who tried to get the eye this last ten years. Indeed, I might, had they not made my life so difficult, keeping guard day and night." His chest rumbled. He plucked a scale from his leg, set it down, and breathed a stream of fire at it. The cavern grew so hot Erec's skin sizzled. Aoquesth stepped on the scale, grinding it into the floor, until it was a pile of black powder. "Rub it all over," Aoquesth said. "With it, you will be able to fly for a day, at least."

"My friend outside needs to come too."

"Share it. There's enough for two, I'm sure." Aoquesth dropped a jar by the powder. Erec scooped the hot, sooty dust into the jar. He rubbed handfuls over his face, hair and clothing. He chuckled. When he left the cave covered in black soot, he would look like a cartoon knight that had been burned by a dragon.

"You *can* leave that scepter here," said Aoquesth.

"Not on your life!" the scepter squealed in Erec's head. "See what trouble you've gotten me in now?"

"I better not." Erec gripped it. "The new king will need it."

"So be it." Aoquesth turned back to his nest. "I think we will meet again someday, Erec Rex. Good-bye."

"Good-bye. And thank you!" Erec left the cave with the scepter, the eye, and the jar of dragon scale dust. All eyes turned toward him. For a moment, everyone froze. He knew he must look as if he were terribly burned.

The king came closer and Erec jumped up off the ground. The air seemed to thicken as he rose, until it felt like water. It was hard to breathe at first. He pulled the souplike wind under his arms and kicked. As he rose higher, King Pluto jumped, waving his arms as if he might catch him. "Get back here! Give me that scepter . . . and the eye!" Kilroy and Rayson stared in shock.

"I don't know if I can," Erec said. "I have something to do first."

CHAPTER TWENTY-TWO
The Eye

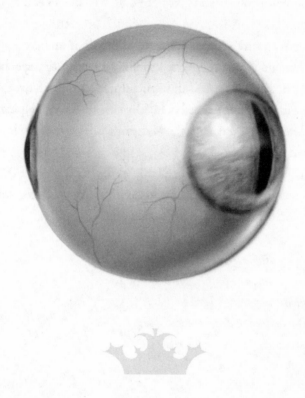

BETHANY ROSE IN the air beside Erec. She was grinning wildly. They were free. As they headed off together, King Pluto and Kilroy disappeared below them.

They flew east, kicking and paddling, away from the mouth of the cave. After they caught the wind, they moved easier. "Thank goodness you didn't give the scepter back. They were going to take the eye, lock you up, and tell everyone that Balor, Damon, and

Rock won the contests. I guess someone took Ward away yesterday, so he's out of the picture." She frowned at him. "Why are you so dirty?"

"Dragon-scale dust. It lets you fly a whole day. You'll need some." They sailed over forests and lakes. "Should we land so you can put it on?"

"I'm not so sure about landing. I'll try to do it up here."

He handed Bethany the jar, carefully holding the eye and the scepter. She rubbed on the dust and dropped the jar over a lake. They flew as straight as they could. The sun set lower, helping them aim, and warming Erec's back as he slid through the air. The wind pummeled his face.

A song crossed his mind: of all things, the lullaby his mother sang since he was small, the one that upset him lately. Shock registered as he remembered the part about the dragon.

> *He's guarding a gift that is just for you.*
> *It came from your daddy, with love so true.*
> *And this special gift, I tell no lie,*
> *Is your very own dragon eye.*
> *It was made for you, it fits right in*
> *So your new life can now begin.*

Erec's breath caught. He squeezed the jar.

"Why can't you use the scepter to get us back?" Bethany asked.

Erec looked at the scepter, surprised. "I didn't think about it," he said.

The scepter made a sound in Erec's head like a yawn. "That doesn't surprise me," it said.

Erec was glad it had kept quiet as long as it did. He waved it toward Bethany and himself, thrilled to use it again. "Send us to King Piter's castle."

Sharp waves of electricity surged through his body, rippling into the scepter. The power was tremendous. For a moment he felt like Emperor of the Universe. A jolt burst through him, and he almost dropped the eye. He felt like a bomb went off, except there he was, standing in the castle entrance with Bethany.

"That was easy," Bethany said.

"For you." Erec looked around the ornate room at the huge golden chandeliers and remarkable tapestries. If only there was somebody he could trust. He wasn't sure what to do next. Keep the eye, of course. Guard it. And keep the scepter, too. Maybe he could take over for King Pluto now. He could use the scepter to make himself king. He had won the contests.

A maid came in, saw them, and scurried away.

"I think we should find King Piter. If he's under a spell, maybe I could reverse it with this." They walked toward the west wing.

Hecate Jekyll walked by. She looked at them, surprised. "My, oh my. Look at you two. Were you sweeping the chimneys or something?" She chuckled and peered closer at their faces. "You two are worn out. Let's make you some chicken soup and maybe a plate of brownies."

Erec was starving, but he had to find King Piter. "Thanks . . . maybe later. I have something to do."

Hecate Jekyll eyed the scepter with suspicion. "That's not yours, you know."

Erec wanted to tell Hecate. Maybe she could help. She was one of the few people that seemed dependable. She had taken his side against Ugry, always been there with plates of treats. And she knew about magical things.

"I found a dragon's eye. It's mine, but King Pluto wants it. Ugry's after me, and Kilroy, and probably Rayson, too. I have to find King Piter."

Hecate put her hands on her hips. "Now, you listen. A dragon eye is serious business. You're right not to give it to anybody. You don't know who to trust. Don't hide it in your room, that's the first place they'll look."

She glanced up and down the hallway. "I saw King Pluto a minute ago. He's in the west wing with King Piter. He's planning to search the castle, and now I see why. I know a safe place where nobody will find you. You better run there, quick. Let him search. When he gives up, you come out and find King Piter. If he sees you now, he'll get the eye for sure." She waved for them to get going.

"It's in the kitchens," she whispered. "A storeroom under a round metal plate carved with an eye. Just say, 'One eye sees all,' and you can climb in and hide."

Erec didn't say he had been there before.

"Grab a snack on your way in," she said. "But run. I'll throw them off your trail."

Nobody followed them as they ran to the kitchens. Erec clutched the scepter and the jar.

When he rounded a corner his arm twisted. In a snap the scepter was wrenched from his grip. Two big men with eye patches grabbed him and Bethany as easily as if they were puppies. A thick man with a scar on his forehead walked toward the dormitories with Bethany kicking and screaming under his arm.

Erec tried to wrench himself from the grip of the huge dark man who carried him down a hallway. The jar with the dragon eye was under his shirt; he hoped the man did not notice it.

If only he had time to hide the eye. How could he give it up after all he had been through . . . after all his father, amazingly, went through for him to have it . . . after all Aoquesth went through. If King Pluto got it, Erec was headed straight for the dungeons, or worse.

Something about his mother's lullaby nagged at his mind. *It was made for you, it fits right in.*

Of course. If only he had thought of it before. He needed to take his glass eye out and put his own eye in. He unscrewed the jar and grabbed the slimy, slippery orb with both hands, so it wouldn't slide from his grasp. The jar dropped to the floor.

The man carrying Erec grabbed the empty jar and shoved Erec into a dark room, slamming the door behind him. Erec gasped. Countless eyes glowed close together with greenish light. It looked like a hundred-eyed monster staring at him in the darkness, each gaze boring into him.

Erec stepped back, shaking. He felt for the doorknob, but it was locked. His trembling fingers flicked on a light switch.

The man before him looked like nobody Erec had ever seen. Eyes covered the skin of his face, arms, chest, and neck. His black sorcerer's robe fell over his arms as the many eyes sank into his skin, making him look like Swiss cheese. Then they vanished altogether. His flesh seemed to swallow them.

For a moment his face was a blank oval of pale skin, and then a crooked nose erupted like a volcano in its center. An angry, sunken, cold blue eye with dark bags beneath burst through at the same time as a thin-lipped mouth split his face. In the place where his other eye should be was a terrible, dark hollow that he quickly covered with an eye patch.

Wispy silver gray hair streamed into his sharp widow's peak. He was tall, with a strong jaw, and sneer lines that dug around his thin lips. His icy blue eye stared at Erec with a cold, steely gaze.

Erec now recognized him. He was the man he had seen on television: the "Crown Prince." The man who had tried to kill him when he was young.

Erec flattened himself against the door. Baskania's eye seemed to probe into his soul. He felt himself weaken as he looked into it. Erec shook his head and grabbed the dragon eye tighter under his shirt.

Baskania cackled. "I see I have no need to introduce myself, Erec Rex. But for the record, I am Thanatos Argus Baskania. You may call me Prince Baskania, for now. Soon, it will be Emperor Baskania, when the new kings give me their scepters. It is my *greatest* pleasure to meet you."

Erec shook. He searched the small room for windows or other ways to escape. There were none.

"Now, please." Baskania held out his hand. "The eye. I have made myself ready." He removed his eye patch. "That's right. I've taken one of my own precious eyes to receive it. Don't worry; I've kept it someplace . . . handy. But I want my dragon eye in place for the coronation ceremony, which will happen in"—he looked at his watch—"three minutes."

"What eye?" Maybe he could stall for time.

"The one you're grabbing under your shirt. I wouldn't have to see through things to know that it's right in front of you. Now hand it to me carefully. Don't ruin it."

"But King Pluto wants it. He's searching for it now."

Baskania loosed a wild, bone-chilling laugh. "He was getting it for me. *I* sent him to the dragon's cave with you to get it." He smirked. "When Pluto found out who you were, he almost let you die in that underground contest of his. Not good thinking. We needed you. With your eye, and the help of Pluto and my assistant in this castle, the world shall soon be *mine*."

Of course. His assistant Balthazar Ugry. Or could it be Kilroy?

"Hand it to me now. I don't want to miss the ceremonies." Erec felt the squishy eye tug from his hand. It was sliding out of his grip. He grabbed harder, squeezing, and the pulling eased off.

"Don't crush it," Baskania said in a hoarse whisper. "It will break. Then neither of us will be happy."

His blue eyes bored into Erec's and his voice slid into low tones.

"What are you afraid of? Don't believe the dragon. They're dumb animals. Give me the eye, and you will rule under me, Erec. You want power to change things. The scepter can be yours. We'll trade: eye for scepter, to use and command as you wish. You could do great things, Erec. I could use somebody powerful like you to help me." Baskania's steely blue eye drove through him. "Your mother said I wanted to harm you. Nothing is further from the truth. I wanted to help you, Erec. To let you reach your full potential. To rule at my side. I can do things nobody else can do. And I'll teach them to you. We will command the very Substance together, make it do our bidding."

Erec's head spun. He began to think about the scepter. He wanted it back.

"Forget your mother. What has *she* made of you? A 'Loser,' as they call those doltish Upper Earthlings, with nothing to your name. You were right not to trust her. She lied to you all along. This is your chance, Erec. Give me the eye, and I will give you all the power you ever wanted, to right the wrongs of the world, to save your family.

"You don't know how to use the eye, anyway. It's useless to you. Hand it to me slowly. I don't want to force it from you and damage it."

Erec stared at him, confused.

"I can see into your mind, Erec. I know what you went through trying to save your mother. You did the right thing, listening to the shadow demon. He was right about her. She was where she belonged."

At the mention of the shadow demon, Erec's mind cleared. He remembered how he had failed, how he believed its slick words.

Erec pulled the eye from under his shirt. On one side of its slippery orb was a shiny blue iris that matched his own. On the other was a large green, glowing circle with a yellow rim and a long black slit that looked like Aoquesth's eye.

He pulled his lower lid down and dug his fingers around his glass eye. It yanked free with a sucking sound and dropped on the floor. Erec pushed the dragon eye into the gap.

The lullaby was right, it fit right in. It felt better than the glass eye . . . but then it started to push and pinch, as if it were growing and making connections. After a sharp sting, he could see through it.

At first everything seemed to glow green, and then Erec could feel the eye move, turn around. He had been looking through the green dragon eye, he was sure, and now it was turning to the other side, his normal eye. After years of having only one eye, everything sprang into three dimensions. He thought of his father and thanked him.

Baskania glared at Erec with his icy blue eye and the awful, dark hole he had made for the dragon eye. "Fool. Now I'll have to kill you to get the eye. You had your chance. But the ceremony is beginning. I want to enjoy it first. You're not going anywhere." A rope sprang from Baskania's palm. It instantly wrapped Erec tight from his shoulders to his knees.

Baskania slid his eye patch on and waved a finger at the wall behind him. It melted away. Noise burst in from the throngs of people behind it. They were in an alcove off the throne room. Baskania raised his face and howled like a wolf. The noise was lost in the crowd.

King Piter sat on his throne above the swarms of people. Apparently there had been enough notice to gather a few hundred from Alypium, if not elsewhere, to watch the ceremony.

The three scepters lay in a clearing before King Piter's throne, bases touching, like a peace sign. Between the poles lay three crowns. Several paces away, Balor Stain, Damon Stain, and Rock Rayson looked smug in long black robes.

Erec struggled against the ropes and almost toppled over. He shouted for help. Baskania did not seem to hear him over the noise.

King Pluto appeared in the alcove near Baskania. The king dropped to one knee and bowed his head. "My liege."

Baskania nodded and King Pluto stood. Baskania put his hand on the king's. "Things are going as planned. You will be rewarded for this beyond your wildest dreams. Without their scepters, your brother and sister will be weaker than slugworms. It will be your turn to show them what power is. As for the boy, I have fixed your mistakes. After the ceremony, the eye will be mine."

King Pluto's eyes narrowed at Erec. "He's using it."

"No matter. When I kill him after the ceremony, it will come back out."

Spartacus Kilroy stood before the throne. His voice echoed. "I am proud to announce . . . the time has come for the second coronation of kings for the great lands of Alypium, Aorth, and Ashona!" The crowd cheered. Erec could not see Bethany anywhere.

"Here are three fine young gentlemen who have shown their strength, nobility, and valor through six difficult trials, with grace, speed, and courage. Let me announce the future king of Alypium . . . Balor Stain!" Mad applause shook the room. "And his brother, the next king of Ashona . . . Damon Stain!" Erec struggled against his tight ropes. They did not budge. "And finally, son of the famous Super A Team bouncer, Stoney Rayson, the future king of the subcontinents of Aorth . . . Rock Rayson!" The crowd went wild.

If only everyone knew it was he who had really won, and that Balor, Damon, and Rock would hand their scepters over to Baskania, who would destroy them. Erec's shouts were lost in the noise of the crowd.

Kilroy continued, "As you all know, to our great misfortune almost ten years ago, the crown triplets, only three years old, and our beloved Queen Hesti, were killed. It should be those three, two boys and a girl, receiving the crowns today." A murmur spread through the crowd. "But they are not here. They cannot be. And life must go on.

So, after Alypium, Aorth, and Ashona's five hundredth anniversary, we have chosen the next kings to follow in the footsteps of our current leaders. Our royalty have been blessed with long life. This year, King Piter, King Pluto, and Queen Posey turned five hundred, along with their countries."

Erec stared at King Pluto's back in amazement. He looked around fifty. With his power, history, and age, how could he bow down to Baskania?

"Our royalty have weathered the years exceptionally well. But they agree, it's time to step down. Few of us were here at the last coronation, four hundred and eighty-five years ago. It was so long ago, even they forget the details." Kilroy glanced at King Piter, who stared impassively at the crowd.

"It is said that during the ceremony the three scepters will rise and fly to those meant to be king or queen. We do not know if that will happen today. It is said that the Lia Fail, the stone at the base of King Piter's throne, will scream when a rightful ruler is crowned. This is probably a myth.

"It used to be thought that future kings and queens needed to perform twelve quests, or labors as they used to be called, before they could receive their scepters and rule. We do not believe this to be true today. These three young men will be kings this very day, receive their scepters, and go off to breathe new life into their kingdoms! Now let the ceremonies begin."

Kilroy stepped back. The lights dimmed. Nine hooded figures in black robes appeared. They carried lit torches and formed a circle around the scepters, humming. Erec started to scream, "Help!" at the top of his lungs, now that the room was quieter. Baskania narrowed his eyes and a cloth appeared over Erec's mouth, holding it shut, before much sound had gotten out. When he tried again he could not make any noise.

Erec sank against the door. At least he could see through two eyes . . . before he died. The dark figures around the scepters, hidden under their hoods, chanted a monotonous song. Erec could not understand their words, but they were mesmerizing.

Their torches glowed in the dimmed room. Candles were lit in sconces on the walls, on big pedestals, and in basins. The room took on a warm, rippling glow. The chant grew louder and louder. It began to sound like a war cry. The throne room, packed with people, was still. Everyone looked mesmerized, even Baskania.

The song ended in a shout. The cloaked figures dropped to their knees.

Silence filled the room. Everyone stared at the scepters and crowns. Balor, Damon, and Rock leaned forward. Baskania bent forward too, arm lifting as if to reach the scepters.

Erec bit his lip. It wasn't supposed to end this way. One scepter twitched upward. Every eye in the throne room watched as it floated slowly off the floor.

CHAPTER TWENTY-THREE

Straightening Up Again

A N EAR-SPLITTING SCREAM erupted, like a banshee. It split through Erec's head. Then it stopped as suddenly as it started, and quiet prevailed. Several people murmured: "The Lia Fail." "The stone screamed." "They're the rightful rulers."

The scepter hovered another moment and then sailed through the air, between Balor and Damon Stain. People in the crowd stared as it flew over their heads. It soared past King

Pluto and Thanatos Baskania . . . and landed at Erec's feet.

"Pleased ta meet ya, mate!" The scepter quivered. The entire throne room crowd was now staring at Erec, bound in rope with a cloth over his mouth.

Baskania seemed stunned. Erec stared at the scepter in shock. This was not the one he had used before, the one that belonged to King Pluto.

"Come on, mate. You better pick me up, I'd say. Look at you."

The words jolted Baskania into action. He started toward Erec.

Erec wanted the scepter desperately. He needed it. He stepped on his heel and slid his foot out of his shoe. The top of his legs were tied together, but he reached as far as he could.

Baskania was steps away.

"C'mon, mate. Reach."

Erec's toes touched the gleaming scepter. Power surged through his foot into his body.

Free me, Erec thought. In a second, Erec's ropes and the cloth over his mouth were gone. The crowd gasped.

"You might want to capture them. Just a thought." The scepter sounded in Erec's head.

Baskania and King Pluto were frozen, wide-eyed. Erec picked the scepter up and aimed it at them.

Eyes flashed open all over Baskania's face, neck, and hands. Erec shuddered at the disgusting sight. Then, before Erec knew it, Baskania and King Pluto vanished.

It happened so quick. If only he had worked faster. But he wouldn't make that mistake twice. A few other people needed to be stopped as well.

Erec lifted the scepter into the air. "Everyone, freeze. Nobody can leave from where they are," he shouted. Power surged and ripped through him and the scepter. It created such shock waves of energy that it was hard to hold. He felt like he was struck by lightning. It took all his strength to hold on. Then all went still.

There was an uproar. People shouted and yelled, but nobody was able to lift a foot from where they stood. Balor Stain stared at Erec with sheer hate, struggling to move.

Erec lifted the scepter. "Balthazar Ugry, rise up and answer my questions." Another surge of power shot through the scepter. Ugry levitated with a menacing look. He seemed perfectly comfortable off the ground. The crowd looked from Erec to Ugry in confusion.

"Tell the truth," Erec shouted.

Ugry glared. "My name is Balthazar Ulric Theodore Ugry. I have a younger brother named Buttleby Ugry. I reside in King Piter's castle in Alypium. I am the AdviSeer to the king. I was born in Alypium and educated at Oxvard before my apprenticeship." Ugry crossed his arms and stared defiantly.

"Keep going."

"It is evening. The sun has set. Alypium has a weather shield to control its temperature." His voice rang out, stony and sarcastic.

"Tell the truth about your plot to take over Alypium." Erec pointed the scepter at Ugry. The power surging through him filled him with pleasure.

"I have no such plot."

"What did you say to Stoney Rayson in the armory, then?"

"I was never *with* Stoney Rayson in the armory."

"Have you been hypnotizing King Piter?"

"Absolutely not."

"Did you order the minotaur to be sent to the middle of the maze?"

"No."

"Well, why were you always around whenever bad things happened?"

"Because . . ." Ugry paused. "I was trying to keep an eye on things. Something was going on. I just had to find out what."

Erec stared. "Then why were you chasing me in the west wing?"

"Because you were running around in the king's quarters, which is forbidden, after having been warned. You deserved to be thrown out of the castle. Who knew what you were up to? And then you illegally used a private Port-O-Door to enter King Pluto's dungeons, no less, to help a prisoner escape."

The crowd gasped. Ugry appeared to enjoy making Erec look bad.

"How did you know I went into King Pluto's dungeons?" Erec asked.

"I figured out before long that you used the Port-O-Door. I followed you in. As I said, it's my job to keep an eye on what goes on in my king's castle, especially when he's not able to do so for himself."

Erec stared at Ugry. "You followed me in. You saw what happened to me with the shadow demon. And then . . ."

Ugry scowled. "I saved you."

"And you didn't want them to take me to the final contest. I heard you arguing with Kilroy. It's because you knew . . ."

"Yes. After what happened in the dungeons I looked in Spartacus's book and figured out who you were. I knew why they were taking you to the dragon's lair. But I could not stop it from happening."

"It's okay," Erec said. "I have my eye now." The room was silent. Balthazar Ugry lowered back into the crowd.

"Spartacus Kilroy, rise and answer my questions," Erec shouted. The scepter buzzed. Kilroy rose in front of the throne. King Piter watched with mild amusement. Kilroy looked afraid of falling, and kept reaching to his feet as if he could get down.

"Spartacus Kilroy, tell the truth about your plot to take over Alypium."

Kilroy looked stunned. "I had no plot to take over anything. Why would you even think that?" Kilroy looked at the throngs below him. "This kid has a screw loose."

"Tell the truth. Were you in the armory with Stoney Rayson?"

"Never! What is that about, anyway?"

"Have you been bewitching King Piter?"

"No! Or . . . not that I know of." He frowned. "Why did I just say that?"

"Weren't you forcing coffee down his throat? Was the coffee laced with something?"

"It's medicated," Kilroy said, exasperated. "The king needs his medications every two hours or he might die, I'm told. I do as instructed. He gets medications every two hours like clockwork, then his evening dose with hot chocolate at eight. It does him wonders. I can see him relax."

"Did you order the minotaur?"

Kilroy sighed and looked down. "Yes. I was told it would be part of the first contest. What a disaster." He hung his head.

"Why were you helping King Pluto get the dragon eye?"

"He said the eye would help our great nations grow." Kilroy sighed. "I was worried about sending you in there. It seemed too dangerous. But he assured me you would be fine. And he was right. He said you broke into his dungeons and let loose a dangerous prisoner. You should be locked up. And then you stole the eye!"

The crowd gasped again. Erec was sure he would be mobbed if they were not all frozen in their spots.

Kilroy sank to the floor. Erec was exasperated. He knocked the scepter onto the floor. "Show me who was bewitching King Piter! Who I heard speak to Stoney Rayson in the armory! Show me the person Baskania called his assistant in Alypium! Raise him for all to see."

At the other end of the room, Hecate Jekyll rose into the air.

Erec bit his lip. The one who helped him hide . . . must have delivered him straight to Baskania. The expert on magical potions and brews. The head of the king's kitchens. She had been there forever.

The scepter burned in Erec's hand. "Tell the truth. How long have you been bewitching King Piter?"

Hecate's face twisted, but she could not hold back her words. "Nearly ten years." Gasps flew around the room.

"And Spartacus Kilroy did your dirty work, giving him 'medications' every two hours?"

"Yes, and I put spells on him every day," she snapped. Kilroy's face was white.

"Why Kilroy?"

"He's trusting and not too smart," she said, glaring. "I chose him when Ruth Cleary, King Piter's old AdviSeer, was killed. Kilroy wasn't qualified and was not a seer, so he had to rely on me. He took orders and kept secrets."

"Then it was you whispering in the armory with Rayson, stealing weapons to take over the Kingdoms of the Keepers."

"Yes, it was me," she hissed.

There was an uproar. Erec pointed the scepter at Hecate Jekyll, and suddenly she was bound with ropes as he had been.

King Piter's head lolled to the side. He would be himself again, when the potions wore off. But not soon enough. Erec pointed the scepter at King Piter. "Let King Piter wake up and be himself."

"Good idea," said the scepter. A flare of power rocketed through Erec. He was getting used to the feeling.

One of King Piter's eyes opened wide. Then it drooped. His other eye did the same. Then he sat up straight on his throne and shook as if he were being electrocuted. When he stopped, he looked around the room with an eyebrow lifted. A smile spread across his face. The room was deadly silent.

King Piter began to laugh. It started as a chuckle and spread over his entire face until tears poured from his eyes. He bent over, pounding his knees. It seemed he had gone mad.

As he sat back up, it looked like the king unfolded before Erec's eyes. His back straightened. Muscles now rippled beneath his royal robes. He looked shockingly big as he filled out his large frame. The king laughed and sniffed. He found a handkerchief in his pocket and blew his nose, then held it out in disgust. "This is ancient." He tossed it to the floor.

"What a doozy." The king's voice echoed deeply. "When I make a mistake, I make it big. And it took a mere boy to fix things. Come here, young man."

Erec made his way forward. People leaned away to let him through but could not move their feet, so he unfortunately stepped on a few toes on his way.

The king's eyes sparkled, almost too full of life. He smiled warmly and pulled him into a hug. "Thank you, Erec," he whispered. "I'm sorry I didn't listen to you."

The king looked around the room and chuckled. "Well, I guess you can't change history. What an interesting chain of events. Things happened so quickly. I was off my guard. My wife was gone. My triplets were gone. Ruth Cleary was gone. Hermit was gone. I had nobody. Something was going to happen, but I didn't know how . . . couldn't avoid it. I had just returned from my friend who was helping . . . take care of something, and a servant brought me a cup of tea . . .

"Now look. Almost ten years have gone by." He mopped his brow, then touched the top of his head and felt his face. "How embarrassing. Have I really let myself look like this? And the castle. I remember the last thing I did was put it on its side, as I was sinking under. What a mess." He winked at Erec. "I remember you encouraging me not to drink the coffee. Good advice. May I have my scepter back?"

"Well . . . I think it's mine now," Erec said, not sure what to do.

King Piter smiled. "It is, in a way. But not yet. You have been found by the scepter and the Lia Fail. But there are some things you must do before the crown and scepter can be yours. Twelve, actually."

Erec slowly handed the scepter to King Piter. He hated to let go. The king waved it with a practiced arm.

Suddenly, the room lurched onto its side, away from the throne. If people had not been stuck to the floor, they would have fallen in heaps on the back wall. Instead, they hung from their feet, their heads toward the wall, swaying and bumping into each other.

Erec, who was not stuck to the floor, flew back into several people. As they flattened against the floor he tumbled over them toward the wall. He caught hold of a hand and held on, dangling.

"Hmm." King Piter hung on to the back of his throne. "Somebody 'fixed' the gravity in here, of course."

He waved the scepter again. Gravity readjusted. People pulled themselves back onto their stuck feet, untangling limbs. The room looked like a giant game of Twister. Erec climbed back to the king, stepping on more feet.

The king's eyelids flickered, and a mirror appeared in his hands. He looked at it with disgust. In a blink, his limp gray hair turned thick and white, his beard full, and he grew taller and cleaner. He still looked old, but also sharp and wise. "Funny. Although I was completely bewitched, I can remember everything, most notably what happened here tonight." With a twitch of his finger, the bound Hecate Jekyll was before him.

The king sighed. "Hecate. You were always such a treasure: smart, organized, educated. You deserved better than this. You chose the wrong path, my dear."

"Your time is over," Hecate sneered. Her bun unwound and long black and gray hair flowed wild over her shoulders. King Piter sighed and tapped his finger. She vanished.

"Where is she?" Erec asked.

"In my dungeons," the king told him sadly.

"Stoney Rayson was working with her, for Baskania," Erec said.

There were gasps. "Impossible." "Not Prince Baskania. He's a good man." "Rayson? He's an athlete, not a criminal."

"Baskania was just here," Erec said. "He's the one who tied me up."

People shook their heads in disbelief. "Must have been someone else. The Sorcerer Prince wouldn't do that."

The king scanned a finger over the crowd. "I'm afraid Mr. Rayson has already left. Some may find it hard to believe Baskania was behind this. He seems to have become quite popular these last ten years." He cleared his throat and eyed Erec's chest strangely. "Those glasses look familiar. Do you mind if I have a look?"

Erec hesitated. "I need them."

"Of course I would give them right back, but if you're not comfortable . . ."

Erec handed them to King Piter. He put them on. His expression changed to delight. His lips tightened and tears rolled down his face. "My darling . . . I'm back . . . Yes, I know . . ." His voice was tender. "It's okay now, that's right. We'll talk tonight." He handed the glasses to Erec. "You did a good job. I hate to think what might have happened if not for you."

Erec coughed uncomfortably. "I need your help. I have a friend, Bethany Evirly. Her uncle is keeping her prisoner. Her parents died, and her uncle makes her work at his newsstand all day long and he doesn't care about her. She really wants to stay in Alypium." Erec was sure he had not explained it right. What adult would help a child run away from home?

316   THE DRAGON'S EYE

"Hmm . . . Her name is Bethany, you say?"

"Yes."

"And her uncle's name?"

"Earl Evirly."

"Ahh. Earl Evirly. I remember him. Funny how much I can recall from my haze. He took directions from Hecate. I remember some of their conversations. Well, let's have a talk with Bethany and her Uncle Earl."

King Piter tapped two fingers on his throne, and Bethany and Earl stood before them. Earl looked around in shock, and then his eyes bugged at Bethany. "There you are, you twerp. You thought you could get the best of me, huh? Sneaking off on your own? Well, I have some mighty big friends, see? Who do you think brought you here? You'll never get far from me. And you'll *pay* for this." His eyes gleamed.

Bethany looked horrified, believing her uncle. Then she saw Erec's big grin, and King Piter, alert and chuckling. She stepped back in shock.

Earl Evirly noticed the king at the same time. His jaw dropped. He looked around wildly.

"You won't find Ms. Jekyll here, if that's who you're looking for," King Piter said. "She'll be spending some time relaxing in my dungeons for a while." Earl turned white and started coughing. "So, you are Bethany's *uncle*, are you?"

"Y-yes." Earl straightened. "I am. She is a runaway and a thief, and needs to come home immediately."

"I see." King Piter stroked his beard. "And her parents are dead?"

"Yes." Earl sounded uncomfortable.

"Is she your sister's child? Or your brother's? What were her parents' names?"

Earl glanced at Bethany for help, but she crossed her arms. The king tilted his scepter toward Earl and said, "I'll follow Erec's lead today. I want you to—how did you say it, Erec? To tell the truth about your relationship with Bethany. Is she your niece?" At the scepter's command, Earl clutched his elbows and squeezed his knees together. "No." Bethany's mouth fell open.

"Why did you have possession of Bethany these last, what . . . ten years?"

Earl squeezed his eyes shut as if he might disappear. Words came from his mouth on their own accord. "Her parents were killed here almost ten years ago. It was thought she might be valuable. I was assigned to watch her until she could be of use."

"Who killed her parents?"

"Dumb thugs following orders. I don't remember their names."

"Of course. Well, you've done your job, Earl. Now the time has come, as you have said, and I will take over the care of Bethany . . . Evirly, is it? Maybe you'll just be Bethany for now." He winked at her. "You look familiar, Bethany. Would you mind living in my castle as part of my family? I don't have any other children here, so pardon me if I spoil you a bit. We'll have lots of parties for you and keep plenty of young friends around."

Bethany burst into tears and threw her arms around the king. Earl's face turned bright red.

"As for you, Earl, what you have done is called kidnapping. I think you'll do well with a corrective memory adjustment." Earl Evirly vanished.

"Where did he go?" Bethany asked.

"To the royal hospital. It will take a few days to recover from his memory adjustment. He'll be shaken up awhile, I think."

"What is a corrective memory adjustment?" Erec asked.

"In Alypium, we don't need prisons. A memory adjustment gives the terrible memory of having spent twenty years or so in a horrible, inhumane prison. Mistreatment, freezing cells, starvation, terrible food . . . Earl will know it didn't really happen, but it won't matter. It will feel completely real because he remembers it so well. There is very little crime here. Of course, there are the dungeons and a few outlying prisons for those hopeless few.

"Now, is there anything else before I release our captive audience?"

Erec had forgotten that the entire room was glued where they stood. From their rapt expressions, it seemed that most of them had forgotten as well. Erec spoke up. "Yes. My family has been on the run. My mother, June O'Hara, just escaped from King Pluto's dungeons. I think he is on Baskania's side."

King Piter nodded. "I'm afraid so. Of course, I will help your mother and you. If you like, you may invite her to live in Alypium, with your entire family. I won't bring them here myself. It would be rather a nasty shock. Why don't you talk to them about it? It might be a good place for you to live, especially if you are interested in becoming Alypium's next king."

Erec's face flushed. The next king!

"Um, excuse me, King Piter?" Bethany said. "That boy, Balor Stain, stole my cat, Cutie Pie. Could I have her back?"

The king smiled. "That wouldn't be the cat on the window sill, would it?"

"Cutie Pie!" The fluffy cat stretched and trotted into Bethany's arms. "When did you escape? Have you been looking for me?" Tears drenched Cutie Pie's fur as she rubbed Bethany's cheek.

Damon pointed. "The cat's out of the bag. Look, the cat's out of the bag."

Balor held his head in his hand. "It *heard* us. That stupid cat tells secrets."

Cutie Pie leapt onto King Piter's shoulder and whispered in his ear. The King nodded, sighing, and shook his head. After what seemed like an eternity, the cat jumped to Bethany.

"It sounds like these three boys here and their friend Ward Gamin were making some wicked plans. Still, I can't punish people for plans, especially if they're only overheard by one cat. But you will have to make amends for stealing the cat." He pointed his scepter at Balor. "What is your most valuable possession here?"

Balor's face was tight. "My watch. If I point it at someone, I can hear what they are saying."

"You must give it to Bethany, in apology. If you try anything else, I will not be so lenient." Balor's watch flew off his wrist into Bethany's palm. Balor cursed under his breath.

Bethany held it with disgust. "Take it," she held it to Erec. "I don't want anything from him."

"You sure?" Erec looked at the buttons and small speaker.

"I'll just throw it away. You've been wanting a watch." Erec put it on.

King Piter wiggled a finger. "You are free to move. I invite you all to a feast tonight in honor of Erec Rex, your future king!"

The crowd broke into applause. King Piter winked at Erec. "We'll talk later. I'm afraid I have some more straightening up to do."

CHAPTER TWENTY-FOUR

The Future King

E REC PUT HIS glasses on in his dormitory room. His mother sat over a sleeping Nell, stroking her hair. The tiny room was filled with cots and sleeping bags.

"Mom?"

"Just a minute," June whispered. She walked into an empty kitchen.

"I did it. I have the dragon eye. Baskania tied me up, but then a scepter flew to me. I used it to get King Piter back to normal. We're safe now! He said we can live in Alypium . . . Do you want to?"

June's eyes were moist. She put her hands over her heart. "We have a lot of decisions to make, don't we?"

Erec thought of his siblings crammed into a tiny room they could not afford. "I bet everyone would like it here," he said.

His mother nodded, lips tight. "Come home tonight, Erec?"

"You bet."

Erec wondered if the festival hall was always this big, or if it was magically expanded to fit the crowds. The feast was delicious, filled with foods from all parts of the magical lands.

People Erec had never seen thanked him profusely for rescuing King Piter. Just when Erec felt like escaping into his dorm room, Bethany appeared. She whisked him onto the dance floor. "Wow. You look great with two matching eyes."

"Just wait till you see how I look with the dragon eye when it's turned around." Erec wasn't sure how to dance to the classical music, but they whirled around the floor, nonetheless. "How did you get away from Earl?"

"I refused to get in the Artery with him at Alypium Station. He pointed a remote control at me, but I grabbed it, and he screamed and ran away. I don't know why I was afraid of him for so long."

A hand on Erec's shoulder halted the dance. It was King Piter. "Pardon me for interrupting. I hate to break up this well-earned dance, but I'd like to talk to you." He led Erec into a small anteroom. "Thanks for saving me from the spell. I shudder when I think what almost happened."

Erec smiled broadly.

"I am sorry you can't have the scepter yet. It is an old tradition that a ruler must perform twelve quests before assuming command. As with most traditions, there is good reason. Each test will teach you something or give you something you will need to rule well.

"The three future kings and queens should perform the tests together, but you are the only one that the folks around here know about now. We can't afford to wait for any others. Nothing says a future king cannot begin the quests without the other two. I suggest you start soon. Hopefully, we will find the two others as you go. In the meantime, you may pick two friends, if you wish, to help with each quest."

"Can you come with me?"

"I'm afraid not. These are tests for the new, not the old. I need to keep watch here as well. And get back to work on those Aitherplanes. The Substance." He shook his head. "If it's the last thing I do I want to right it. But maybe you'll have better luck." He winked.

"As you know, the scepter is quite powerful," continued the king. "Without training, it could take you over and rule you rather than you ruling with it. You may have gotten the wrong impression today. I only use it when I absolutely must. Today I used it more than was safe even for me."

The king tapped his chin. "I wonder if the ceremony today could have tricked the scepters into being used by someone other than their true rulers. If it did, the results could have been disastrous. Thanatos Argus Baskania is deranged. The scepters would have driven him into complete, destructive insanity. He is much older than I am. He created the Kingdoms of the Keepers and wanted to rule them from the start. When it was prophesied we would rule, he waited too long to kill us. We had done a number of the twelve labors and had become too powerful."

"Why is he so rich and famous in Upper Earth?"

"He breaks one of our cardinal rules: Interestingly, it is one that he came up with himself. No magic is to be done in Upper Earth. He uses magic of all kinds in his factories and businesses, from creating goods at no cost to making the public crave his products, however poorly they are made. He was the main force behind severing our contact with Upper Earth and keeping them in the dark about magic. He wants to divide the Keepers from the Forgetters so no one knows of his doings there.

"In the meantime, he has developed quite a following here. My plants have already confirmed that many of my dearest friends have already gone over to his side. It seems most have all but forgotten there were sides at all. Well, I made quite a mistake, letting myself get sidelined all these years, but thank goodness all is not lost.

"I do worry, though. I shall make one more mistake. You should remember that. The fates have said that both the sorcerer prince and the crowned king of air will make three mistakes. This was my second."

"How many mistakes has Baskania made?"

"I don't know. I'd say tonight might be considered a mistake for him, however."

Erec gazed around the room, still amazed at the view with two eyes. "Does my dragon eye have special powers?"

"Oh, most certainly. With it, you may look into the future. But you must learn how to use it." King Piter smiled. "Are you ready to go home?"

Erec nodded.

"Good. I've had enough with crowds for tonight. I'm looking forward to my first good sleep in ten years." The king handed Erec a small bag containing a few pieces of chalk. "This is for your mother, in case she decides not to come here. She can draw a ring of safety around your home."

Erec found Bethany and said good-bye. "I'll be back soon. Maybe we'll all move here. Could you take care of Wolfboy while I'm gone? You know what to do when there's a full moon."

"Sure. Thanks for everything, King Erec."

"Cut it out." Erec said, grinning. "I'll see you soon."

King Piter led Erec to the Port-O-Door by his chambers. Erec found the corner of Straight Street and Way Lane on the map of Upper Earth, under the section marked, "Other." He walked through. As the door closed, he remembered he had left his Magiclight, Sneakers, and the big bag of gold, silver, and bronze back in the dormitories.

The setting sun shone through the branches of trees lining the street, casting a dancing shadow at his feet. As he walked to the tall, skinny apartment building on 341 Straight Street, he noticed how beautiful even the dusty facade was, and how light he felt traveling with empty hands.

Ten Years Earlier

D APHNE FLORA, THE queen's favorite handmaiden, ran through the west wing of King Piter's castle. She was chased by a coat. True, the coat was a very attractive, tall tuxedo jacket, with tails that it ran on like two spindly legs. But, to Daphne, it was annoying. Her long brown curls flounced at her sides as she looked for an open door or a hallway to dart down.

Darn that Balthazar Ugry. He was away for the first time in ages and had forgotten to lock his jacket in the closet. Ugry had special-ordered the thing from Heph Vulcan himself. It was made to guide his moves on the dance floor, steering him so he would no longer embarrass himself at palace balls.

Unfortunately, the coat turned out to be something of a skirt chaser. It had put Ugry in a few awkward situations. Daphne wondered if that was bad. Ugry needed loosening up.

The coat had its eye on Daphne, and it found her whenever it escaped. Now, catching up with her outside of the royal chambers, it wrapped a slim black tail around her ankle. She fell on her face. It pulled her up to embrace her.

Daphne giggled, thinking how ridiculous she must look. The jacket tickled, so she laughed louder still.

Then the chamber door flew open. Queen Hesti appeared, curly brown hair rumpled. Daphne's hand shot to her mouth like a magnet. Now she had done it. She had woken the queen. The jacket froze. Daphne perched on tiptoes, ready to explain, but Queen Hesti did not notice her.

Face pale, eyes wide, and lips pressed tight, the queen looked like she had seen a bronze ghost. She threw open a closet door, slipped shoes on, and ran down a corridor. Daphne's heart pounded. Something was wrong. The queen ran fast and noiselessly but Daphne chased her, Ugry's coat at her side. The queen might need help.

Queen Hesti ran into the triplets' nursery. The door slammed. Terrible bangs and yells came from the room.

Daphne grabbed the doorknob. It was locked. Moments later, an anguished cry rang out, and the door flew open.

Two men ran out, knocking Daphne out of their way. One carried a big rolled blanket. Ugry's jacket flung itself valiantly onto the blanket. The man carrying it flicked a remote control. Blanket, jacket, and men disappeared.

The queen burst from the room, looking around wildly. "Come back here!" she shrieked with rage. Tears poured down her face. "Come back!" She melted into the doorjamb, sobbing.

A moment later she sniffed and glanced into the room. Her face softened.

Daphne could hardly breathe. Queen Hesti seemed to see her for the first time. She sounded hoarse. "Daphne. Go tell everyone the triplets are dead."

Daphne dropped to her knees. Not the queen's three-year-old triplets. Why was the queen so calm? She did not understand.

"Now! Hurry, Daphne!" The queen shouted.

Daphne, terrified, scrambled to her feet. Hot tears slid down her face. Since Ugry was gone, she banged on the door of Ruth Cleary, the king's other AdviSeer. Nobody answered. She pounded harder. How could Ruth, her husband Tre, their twelve-year-old son, and their three-year-old daughter, not hear her? Their new baby didn't even cry—and he always howled. Where could they be?

Daphne took a breath and ran to the royal chambers. She would have to wake the king herself.

King Piter snored, his long white beard flowing over the sheets.

She touched his shoulder. A sharp sob came from her chest. The king sat up and looked at her with surprise.

Tears poured from her eyes. The words were locked in her throat.

"What's wrong, Daphne?" King Piter's voice was calming. He looked at the sheets where Queen Hesti had been.

Daphne took a breath. "The queen . . . she ran to the nursery. Something terrible happened to . . . the . . ." She melted in sobs.

King Piter threw off his sheets, grabbed his robe and scepter, and shot toward the nursery. Daphne ran behind him. King Piter could do anything. Maybe even save the triplets.

He burst into the nursery and Daphne followed him. It was empty. No triplets, no queen. Daphne did not understand. She looked under their sheets as if she might be mistaken.

King Piter shook his head in wonder. His face was pale. He murmured, "He told me. Why didn't I listen?"

"Who told you about this?" Daphne could not believe the king had been warned and still let this happen.

King Piter sat on the floor and dropped his scepter. "Erec."

He buried his head in his arms.

BONUS: NEW CHAPTER

BONUS CHAPTER

Ghost Stories

DEEP IN THE CATACOMBS below the Castle Alypium, in a room nearly lost within a maze of twisty passages, there floated a ghost named Homer. Homer was not just an ordinary ghost. No, he was a very rare type of ghost indeed. Homer was a golden ghost, one of the last of a nearly extinct breed.

The Golden Ones, as he and his friends used to be called, once ruled the planet with very kind and loving, yet iron, fists. Since the dawn of mankind the Golden Ones kept watch over the wars and petty disputes, the weddings and politics, and the general ebb and flow of life on earth.

The animals of the planet did not need much interference. They slept, ate, hunted, and fought over mates; nothing that the Golden Ones needed to change. But the humans kept getting themselves into trouble. It was the Golden Ones charge to make sure that humans remained ethical, moral, and basically good.

This was an easy task, as the Golden Ones were nearly all-powerful. The magic of a scepter paled in comparison to what this ancient race could do. The world held no secrets from them. Creating new species, reversing time, breathing life back into the dead, were all simple for them. But because they were completely good, they only used their powers when absolutely needed, which was rare.

Homer had loved his life as one of the Golden Ones. It was filled with the beauty of the universe. Every bird soaring by was a miracle. He could see the blood pumping through its arteries, the cells working in tandem to fight germs, the way the air rippled around its wings—the miracle of its flight. There was nothing Homer missed. It would have been exciting enough for him to spend all of his time just watching one raindrop, admiring the glow of the bonded atoms that made it up, and caught up in the suspense of the teams of life budding inside of it. Which feisty little bacteria tribe would make it? How fast would they grow? Where would they end up after the drop splashed on a tree leaf?

But there was so much more for Homer to do back then that he rarely had the time to enjoy these observations. Reading into the future and past of societies and individuals, and keeping people on the right path, was a full-time job. Not that he could have complained. It was just as beautiful and miraculous as everything else. Even the mistakes people made were beautiful, they were such bumbling, intricate creatures, well-meaning yet confused all at the same time.

Maybe knowing that it would all soon end made his time on earth even sweeter. For the Golden Ones were able to see into their own future as well. So they knew what was coming.

Like most things that were put on earth from the heavens, they had limitations. Specifically, six very powerful limitations in the form of sisters: the three Fates and the three Furies. Even more powerful than the Golden Ones, the Fates and Furies saw that humans must soon be responsible for their own mistakes, and thus must be allowed to make them. They disagreed with how the Golden Ones protected humans. It was known by both sides that at a certain time the Fates would end the Golden Ones' reign on Earth, turning them all into ghosts.

When that happened, many of the Golden Ones, now golden

ghosts, decided that they no longer wished to remain. Even though they were not fully stripped of their powers, their main job had been taken away from them—protecting humans from their typical bad choices. Deprived of this, most felt it was time to pass on.

But a few stayed, like Homer. He found he could still help people just a little if he was careful not to interfere too much. It wasn't worth raising the suspicions of the Fates. Like now, he was helping an old human friend, playing watchdog for a while. Plus, with the big job of babysitting mankind taken out of the way, he now had time to enjoy watching the tiny miracles that made up the world.

But what was there for Homer to watch deep in the catacombs under the Castle Alypium? The room he was in was empty, aside from the one thing he was guarding, and there was nothing else to look at aside from four stone walls. Most of the light in the room came from Homer's own glow, or the room would have been only dimly lit.

Surprisingly, there was more for Homer to observe and enjoy in this empty little room than even he suspected. The battles and arguments of the mice and rats living there were an endless source of amusement. And the insects were stunning, down to their gossamer wings and strong stick legs.

After he arrived, a form of lichen began to grow on one of the rock walls. It fed off of the light glowing from Homer as if he were the sun. Like other lichens, it was made from two species joined in a pact—an algae and a fungus living together and protecting each other. Their beauty, and the relationship between them, the way they thought so differently yet allowed for each other's views, took Homer's breath away.

Even though there was so much to ponder here in this little room, there were still times when Homer was drawn to look elsewhere. All he had to do was close his eyes, and choose a time and place, past or future. He would see what was happening there as though he was living it.

Sometimes he picked random times in history, or in the distant future, for fun. But he also liked to keep up with things that were important to humans. Watching over them was a hard habit to give up. Even though he knew he couldn't do much about what he saw, he still wanted to be aware of everything significant.

Which was why, today, he decided to take a look at what was happening with one of the key players who was now in Upper Earth. A misguided man who was becoming more misguided by the minute. Homer shook his head and smiled. Those humans. It was always something.

He closed his eyes and let his mind take over.

Jesper Konungsson took the night train from Stockholm, Sweden, where he lived, to Copenhagen, Denmark. It was the same train that he had taken countless times for work, but this time he'd rather be going anywhere else.

He still could not believe what had happened. It was hard for him to think about anything right now. He was sick, stunned. This should have been the best day of his life, and instead it was the worst.

Jesper had just been elected president of the United Nations, with delegates from nearly two hundred countries. This had been his life's dream. Why, today, did everything have to fall apart?

Thoughts flitted through his spinning head, the awful rumors that flew around at the United Nations' headquarters in New York City. He refused to believe that they were true. Typical Americans, trying to blow everything up into a big drama, like a Hollywood movie.

All the same, he had to admit it was strange that all of the UN presidents had horrible luck at the beginning of their terms.

Last year's president, Colm O'Keogh, from Ireland, seemed to believe in the rumors. He couldn't pass the torch to Jesper soon enough. Jesper remembered Colm having some trouble with his wife getting sick last year when he was elected, but it all seemed to turn out okay for him. Nothing compared to what Jesper was going through, anyway.

No. On the best day of his life, he got a phone call that his wife, Rebecka, had a terrible car accident in Copenhagen. She had been looking for a house, so they could live closer to the UN agency there. Then, one anguishing hour later, he got the phone call that she had died.

Jesper took the first plane to Stockholm to pick up his daughter, Annika, who was staying with a friend. He dreaded seeing her, his only child—what would he say? It was beyond horrible. He couldn't even bring himself to call the friends watching her until his plane landed in Stockholm.

As much as he dreaded the phone call, he was not prepared for what he was about to hear. The friends had not known about the accident. They shakily told Jesper that Annika had gone with her mother to Stockholm.

He prayed that she was all right, and phoned the hospital there immediately. After many apologies, and nurses passing the phone from one to the other as if nobody wanted to be the one to speak to him, a voice finally told him what he didn't want to hear.

Annika had been in the car. Nobody had mentioned her before, as she seemed fine. But soon she felt dizzy, then sick. The doctors had not determined why yet, but she had died as well.

Jesper felt like he was in a nightmare, and kept waiting to wake up. At one point on the train he fell asleep. When he awoke he was confused, not knowing where he was. And then he remembered, and it felt like someone stuck a knife in his heart. He would have to give up his post as president of the UN. There was no way he would be able to function. Plus, what was the point, anyway? He had no family that cared anymore.

Somehow he managed to stumble out of the Copenhagen Central Station into the crisp wind outside. The station had a huge, tall, ribbed ceiling, and was so open and airy that the terrible events seemed even more unreal. He glanced up and down Bernstorffsgade, the street he was on, forgetting the simplest things, how to get around the city.

Tivoli Gardens was right across the street, but he tried to keep from looking at it. The last time he had been here he had taken Annika on the wooden roller coaster there. Rebecka had waited, then gone with them on the fantastic carousel after, which was more her speed. He nearly choked thinking about her.

A man with short blond hair and an eye patch nodded at him. Jesper recognized him from the train. He was hard to miss, with a two-inch stripe of dark hair running from front to back through his blond curls, like a skunk. The man asked Jesper if he needed help.

Jesper nodded. "I need a cab." He looked around aimlessly.

The man smiled and put a hand on his shoulder. "You look like a mess. Where are you going?"

Jesper clenched his teeth to fight off a wave of tears. "To Rigshospitalet. It's a hospital in Copenhagen."

"No worries, friend. Come with me, I have a car waiting. Get you there in a jiffy."

Jesper followed him blindly down Bernstorffsgade. There was no room in his head for any thoughts about safety, or how this man could have a car waiting if he had just come in on the same train. But even if he could think about safety he probably wouldn't care. What was there to live for, anyway?

A limousine waited on Tietgensgade, the next street. Jesper

climbed inside after the man with the eye patch, glad not to think. His head ached.

The man smiled consolingly. "Looks like you've had a long day. My name is Ajax Hunter, by the way. Pleased to make your acquaintance."

Ajax had a slight British accent, but sounded like he had been living in America a while. "I know this sounds hard to believe," he said, "but I know what happened to your wife and daughter. I'm friends with their doctor." He shrugged, an apologetic grin on his face. "Don't worry. I think things are going to turn out just fine."

A wave of confusion washed through Jesper. It seemed impossible, this stranger claiming to know what happened to his family. How could he? He had said "your wife and daughter," so he must have heard something.

No, Jesper realized. "You must be confusing me with someone else." His voice cracked. "Things aren't going to turn out fine for me."

"Really, mate. I think it will." Ajax smiled encouragingly.

Jesper dropped his face into his hands. Something seemed to crack inside him, threatening to let all of his pain spill right out. "No, Ajax. It won't. I'm too late. They had a car accident and they're both . . ."

"Dead?" Ajax laughed, which made Jesper's stomach turn. How dare he?

Ajax shook his head. "No, they'll be okay. Really. Like I say, I'm friends with their doctor. I'll take you to see him straight away. He's not at the hospital anymore, though. He's got your wife and daughter safely in his lab. Dr. B is a master surgeon, I'll tell you. If anyone can save them, he can."

Hope surged unexpectedly through Jesper. Maybe the hospital had been wrong! He was afraid to believe it, sure that he'd be disappointed and have to go through worse pain when he found out.

The whole thing was confusing and hard to grasp with his mind spinning. Ajax knew the doctor? Was it a coincidence that he had been on the same train then? "Are you sure you have the right person? How do you know all of this?" Jesper asked.

Ajax leaned back against his seat and closed his uncovered eye as if he didn't hear the questions.

Jesper began to panic. "Are you sure they're okay?" He shook Ajax. "Tell me how you know. Where are they?"

Then a fear shot into his heart like an arrow. Could someone have sabotaged his family because he had become the UN president? Would anyone really do that? He was dizzy with shock and grief. Maybe he was getting paranoid.

Before his head stopped spinning, the limousine pulled into the driveway of an immense building.

Ajax led Jesper through the building's corridors. It was plush, and looked nothing like a hospital or laboratory. The doctor was waiting behind a large oak desk in an ornate room filled with gold statues and art. Even sitting, Jasper could tell he was tall, an imposing man with silver hair that dipped into a sharp widow's peak. He had an eye patch on, like Ajax did, which struck Jesper as peculiar.

The doctor's thin lips stretched into a smile, but his uncovered blue eye regarded Jesper coldly. "President Jesper Konungsson. I hear congratulations are in order."

"I should think not," Jesper spit out. "Where are Rebecka and Annika? Are they . . . okay?"

"They should make it, I think," the doctor said. "Only with your help, though." He cleared his throat. "Please excuse me. I've had a few disappointments this week. I lost an eye." He pointed at his eye patch. "And I'm not at my best. May I introduce myself? I am Thanatos Baskania. You may have heard of me—the Crown Prince of Peace? I hope that we will become good friends this year, like I have with the former presidents of the UN."

The Crown Prince of Peace? This couldn't be. Jesper shook his head. This was the head of Eye of the World, the peace organization that just took over as the ruling body of the United Nations? The man who owned so many multinational corporations that he nearly owned the world? And he was a doctor?

Obviously not. This was some kind of scheme to control Jesper. He had planned to kick Eye of the World out as his first move as president. It seemed hard to believe that anyone would stoop to this level. This was going too far.

Baskania seemed to have read his mind. "It's all in how you look at it, Jesper. Everything will be fine soon for your family. More than fine. You will have a wonderful term as president. You will support me and Eye of the World fully, and learn to appreciate what I am doing for world peace. And you will find that with my support you will be able to accomplish everything else you want, and more. No harm done at all.

"That is, if you cooperate. For you see, I am a doctor, Jesper. And it was lucky that I was here when this accident happened. I was able to save both of their lives after everyone else had given up. They will be completely fine, now. All I need is your agreement to help me in return. A simple operation." He paused. "Would you like to see them?"

"Yes." Jesper's heart leapt into his throat as he followed the doctor and Ajax down the hallway into a large room with white tiled walls and floor. Rebecka and Annika rested on tables in the middle of the room. They looked peaceful, asleep. No tubes or catheters were in sight. Not even a bruise.

Jesper saw them both breathing and his body relaxed so quickly he almost fell. Choking back a sob, he rested his hand on his wife's cheek. "Rebecka? Wake up, honey. I'm here now."

Rebecka didn't move. Jesper shook her a bit. "Honey? Are you okay?"

"She won't be able to hear you," Baskania said. "You need to understand. I will not be able to wake them up, ever, unless you cooperate with me."

Jesper struggled to fight his anger. "What do you need? Let's get this over with."

Baskania tsked. "Attitude. That's not going to help." He frowned. "You will pledge your allegiance to me. You will do as I tell you. You will report to me. And you will give me your eye."

"My . . ." Jesper's hand flew to his face. "Are you taking my eye since you just lost yours?"

"No." Baskania chuckled. "Yours is not important enough for this spot on my face." He tapped his eye patch. "I'm saving this for a special eye that should have been mine by now. Yours will just be another at my disposal.

"When you give me your eye you will become part of my Watch Guard. I will be able to see what you are doing at any time, keep tabs on you. Your eye will be inside of me. I will bring it to the surface when I want to see through your other eye, communicate with you, or show you something where I am. I may send you on missions to show me things I need to see through your remaining eye."

Jesper could feel his stomach lurch into his chest. Baskania was a madman. He actually wanted to take an eye from Jesper, and believed that he'd be able to see through Jesper's other one? This was insane.

The only thing he could do now was play along, get him to release Rebecka and Annika. If he could only do it without losing an eye. . . . In either case, as soon as he got his wife and daughter safely out of here he would turn Baskania in to every authority that existed—

Baskania sighed loudly. "As usual, you losers in Upper Earth show such a poor imagination. Like your predecessor, Colm O'Keogh, I will have to prove to you that I mean what I say. I believe after this I shall have no more trouble with you."

In a moment, the most gruesome and unbelievable thing happened before Jesper's eyes. Baskania removed his patch, revealing a dark gap beneath it. Then his features, his other eye, eyebrows, nose, and mouth, all sunk deep into his face, leaving deep pits that moved around and turned into even more pits. Jesper choked, grabbing his stomach. All he could think was that Baskania had turned into a white bowling ball with far too many finger holes.

But then, even worse, eyes started appearing on Baskania's face where the holes had been. Each of the eyes looked different in shape and color, as if they had, indeed, come from different owners. Jesper gasped as Baskania pulled his sleeves up. Eyes covered his arms. Some were glancing all around the room, others stared pointedly at him.

Jesper felt his knees buckle. Ajax appeared at his side, holding him up. "S'okay, Mr. President," he said. "It looks strange at first, but you'll get used to it. Mr. Baskania here is doing everything he can for the good of the people of the world, protecting them from bad governments. We just want to make sure you're on our side."

Jesper nodded, as if there was a choice. Baskania's eyes were disappearing into holes in his face again, and his normal features erupted on its surface. He waved an arm at Rebecka and Annika, and suddenly both of them sat straight up on their tables, eyes open.

They looked at Jesper and said in unison, "You need to help the Crown Prince of Peace if you want us to live." Then they both lay back down and closed their eyes again.

Jesper felt his knees shaking. No wonder Colm couldn't wait to hand over this job. "Can't I just resign now, let someone else do this?"

"I'm afraid that's not an option," Baskania said. "If you want to keep your family. And I wouldn't bother telling anybody about this. I don't think they would believe you. Even your family—they won't remember a thing that's happened here. You'll get one of the new glass eye replacements. They look completely real, nobody will know."

Jesper nodded. In just one year he'd be out of this predicament. At least Baskania would have less reason to plague him, he hoped. It was time to save his family. "Take the eye then. Let's get this over with."

Jesper was unusually quiet on the train ride back to Stockholm.

"Are you okay, sweetheart?" Rebecka asked. "It was so nice of you to come down and get us. You really didn't need to."

He nodded and pulled her close, squeezing Annika in for the hug. It would all be okay, he told himself. It would take a while to get used to seeing out of only one eye, but that was nothing compared to having his family back.

It wasn't until the following week, at his first UN meeting as president, that he felt a burning in his good eye. He knew who was watching.

Homer let the vision fade. Maybe it was a good thing that he wasn't responsible for humans any more. It was too much work.

READING GROUP GUIDE

Reading Group Discussion Questions

1. Kaza Kingsley used names, objects, and stories from mythology throughout the book. How many references can you find?

2. The citizens of Alypium and the Kingdoms of the Keepers debate whether to let the "Losers" in Upper Earth know about the magic they lost. Supposing we did once have magic, would we deserve to know how to use it again? Is there such a thing as dangerous knowledge? What things might you hide from people to keep from hurting them?

3. Why do you think Erec's cloudy thoughts make him sick at the beginning of the book but not at the end? Would you like to have cloudy thoughts? Are they a gift or a curse?

4. Erec is overly confident in his ability to face the shadow demon in King Pluto's dungeons. Did you think he would succeed in walking through the shadow demon and rescue his mother? When you finished reading the chapter, did you think he or his mother had been killed? Who would frighten you more, the destroyers or the shadow demon?

5. Erec changes over the course of the story. How do his internal struggles relate to his outer struggles?

6. If King Pluto is a powerful king, why does he have Baskania for a master? What do you think he is getting out of that deal? Is there any good in him?

7. Erec has a strong sense of justice. Baskania and Balor, on the other hand, will do whatever it takes to get power. Can justice and power coexist? Are people in power too interested in keeping it to be truly just?

8. What kind of powers do you think the dragon's eye holds? What about the scepter? Will these things be good for Erec or not?

9. During the coronation ceremony, why did the scepter fly to Erec and the Lia Fail scream? Is Erec meant to be king because he won the contests, or is there some other reason?

10. Is Aoquesth kind even though he eats humans who invade his cave? Would you like to meet him? Were you surprised when he told Erec that the eye he was guarding belonged to Erec?

11. The Epilogue, "Ten Years Earlier," reveals what happened when King Piter's triplets disappeared, but it raises many questions. Why did the king say "Erec" at the end? Was the queen telling the truth when she told Daphne the triplets were dead? What do you think happened to Ugry's tuxedo jacket? What might it have seen?

12. Bethany has been a good friend to Erec. What will her role be in future books? Is she destined to be something other than a sidekick?

A CONVERSATION
WITH KAZA KINGSLEY

Kaza, what drew you to fantasy as a writer?

KK: I think it was the part of me that never wanted to grow up. I always had a wild imagination and believed in things strongly. For example, when I was a child I was sure I could fly if I just worked hard enough at it. I jumped off my parents' couch every day, convinced I was going a little farther each time, and I would soon learn to control it and take off into the air. And I still like to believe in crazy things. Like superstitions. I have to knock on wood when I hear good things, and I always say "God forbid" when someone mentions something bad. Good thing I never got into the throwing salt habit. If I had a choice, I'd live in a fantasy world any day. I try to make my life as fantastical as I can. So of course that's what I'm drawn to when I start writing.

Did you learn anything writing Erec Rex*?*

KK: Absolutely. On one level, I did a lot of research into Greek, Roman, Celtic, and Norse mythology for the series, so I learned a lot there. And on another level, I learned about myself, what persistence can accomplish, and how deeply the lives of my characters can affect me. A funny thing I noticed, before I wrote *The Dragon's Eye*, I used to get so worked up from scary books and movies that I'd be afraid to go to sleep. And then I'd have nightmares. After I wrote the book, though, those things no longer affected me. Something deep inside of me finally realized the things I was afraid of aren't real.

So you researched mythology. How did you use it in the book?

KK: Mythology references are everywhere in Erec Rex. Sometimes they are blatant, like the Lia Fail, which is a stone straight out of Celtic mythology that screams in the presence of a rightful ruler. Other references might be a bit harder to spot. For example, King Piter, Queen Posey, and King Pluto relate to certain Roman gods. King Piter is named after Ju-Piter, king of the skies (Alypium being derived from Olympia); Queen Posey of Ashona is named after Poseidon, king of the seas; and Pluto was the name of the Roman god of the Underworld (Aorth being underground). I could go on and on.

Oh really? What other names did you draw from mythology?

KK: Erec's name, aside from being a Celtic spelling, is derived from Heracles, the Greek word for Hercules. And like Hercules, Erec has to perform twelve quests to prove himself. Balor is the name of a powerful evil being with one eye from Celtic mythology. I have a lot of eye references too, like Thanatos Argus Baskania. His first name is the Greek god of death; his middle name is a creature with one hundred eyes; and Baskania is Greek for "the evil eye." Most of the characters in my books have names with some sort of meaning.

This is your first published fiction book. Have you always wanted to write?

KK: I've written for as long as I can remember. I wrote my first book when I was in third grade. It was about a terrifying octopus that shot ink at people and made them do math. It involved a new way of doing math called "octoprillopus." Strange, as I think of it, in Erec Rex, Bethany loves math, and being a seer has to do with understanding math. I'm starting to wonder if I have math issues.

***Are there books that have inspired your writing, recently or in the
past?***

KK: I read as much as I can, but I get as much inspiration from life
as I do from literature. When I was a kid, I loved the Wizard
of Oz series by L. Frank Baum. Dorothy returned to Oz
repeatedly and had fun adventures there. With my overactive
imagination, I was sure I could find the next portal to Oz
under a rock and go meet all my favorite characters. So those
books inspired me the most. *Alice's Adventures in Wonderland*
and *Through the Looking Glass* were close follow-ups. I still
love to read *Alice* and all the crazy poems Lewis Carroll wrote.
I finally got to taste treacle, in honor of the Dormouse, a few
months ago. It was delicious!

***It seems that reviewers keep comparing the Erec Rex series to Harry
Potter. The reviews are great, saying you're original and fresh, but
Harry's name keeps sneaking in there. Does this bother you or are
you happy with the comparison?***

KK: I've talked about this in several television interviews that
are posted on YouTube and other places online. I think it's
inevitable that all fantasy books are going to be compared to
Harry Potter because of the fame and success that series has
enjoyed. But it's like going on a date with a guy who keeps
comparing you to his gorgeous ex-girlfriend. You love that
he thinks you're so great, beautiful, etc., and that's really a
compliment. But after a while, you start to think, "Hey, look
at me! I'm my own person, not her. I've got my own things
to offer." I mean, the story line of my first book is about a

boy trying to save his mother and finding out he's a future king. And my second book has a battle, Erec is lost in the wilderness, addicted to the scepter . . . not something that compares to other books that I know of.

Is there any advice you would like to give readers or others who want to write a book?

KK: Yes. It does not matter what you want to do, just do it with all your heart. Give up the excuses, reasons why it can't work. And don't listen to what others say. Plunge in with joy and love, and speak from the deepest, most hidden parts of yourself. That's the part we all need to hear from, to help each other through the craziness of this world.

ABOUT THE AUTHOR

When **Kaza Kingsley** was born in Cleveland, Ohio, they say the resident doctor who delivered her had been up all night studying. She yawned just at the wrong moment, and baby Kaza slipped right through her fingers! But the resident's open textbook lay on the floor, shielding Kaza from a hard fall. Baby Kaza supposedly wailed for a moment but then stopped, lovingly gazing at the pages and words draped around her.

We think this was the beginning of the end.

Kaza (rhymes with Jazz-a) loved to write since she was old enough to pick up a pen. After playing tag and other normal kid games, she used to drag friends into her backyard to write books at her picnic table for as long as they could stand it. Her first book was about a terrifying octopus that shot ink at people and made them do math. Since then she has written pretty much anything she can, including poetry, short stories, and nonfiction.

Erec Rex is Kaza's first series of books.